DEATH

OF A

MESSENGER

ALSO BY ROBERT MCCAW

Koa Kāne Hawaiian Mysteries

Off the Grid

Fire and Vengeance

Treachery Times Two

DEATH

OF A

MESSENGER

A KOA KĀNE HAWAIIAN MYSTERY

ROBERT McCAW

OCEANVIEW (PUBLISHING

SARASOTA, FLORIDA

While this novel draws on the spirit and history of Hawai'i, it is a work of fiction. The characters, institutions, and events portrayed are either the product of the author's imagination, or are used fictitiously. Any resemblance to actual events, locales, or persons, living or dead, is coincidental.

ISBN 978-1-60809-478-3

Published in the United States of America by Oceanview Publishing

Sarasota, Florida

www.oceanviewpub.com

10 9 8 7 6 5 4 3 2

PRINTED IN THE UNITED STATES OF AMERICA

For my mother, Sally, who inspired me to read . . . and write.
And who so much wanted to see this book in print.

ACKNOWLEDGEMENTS

Among the many people who helped make this book possible are my dear friends in Hawaiʻi who generously shared their knowledge of the culture, history, and language of the Hawaiian people. To them I owe an enormous debt of gratitude.

Special thanks must also go to Makela Bruno-Kidani, who has tirelessly reviewed my use of the Hawaiian language, correcting my many mistakes. Where the Hawaiian words and phrases are correct, she deserves the credit. Any errors are entirely of my doing.

Lastly, this book would not have been reprinted without the amazing support of my agent, Mel Parker of Mel Parker Books, LLC. His faith in my work and his tireless efforts made the publication of this story possible. I would also be remiss if I failed to acknowledge the support of Pat and Bob Gussin, owners of Oceanview Publishing, who have devoted their phenomenal energies to supporting and publishing my work and that of many other aspiring mystery and thriller writers.

DEATH
OF A
MESSENGER

CHAPTER ONE

HAWAI'I COUNTY CHIEF Detective Koa Kāne strapped in, and the US Army UH-72A Lakota helicopter lifted off the Hilo tarmac. An anonymous 911 call to the Hawai'i County Emergency Command Center had reported a corpse at Pōhakuloa, the Army's remote live-fire training area, or PTA. Sergeant Basa had alerted Koa, and was now sitting next to him as the chopper headed for the Army reservation in the Humu'ula Saddle between Mauna Kea and Mauna Loa, two of the five volcanoes that form the Big Island of Hawai'i.

The chopper turned west and climbed toward the saddle. Koa barely noticed, though. The mad dash to catch the chopper had aggravated the pinched nerve in his neck, and he sat stiffly erect to avoid further jolts of pain.

As they passed over an ambulance heading up the Saddle Road, Sergeant Basa leaned over, shouting above the roar of the engines, "That's the county physician and the crime scene techs down there. I told them to get their butts up to Pōhakuloa."

Koa spotted flashing lights in the distance and felt a spark of excitement. A crime scene did that to him. He counted ten vehicles: military police jeeps, EOD (explosive ordnance disposal) vehicles, a tracked ambulance, and a fire truck. As the helicopter approached,

Koa saw that the vehicles were spread out along a barely visible jeep trail that meandered east of a sizable cinder cone. Yellow tape marked a path cleared by EOD personnel. Several men stood near an oval pit at the end of the tape.

As the chopper settled between two MP vehicles, a military policeman dressed in camo with a silver first lieutenant's bar broke away from the cluster near the pit and hurried toward the chopper. Jerry Zeigler's ferret-like face and crooked nose identified him as the commander of the military police detachment at Pōhakuloa.

"Hello, Jerry." Koa shook hands with the twenty-five-year-old military police officer. Though they came from different backgrounds, they shared a common bond. Both had grown up dirt poor. The Kāne family had been respected in ancient times, but Koa's father and grandfather had been virtual slaves at the Hāmākua Sugar Mill. Zeigler had been a South Dakota farm boy. Both had known hardship growing up, and both had been rescued by the US Army—Koa with the Fifth Special Forces Group and Jerry by the military police. They'd worked together a half-dozen times when the Army had pitched in on disaster relief, and bonded while helping folks after a big earthquake hit the west side of the island, wrecking hundreds of homes and schools.

Koa remained smiling even as Jerry's vigorous handshake sent a blazing streak of pain radiating down his right arm. Without being obvious, he placed both hands behind his neck and arched his back. The pinched nerve was getting worse, just as the doctor had said it would. He dreaded the thought of spinal surgery, but it might be better than the damn pain. He wasn't supposed to feel this old at forty-three.

Mercifully, the helicopter pilot shut down his twin engines and Koa could make himself heard. "You got a body?" he asked Jerry.

Zeigler nodded. "Stay inside the yellow tape. There are unexploded shells all over the PTA and tons of them around this area." Zeigler led the policemen between two yellow tapes. "Got Sergeant Basa's call about eleven thirty this morning, and we put an observer up in a chopper. My man had no trouble spotting the probable site, but it took us awhile to get here. The bomb disposal boys blew a dud on the way in," he said, wending his way across the uneven ground.

"The 911 caller nailed it. It's in a lava tube, mutilated and decomposed—a human male, but it's gonna take a medic to reconstruct much more. Nobody but me has been in there, and I didn't venture far or touch anything." Thousands of lava tubes—underground passages where lava once flowed but then drained away—permeated the Big Island, some extending only a few feet while others ran for miles and were wide enough to hide an eighteen-wheeler. Koa, like all Hawaiians, knew his ancestors buried their dead in lava tubes, often in mass graves, but he'd never been to a murder scene inside one of these natural tunnels.

Zeigler was a good cop, and Koa listened as the MP related what he'd seen. "There are some odd boot marks on the ground outside the mouth of the tube. The ground's been chewed up, recently too. You're lucky it rained . . . the boot heels left clear impressions. As for the body, it's been there for days, that's for sure. I figure someone stumbled on it, got frightened, and fled."

Keeping his core tight and his shoulders back to minimize the stress on his neck, Koa climbed down into the pit with an electric torch. He examined the disturbed ground and boot marks. The heels had cut deep, leaving sharp impressions, rounded on the back and flat toward the toe with horseshoe-shaped taps on the heels. Cowboy boots for a man on horseback. The man—he guessed it to be a man from the depth of the marks—wore specialty boots, likely handmade and expensive. He wondered if the boot tracks could be traced to a boot maker.

He glanced around the desolate area. Who would be out here? A hunter? Only a fool would hunt in the restricted area with all the unexploded ordnance around. And why would a hunter be down in a pit? He peered at the dark opening. Why would a hunter have ventured into this particular lava tube? Koa saw nothing unusual about it. He searched the ground for anything that might give him answers. Not much. Just the heel marks and disturbed rock.

He directed his beam of light into the lava tube. He didn't like caves—they held too many unpleasant surprises. Carefully, he picked his way into the darkness. A putrid smell assaulted him instantly. "Oh God," he exclaimed, pulling a handkerchief from his pocket and fastening it across his nose and mouth. Then he saw the body.

Koa stepped closer and stopped short. Even as a veteran of the Special Forces in Somalia and a witness to more than a few murder scenes, he struggled to suppress his nausea. *Control. Stay in control. Block emotion. Concentrate.* He clenched his teeth until they hurt. His nausea receded.

It was a horrendous crime scene, and Koa sensed that catching the killer would require all of his resources. He'd have to focus his military and police training, his intense powers of observation, and his own criminal experience—as a teenager he'd killed the man who'd tormented and ultimately killed his father and gotten away with it—to find the perverted killer who left this corpse.

In the dozen years since 2003, when he'd left the Army to join the police, Koa had heard about ritual killings, but had never actually seen one. Until now. The naked body lay with its legs toward him, feet slightly separated. The trunk was bloated from putrefaction. The skin had blackened. The genitals had shrunk into the body, but the deceased was unmistakably male. The sight, the smell, and the walls squeezed in upon Koa.

The victim's arms had been drawn out to the sides. The upper arms were swollen, but below the elbows the flesh had shriveled. Bones protruded from shredded hands and smashed fingers. Slash marks cut wide ribbons across the distended chest. The incisions must have been deep, he judged, for the swelling to open up the flesh in those straight, wide tracks. A sharp knife or, perhaps, a straight razor. Something with a real edge. It wasn't easy to slice human flesh. The killer had been strong. Koa looked around for a knife but saw none.

The face had blackened to pulp, much of it bludgeoned beyond recognition. The lower facial bones had been shattered. Nose broken. Jaw smashed. Most of the teeth knocked out. The killer must have directed numerous blows at the victim's mouth. Dental identification would be difficult, maybe impossible.

An empty socket leered at Koa from the left side of the dead man's face. A gaping blackened hole surrounded by withered flesh. The hole on the left side of the skull seemed to fix upon him. Koa's own eye, his left eye, began to hurt. He shook his head to dislodge the false pain. Mutilated hands, battered faces—he'd seen those before, but desecration of an eye was something new. The killer must have gouged out the eyeball.

But why? Why pluck out the left eye? Some savage had derived great pleasure from acting out this rite. That was Koa's job, to stop people from acting like ancient savages.

Koa swung the light back and forth, searching for any other evidence. Trying to absorb every aspect of the scene. To miss nothing. To avoid being misled by false clues. No clothes. No shoes. Where were the victim's clothes? The killer must have taken them.

Farther back in the cave his light revealed piles of small rock fragments. A blackened spot. Remnants of charcoal. A fire ring. A long-doused fire. It looked as though it had been there for ages.

The light fell on a peculiarly shaped dark gray or black rock next to the victim's left leg. It was rectangular at one end, angled in the middle, and tapered to an edge at the other end, like a cutting instrument. A man-made shape, not a natural rock form. Some kind of primitive stone tool. The ancient fire and now this strange rock. Maybe this place had some historical significance. Koa made a note to call the state archaeologist.

He stooped down, keeping his back straight, and directed his beam of light to examine the object more closely. Dried blood covered part of the dark gray stone.

Blood? He examined the floor around the corpse. Blood was only in one small place, where a puddle had congealed and dried. He looked more closely. Not much blood. Odd. There should be more blood—a lot more blood—given the carnage wreaked upon the body.

Koa walked out into the sunlight. Tearing the handkerchief from his face, he sucked in the clean, dry air. Questions ricocheted in his mind. It was always like that at the beginning of an investigation, and he'd learned to let the questions accumulate unanswered. Questions opened the mind to unlikely possibilities. That and his own secret criminal history were what made him such a good investigator.

CHAPTER TWO

KOA'S CELL PHONE sounded the "Star-Spangled Banner," the ring-tone reserved for his boss. Chief Lannua inevitably picked the worst time to call, but he wasn't to be denied. "Detective Kāne here," Koa answered.

"Where the hell are you? The budget meeting started fifteen min-utes ago."

"I'm up at Pōhakuloa at the scene of a grisly murder."

"And you didn't bother to let me know?"

During the mad dash to the helicopter he'd asked Piki, the young-est of his detectives, to tell the chief that he'd been called to a crime scene. For some reason the message hadn't gotten through, but Koa wasn't about to hang his junior out to dry. "Sorry, Chief, I should have remembered the meeting when the balloon went up."

"Your numbers are way out of line." The chief got to what was really bothering him.

This was the part of his job Koa hated the most . . . begging for money. He didn't have enough detectives, his men were underpaid, the department was light-years behind the mainland police in tech-nology, and crime was getting worse, especially with the spread of illegal methamphetamine labs. Some days he wished he'd stayed in the Special Forces. At least they got budget priority. "I can justify every dollar, Chief. Let me get through here and I'll walk you through it line by line."

"Call me when you get back, but figure out how to cut seven percent, unless you want me to apply it across the board."

Ouch, Koa thought, 7 percent. He'd built in a 2 percent cushion, knowing the chief would cut, but seven was going to be a bitch and across-the-board was out of the question. Still, now wasn't the time to argue.

"Okay, Chief, I'll come up with a proposal."

"It better be good," the chief retorted before hanging up.

Like a car changing gears, Koa's mind shifted back to the crime scene. He needed a medical examiner—yet Hawai'i County had none. A county physician, Shizuo Hiro, doubled as coroner when he wasn't delivering babies, yet the seventy-five-year-old Japanese obstetrician wasn't up to this kind of a case. The old man could barely fend off the cross-examination of defense counsel in murder cases where bullet holes established the cause of death. God help them if they had to rely on Shizuo for forensic evidence in a case like this one.

Koa knew the importance of forensic evidence. He'd escaped punishment for his own crime only because he'd staged a suicide by hanging and no competent coroner had ever visited the scene or properly autopsied the body.

As he looked around, the white cross of the military ambulance caught his attention. That gave him an idea. He joined Lieutenant Zeigler. "Jerry, the county physician isn't up to a case like this. I need a competent medical examiner. Any chance of getting an Army doctor up here?"

"I don't know, but I can find out."

Koa was a pro at overcoming initial hesitation. "Get on it, will you?"

"Will do." The military police officer returned to his jeep and used the radio. He soon came back with an answer. "We don't have a doctor up here with mortuary experience, but Lieutenant Colonel Samuel Cater, the deputy scientific director of the Army Central Identification Laboratory on Oʻahu, has a lot of forensic pathology experience. We could hook him in by phone, maybe even with video. Then he'll fly over to assist with the autopsy."

"Okay. Get the communications hookup ready and tell Cater to handle Shizuo with kid gloves. The old man's going to shit a brick over an outsider, especially a forensics expert, moving in on his turf." Koa formulated a plan as he spoke. "If necessary, I'm going to tell Shizuo that the Army insists on participating in the autopsy because the body's on federal property." Zeigler gave him a sly grin and hurried off.

Sergeant Basa stepped up as Zeigler left. Basa hailed from a large Portuguese family. They'd originally come to the islands to work as engineers on the sugar and pineapple plantations, but nowadays his nine brothers were into everything from shipping to cement manufacturing. Koa had once joined the sergeant at a Basa family reunion and met some of his colleague's 250 relatives. The whole family, Basa in the forefront, played sports with fearsome competitiveness.

Basa himself had worked his way up the police ranks from patrolman to one of the key leadership positions, and Koa trusted him to be thorough. They had developed a sort of partnership that made both of them more efficient. Yet that didn't stop the two of them from going after each other in their favorite sport, open-ocean canoe racing. Koa always joked that Basa used more muscle than insight into the ocean currents. At least until lately, when his neck had started plaguing him. Now he let a lot more of Basa's barbs go unchallenged.

After working together for a dozen years, the bear-like sergeant knew how Koa liked to process a crime scene. "Koa, it's gonna take manpower to search this whole area." Basa paused before continuing. "Want me to talk to Zeigler and see if I can get the bomb boys to start checking for ordnance?" Basa had made no bones about his admiration for Koa's skills as an investigator or his own ambition to become a detective.

"Good idea, go for it."

Shizuo Hiro and the rest of the Hilo crime scene team arrived by jeep, having left the county's red ambulance on the Saddle Road. Koa immediately drew the diminutive county physician aside, well out of earshot of everyone else. He took a deep breath. This was going to be tricky. Shizuo was all about his own self-importance. You called him Doctor, not Doc, unless you wanted to get under his skin, which Koa relished from time to time. You paid lip service to his authority as the makeshift coroner, even though he had the job only because he lost one poker pot after another at the mayor's Thursday night smokers.

"Shizuo, this is a bad one. Mutilated victim. Smashed face and hands. An eye's been gouged out. We're going to need sophisticated tests. When we catch the murderer, we'll need courtroom—"

"What are you saying? You think I can't handle the medical exam?"

"Sure you can, Shizuo, but we've arranged for you to work with an Army doctor, an expert in forensic pathology."

"No, sir." The little Japanese doctor stiffened, like a peacock. "I'm the county physician. This is my job."

"Shizuo, we're on a military reservation. Lieutenant Zeigler and I are jointly in charge of this investigation." Koa assumed that Shizuo didn't know that the Army only rented the Pōhakuloa Training Area and that the state of Hawai'i retained criminal jurisdiction. Such details were beneath the good doctor's notice. "Zeigler checked with his superiors, and we've agreed on this approach. It's going to be a joint autopsy."

"No, sir. You have no . . . no authority to agree."

The nice approach wasn't working; luckily, Koa had no problem taking a stiffer line. "Calm down, Shizuo. Without an agreement, the Army will take charge of the autopsy. This way, we—you'll—still have a principal role."

Shizuo reflected upon Koa's words before giving a curt nod.

"Where is this Army doctor?" Shizuo looked around at the military personnel, searching for medical corps insignia.

"He's on O'ahu, at the Army Central Identification Laboratory. He's going to participate by videophone."

"Let me talk to him."

Koa signaled to Zeigler, who approached carrying a headset and trailing wire from a small communications van. He handed the headset to Shizuo. "It's a secure two-way channel. You can talk to Dr. Cater just like he was standing next to you."

Shizuo glared at the military police officer before grabbing the headset and fitting it in place. Koa stepped back and motioned Zeigler to do likewise. While Shizuo spoke to Dr. Cater, Koa whispered, "You warned him?"

Zeigler nodded.

Several minutes later, Shizuo turned with rigid precision to face Zeigler. "You have the video communications ready, Lieutenant?" Shizuo uttered the last word with such distaste that Koa bit his lip to stifle a response, but the insult had no perceivable effect on Zeigler. A thin skin wasn't an asset in either the military or the police.

"We'll be ready for you in five minutes."

"We will need lights too, Lieutenant." Again, disdain dripped from Shizuo's voice.

"We've already set up arc lights, Doctor."

Shizuo removed the headset and thrust it at Lieutenant Zeigler. "Inform me when everything is ready." He strutted toward the jeep to retrieve his medical kit.

Koa said sotto voce, "That was inexcusable. I apologize."

"Don't. The Army probably killed his relatives during the war. At least, I hope so."

The two men shared a brief smile.

Koa assembled all the military and police personnel. "Here's the routine," he said. "Everybody will wear masks. The body is badly decomposed . . . the smell is god-awful." Koa pointed to Ron Woo, the pencil-thin police photographer. "I'll go in first with Ron. He'll get pictures. By then Lieutenant Zeigler should have the telecommunications hookup ready and the medical types can do their thing. When they're done, the crime scene team goes in. Everybody understand?" Koa paused, and when those around him nodded, he added, "Okay, let's do it."

Basa already had the ordnance techs sweeping for unexploded duds. They discussed manpower needs with Zeigler, and Koa asked Basa to take command of the search operation. "Tell 'em to be careful," Koa warned. "We've already got one body. We don't need another one."

Shizuo passed out surgical masks, and the military police illuminated generator-powered arc lamps. Once light flooded the underground cavern, Ron Woo and Koa donned masks and entered the cave. Bright flashes bounced off the walls of the ancient lava tube, giving a kind of strobe-light effect to the scene. Woo photographed the body from every angle, then calmly turned his camera on the stone implement, the stone chips, and the ancient fire ring. Koa always marveled that Ron could photograph the most grotesque of crime scenes without the slightest trace of revulsion.

By the time Koa and the photographer finished, Zeigler's MPs had strung coaxial video cabling from the communications van to a video camera in the cave. Shizuo entered the lava tube, wearing both a mask and a communications headset.

"Okay, Doc, you're the executive producer. Just tell me where to point the camera," the video technician announced.

Shizuo glared at the technician, who'd dared to call him Doc, and Koa thought the Japanese physician might blow a gasket. Then the baby doctor got control of himself. "First, pan the whole corpse so Dr. Cater can see the body *in situ*. Then point the camera where I point my left index finger. My left index finger." Shizuo held up his finger. "Understand, soldier?"

"Yes, sir." The technician slowly recorded the scene for the forensic pathologist two hundred miles away.

Shizuo spoke softly into his microphone, using clinical words to describe the corpse—blunt force trauma . . . lacerations. Koa moved away, giving the doctor room to work, so he heard only intermittent snatches. Shizuo examined the corpse, using his left index finger to direct the video camera at the legs, the trunk, the slashes across the chest, the battered hands, the mauled face, the empty eye socket, and the remaining eye.

The presence of men in white surgical masks, bright arc lamps, Shizuo's bag of medical instruments, wires trailing from Shizuo's headset, and the video camera all seemed like some desperate attempt to pump life back into the naked corpse spread-eagled on the floor of the rocky cavern. Koa had a momentary thought of Frankenstein at work in the bowels of his castle.

Shizuo inserted a thermometer, measuring the rectal temperature of the corpse. Using thick needles affixed to syringes, the physician drew a variety of body fluids, including blood and spinal fluid. When he dispassionately pierced the victim's remaining eyeball, Koa walked outside to check on the progress of the search.

When the old doctor finished, Lieutenant Zeigler's troops placed the victim into a black plastic body bag. Three soldiers carried the dead man to the military ambulance. The APC's engine roared, belching black diesel smoke into the breeze as it carried the corpse off toward the morgue in Hilo.

Koa joined the county physician. The old man had a wilted look, and Koa wondered whether the strain of the exam or injury to his authority had sapped him. "Well, Shizuo, what can you tell me?"

The little man straightened, but his military snap had vanished. He shook his head. "All this technology." He spat the word with nearly as much venom as he previously applied to the lieutenant. "Video cameras. Spectrometry. Vitreous fluid. Insects. That Army doctor wants samples of the larvae growing in the corpse. Bugs, for God's sake. It is not the way to do a medical examination."

"Shizuo, the crime scene is inside the PTA. We have to work with the military."

"He's flying over now. Wants to work through the night. Through the night!" Shizuo exclaimed. He shook his head. "What's the rush? It's a corpse. It'll still be a corpse in the morning."

Koa kept his face impassive, but inside he congratulated himself for bringing a competent medical examiner into the picture. Shizuo's complaining only strengthened his conviction that the baby doctor couldn't handle the case.

"Give me the preliminaries, Doctor."

"Well, there's not much. The body's been there for days. No way to establish time of death. Definitely male. Adult. Between twenty and forty-five, but probably closer to thirty. Deliberate effort to conceal the victim's identity—dental X-rays will be useless. Looks like a ritual killing . . . got to be some kind of whacko thing."

Koa had already figured that out for himself. "When will you have more?"

"A couple of days. The Army doctor wants tests. Fancy stuff I've never heard of, and that'll take time. The samples have to go to O'ahu. Waste of time and money, and you don't get quick results."

Shizuo turned on his heel and walked away as Lieutenant Zeigler approached.

"Learn anything new from your doctor?" The mocking tone in Zeigler's voice matched the smirk on his face.

"Not a goddamn thing. He's the only quack I know of who can commit malpractice on a corpse."

"I had a word with Colonel Cater before he disconnected. He's not impressed with your baby doctor either," said Zeigler.

"Why am I not surprised? Did he have any idea about the time of death?"

"No, not from the scene, but he's running a test that might fix the time. He expressed surprise at the lack of blood. Did you notice?"

"Yeah, what do you make of it?"

"Killed elsewhere and moved here?" Koa nodded.

"Possible, even likely."

By the time the crime scene team finished, the sun hung just above the western horizon, gold rims adorned scattered pink clouds, and the *pu'us*, or cinder cone hills, cast fantastic elongated shadows. The ground search had gone slowly, and they couldn't continue in the dark. Koa asked everyone to reconvene at dawn, and Zeigler assigned several soldiers to secure the site.

Koa and Basa borrowed an office from the military police and set to work. Koa asked Basa to arrange for clerks at headquarters to assemble all local missing-persons reports for the past month and to send inquiries to police on the other islands. "Get every case file on a ritual killing during the past thirty years," Koa directed. He yawned. "I'm beat and I'm going to stay over in the barracks here. You want me to have Zeigler get you a room?"

"Yeah. That's a good idea. It's already way too late to see the kids." Basa was a devoted family man, who doted on his ten-year-old daughter, Samantha, and his seven-year-old son, Jason, both of

whom were already learning to paddle outrigger canoes. He'd
brought both kids, dressed as miniature police officers, to headquarters a number of times, and they called Koa "uncle," as was the Hawaiian custom in addressing esteemed elders. "You know tomorrow's
Saturday. You're gonna miss your workout with the canoe team.
That's the second week in a row. An old man like you has to work
out regularly or he loses a step or two."

Koa winced, feeling a need to massage his neck and upper arm
but not giving in. He didn't like the idea of aging, let alone losing a
step. "Yeah, yeah. I'm only reaching my prime. Let me point out that
my team didn't *huli* two weeks ago," he said, making a flip-flop gesture with his hand. Basa's racing canoe had capsized in the ocean.

"Oh, Jesus, do you have to bring that up? Anybody can get rolled
by a freak wave."

"And the ocean isn't full of freak waves?"

Basa started to retort, then stopped. Koa wondered if the sergeant had somehow spotted his pain and was pulling his punches
out of respect. Of course, it made sense. He had been moving gin-
gerly all day, and Basa had proven himself quite observant.

Koa slipped into the next room, closed the door, and stretched
out on the floor with his hands above his head, the one position
guaranteed to provide relief for the throbbing in his neck, shoulder,
and arm. The doctor had shown him his MRI, pointing out the cal-
cified spinal deposits pinching the nerve that controlled his right
arm. The specialist had been definitive about the need for surgery
before the muscles in Koa's arm began to atrophy and he lost the use
of it altogether. But what if the surgery failed, and he woke up crippled, or maybe not at all? That thought had made him lose a lot of
sleep lately.

He thought about the fire ring and the stone chips at the back of
the cave. Another detective might have dismissed them as irrelevant,

but Koa's personal criminal experience made him paranoid that he might miss something. The fire ring and stone chips might lead nowhere, but he'd take that risk.

After a while, he got up and called the state archaeologist in Honolulu, only to find that the man was away on vacation. Thwarted in following official channels, he wondered if his live-in girlfriend, Nālani, might know an archaeologist. She worked as a technician at the Alice Observatories—home of the world's largest optical telescope, located atop Mauna Kea—and was plugged into the island's scientific community. Feeling guilty for not having checked in with her earlier, he called.

"*Aloha, ipo.*" He knew she liked the Hawaiian term of endearment.

"Where are you?"

Koa winced at the reserve in her voice. "I've had a tough afternoon. Sorry I didn't call earlier. I'm up at Pōhakuloa. We got a mutilated corpse inside the live-fire area. Looks like some kind of ritual killing. I don't want to gross you out, but it's bad, not as bad as what I saw in Somalia, but close."

"Jesus, are you okay?"

"Yeah, nothing a night's sleep won't cure. But I've got to stay up here tonight. Zeigler's got a place for me. Listen, we found some kind of stone tool next to the body in a lava tube. There's an old fire ring and a bunch of little stone chips. You know anything about ancient caves in the saddle area?"

"Not really. Archaeology isn't my field."

"I tried the state archaeologist, but he's on the mainland vacationing. Do you know an archaeologist? Somebody I could talk to?"

There was a pause on the other end of the line. "Sure." Nālani's voice brightened. "I know just the guy . . . met him up on the mountain when he was working out at the stone quarries. He's an expert. Jimmy Hikorea, that's his name. You want me to call him for you?"

"That would be great. Have him call me here no matter how late."

"Don't be put off. He's as sharp as a razor," Nālani warned.

After a day spent with Shizuo, Koa was a model of patience. "Okay. I'm forewarned."

Nālani lingered in his mind's eye after he put down the phone—Nālani in that outrageous bikini at the Green Sand Beach, Nālani with the wind tangling her hair on the Kīlauea Iki Trail in Hawai'i Volcanoes National Park, sleepy-eyed, half-naked Nālani waking up in the morning. He wondered how he could be so lucky and worried that his job—and now his damaged neck—were straining their relationship. Although he had eight years on her, he didn't feel old when he was with her. Yet he wasn't sure how she felt deep inside about living with a forty-plus year-old cop. Insecurity was a funny thing . . . it hit you hardest when you had something to lose.

He was tired and knew he was letting his fear of spinal surgery get to him. Basa's remark about losing a step hadn't helped. He was going to have to face the inevitable. Hell, he'd faced tougher obstacles in the service. Ranger training had been no picnic, nor had putting buddies into medevac choppers, but at least then he'd had some measure of control. Maybe that's what bothered him most about going under the knife—his life would be in some stranger's hands.

It was after midnight when his phone rang. "Koa Kāne here."

"Hi. It's Jimmy Hikorea. Nālani asked me to call. Said you had some kind of archaeological find."

The voice had a squeaky quality, and Koa pictured an emaciated academic on the other end of the line. What had Nālani said? Don't be put off. Had she been referring to his voice?

"Well, I'm really not sure. We're investigating a homicide in a lava tube in the Pōhakuloa Training Area. We found some kind of stone tool, an old fire ring, and some stone chips. We need some expert help to understand if the site might be connected to the homicide."

"Ahhh . . . the stone tool, is it wedge-shaped, like the head of a small hoe?"

Koa found the man's patronizing voice irritating. The man's tone must have prompted Nālani's warning. "Yeah, exactly."

"Sounds like you stumbled on a cave used by the ancient stone workers who transported preforms from the Mauna Kea quarry."

"Preforms? What's a preform?"

"You've never had any training in archaeology, have you?"

Koa felt bone weary and in no mood to tolerate an arrogant academic with a shrill voice. "No, I'm just a dumb cop."

"Sorry. I didn't mean it that way. A preform is a partially shaped cutting tool, usually an adze head. A kind of blank without its final edge." Despite the apology, Jimmy's high-pitched voice hadn't lost its pedantic quality. Koa had to force himself into the role of student.

"Tell me about this quarry."

"There's a bunch of old quarry sites on the upper flank of Mauna Kea. Stone workers mined a dense rock called hawaiite for adzes and other implements. They carried their preforms, half-finished stone tools, down the southern slope of the volcano and into the saddle area. That area was a kind of crossroads."

Now Koa got more interested. He, like so many other island natives, had great pride in his people's history. "Are there caves used by the stone workers in the saddle area?"

"People doing archaeological survey work for the Army found two or three small lava cave shelters in the Humuʻula Saddle. Sounds to me like you've found another one. You want me to come out in the morning and take a look?"

"I'd appreciate it, if it's not too much trouble."

"No trouble at all."

"Come as early as you can. Look for the military police on the Saddle Road near the eastern end of the PTA. Ask for Lieutenant Zeigler if you have a problem."

"Great. I'll be there . . . ummm . . . by mid-morning."

When Koa finally collapsed on a borrowed Army bunk, he was slow to find the peace of sleep. The mutilated face with the blackened eye socket haunted his dreams, coming at him out of the shadowy darkness of the lava tube. Over and over, the mangled face advanced and receded, back and forth, coming closer and closer in his mind's eye until the face came alive. With its good eye gleaming and its mouth contorting, it uttered a long, silent scream.

Then the dream began again with the brutalized face approaching from inky blackness. The face bright, sharp in contrast to the surrounding void. Closer. Closer. The good eye shining. The empty socket large and black, like a hole straight through the head. The dream repeated itself until Koa could feel the heat of the corpse's breath upon his face. The torn lips moved, exposing stumps of jagged, broken teeth.

Desperate to speak, the disfigured face mouthed a single word: *Kōkua!* The word echoed in Koa's mind. Help . . . the poor bastard was screaming for help.

CHAPTER THREE

KOA WAS UP at five and in the mess hall by five thirty. The place was swarming with artillerymen, chopper pilots, and grunts in from O'ahu for a combined arms live-fire exercise. The air was thick with testosterone, and when the rotorheads discovered Koa was a former snake eater who'd lived through the *Black Hawk Down* episode, they had him retelling the tale. Even years later, it still hurt to describe the brutal firefight in which he'd lost two of his service buddies, including Jerry.

Jerry, the fellow soldier who'd helped him through ranger school and become his best friend, had died in Koa's arms, killed by a sniper's bullet meant for Koa. That had been the second turning point in Koa's life. Jerry had always planned to become a cop, and since Koa owed his life to Jerry, Koa committed himself to fulfilling Jerry's life ambition. Devoting himself to the pursuit of justice salved his guilt at having killed his father's nemesis.

Time had blurred the pain, but not his anger at the damn politicians who had sent his unit into harm's way without adequate backup. Somalia was one of his darkest memories.

In the ensuing banter, he was amazed at how in just a few short years technology had revolutionized the battlefield, but left soldiers with the same old gripes—dull food, inadequate equipment, lack of spare parts, insensitive commanders, and the infamous hurry-up-and-wait approach to everything. Maybe, he thought, as he finally walked out of the mess hall, the life of a Hilo detective had its advantages.

Koa and Zeigler, along with their respective teams, reassembled at the crime scene just after dawn. A dead *māmane* tree, silhouetted against the eastern sky, stood like a tombstone over the murder site. Koa eyed its twisted branches, idly hoping for some glimmer of motive for the murder, but he wasn't surprised when it remained just a dead tree. That sort of stuff worked only in old Hawaiian folktales.

Zeigler had requisitioned a helicopter and pilot for an aerial tour of the crime scene. Once they were strapped into their seats, Zeigler handed Koa a headset and a pair of binoculars. Once again, Koa braced his back as the pilot took off. "Can you hold here?" Koa shouted into his microphone as the chopper passed just east of the murder site. The chopper slowed to a halt and steadied.

Below, the entrance to the lava tube lay in a pit thirty yards west of the rutted jeep trail and 150 yards east of a small *pu'u*. Rough ground surrounded the pit, but as Koa studied the terrain from above, he noted a possible route—between a small ravine and some scrub trees—that appeared to offer access. The killer or killers must have driven along the cinder jeep trail, cut off on the rough track nearest the lava tube, and walked the last thirty yards. Koa made a quick sketch of the scene.

"They must have driven out here. Too far from anywhere to walk." Zeigler's voice boomed in Koa's headset.

"You're right, but wouldn't the MPs notice a vehicle?"

"It would be pretty hard for a vehicle to escape detection during the day. Most days, the command's got choppers up, and the pilots know to report intrusions. Still, it's different at night. You could run a moving van in and out of here after dark. Nobody would ever spot you."

"But to rendezvous out here at night . . . walking over that lava in the dark would be begging for a busted ankle or worse."

"Yeah, but out here in the east end—six, maybe eight miles from the barracks, you could use lights." Zeigler pointed toward the PTA headquarters to the northwest. "Nobody would spot flashlights or even car lights."

Koa spun it out further. "If the killer met the victim out here then they must have come in separate vehicles. Separate vehicles mean two killers—or an accomplice—because somebody had to drive the victim's car out of here."

"Yeah, I guess that's right, Koa, but I have trouble seeing two killers. I mean, Jesus, the scene inside that tube . . . I'm no criminologist, but it takes a twisted mind to cut a man up and mess with his eye. Doesn't seem like a group effort."

Koa saw his point. "If you're right, the killer and the victim came together . . . maybe with the victim unconscious or restrained." Koa turned to look at the young Army officer, catching a particularly unflattering profile of the former hockey player's uneven nose.

"Jesus. Can you imagine cutting up a friend or at least somebody you knew? Gives me the creeps."

Koa had seen worse sights, some of which still haunted his dreams. Like the time in a tiny Afghan town where he'd watched as villagers stoned a girl to death for loving a boy from the wrong family. More recently he'd found a young man stabbed over fifty times in a Hilo back alley. Images of the man's flayed face still came flaring up out of nowhere in his nightmares. Still, he too had trouble imagining how anyone could slice up and abandon a friend in a lava tube. "I don't know, Jerry. Some people are capable of incomprehensible violence."

As the helicopter approached the dirt road just outside the search area, Koa saw Sergeant Basa waving. After landing, Koa joined Basa and a young enlisted man about halfway between the closest trail and the lava tube. Several scrub trees dotted the slope on his right, and a rocky gully posed an obstacle to his left. They were close to the possible access route Koa had spotted from the air. A man walking from the trail to the lava tube might well have passed the exact point where they stood.

"This is Pedro," said Basa. "He's one of Zeigler's MPs, from Texas. Been here on the island only a couple a months, but he's got sharp eyes. He spotted this key lying on the ground. We haven't touched it. I thought you'd better have a look." Basa pointed at a single detached key.

"Good work, soldier," Koa said.

"Thank you, sir."

Keeping his back straight, Koa stooped to inspect the silver key on porous gray-white lava, half-concealed beneath a leafy shrub. He ordered it photographed. Although the standard Yale key bore no identifying marks, it was clean and shiny. A fingerprint check yielded only a badly smeared partial print of dubious identification value. Yet the oily print was enough to confirm that the key had been dropped recently. Maybe, Koa thought, it had fallen from the victim's pocket, if his body had been carried.

Just before eleven o'clock, the MPs radioed that Jimmy Hikorea, the park service archaeologist, wanted access to the crime scene. A bright red Ford Bronco soon bounced up the rutted trail. Koa started toward the vehicle as it jerked to a halt but stopped short as the driver swung the door open. Koa watched intently as Hikorea reached into the back to lift out a wheelchair, placed a cushion on the seat, and swung himself down.

The shrill voice from the previous evening's telephone call flashed into Koa's mind. He remembered how the archaeologist responded to his invitation to drive forty miles across the island to Pōhakuloa: "No trouble at all."

Koa smiled. This was going to be interesting.

The barrel-chested man maneuvered the wheelchair, which twisted and bounced like an amusement park ride, over the rugged terrain. How many wheelchairs does this guy destroy in a month? Koa wondered. Jimmy's upper arms were huge, yet his legs ended above his missing knees in thick rubberized stubs. As if in sympathy, a spear of pain shot down Koa's right arm. Hikorea's vehicle, Koa thought, had to be equipped with hand-controlled brakes and accelerator.

He wore a black windbreaker with the National Park Service logo, beneath which appeared the words "Federal Archaeologist" in yellow letters. He sported a black baseball cap with the Marine Corps logo in gold. It looked incongruous with his shoulder-length black hair.

"Jimmy Hikorea here. Are you Detective Koa Kāne?" Jimmy extended his right hand while continuing to drive the chair forward with his oversized left arm. Never once did he take his hard-black eyes off Koa's face. Koa recognized the high-pitched squeak, and somehow knew it wasn't natural; it was the legacy of some injury. Had Jimmy really been a marine? The lines in Jimmy's chiseled face told Koa that he was old enough to have served in Iraq despite his long hair.

When they shook hands, Koa felt the man's life-force crush his grip. He seemed to radiate power.

"Yeah, I'm Koa. I appreciate your coming out here on such short notice."

"No trouble. I'd walk to hell and back for a new dig."

Koa studied the archaeologist. He had light brown skin and, despite his masculinity, the finely sculptured features of an Indian princess.

Jimmy's smile disappeared and his eyes darkened as Lieutenant Zeigler joined them. A vein in Jimmy's neck bulged. Zeigler held out his hand to the newcomer, but the archaeologist ignored the military policeman. Zeigler stood awkwardly for a moment before slowly withdrawing his hand. A puzzled look came over his face.

"I came up here out of respect for Nālani and to help the county police. I'm not here to help the goddamn Army." Jimmy glowered at Zeigler as though the man had committed a crime.

"Whoa! I know when I'm not wanted." Zeigler took two steps backward, turned on his heel, and strode back toward his jeep.

"Bastards," Jimmy snarled.

Koa resisted the urge to go after his friend, and instead informed the crippled archaeologist, "That wasn't necessary. Zeigler's a good man."

"I've had my fill of the fucking Army. Show me what you've found." Although the voice squeaked, the words came out with the assurance of a man used to being in command. Nālani's words came back to Koa: "Don't be put off; he's as sharp as a razor." Had Nālani been referring to Jimmy's intellect or his personality?

Koa hesitated, weighing the man's odd behavior against the needs of his investigation. The Army must have had something to do with Jimmy's injuries. On the other hand, Koa needed Zeigler's cooperation. Plus, he resented the mistreatment of his friend. And he wasn't about to cede control to this archaeologist. "Maybe I made a mistake in inviting you out here, Mr. Hikorea." Koa held the man's gaze. "Either play nice or climb back in your truck and head out of here."

Jimmy straightened in his chair, eyebrows raised, a look of surprise on his face. He wasn't used to being challenged. The two men glared at each other until a smile slowly spread across Jimmy's face. "Nālani told me you were one tough cop," he said. "Shall we start over?"

Koa decided to give the archaeologist a second chance. "The body's in a lava tube off the bottom of a pit. We'll have to carry you down."

"Fine by me, if you're up to it."

A year ago, Koa would have grabbed one side of the wheelchair, but with his neck problem, he let one of the soldiers help Basa carry Jimmy. Gradually, they jostled the archaeologist down the sloping side of the pit. Once on level ground, Jimmy powered his wheelchair into the lava tube, which was still illuminated by arc lights. Koa followed, leaving the others outside, and handed Jimmy a glossy color photograph. "We found this next to the corpse."

Jimmy studied the picture.

"It's an adze preform, like I told you last night—the unfinished head of a stone hatchet. The color says it came from the adze quarry up the slopes of Mauna Kea."

Jimmy rolled his wheelchair around the site. Around and around he circled, his black eyes darting from place to place. When he reached the piles of stone chips for the third time, Jimmy locked the wheels of the chair, eased himself forward, flipped the seat cushion onto the floor, and lowered himself down. Producing a magnifying glass from a pouch attached to his belt, he examined the stone fragments while Koa moved one of the arc lights closer.

Incongruous, Koa thought. Barrel chested and a squeaky voice. Hates the Army, but he drives halfway across the island to an Army training area. A football player's neck, yet he handles a magnifying glass with the finesse of a jeweler. Jimmy sat next to the pile of stones, staring off into the floodlit space.

"Something wrong?" Koa's voice reflected his rising impatience. He still questioned the wisdom of bringing this strange man into the investigation.

"These are quarry flakes—pieces of rock that flake off when a workman shapes stone. Here, see these fluted edges?" Jimmy held out one of the stone chips for Koa's inspection. "Those edges are characteristic of quarry flakes."

"So?"

"So, stone workers quarried and shaped stone on the mountain. Why are there piles of stone flakes here in this cave?"

"You tell me."

"I can't. That's what bothers me."

Jimmy moved farther back into the lava tube. Placing his hands firmly on the rough floor, he nudged the cushion forward and swung himself onto it, covering the uneven floor with the measured hops of a monstrous frog. Koa would have laughed at the odd movement had the man not been disabled.

Hop by hop, Jimmy jumped his way into the narrow, low-ceilinged area at the back of the cave where it ended in a jumble of broken rocks. Koa followed with an arc light and stooped to watch the archaeologist sitting in the confined space. Koa eased himself down onto his haunches as Jimmy continued to sit immobile, staring at the back of the cave. Seconds passed. A minute passed. Koa shifted impatiently.

Jimmy withdrew a matchbook from his pouch. Koa expected the archaeologist to light a cigarette, but instead he struck a match and held it aloft, watching the tiny flame dance as if caught in a breeze. Koa watched the flickering light reflected in Jimmy's bright black eyes. What was this strange man thinking? The flame ate away at the match. Was Jimmy checking for gas? Koa thought the archaeologist would scorch his fingers, but the man snuffed the match out just in time.

Jimmy reached upward and began to push and pull upon a large rock near the ceiling. The rock shifted. Jimmy wiggled it. Back and forth. Back and forth. Koa watched, puzzled by the archaeologist's actions. Gradually, Jimmy worked the rock loose. As it began to slide free in a shower of loose dirt, Koa saw that it weighed seventy-five, maybe a hundred, pounds. Yet Jimmy pulled it loose and set it to the side as though it were a pebble.

With the first rock removed, Koa realized there was an open space behind the rocks and joined Jimmy. Working together, they quickly shifted rock after rock from the back of the lava tube until they'd opened a hole nearly two feet in diameter. Koa pointed his light through the hole. The jumble of rocks that had appeared to be the end of the lava tube was only a rockfall. The lava tube extended much farther, far enough that the inky depths absorbed the beam of light, making it impossible to judge the depth of the tunnel.

The two men worked together to clear away additional rocks until they had an opening large enough to crawl through. Koa scrambled forward first, ignoring the pain in his shoulder. *Scrape. Scrape.* Koa heard Jimmy's cushion slide across the rough floor as he followed. Koa crawled two dozen feet along a narrow tube until it opened into a rock chamber the size of a small room. Koa blinked rapidly, trying to assess the strange sight revealed in the narrow beam of his light.

He illuminated a long, curved object, like a log from some long-fallen tree. From its center a black stone figure spiked upward. Koa stared transfixed at the thing. Its form was recognizable as female through the dust—heavy breasts, weighted down with age, nipples drooping; legs open, crooked outward at the knees. Human, yet not human. A great beak jutted from the center of its elongated head and its huge unseeing eyes seemed to glower with a warning. Beneath a covering of dust, the unornamented figure had the glow of polished obsidian.

Koa felt the hair on the back of his neck rise. He could almost hear the bird woman screaming, demanding to know who dared intrude upon her secrets.

"What is it?" Koa asked, as Jimmy pulled up next to him.

The archaeologist had a wide-eyed expression and seemed as stunned as Koa. "A talisman . . . but unlike any other in the islands."

"It's awe-inspiring. She must have perched there for centuries." Koa heard the reverence in his own voice. His heritage stared him in the eye, bringing back his grandfather's stories about a time when men worshiped idols. Slowly, he shifted the light down below the base of the figure to the object below. As he moved the light from side to side, Koa recognized the shape. The raised bowsprit and curved gunnels had the unmistakable shape of a Hawaiian war canoe. "It's a canoe."

"Painted red . . . the color of the gods," Jimmy added.

"What's a canoe doing here in a cave in the saddle, miles from any water?" Koa's voice echoed eerily from the walls of the small cavern.

"It's a coffin."

"A coffin?" Koa nearly choked on the word.

"We've entered the secret royal burial crypt of some ancient *ali'i*, some man of enormous power in his time."

"You mean, there are bones inside the canoe?" Excitement registered in Koa's voice. "The bones of a Hawaiian king?"

"Yes. Every royal family had a trusted retainer charged with hiding the bones of deceased kings," Jimmy squeaked. "The canoe was probably already placed here, poised to transport the spirit of the *ali'i* forever."

Koa turned toward Jimmy. "What king?" Koa asked, a feeling of excitement rippling through him.

"The talisman should tell us," Jimmy said, his high- pitched voice becoming tentative again, "but I've never seen such a female bird figure."

"Could this burial site have anything to do with the dead body?"

"I don't know. It didn't look as though anyone had disturbed those rocks in recent years. But I can tell you that in pre-contact times, before the *haole* missionaries arrived, almost any member of a deceased *ali'i*'s family would have killed to prevent the theft of his bones."

Koa studied Jimmy's animated face, searching for some hint that the man was joking.

"You're serious?"

"Quite. Under the old system of beliefs, the family or a loyal retainer protected the bones forever."

"What happened when the retainer died?" Koa asked.

"The man who secreted these bones would, as he neared death, have revealed their location to a trusted member of the next generation."

At this point, Koa's native fascination began to drain away. He could buy into the old traditions only so far. "No one still believes power can be secured from the bones of a king or prince who died hundreds of years ago."

"Don't be so sure," Jimmy challenged. "The Polynesian idea is neither unique in human history nor outmoded. The Catholic Church sanctified Father Damien's St. Philomena's Church on Moloka'i by sealing the bones of his right hand in a crypt. Many human relics still attract pilgrimages in Europe and the Middle East."

Koa tried to puzzle out all this information. It was all too fantastic: The mutilated corpse. The missing eye. Now this secret burial vault. Could it be that someone had killed to preserve the tomb of his kin? Impossible? Perhaps not.

After killing Hazzard, Koa had thought he'd never escape punishment, yet he'd successfully faked the mill manager's suicide. Nothing was impossible.

"What would you say if I told you the corpse we found outside had been mutilated? Missing its left eye?"

Jimmy's head snapped around. "The left eye . . . just the left one?"

"Yes. The left eye was gouged out. The right eye was intact."

"A sacrificial warning," Jimmy squeaked hesitantly as though he were struggling with the thought.

"What do you mean?"

"Ancient Polynesians, including the Hawaiians, made human sacrifices and often gouged out the left eye. They displayed sacrifice victims as warnings to others who might break some *kapu*, some law or custom."

"Jesus." Koa struggled to maintain his calm. "The secret must have died a hundred years ago."

"Perhaps, but I know of Hawaiians living today who possess such secrets. Your victim could have been killed to warn others against intruding on this burial site."

CHAPTER FOUR

As Koa stood before the canoe, the memory was vivid, like a movie playing in his mind. When he was six or seven he'd sat at his great-grandfather's feet, staring wide-eyed as the old man talked story of the *kahuna kālai waʻa*, the expert canoe builders who were Koa's ancestors. Singsong prayers and the roasting of special fishes readied his father's father four generations past to climb into the forests where the great *koa* trees made the finest canoes. Like a priest listening for signs, each of the ancient Kāne men was alert for the hollow tapping sound of the *ʻelepaio* bird. The bird signaled a rotten tree—always to be avoided. *ʻUā ʻelepaio ʻia ka waʻa*—the canoe is marked out by the *ʻelepaio*.

Even with chanted prayers, it took the Kāne men many hundreds of blows with a stone adze to fell a forest giant. Then came the women to tend the fires and cook for the dozens of men who hauled the great log down the mountain, ridden by a guide to keep it safe from harm on the steeper slopes. As a child Koa had always wanted to ride one of those canoe logs. Now he wondered if his ancestors had carved this red burial canoe, painted the color of the gods.

"Remember the match, Detective?" Jimmy interrupted his reverie.

Jerked back to the present, Koa thought not of the match itself, but of its dancing reflection in Jimmy's eyes.

"Yeah." Koa kept his voice even, suppressing his irritation at Jimmy's obliqueness.

"Remember how the flame danced around?"

A light dawned in Koa's mind. "Airflow. That's why you moved the rocks."

"Dead-on, Detective . . . and the airflow is even stronger in here." Koa recognized the freshness of the air, even before the archaeologist finished speaking.

"I should have figured. There's another entrance."

"Don't kick yourself. I've been in these burial caves a bunch of times. Multiple burial sites often branch off of the same tube."

Koa advanced beyond the canoe to a recessed area in the opposite wall, and Jimmy hopped along after him. Koa knelt, pressing both hands against the wall and straining against the rock. Nothing happened, except for the pain clawing at his shoulder. Jimmy joined him, and they pushed again. Still no movement.

"I don't think it's going to budge." Despite the airflow, Koa doubted that the cave extended farther. "One more time. Let's push together."

Both of them heaved against the rock wall. As they strained and Koa clenched his teeth to control the pain, a section of the wall began to shiver. Barely discernible at first, the movement accelerated, leaving a gaping hole.

Koa's arm and shoulder hurt like blazes, and he stopped for a moment to choke down two pain pills, dry swallowing, before following his light through the opening into another cavern. The place was immense, so big that the dim light faded in every direction.

Koa's eyes followed the beam. The circle of artificial light illuminated a large, flat boulder. The rock, nearly four feet long and two and a half feet high, stood like a stone table. A mound of chips surrounded its base. The chips appeared to be nearly a foot deep near the stone and tapered down to a loose carpet a dozen feet away from the boulder. Several round stones, about the size of baseballs, lay atop and intermingled with the flakes.

Jimmy hopped over next to Koa. "Sweet Jesus, an adze maker's workshop, untouched by the hands of time." Koa shifted the light farther down the wall, revealing another large, flat boulder, also surrounded by stone chips. Beyond that rock stood a third stone table and a fourth. The light wouldn't penetrate the farthest recesses of the cavern.

"It's huge." Koa heard the awe in his own voice. "Dozens of men must have worked in here."

Jimmy seemed equally amazed. "It changes our understanding of history."

"What understanding of history?" Koa asked.

"Jesus. We knew only half the story. The flat rocks surrounded by stone chips are workbenches. The round rocks scattered among the stone flakes are hammerstones, used to chip away stone fragments as they shaped the preforms." Jimmy paused. "This workshop is where the adze makers worked in the wintertime when freezing weather stopped work on the summit."

Koa found this giant underground cavern fascinating, but he'd become chief detective only through an unrelenting focus on solving crimes. For him the mission was foremost. He wanted to know if this workshop was connected to the poor tortured soul whose death had brought them out here. He played his light across the floor, looking for anything that might answer that question. He'd trained his eye to look for an oddity, a discordant note, the one thing that didn't belong in any crime scene.

Something shiny near the base of the closest stone table reflected the beam of his flashlight. He moved closer and searched for the source of the glimmer. Nothing. He shifted position and directed the beam of light into the pile of stones. There. He knelt to examine the source of the reflection—a tiny piece of cellophane with a thin blue stripe. Packaging... it was a remnant of the wrapper of some modern product ... and it instantly changed his whole approach to the cavern. This was more than an ancient workshop, untouched by the hands of time. Someone had been here in contemporary times ... maybe only recently. This place might really be related to the murder.

After searching the immediate floor area for other clues, Koa swung his light up over the cave walls, stopping the beam on a rocky outcropping from which a small piece of broken stick protruded. Although hard to see in the poor light, the stick appeared blackened. "What did they use for light in this cave?"

"I'd guess that we'll find the work areas ringed with *kukui* nut lamps."

Koa nodded. Old Hawaiians crushed the nuts of the *kukui*, or candlenut tree, and burned the oil in hollowed stones, called *kukui* nut lamps. He turned the light toward the curved roof of the cave. A thick vein of soot blackened the chocolate-colored lava rock wall above the torch holder. "Whatever it was, they burned an awful lot of it, and it smoked."

Koa suddenly thought of his last adventure in a cave. He and Basa, along with a half-dozen patrolmen, had cornered an escaped convict in an isolated lava tube. It had taken them three days to root the half-crazed and heavily armed man out of the dark, winding passages. He hoped he wouldn't have to spend three days in this cavern, but at least here nobody was shooting at him.

The flickering flame of Jimmy's match, the airflow in the burial chamber, the clean smell of the air in this huge cavern ... all flashed together in Koa's mind. "There's got to be another entrance to this place."

"Dead-on, Detective."

"Someplace down there, I suppose." Koa pointed the light toward the back of the huge cavern, but the powerful beam dissipated in the darkness.

Koa swung his light from side to side, examining the workshop. Suddenly, the beam revealed a huge patch of wall where the rough lava rock had been painstakingly smoothed. In the middle of this flattened surface a crude figure stood carved in high relief. A human stick figure.

A giant X outlined the body and legs of a man. A line across the top of the X formed the arms, while an inverted J created the neck and head. The figure's right hand held a stick with a square top, while the left hand held what might have been a ball sprouting V-shaped lines. Above the stick figure, a ridge of protruding rock formed a gigantic upside-down V, like a ragged triangular roof. "It's a petroglyph!" Koa exclaimed. "It's magnificent—"

"A relief carving," Jimmy interrupted. "Petroglyphs are scratched into smooth lava rock surfaces. This figure is raised." Jimmy's shrill voice took on a pedantic tone. "Stonecutters chipped away all the surrounding rock, leaving the original rock to make the picture in raised relief. This technique is different and vastly more sophisticated than the traditional Hawaiian petroglyph."

"This place is extraordinary. Unbelievable." Koa could barely control his excitement. He'd never imagined he would be part of a historic discovery. Even without specialized training, he knew he'd made a spectacular find. "What's the figure holding?" Koa held his light on the figure's right hand. "The right hand could be holding an adze."

"Gee, I'll bet that's right," Jimmy conceded. "It looks sort of like a hammer or a hatchet. What about the left hand?"

Koa shifted the light to the figure's left side. "That's harder. The upper part could be the sides of a cup or a bowl. Maybe it's a bird." Even as Koa spoke, he knew he had nailed it.

Jimmy turned to Koa with an astonished look. "My God, you're right, Detective. It's a petrel, a dark-rumped petrel . . ."

"Seabirds? The ones that loiter about behind ships?" Koa asked.

"Yes, seabirds . . . seabirds that nest on the ground. The Hawaiians called them 'ua'a. You won't find many around here today, but in ancient times hundreds of thousands of petrels nested in the saddle lands. Even when the first *haoles* arrived, thousands of petrels nested here."

"The Hawaiians hunted them for food?" Koa continued to hold the light on the figure's upraised arm.

"Yes. The chicks still dressed in down were a delicacy, a treat reserved for the chiefs."

"So what do you make of this guy holding the petrel aloft?"

"An adze and a petrel. It's a celebration of ancient natural resources in this part of the island."

"And the talisman, the bird woman . . . did she have the head of a petrel?" Koa guessed.

"Dead-on. You missed your calling, Detective. You should have been an archaeologist."

Koa grinned, pleased with the compliment. "This place is a major historical and archaeological find, isn't it?"

"The combination of that grave and this massive underground workshop represents a previously unknown power center. Think of the work required to build and maintain this place. Food for the workers. Oil for the lamps. Stone for the stonecutters. Wood for the adze handles. Think of the social organization and power structure required to control the manpower. People developed the skills and devoted the time to make that rock carving and the bird woman talisman. A powerful man or group of men governed this place. Power derived from stone. Stone implements. And we had no idea before today—"

Jimmy stopped talking as Sergeant Basa and Lieutenant Zeigler came crawling through the tunnel into the cavern, followed by one of Zeigler's soldiers, dragging an electric arc light with its trailing electric cable. Jimmy's body stiffened and he scowled. Before the archaeologist could open his mouth to speak, Koa placed a hand on the man's shoulder. Jimmy tried to shake off the restraining hand, but Koa tightened his grip.

Koa spoke in a low, urgent tone. "Jimmy, I don't know what the Army did to you—"

"The fucking Army killed my buddies an' took my legs. Pissant lieutenant called in the artillery on us." Jimmy leaned forward as though straining to rise off his cushion. His high-pitched voice quavered with uncontrolled rage.

"I'm sorry for that, but Lieutenant Zeigler didn't do it." Koa spoke slowly, trying to appeal to Jimmy's rational side. "He's a good man."

"There ain't no good Army lieutenants. They're all bastards."

"Don't be a fool," Koa snapped, before forcing himself to speak slowly. "You're going to need Zeigler's help to study this site. It's on Army land. You would like to be the archaeologist who reveals this workshop to the world, wouldn't you?"

That had the desired effect. Jimmy slowly rocked backward on his cushion. Koa, who continued to grip Jimmy's shoulder, felt the tension drain out of the man's body. The angry mask of Jimmy's face began to dissolve, replaced by a crooked half smile. "You know how to get what you want, don't you, Detective."

"Dead-on, Jimmy." Koa returned Jimmy's half smile as he released his grip on the archaeologist's shoulder.

Koa signaled to the newcomers and they gathered around him. He told them about the small piece of cellophane he'd found. "We're here to check for any evidence that might connect this cavern to our murder site. Beyond that we don't disturb anything." His voice had the hard ring of authority, like a troop commander. "We'll report this archaeological site to the state and federal governments."

"The National Park Service and the Hawaiian government are going to request the Army to suspend military operations here until this site can be properly evaluated and perhaps even excavated," Jimmy squeaked as he looked malevolently at Lieutenant Zeigler.

"Christ, that's beyond my pay grade," said Zeigler. "I'm just a lowly lieutenant."

Koa held up his hand for silence. "We're out here on a murder investigation. We need to know why a ritual killing occurred in the shadow of an undiscovered archaeological site."

"Hell, this cavern would sure as hell explain someone sneaking past my MPs at night," Zeigler said, spreading his arms, indicating the scope of the cave.

"Agreed, if—and it's a big if—the victim or the killer knew about this underground workshop," Koa said. "But as near as we could tell, nobody had disturbed that rockfall before Jimmy arrived."

The men moved deeper into the cavern, crunching over the loose carpet of stone chips as they passed the four large stone tables. For a moment, Koa thought he spied a fifth worktable, but as they approached, he realized that the boulder was neither flat on top nor surrounded by stone flakes. Then he saw the opening in the wall and hurried forward. Directing his light through the opening, he saw not another entrance, as he had expected, but a second burial crypt. A disturbed burial crypt. Empty, aside from a pile of bones. Jimmy hopped up next to him.

"What do you make of this?" Koa moved the light around the desolate chamber.

"An archaeologist's worst nightmare."

"Vandalism?"

"Looks like it. The ancients never buried their dead like that."

"The question is when. Is this the work of modern hands or was this crypt robbed eons ago?" Koa held the light on the jumble of bones.

"Can't say. Grave robbing is as old as time." Koa heard melancholy in Jimmy's voice.

As they approached the far end of the cavern, all four men felt the steady flow of air emanating from another tunnel.

"There's a good breeze blowing in here. This tunnel has to have another outlet," Zeigler commented.

"Where do you suppose it comes out?" Basa responded.

"It's anybody's guess. We won't know until we explore it." Jimmy grinned, obviously eager to continue exploring.

"Koa, look at this!" Zeigler had moved into the mouth of the tunnel. Koa moved to the lieutenant's side and knelt. He removed a plastic evidence envelope from his pocket and used it to pick up a small cylindrical object. Suddenly, he made the connection—butt and cellophane wrapper—both from a package of cigarettes.

"These two things increase the likelihood of a connection between what we've found and our murder," Koa announced.

"What is it?" Basa stepped forward, looking at the object in the small plastic bag.

"A cigarette butt." Koa held the unfiltered butt for the others to see. The stub bore a marking identifying it as a Gauloises, a European cigarette. "That's not a common smoke out here . . . maybe we can trace it."

"Suggests a modern grave robber, doesn't it?" The melancholy in Jimmy's voice had turned to anger.

Although the vast majority of Koa's work involved burglaries, street crimes, and drug cases, he knew a bit about the black market. "Things from this cave would be pretty valuable on the black market, wouldn't they?" Koa looked toward Jimmy.

"Oh, they're valuable. The burial canoe and the talisman are priceless. Archaeological history is unfortunately full of murderous grave robbers. That part of *Raiders of the Lost Ark* was real enough."

Koa directed his light down the tunnel. "Exploring that tunnel just became a part of our murder investigation."

CHAPTER FIVE

ARC LIGHTS BLAZED at the far end of the ancient underground workshop. Koa, Basa, Zeigler, and Detective Piki, Koa's most junior detective, who'd been on cave-exploring expeditions, assembled the ropes, hand lights, and safety equipment necessary to explore the tunnel that fed fresh air into the stone workers' cavern. Jimmy Hikorea joined them, riding a small three-wheeled scooter, retrieved from the back of his Bronco.

"'Natural sewers,' that's what the pros call these here lava tubes," Piki said, his boyish face and crew cut making him look no more than nineteen years old. They perfectly matched his exuberant voice and inability to stop moving around.

"Well, if this tube is one of Piki's natural sewers, its lava came from Mauna Kea, and the tunnel leads back that way," Jimmy said in his squeaky academic voice.

"Yeah, the airflow is real, real strong. That's peculiar." Piki made a speeding motion with his hand.

All of them turned to look at Piki. "Why?" Zeigler asked.

"Well, air don't flow for no reason. I figure Dr. Hikorea's got it right. This here tube carried lava from Mauna Kea. The other entrance must be somewhere up the side of the mountain where the air is cooler. Cooler air is heavier. Temperature difference might explain a light breeze, but this air is really movin'. It's more like a wind tunnel. It's real peculiar." Piki made another swooping gesture with his hand.

"Dead-on, Sherlock." Jimmy looked appreciatively at the young detective. "You ever think about becoming an archaeologist?"

Piki couldn't contain his pride. "No, sir, but I've read books about grave robbers."

Jimmy frowned. "Not exactly what I had in mind." His voice betrayed more than a touch of sarcasm, and Koa shook his head.

Coils of rope, cord, and wire lay stacked on the cavern floor. The arc lamps sent light piercing far into the tunnel's depths. Zeigler carried a portable field telephone, linked by wire to a communications set on the surface. They were ready. The mouth of the tunnel beckoned.

The five men moved easily down the wide underground passage trailing a white nylon cord, knotted at hundred-yard intervals, as well as the communications wire linking them to their support team on the surface. Jimmy rode his scooter, rocking back and forth as the fat rubber tires gained traction over the uneven floor. Each man carried a battery-powered halogen light.

"Twenty-two, twenty-three, twenty-four . . ." Basa kept count of the knots as Piki played out the nylon cord behind them. Suddenly he paused. "Oh my God."

They all heard the growing rumble. Particles of dust separated from the walls of the cave, sparkling in the beams of their halogen lights. Everyone stopped moving and stood, statue-like, in the middle of the cave. "Oh, God! It's an earthquake," Zeigler shouted.

"Christ, we'll be trapped in here," Piki yelled, his voice reverberating through the tunnel.

"Get flat against the walls," Koa commanded. Everyone save Jimmy sprang to obey and crouched against the sides of the tunnel.

The rumbling rose, growing louder and deeper. Louder and deeper. Bearing down upon them like a speeding locomotive growling through a tunnel, the sound reverberated, echoing off the walls, reinforcing itself and growing ever louder.

"Mayday! Mayday! Earthquake! We're caught in a strong earthquake," said Zeigler, speaking urgently into the field telephone and huddling against the cave wall. "We're about twenty-four hundred yards in. Explorer base, do you copy? Over."

There was no reply. Zeigler desperately repeated the mayday call, his voice rising to be heard above the din. Still there was no answer. A frightened look creased his face. "I can't get through."

Basa, a devout Catholic, crossed himself. He sang baritone in the church choir whenever work permitted and rarely missed going to mass. His lips now moved in an obvious prayer none of the rest of them could hear above the awful noise. Koa guessed he was praying for his wife and kids.

Louder. Louder. Rumbling. The sound seemed to be almost on top of them. The ground trembled. Dust particles flaked off the lava and clouded the air, growing thicker by the second. The noise became deafening. Piki screamed. Shaking like a tree branch in a hurricane, he broke from the wall into a stumbling run back the way they'd come. Koa thought about going after him but knew you couldn't outrun an earthquake.

Piki's scream and the rising volume of the ominous roar reminded Koa of the Olympic Hotel in Mogadishu, where his rescue unit had come under heavy machine gun and rocket fire from Somali militia. Two of his men had died that day. Odd, he thought, to survive that disaster only to die in a lava tube. He knew now why he'd always hated caves. Someone in the great beyond had been warning him.

Through it all, Jimmy sat on his scooter in the middle of the cave with his head cocked to one side, listening intently.

The rumbling rose to a thundering crescendo . . . and peaked.

The sound began to gradually fade. Softer. And softer still. The din slowly faded away to an intense silence. Koa felt his heart racing and realized he'd been holding his breath. Zeigler too had stopped breathing.

"What the hell was that?" Basa exclaimed.

"A truck," Jimmy proclaimed dispassionately. Poised upon his wheels in the middle of the tunnel, he alone sat completely unruffled by the terror they'd experienced. They all looked at him as though he'd lost his mind.

"We're directly under the Saddle Road," he piped with a self-satisfied grin. "You just got run over by an eighteen-wheeler."

The sound came again, only softer this time, rising and fading, like an oncoming vehicle crossing above them.

"That must have been a damn car," Zeigler said. He laughed. Basa joined him. They all laughed, even Jimmy.

Koa knew that laugh well. He'd heard it many times in the military. It had nothing to do with humor.

One by one Koa, Basa, and Zeigler unfolded themselves from their crouched positions against the cave walls and slapped dust from their clothing. Piki, now red as a fire truck with mortification, rejoined the group. Zeigler, choking down his embarrassment, cancelled the mayday call.

"Wow, that was scary. I thought I was about to meet my maker," Basa, who was normally unflappable, commented.

"Yeah," Koa conceded.

The five explorers slowly moved forward again. As they advanced, the tube became narrower. The airflow going past them grew stronger and cooler. The floor of the tube sloped upward, and Jimmy had an increasingly difficult time maneuvering his scooter. Finally, they came to a point where the passage narrowed to the width of a man. They had to proceed single file, and Jimmy had to abandon his scooter.

"You want one of us to go back with you?" Basa knew the answer, but somehow felt compelled to offer.

"Hell no, my arms need the exercise. Besides, I wouldn't miss the end of this expedition for a week's R and R in Bahrain."

The five men forged through the narrow, now-twisting underground passage. Jimmy hopped along behind at a surprisingly rapid pace. Their route turned sharply upward. The tunnel veered ninety degrees to the right, then ninety degrees to the left. Koa suddenly saw light ahead, glimmering off the lava walls.

He emerged from a tiny portal behind a giant boulder inside a cinder cone. He saw that the wall of the cinder cone rose almost straight up an eighty-foot cliff to the west, while the eastern side of the cone had disintegrated. One by one the others emerged from the cavity, blinking in the brightness of daylight, leaving Jimmy behind.

"Hey, Koa," they heard Jimmy exclaim, "come look at this."

Jimmy sat inside the mouth of the lava tube on his pad and pointed toward a spot on the wall about eighteen inches off the ground. Koa, mindful of his neck, knelt and bent over to see. Recessed into the wall below a small rock shelf, he spotted a small metal plate with a tiny dim red light. Jimmy pointed to a similarly small plate with a crystalline patch on the opposite wall. Both were impossible to see when standing.

"What do you make of it, Jimmy?"

"Looks like an infrared light beam designed to detect the presence of anyone entering or exiting this tunnel. And it's positioned so anyone walking normally would miss it. Whoever installed it didn't count on someone looking at the world from my vantage point."

"And we've just tripped it."

"Dead-on, Detective."

Jimmy finally hopped out of the crevice behind the boulder screening the mouth of the tunnel. Koa pointed up toward the western wall of the cinder cone.

"Those old adze makers could teach modern engineers a thing or two. There's the answer to your airflow mystery. The western wall of this cone acts like a sail. It catches the predominantly easterly winds and funnels the air down the wall into the lava tube. Nature has created a near-perfect ventilation system for the underground workshop two and a half miles away beneath the floor of the saddle."

"Wow. That's way cool," Piki said. He grinned, the cherry-red blush of embarrassment having faded to a dull rouge.

Koa led them southeast toward the collapsed side of the old cone. They climbed to the crest of a small rise and were greeted by a breathtaking view. Looking south, they peered down the slope of Mauna Kea, back across the Humu'ula Saddle, and over the Saddle Road. Their starting point was identified by Jimmy's bright red Bronco, which sat among a collection of military vehicles. The broad shield of Mauna Loa rose to a snowcap on the other side of the saddle.

Basa voiced their shared feelings. "I'm never gonna feel the same way about that damn road. That truck scared the shit out of me."

A shout came from Detective Piki about twenty yards down the hill. Koa hurried toward the young detective, who knelt over a small pit on the slope of the mountain.

"What have you found?"

"Dunno. Looks like somebody's been blasting." Piki held up a short piece of frayed cord and a fragment of heavy yellowish paper. Koa examined both the cord and the paper. The detective was right. The cord appeared to be fuse material, while the paper had the waxy texture of explosives packaging.

"What do you make of it, Piki?"

"There's no reason for blasting . . . except maybe the survey crew for the Saddle Road improvement project?"

Koa shook his head at the young detective's wild guess. He tried to make sense of it all. The mutilated body, the series of caves, the disturbed grave, and now this explosives residue. What the hell was going on? Who would go to all this trouble, with all these elaborate ritual preparations, to kill someone? And leave a body, he reminded himself, he hadn't yet identified?

CHAPTER SIX

AFTER TWO LONG days away from home, Koa was thrilled to be back in his own cottage waiting for his sweetheart, Nālani. It felt right to leave the case behind and play chef for her, even if the respite was only temporary. He cut the deep red sushi-grade ʻahi into long square strips, added salt and pepper, and coated them with a mayonnaise wasabi mixture. With the panache of a sushi chef, or so he liked to imagine, he added enoki mushrooms and wrapped each strip in a sheet of seaweed nori. Setting aside the ʻahi, Koa prepared the tempura batter and placed it in the refrigerator.

Nālani burst through the door and danced across the great room, whirling around and moving her arms in graceful arcs. As her long black hair swirled around her body, her oval face lit with a mischievous smile like the one that had first attracted him.

"I gather the job interview went well," he remarked wryly. The two were so different—a forty-plus-year-old cop and a thirty-four-year-old biologist . . . she so trim, so lithe, so gentle in her movements, while he resembled the muscular football player from his high school days. Given how independent they both were, it was a small miracle their romance had blossomed. Luckily, her free spirit made her tolerant of the demands of his police duties.

"Fantastic!" She twirled around again. "There's going to be an opening in four months, and I'm the number one candidate . . . numero uno!"

After graduate school in California and a stint in the research department of a big pharmaceutical company, Nālani had worked as a park ranger at Yosemite for four years before returning to Hawai'i. Unable to secure her dream job at Hawai'i Volcanoes National Park, she'd lucked into a technical support job at the Alice Observatories on Mauna Kea. While she'd loved her nine months at Alice, she'd kept pursuing her dream, applying for an opening at Hawai'i Volcanoes National Park and finally winning an interview. Now a job had opened up, and she stood on the brink of grabbing it.

Koa poured two glasses of Russian River chardonnay, and they toasted to her success before he pulled her close for a long kiss. "Now, or after dinner?" she teased, fiddling with the top button of his shirt. Her eyes twinkled with naughty delight before she playfully pushed him away.

"No, you should feed me first. I'm famished."

Koa smiled at her tease. It was one of the many qualities that drew him to her. She was his miracle. Attracted from the first time he'd seen her smile at a charity cocktail party, he'd doubted such a sexy woman could possibly fall for an older, hard-boiled cop. But against all odds, it had happened. They'd been introduced by a mutual friend, dated, and found excitement in being together.

Both loved the outdoors, and most of their dates had involved hiking, surfing, and overnight camping. They'd spent hours exploring the national park, and she'd taught him more about native birds and plants than he could ever have imagined. Making their dream romance almost too good to be true, she was the most sensuous and creative lover he'd ever known. She even left the cooking to him, which might have bothered some men, but suited him to a T. After dating for three months, he'd carried her over the threshold of his little Volcano cottage to stay. He lived in constant fear she'd tire of him and cherished every moment they were together.

Returning to the stove, Koa brought the mixture of wine, vinegar, lemon juice, butter, soy sauce, and wasabi to a simmer. Nālani, always flirtatious, had plainly missed him, and he relished what was coming after dinner.

Nālani suddenly became serious. "I'll be glad to leave Alice."

He knew the nuances of her voice, and this one sounded off, somehow forced. "Oh, why is that?"

"It's not always what it's supposed to be."

He wasn't liking the sound of this mysterious "it." "And why is that?" he asked.

"You remember Charlie Harper?"

"Vaguely. He's one of the assistant directors, isn't he?"

"Yeah, that's right."

He sensed hesitation on her part and turned to face her. "What about him?"

"He's got roving hands."

Koa stiffened. "Has he hit on you?"

"Yeah. A couple of times." Looking away, her face colored.

A couple of times, Koa thought, and she hadn't said anything. "You haven't told me about anything like that," he said mildly, trying not to press her. He didn't like to bring his interrogation tactics home.

"You haven't been around much."

That was true. He'd had a series of demanding cases and late nights even before spending two nights away at Pōhakuloa. "It's been pretty hectic," he responded, kicking himself for sounding lame. "So what happened?"

"The first time he came in while I was alone in the mirror cleaning shop—you know, where we re-aluminize the hexagonal pieces that make up the telescope's mirror—and made a pass at me. I told him to get lost and didn't think too much of it." She turned to face him, glad to have the issue out in the open. "Then a week ago, he put his hands on me."

Her words jolted Koa. A week ago. Why had she waited a week to tell him about it? A sneaking part of him couldn't help wondering what had motivated Harper to hit on her. Her impish sexuality had attracted Koa, and he'd seen it turn male heads when she walked into a bar.

"And?"

"I slapped him across the face and told him to keep his paws off me. That's when he told me he liked a feisty bitch."

"What?" Koa thundered.

"Yeah," she said. She must have sensed his doubt, because she added, "He's done the same thing to a couple of the women astronomers."

"Jesus," Koa growled, and shifted position. Pain shot down his arm. He suddenly felt much older than Nālani, and worried that she might not be so attracted to a decrepit cop facing spinal surgery. He tried to dismiss the thought, but it wouldn't go away. He'd lost a step. He'd felt it out at Pōhakuloa. Basa, he was now sure, had seen it. Nālani too must see him as less of a man. That couldn't be good for their relationship.

"He thinks he's God's gift to women. He's such a perv. I feel sorry for his wife, even though she's a total doormat. I need to shower after being around the guy."

"Does Director Masters know about Harper's sexual harassment?" Koa had never met Masters but knew of him through Nālani. He'd had a celebrated career as an air force defense contractor working on President Reagan's Star Wars anti-missile program before becoming the top dog at the Alice Observatories. He'd been at Alice for a number of years and was frequently in the news. Although as a lowly technician, and not an astronomer, Nālani had limited contact with Masters, she never had anything but good things to say about him.

"Oh, God, no. Masters would fire Harper if he got wind of it. I mean, Masters went out of his way to give me a job, and he's one hundred percent supportive of the women astronomers and techs."

"So why don't you talk to Masters? If he's as supportive as you say, he'd make short work of Mr. Harper." Koa was thinking that Masters should cut off Charlie's roving hands, but as a cop he couldn't say that.

She gave Koa a surprised look. "You think I should?"

Why would she be reluctant to go to Masters? the cop voice inside him wondered. Was there more to this story? "Don't you want somebody to stop this snake?"

"I don't know. Seems like . . . well, I should fight my own battles."

"Harper hasn't tried anything else with you, has he?"

"No, not really, but he followed me into the control room today and may have been stalking me, so I told him I had Mace in my purse, and I'd use it on him."

"Did you really have a can of Mace?"

"Actually, it's pepper spray, but it would do the trick."

She walked across to the table where she had dropped her purse and pulled out a can of pepper spray. She tossed it across the room to him.

He felt a surge of relief. No matter what had provoked Harper in the first place, Nālani plainly intended to put an end to his advances. He felt bad for doubting her fidelity and guilty for not being around to protect her, but mostly he was concerned for her future safety. "Christ, I'd like to go up there and teach the asshole some manners."

She looked alarmed, and he realized why she hadn't told him in the first place. "Please, Koa. I'm leaving Alice, and I want it to be on good terms. I'll spray the bastard if he tries anything, but I don't want to create an incident if I can avoid it."

He couldn't disagree with that. "Okay, but keep this with you." He tossed the can back to her and watched her put it back in her purse. "And call me immediately if he tries anything. Promise?"

"Promise."

Still bothered by the issue, but knowing it was beyond his control, he turned back to his cooking. Yet he was so unnerved, he immediately knocked a knife off the counter. He jumped back to avoid getting skewered, and his abrupt movement triggered a burst of pain. The jolt shot all the way down his arm to his fingers. He winced and grabbed his neck.

"Koa Kāne."

Nālani never used his full name. He turned to see her staring at him with her arms folded across her chest.

"When are you going to schedule that surgery?"

"I'm seeing the surgeon the day after tomorrow, but—"

"But what, Koa?" she demanded sternly.

He didn't like being pinned down like this, but he saw no way out. "I don't know. I'm just not sure."

"Not sure about what?" She had a fierce look in her eyes. "You've got two opinions; and both doctors agree. Do you really want to lose the use of your right arm?" Then both her face and her voice softened. "We've got years ahead of us, Koa. Neither of us wants you disabled."

Her words struck a blow. She didn't want him . . . disabled. He felt cornered but fought the instinct to be combative. "Okay. I'll schedule the surgery."

"Good. That's settled." She grinned. "Now mister master chef, fix me some grub."

He put the issue aside for the moment and concentrated on coat-
ing the nori-wrapped *'ahi* in the cold tempura batter before placing
it into the hot oil sizzling in the wok. He turned the fish repeatedly.
When the outside had turned crisp, but the *'ahi* remained rare inside, he sliced the rolls and arranged the pieces on plates before adding capers along with a beurre blanc sauce. He served the seared *'ahi*
with salad, edamame, and more chilled chardonnay. The dish ranked
among Nālani's all-time favorites.

"Did you identify the victim of that god-awful killing out at
Pōhakuloa?" Nālani asked.

Koa was glad she had switched to a new, more familiar topic. "No,
not yet. But you won't believe what we found." He described the
canoe coffin, the bird woman, and the workshop. "Your guy, Jimmy
Hikorea, says it's a major archaeological find. And, I'll have you
know, yours truly participated in the discovery."

"That's fabulous. I'm sorry I wasn't there too." Her face blossomed
into a huge smile, and he felt absurdly pleased. She too saw the oddity of a police detective dabbling in archaeology. "What was it like,
you know, the moment you realized the importance of the cave?"

"It's hard to describe, but down in that cave, I felt a *pilina*, a connection, to my roots . . . to my ancestors. I haven't felt anything like
that in a long time."

"That's neat," she encouraged. "Describe it for me."

"Those men . . . their lives were so brutal, but they made things of
exquisite beauty. I mean, the bird woman just grabbed me. And the
canoe, painted red, the color of the gods, reminded me of my grandfather's stories."

"That's cool, Koa. That's our heritage." Like many poor Hawaiian
children, Nālani was raised by her grandmother. *Tūtū*, as Nālani
invariably called her, had nurtured a multitude of children and was
quick to spot the spark that set Nālani apart. Whether playing at

'ōlelo nane, a game of riddles, or surfing the big ones, tūtū accepted nothing less than the best from her favorite granddaughter. And so Nālani learned to excel. Only years later after graduate school did Nālani understand just how much she owed to her uncompromising tūtū. And tūtū inspired the love of Hawai'i's unique natural beauty and culture that inevitably drew Nālani back to the Big Island despite lucrative opportunities on the mainland.

"Yeah," he said, caught up in the excitement. "I remember my grandfather, and even my father sometimes, used to fascinate me with stories of the kahuna kālai wa'a," he said, referring to the expert canoe makers of the ancient Kāne clan.

"I wish I'd known your grandfather. He sounds a lot like my tūtū," Nālani mused as she savored a slice of 'ahi. Koa wasn't one to talk much about his past. During their courtship and even after they began living together, he'd regaled Nālani with stories of his military service and his detective work, but hadn't talked much about his family. His hesitancy stemmed partly from chagrin at his lowly roots and partly from reluctance to discuss his youngest brother, Ikaika, who'd been a juvenile delinquent before graduating to serious crime and serving time in the slammer. But the real reason had been his secret criminal history. He couldn't tell her about the most devastating event in his life, one that helped drive him to become a cop and motivated him to pursue justice for victims for crimes.

"My dad worked the sugar mills and died in an accident when I was sixteen. He was only forty, but after twenty-two years in that damn place, he walked bent over, like a crippled old man. I hated that goddamn mill—God, how I hated it—and I swore I wasn't going to let a lousy dead-end job suck the life out of me." Koa realized he'd never shown her the picture and grabbed his billfold. He pulled out a dog-eared photo of the old Hāmākua Sugar Mill. "I carry this picture with me always to remind me never to end up like he did."

He left the story there, not reciting how he'd suspected Anthony Hazzard, the mill manager, of arranging his father death or how he tracked the man to a remote hunting cabin in the Kohala mountains, started a fight, and accidently killed the man. He'd never shared that personal history with anyone and wasn't about to tell Nālani.

Nālani's face softened and her eyes seemed to glow. "He'd be proud of what you've accomplished, Koa."

"Yeah, I guess." Koa gave her a wry smile. "Even though, like many Hawaiians of his generation, he never had much use for the police."

They fell silent as they ate the *'ahi.*

Koa reached across the table, softly covering Nālani's hand. "You're going to leave in a couple of months. Why not just quit now?"

She shook her head. "I don't want to sit around for four months, and besides, the park service hasn't actually hired me yet."

"What if Harper tries something, and you can't get to your spray?"

"I'll be careful, Koa. I promise."

This uninspiring reply left him uncomfortable, just like the whole affair left a sour taste in his mouth. Men who harassed women didn't just stop . . . that's what made them harassers. He respected Nālani's desire to leave Alice on good terms, but if Charlie Harper made another unwanted pass at her, he'd teach the creep a lesson or two.

CHAPTER SEVEN

KOA RACED HIS dark blue Ford Explorer up the Belt Road toward
Hilo. His friend, Hook Hao—fisherman, auctioneer, Hilo legend—
had phoned with despair in his voice while Koa had been up at
Pōhakuloa. "He's hurt, Koa. Hurt bad."

"Who? Reggie? Reggie's hurt?" Reggie was Hook's twenty-two-
year-old son.

"He's in a coma." Hook sounded exhausted. The usual spark was
gone from his voice.

"Where? Hilo Memorial?"

"No, over on Maui."

"How? Was he in a car accident?"

"No. He was on the abandoned Navy bombing range on Kaho'olawe. An old bomb blew up." The small island of Kaho'olawe
south of Maui had been taken over by the Navy as a bombing range
during World War II. Although no longer in use, it was littered with
bombs that had failed to explode.

"Jesus, Hook. How bad is he hurt?"

"He's unconscious, some kind of concussion. They're not sure
when, or if, he's going to come around." Hook choked on the words.

"What was he doing on Kaho'olawe?"

"I don't have much. Reggie can't talk, but the police say he and some guys went exploring. I don't have details."

None of this made sense to Koa, but he did know one thing. He wasn't going to let Hook down. "I'll come by after the auction."

"*Mahalo*, Koa . . . *mahalo*."

As he reached the outskirts of Hilo, Koa's mind shifted to the identity of the Pōhakuloa victim. Figuring out the identity was the critical first step. Scene-of-the-crime evidence might be crucial to a conviction, but the victim's background typically provided the first clues to the identity of the killer.

Koa puzzled over unanswered questions. Most people had family and friends. Why hadn't a friend or relative reported the man missing? Most people worked for a living. Why hadn't an employer called the police? *West Hawaii Today* and the Hilo newspapers had run stories about the discovery of an unidentified body in the saddle area. Why hadn't someone called?

Had the victim been homeless? He brought the victim's mangled face—his forehead, his hair—into mental focus. Above the smashed face, the hair, although matted, had been short along the sides and trimmed around the ears. The man couldn't have been without a haircut for more than a month. So probably not homeless. A tourist traveling alone? Possible, but somehow it didn't fit. If someone had kidnapped and killed a tourist, why conceal the victim's identity? Koa nevertheless made a mental note to have patrol officers check hotels for a missing guest, perhaps with an unpaid bill.

Maybe the victim had been someone who could be expected to stay out of touch for days at a time. A traveling salesman? A free-lance writer? A drug courier? *Pakalolo* or marijuana, known locally as "Puna butter" and "Kona gold," remained the island's largest cash crop. Peace had generally reigned lately among Hawai'i's drug traffickers, but almost anything could trigger a feud among them. If the victim had associated with criminals, that would explain the lack of a missing-persons report.

Was the victim connected to the adjacent royal tomb or the stonecutters' cave? Both walls—the one from the cave into the tomb and the one from the tomb into the stonecutters' workshop—had appeared intact, undisturbed for decades. But someone had been in the workshop and looted a burial crypt. Was the proximity of the victim to the stonecutters' workshop mere coincidence? Possibly, but Koa hadn't become chief detective by trusting in coincidences.

The deceased's involvement in illegal archaeology would provide motive. Artifacts like the bird woman had great value on the black market. Koa had seen men killed for less. The man's participation in a criminal conspiracy would explain why his co-conspirators hadn't called the police. It might even explain the mutilation: suppose the deceased were an archaeologist or an antiquities smuggler; the killer might want to conceal his identity. But why would the killer leave the victim so close to the treasure? Questions and more questions without answers.

In the end, Koa decided he needed an entrée into the local antiquities community. Jimmy Hikorea might be able to provide the contact.

Koa turned a corner onto Lihiwai Street in front of a weathered one-story storefront and fish market. After parking his Explorer, he crossed the street, heading toward the crowd collected around the big open-air stall at the end of the building. Unshaven fishermen in grungy overalls and knee-high black rubber boots mingled with drivers from trucks scattered along the street. Buyers from the island's restaurants, hotels, and grocery chains, dressed in slacks and short-sleeve shirts, rounded out the regulars.

Koa liked the rituals of the fish auction, its timeless authenticity. Fishermen sipping quart-sized cups of takeout coffee, swapping sea stories while eyeing each other's catch. Here, as much as anywhere in the islands, multilingual pidgin filled the air, mixed with the smell of steaming coffee, saltwater, and fish offal.

Neat rows of ribbed fiberglass pallets held *'ahi*—whole black tuna, weighing anywhere from seventy-five to 250 pounds each. Smaller *'ahi*, grouped head down in twenty-gallon white plastic buckets, would be sold in lots. Mustard-colored *mahimahi*, some over six feet long, lay side by side on another row of pallets.

At just over seven feet, Hook Hao towered over the next tallest man in sight, and his outsized head, bald and shiny, gave true meaning to the phrase "a head taller." Hook wore his usual uniform— threadbare T-shirt, blood stained blue jeans, and snowshoe-sized black rubber boots. He wielded a short-shanked gaff, which accounted for his nickname, like an extension of his hand. Yet what Koa saw were the dark circles under the giant's eyes. Reggie's troubles had taken their toll on the old fisherman.

As Koa watched, Hook's gaff shot into an ice chest and jerked back, dragging a hundred-pound *'ahi*. With a flick of his wrist, Hook affixed the fish to an electronic scale suspended from a ceiling track. A helper called out the weight to a worker, who wrote it and the owner's mark on a slip of paper he slapped onto the fish, using its natural moisture as glue.

While one of the helpers dragged the freshly weighed tuna to an empty place next to its kin on one of the pallets, Hook drove his gaff back into the ice chest. To the surprise of nearly everyone on the auction floor, the gaff brought forth a moray eel. Hook held the mottled brown sea snake aloft to get a measure of the beast—a good eight feet.

At that moment, Hook caught sight of Koa and their eyes locked in a familiar gaze. Despite his weariness, a smile crept into Hook's eyes. They went way back together, back to a time when Reggie had found a different way to get into trouble.

Koa had been a junior detective that first time they'd met, having just returned from arresting a half-dozen high school kids for growing pot behind the Hilo high school stadium. Somehow, Hook got word of the arrest and showed up at the police lockup. The hulking beast of a man, dressed in fishermen's gear, smelling of stale fish, and chomping on a stubby remnant of a cigar, approached Koa, suggesting they have a word in an empty interrogation room.

"Detective, you don't know me, but I know of you. You are *hanohano*."

Koa hadn't been afraid of the man, but he couldn't help feeling a little intimidated by his size. "You find me honorable?"

"I have come to you."

"Why?"

"Do you know the story of the *puhi*, who stole from the sacred fishpond of the *ali'i* at Kohala, the place of the whale?"

Koa stared at the huge man, repulsed by his unkempt wharf odors, yet curious at his bizarre approach. "No, Mr.—"

"Hao. Hook Hao."

"Ahhh, that's your son in the lockup?"

"*He pula, o ka 'ānai ka mea nui.*"

Koa smiled at the Hawaiian saying. Translated literally, the words meant: A speck of dust in the eye causes a lot of rubbing. Yet Hook meant the wrong of one family member brought shame to all. "No, Mr. Hao, I don't know the story of the *puhi*. Does this have something to do with tonight's drug bust?"

"You might profit from its ancient instruction."

Intrigued by the man, Koa sat down at the table and motioned the larger-than-life fisherman to the opposite seat. "Okay, Mr. Hao, I have a minute. Tell me the story of the eel."

Hook laid the stub of his cigar on the table and drew himself up to begin. "The fishponds of the *ali'i* at Kohala were sacred *kapu* to all, save the old *lawaiʻa*, the old fisherman, who tended the ponds. But one day the *lawaiʻa* noticed a *puhi*, a great speckled snake of an eel, wiggling through an opening in the seawall. As big around as a small tree and longer than a canoe, the eel bore down on one of the fattest of the *aku*, and, right before the *lawaiʻa's* eyes, took the prized fish and vanished into the sea." Hook had the islander's gift of storytelling, and Koa felt the man's rhythmic cadence drawing him into the tale.

"'I have seen the thief and I will catch him,' promised the *lawaiʻa*. That night the *lawaiʻa* tied the end of the *hau* rope to a tree and lay near the seawall with his stone club. He dangled the hook beside the hole and waited for the *kapu* breaker to come from the sea. The old fisherman waited, sure that the *puhi* would come. And come it did." Hook paused for effect.

"As the *puhi* reached the seawall, he took the bait. The water swirled as the *puhi* tried to free itself from the fishhook. All night the *lawaiʻa* struggled until, with the coming of dawn, he finally pulled the *puhi* onto the rocks. Both man and beast were exhausted, but the old fisherman lifted his stone club high, ready to smash it down upon the *puhi*." Hook seemed to breathe harder as he described the struggle.

"To his amazement, the *puhi* spoke. 'It is true, old *lawaiʻa*, that you have won and have the right to kill me, but that would be most unwise.' The astonished *lawaiʻa* stared at this strange talking *puhi*.

"'And why would it be unwise?' the *lawaiʻa* croaked.

"Again, the *puhi* spoke. 'If you let me go free, I, myself, will guard your fishponds and keep them safe from all the other *puhi* in the sea.'

"'How do I know that you, a thief, will keep your word?'

"A third time the *puhi* spoke. 'Because I will entrust something to you more precious than my own life.' The *puhi* made a sound—*click, click*—barely heard, and another smaller *puhi* appeared. 'This is my son, my first and only son. He will come and live within your fishponds.'

"And so the *lawai'a* allowed the *puhi* to go free, a decision he never came to regret. For the old *puhi* kept his word." Hook made a circling motion with his hands, signaling that all had come out right in the end. "That is the story of how the *puhi* became the protector of fishponds at Kohala."

His story finished, Hook Hao picked up his cigar and sat staring at Koa. His black eyes were intelligent and clear. He had a forthright look, despite the smell of salt and fish offal. Koa contemplated the man, trying to make up his mind. The fisherman seemed content to let the detective's evaluation run its course.

"You would be of service, like the old *puhi*?"

"I would."

"What service?"

"I work on the docks, around delivery trucks. I know masters, mates, deckhands, truckers, buyers. I see things, I hear things . . . things that are no good for the island . . ."

"You would tell me these things?"

"When it would help the fishpond."

"Help the fishpond?"

"When it would be good for the island . . . good for the few who have not been poisoned by the Westerners."

Koa understood the value of such an informant. "I can trust you to do this?"

"My son, my first and only son, will remain here in this pond . . . on this island . . . and you will have no further trouble from him. On that you have my word."

"Wait here."

Koa retrieved the badly shaken boy, then fourteen, from the lockup. When Koa guided him into the interrogation room, the fisherman's son stood, eyes cast downward, unable to meet his father's gaze. Koa left them together for over an hour. Hook's arm embraced the boy's shoulders when the two of them finally walked out of the police station.

Three weeks later, the big man presented Koa with a magnificent sixty-pound *ʻahi*, its rich red flesh still glistening from the sea. In the cavity of the fish, Koa found a note detailing the location and operation of an illegal drug lab in the Kaʻū district. The police raided it two days later and arrested six people for the illegal manufacture and distribution of amphetamines.

Hook Hao became a friend in the intervening years. His natural intelligence and ambition served him well—from fisherman to mate to trawler captain, from owner of one vessel to owner of two, then into leadership of the Suisan wholesale fish business. In the meantime, Reggie had grown up. While he had stayed out of the criminal courts, his father's success had eluded him. He ran a semi-solvent charter fishing business. Except now Reggie was hospitalized in a coma.

The sound of a bell broke Koa's reverie. Hook gave the buyers only a few moments to formulate their bids. Then he lowered his steel gaff to the first *ʻahi* to start the auction. "Lesgo, lesgo, lesgo."

"Three dolla," came the first bid.

"Lesgo, mo'better, mo'better fo' da *ʻahi*. Geevum, geevum, brah." Hook's quick voice packed the words into a blur.

"Three-fifty."

"Three an' sixty."

"Mo'better, brah, mo'better, mo'better, mo'better, brah."

"Three-seventy."

"Three-seventy . . . Three-seventy . . . an'den . . . an'den . . . lesgo, brah."

"Three-ninety."

"Three-ninety . . . three-ninety . . . no mo'better . . . three-ninety . . . *pau*." A step forward and the hook touched the next '*ahi*, leaving the winning bidder to write the price and his mark on a scrap of paper to be patted onto the damp fish. Settling up would await the end of the auction. "Lesgo, brah . . . lesgo . . ."

Sometime later, Koa climbed down to the quay. The last step was a long one, and he held his neck as he eased himself down. Boarding Hook's boat, the *Ka'upu*, the albatross, he slipped into the wheelhouse of the weatherworn fishing vessel. He crossed to the back of the small cabin to examine the photograph on the bulkhead over the chart table. It showed a young man whose innocent eyes peeked out from under a shaggy mop of hair. The black-and-white photo of Reggie Hao, taken within the past year, was the latest in a progression that had occupied the place of honor over the *Ka'upu*'s chart table.

Heavy footfalls on the deck—thuds, followed by the squish of rubber boots—announced Hook's arrival. With a fluid motion Hook lowered himself into the captain's chair behind the helm.

"Good auction, Hook?"

"Okay," he said with a grimace, "but not like the old days." The pidgin had disappeared from the big man's vocabulary, as though he had switched personalities upon leaving the auction floor. "But you're not here to talk fish."

"No. I came to talk about Reggie." Koa paused. "He's still in a coma?"

The weariness in Hook's eyes answered Koa's question.

"*Mahalo* for coming."

"Sorry that I couldn't come sooner."

"It doesn't matter. The doctors have told me very little. His vital signs are normal, but his brain is asleep. They can't tell me how long. Maybe an hour, maybe a day . . . maybe forever." Hook's voice cracked.

"Have you talked to a specialist?"

"Yes, a neurologist from Honolulu. There's nothing they can do, except wait."

"What was he doing on Kahoʻolawe?"

Hook's mouth twisted slightly. "He was in with a group committed to *kanaka maoli*," he said, referring to the restoration of native sovereignty. "Kahoʻolawe was a sacred place for our ancestors. It was the gathering place of the *kahuna* ... the center for their study of the stars and navigation. Reggie and his friends were trying to rescue *mea makamae*, treasures, from Kahoʻolawe."

Koa instantly saw the folly in such a mission. "But that's crazy. Everybody knows that Kahoʻolawe was a Navy bombing range, littered with unexploded duds, just waiting to go off."

"The *hoʻihoʻi i ke ea* groups have always been a little reckless, you know that, Koa. You remember, they sent swimmers out to Kahoʻolawe while Navy planes were still dropping bombs. Yeah, they're reckless." The giant fisherman clenched his fists. "Too reckless. *Damn*, I wish he hadn't."

"I'm sorry, Hook ... so sorry." Koa paused to let the old fisherman get control of his emotions. "So who was in this group?"

"Reggie never told me. I heard him refer to the *ʻohana huna*, the secret family, but I never paid a lot of attention. I just kept telling him to stop going out there ..."

"He went more than once?"

"Oh, yeah ... maybe five times ... or ten ... I really don't know ..."

"And they found ... ancient treasures?"

"Yeah. Kahoʻolawe was a place of many shrines, many carvings, many gods ... you know that. It holds many *mea makamae* of old Hawaiʻi, at least to the extent the Navy hasn't bombed everything." The big man's voice took on an angry tone, and Koa understood. As a Hawaiian, he too respected his island heritage. The navy had wrecked Kahoʻolawe, and the *haoles* didn't care.

"Were they working with the Bishop Museum or one of its archaeologists?"

The look in Hook's eyes answered Koa's question even before the fisherman spoke. "The *ho'iho'i i ke ea* don't have much use for museums."

"So I suppose Reggie and his friends hid what they found . . . hid it away in caves somewhere here on the Big Island?" Koa knew he was treading on sensitive ground.

"There could be a legal problem for Reggie, yes?"

"Yes. Trespassing because Kaho'olawe is still off-limits, but that's a misdemeanor and prosecution isn't too likely in any event. Theft of protected antiquities could be a bigger problem. That's a state and federal felony. Have the Maui police said anything about charges?"

"If the police know, they aren't telling me."

"What have they told you?"

"There were three of them—Reggie, Aikue 'Ōpua . . ."

"The sovereignty activist . . . the guy who's always quoted in the papers about the restoration of native rights?"

"That's him, Aikue 'Ōpua, and a Garvie somebody."

"What do Aikue and this Garvie guy say? The police must have talked to them."

"That's the strange part. 'Ōpua says they were trying to protect their native heritage . . . working to protect Hawaiian treasures from the *haoles*. They were digging when a dud blew. All three of them got knocked down, and Reggie didn't get up. 'Ōpua tried to revive him and then went for help." A shadow crossed Hook's face. "But Garvie refuses to talk to the police."

"You mean he's invoked his Fifth Amendment rights?"

"Yeah . . . and the police say he has some kind of a criminal record."

This news surprised Koa. Unless the crime was trespassing or something similar, it didn't fit the usual activist, filled with virtue for the cause. "What kind of a criminal record?"

"The police haven't exactly been forthcoming." Hook's eyes flickered, and Koa realized that he would have to check out this Garvie character. "I'm worried. I'm worried that even if Reggie recovers, he could face some kind of criminal charges."

"That's not impossible, but the courts always go easy on sovereignty types. Hell, I doubt they could get a jury to convict."

"It's more than that. Can I say something in confidence?"

They had come to this boundary before, and Koa gently reminded his friend, "Yes, Hook, I will do everything in my power to preserve your confidences. But you know I'm a cop . . . I've got certain obligations."

It was Hook's turn to pause. Then he nodded. "Reggie's charter business is failing. He's on the verge of bankruptcy. I hope . . . I just hope he was out there protecting our heritage and not selling treasures to rescue his business. It scares me. It really scares me."

Koa stared out at the ocean, taking in the long, rolling swells without really seeing them. An unbidden thought leaped to his mind. Could there be a connection between Reggie's Kahoʻolawe trips and the Pōhakuloa investigation? Was it mere coincidence that two separate incidents involving stolen artifacts surfaced in the same week? Koa suddenly had a bad feeling about Reggie's trips to Kahoʻolawe.

"Hook, if Reggie was selling things dug up from Kahoʻolawe, how would he do it? Anybody you know fence that sort of stuff?"

Hook frowned as he pondered this new angle. "Sell archaeological treasures . . . I don't know. There's nobody on the island handling that kind of stuff . . . nobody I ever had a line on. Maybe Honolulu. There might be some low-down dealers in Honolulu, but most likely it would be mainland or foreign."

Koa could hear the desperation in Hook's voice. Though Hook had the pulse of Hilo and a good many of the other ports around the islands, his reach didn't extend too far beyond the docks. "You want me to look into Reggie's situation, Hook?"

"Could you do that?"

"Yeah. I'll call a friend on the Maui force. The Maui police owe me a couple of favors."

"You are *hanohano*."

Koa smiled. Being a cop, natives rarely paid him such a tribute. "There is no higher compliment."

The two men once again lapsed into silence, taking in the sounds of the sea and the harbor. Minutes passed before Hook broke the silence.

"You been up at Pōhakuloa?"

"Yeah," Koa said. "Hear anything about the body?"

"Nothing. Saw the piece in the paper. Even did a little trolling. There's nothing about that saddle business on the docks. Not even a whisper. Who died up there, anyway? Anybody I'm supposed to know?"

"That's the problem, Hook. We don't have an identification. Heard anything—anything at all—about somebody gone missing?"

"None of the locals have disappeared . . . least that I know of. Must be an outsider from one of the other islands. Or the mainland. Maybe foreign. What does this dude look like? That might help."

They had reached the boundary again, and Koa stood firm. "Right now, we're going with what was in the papers. We may have more later."

Hook looked hard at Koa. "You got a killing an' you don't know what the pigeon looks like?"

Koa nodded.

"And you haven't got fingerprints either, have you?"

Again, Koa nodded.

"Some kind of professional hit?"

"Could be. Look, Hook, just suppose . . . I'm not saying it's so, I'm just supposing . . . that the victim up in the saddle was into something illegal . . ."

"Like I told you last month, the *pakalolo* crop is gonna bust some kind of a record."

"It could be smuggling, but how 'bout kooks? Human sacrifice . . . ritual killing . . . that sort of stuff?"

Hook drew back, his face mirroring the way Koa had felt back in the cave. "Ritual sacrifice? You gotta be kidding. There's been nothing like that since that bunch of bikers raped and killed that girl three, maybe four, years ago."

"It's no joke, my friend."

"Christ, this one's real heavy, ain't it?"

"Yeah, it's heavy, but I don't want that word on the street, Hook. Wouldn't help tourism, you know."

"You know me. I'm all ears and no mouth."

"Odd description for an auctioneer." Both men laughed.

So, Koa thought, as he returned to his Explorer, I struck out with the man who has ears to the ground everywhere. He pushed the remote locking gadget when he was still a distance away, popping open the driver's door. He'd have to go back to the evidence. Maybe a dead man could tell them something, after all.

CHAPTER EIGHT

LATER THAT MORNING Koa drove to Hilo Memorial Hospital, running twenty minutes late for his eleven o'clock appointment with the county physician to witness the autopsy. He found Shizuo Hiro behind his desk in a tiny, cramped second-floor office. X-ray light boxes, several holding large panels of film, covered one swath of the wall behind Shizuo. The white room, with its white desk and white-frocked doctor, had an antiseptic smell that reminded Koa how thoroughly he disliked hospitals. Not to mention the doctors who hung out there.

"Hello, Shizuo." Koa put on his best public demeanor for the Japanese obstetrician.

"You lose your watch?" snarled Shizuo. "You said you'd be here at eleven."

"I got held up."

"I hear you found a bunch of old Hawaiian junk out at Pōhakuloa."

Koa felt the color rise in his face and his jaw harden. "No, Shizuo. We found a royal grave and an underground workshop from the 1600s. It's a significant discovery."

"The 1600s . . . that's nothing. Japanese culture extends back to 30,000 BC."

Koa wanted to shove the arrogant Japanese doctor's head inside
one of his light boxes, but he restrained himself. "Is Dr. Cater here?"

"Down the hall. But make it damn fast. I've got one in the labor
room. Any time now."

"Good. You should stick to what you do . . ." Koa faltered. He
couldn't imagine the man did anything "best," and left the sentence
unfinished as he turned away.

Two doors down the hall, Koa found a man in a white hospital
coat with miniature medical corps insignia on one lapel and a tiny
silver oak leaf on the other. Red-faced and heavyset with baggy jowls,
the man plainly knew his way to the officers' club bar. "Dr. Cater?"

"That's me." He spoke with an Irish brogue thick as tar. "You must
be Chief Detective Kāne?"

"Koa . . . my friends call me Koa." Koa offered a hand, which the
Irishman shook vigorously. As pain radiated through his shoulder,
Koa wished people would back off the power handshakes.

"Sean McHaney from the Honolulu force sends his regards."

Sean had been on the Hilo force back when Koa had returned
from overseas to be with his sick mother—the one rock-solid pillar
in his life. A native healer of some local renown, she'd used all her
connections to get Koa into the prestigious Kamehameha schools
for children of Hawaiian descent and prodded him to perform. In
the tug-of-war between his father's failure and his mother's hope,
she'd won. It was a debt he could never repay.

He'd never thought of leaving the Special Forces until his friend
Jerry, who'd always wanted to be a policeman, had died in Koa's arms
and Sean had suggested he come home to join the Hilo police force.
The need to be with his ailing mom and the necessity for someone
to exert some measure of control over his seriously wayward, frequently incarcerated brother had sealed the deal. Sean's career had
later stalled, while Koa's had kept charging ahead.

"Sean McHaney . . . that old Irish cop got me started in police work. How do you know Sean?"

"The Army's teamed up with the Honolulu police many times, and Sean has a nose for the tough ones. We'd better go see your so-called coroner. He's on OB call and doesn't have much time." The venomous tone in Dr. Cater's voice took Koa aback, but the doctor hustled out the door and down the hall to Shizuo's office before Koa had a chance to question the source of his hostility. But something, Koa sensed, was seriously wrong.

"Ready to do the autopsy?" Koa asked as he and Cater reentered Shizuo's office.

"It's already done," Shizuo said with a gleeful little snarl.

"What?" Koa demanded. Christ, this was an unwelcome surprise.

"Yes, sir," Shizuo chirped. "I'm seeing OB patients this morning, so I did the autopsy last night."

"Damn! You knew I wanted to witness it." Koa could barely contain his anger.

"Cops don't add much to autopsies . . . they just get in the way," Shizuo responded dismissively.

Fuck, Koa thought to himself. When am I ever going to be rid of this arrogant asshole, this make-believe coroner? Shizuo was one of the ironies of Koa's life. He'd avoided prosecution for his own crime because of an incompetent medical examiner, and now he was stuck working with an equally unskilled medical hack.

His control reasserted itself. What was done, however wrong, was done. He'd simply have to make the best of it. "So what did you find?"

"I'll make this quick." Shizuo picked up a red folder from his desk. "I've got some surprises." The Japanese obstetrician held up a single finger and paused for effect. Koa grimaced at the clichéd gesture. He'd seen defense lawyers mimic that same pose—just before they tore Shizuo apart on cross-examination. "First, the visible

wounds were not fatal. Any premortem damage to the facial structure and the hands was painful, but not fatal."

Shizuo raised a second finger. "Second, there was inadequate blood
in situ. The degree of hemorrhage is not consistent with the tissue
damage. That evidences postmortem trauma. It is my opinion"—
Shizuo didn't bother to acknowledge his military colleague—"that
your victim was dead for at least two hours before the lacerations
were inflicted."

"Then what was the cause of death?"

"We—" Dr. Cater tried to interrupt.

Shizuo held up his hand, cutting Dr. Cater off. "I am the county
physician. This is my report." Koa bit his tongue to control his
frustration.

"Proceed, Dr. Hiro." Exasperation hung heavy in Dr. Cater's voice.

"Asphyxiation is the cause of death."

It was the last cause of death Koa expected. From the looks of the
corpse, he'd assumed the man had died from one of the many blows
to his head. "Asphyxiation?"

"Yes, a fractured hyoid bone blocks the tracheae." Shizuo swiveled
in his chair and stood up, stabbing a finger to the center X-ray film
on the light boxes behind him.

"This X-ray shows your victim's neck and head." Shizuo ran his
finger up and down the picture in front of the spinal column. "Here's
the trachea. The hyoid bone is here." He jabbed the X-ray with his
finger. "The hyoid is laterally displaced into the trachea, interfering
with the respiratory function and causing asphyxia. It's a choke hold
injury, most common in police brutality—"

An insistent beeping prompted Shizuo to grab his electronic
pager and examine its message window. "My delivery calls," he announced and strutted out of the room.

Dr. Cater shook his head. "I feel sorry for the baby."

"I usually feel sorry for the corpse. And for me."

"At least he does OB work. Otherwise, he'd be bleeding patients."

The men shared a look of consternation before Koa continued. "Seriously, we appreciate your help with less than ideal cooperation."

Dr. Cater nearly choked. "You've got a gift for understatement, Detective."

"Were you able to learn anything from the autopsy?"

"Only a little, I'm afraid. Your baby doctor"—Cater inclined his head toward the door—"started the autopsy before I arrived."

Koa should have known. "Christ. It never occurred to me . . ."

"He made a mess of it. First-year medical students know more about forensic medicine."

"So you've got nothing for me."

"I didn't say that. I just want you to understand I did a salvage job. It's tough enough to autopsy a decomposed body without treading in the tracks of an obstetrician who hasn't cracked a medical text printed after World War II."

Although he agreed with this opinion, Koa couldn't help noticing Dr. Cater's own tone of superiority. Doctors were a tribe of arrogant know-it-alls. "I hear you. Tell me what you can."

"All right, let's start with the cause of death. Your baby doctor's right about the fractured hyoid bone, but I'm not convinced that's the cause of death."

"Why?"

"The blood chemistry doesn't square with asphyxiation."

"You can tell despite the decomposition?"

"Yes, with the right sampling technique."

"Then this hyoid bone"—Koa stepped to the X-ray and pointed to the top of the windpipe—"was broken by a postmortem blow?"

"I don't think so." Cater exhaled as he spoke. "Despite the decomposition, we found no evidence of broken skin or torn flesh on the neck. The postmortem blows seem to have been confined to the head and hands."

Koa had lots of experience with injuries causing death, but he wasn't following. "I don't understand. If the hyoid bone wasn't fractured postmortem . . ."

"The extreme, but largely superficial, nature of the visible injuries, the lack of hemorrhaging, and the fractured hyoid all suggest strangulation. If the blood chemistry were right, I would conclude, as your baby doctor did, that strangulation was the cause of death. But the blood chemistry doesn't fit."

"You're saying that the deceased was choked, but that strangulation wasn't the cause of death?"

"You got it."

The light started to dawn. "You think the killer might have subdued the deceased with a choke hold before inflicting the fatal injury?"

"That's . . . that's my hypothesis."

"Then what was the cause of death?"

"I suspect some sort of trauma to the brain, but I haven't been able to pinpoint the physiology because your baby doctor opened up the skull before I arrived."

"Damn," Koa swore.

"My sentiments exactly."

"How do you account for the lack of blood *in situ*, as my baby doctor refers to the crime scene?"

"That's a puzzle. Putting aside improbables, such as anticoagulants and extreme cold, it would appear that the victim may have been dead for an hour or two before the killer inflicted the external injuries. In fact, it's possible—we can't tell for sure—that the killer may have choked and killed the deceased somewhere else, moved the body into the lava tube, and then mutilated the corpse, most likely to conceal his identity."

Koa whistled softly. "So the killer either spent a couple of hours in that lava hole killing the victim, waiting all that time, and then mutilating him, or else he killed the victim somewhere else and carried the body out to Pōhakuloa, mutilated it, and then left."

"Exactly." Dr. Cater nodded.

"What about the date and time of death?"

"None of the standard methods for determining time of death works. When the victim's been dead for days, temperature, rigor mortis, and skin color tell us nothing."

Koa really wanted a time of death. That way he could match it with the disappearance of any missing persons, and later with the actions of possible suspects. "You mean you can't give me any kind of estimate? None at all?"

"I never said that. The standard methods don't work, Detective, so I used a relatively new technique called the vitreous fluid potassium test. You see, after death the red cells in the blood break down. Potassium, one of the resulting chemicals, seeps into the vitreous fluid inside the eyeball." Dr. Cater produced a graph showing the expected increase in potassium with the lapse of time. "The process occurs slowly." He ran his finger over the graph.

"Unfortunately, the vitreous fluid test has a wider margin of error than traditional methods, but when properly conducted in an adult victim, the test results are accurate to within twenty-four hours in the first 200 hours postmortem. Based on the amount of potassium in the eye fluid and the temperature in the lava tube, I estimate that your victim died between 208 and 256 hours before the police found the body and Dr. Hiro drew the vitreous fluid sample. So about eight to ten days. That would put the time of death between 1:00 a.m. on January 20 and 1:00 a.m. on January 22."

That was more like it. Koa could work within that window.

"Moreover, his stomach contents show he died about five to six hours after eating lamb. That's a guess, but it's not too far off the mark. If the deceased ate a lamb dinner between 5:00 p.m. and 8:00 p.m., that would put his death in the 10:00 p.m. to 2:00 a.m. time range.

"Combining these data, your victim likely died during the early morning hours of Tuesday, January 20; Wednesday, January 21; or Thursday, January 22. Pinning down exactly when he ate lamb would allow you to fix the date and time more precisely."

"Excellent, Doc." That could prove to be crucial information. "What about the cuts? I figure a razor or knife with a sharp edge."

"Without a doubt. And brace yourself, Detective—it was used on the genitals, too."

The words came at Koa like a body blow. "Jesus. That's all I need . . . a ritual sex killing."

"The killer cut off the head of the victim's penis, an act that should tell you a good deal about the mental state of your killer. I'm not a psychiatrist, but . . ."

"Christ." Koa frowned. "If the newspapers get hold of this . . . You better keep the file locked up and caution all your medical personnel who are privy to this information."

"There'll be no leak from my end, but you'll have to put a lid on your baby doctor."

"I'll talk to Shizuo," Koa muttered. "Say, you got anything for me on identity?"

"Not much." Cater opened a red folder and started to read from his notes:

"Almost certainly a Hawaiian male . . ."

"How can you tell?"

"Ethnic identification is hard. But, given the nature of this killing, we used DNA tests. Went to military data banks for DNA comparables. They give us a high degree of confidence that the deceased was of Hawaiian ancestry."

Koa couldn't understand that at all. "That only adds to the puzzle."

"Why?"

"If the deceased was Hawaiian, that increases the chances he was local. Family, friends, an employer... someone should have reported the victim missing. Why no missing-persons report?"

"Can't help you on that one, Detective."

Koa realized he was thinking out loud. He couldn't expect this doctor to know that side of the investigation. "Your exam tell you anything about the killer?"

"Yes, at least I can offer you a couple of tentative guesses."

"Like what?"

Dr. Cater closed the red folder. "You understand, these are just guesses."

"Sure."

"There was no evidence of external trauma to the neck, such as would have been present if the victim had been strangled with a rope or garroted with a wire. Therefore, I'd guess that he was strangled from behind using a choke hold."

"So? Spell it out for me."

"The hyoid bone is at the top of the windpipe. It would most likely be broken by pressure angled back and up. To get upward pressure with a choke hold, the killer must have been taller than the deceased."

"How tall was the victim?"

"Five feet, nine inches."

"How tall would the killer have to be?"

"I figure at least six feet, minimum, maybe even six-two. That, of course, assumes that the killer and the victim were both standing on level ground. It is possible that the killer could have pulled the victim over backward and applied the upward pressure while the victim was falling."

Koa knew all about choke holds. The department frowned on their use because of the risk of killing the perp, but sometimes with a big, drug-crazed moron a cop had no other way to bring the offender down without undue personal risk. You simply got behind the subject, wrapped an arm around the neck beneath the chin, and pulled backward. The more the perp struggled, the more you tightened your hold. It was even easier if you started on a higher level than the bad guy.

"But your best guess is that the killer was six feet or taller?"

"Yes, and strong too, Koa. You have to be pretty strong to strangle an able-bodied adult male. Even with a sharp knife, it takes a strong, steady hand to slice up a man's chest that way. I have little doubt that your killer is physically powerful."

"Anything else?"

"Just that the killer has nerves of steel."

"Why?"

"Those cuts across the chest—they were straight, like railroad tracks—could have been made with a razor and a straightedge. Those cuts were administered almost professionally . . . without the slightest sign of nervousness or panic."

"Great. So I've got a tall, strong, psychologically unbalanced killer with nerves of steel. The perp from hell."

Koa racked his brain trying to figure how a Hawaiian had been killed and missing for more than eight days without a missing-persons report. That most likely pointed to a native who had left the islands and recently returned. Maybe a native connected to archaeology. He needed to explore that angle. Maybe Jimmy Hikorea had a missing colleague.

CHAPTER NINE

KOA FELT A keen sense of anticipation as he and Jimmy drove up the winding forest drive. Koa had asked Jimmy for an introduction to an expert in Hawaiian artifacts and possible black-market outlets for antiquities. Jimmy had suggested Prince Kamehameha, a remote descendant of the most powerful king in Hawaiian history. It wasn't every day Koa got to shake hands with a prince. However, he tamped down his expectations, reminding himself that he'd come to gather facts for his murder investigation. As always, he was determined to focus on his mission.

Although the prince still used his *ali'i*, or royal title, he had no governmental function. Still, many old Hawaiians revered his family heritage and paid special attention to his views. Thus, his considerable influence derived from his wealth, his illustrious name, and his behind-the-scenes role in community affairs.

They entered the prince's secluded villa on the slopes of Mauna Kea through wooden gates in the north wall. Verdant green lawns extended on either side of the road. In the center of the garden stood a black wrought iron aviary, perhaps sixty feet high. Squat royal poinciana trees with long, spreading branches sprouting flamboyant clusters of crimson flowers ringed the ornate cage.

Inside the aviary three *'ios*, Hawaiian hawks, perched; and Koa asked Jimmy to stop so he could take in the scene. *"He 'io au 'a'ohe lāmā kea 'ole* ... I am a hawk; there is no branch on which I cannot perch." The ancient words came to Koa from the recesses of his mind, surprising him with his own memory.

"The symbol of Hawaiian royalty," Jimmy replied in the same reverent tone. The hawks held themselves regally, surveying their visitors with stony black eyes.

"They shouldn't be in captivity," Koa said sharply. His intensity drew a concerned look from Jimmy.

"Please..."

"Don't worry. I won't embarrass you with our host."

Past the aviary, a tall man with snowy-white hair and a cream-colored shirt, who looked to be in his seventies, stood on the lawn, facing away from the road. A wicker box lay on the grass near his feet. The solitary figure's rigid posture projected tension, and when he turned, Koa saw an *'io* perched on the man's black-gloved hand. The hawk sat regally erect, bound by the legs to a thin leather leash and blinded by a tasseled hood of intricately dyed leather.

The sight took Koa back in time to a darkened movie theater, where he had first seen a man, or rather a boy, launch a hawk into the air. The movie had been *The Falcon and the Snowman*. He remembered watching the great bird, its hood suddenly removed, seeing daylight and blue sky, sensing the freedom to spread its wings and fly. He'd grown up watching *'ios* sailing majestically over mountain slopes, symbols of the grace of creation. Before the movie he had never imagined a hawk in captivity, let alone submitting voluntarily to hooded darkness. The idea repulsed him now as it had then.

The broad-shouldered man on the green unclipped the leash from the jesses and loosened the strings fastening the leather hood. The hook-beaked bird, its eyes still sheathed, tensed. Taking hold of the tassel, the man lifted the hood, restoring the bird's sight. The raptor quivered, spreading its wings before resuming an alert pose. The man's arm shot forward, carrying his gloved fist above shoulder height.

The hawk launched into the air, its powerful wings driving it upward. Sweep after sweep of its wings carried the predator higher. The princely bird, its wedge-shaped tail extended and its wings spread nearly forty inches, rode thermal updrafts over the mountain slope. Only the narrow straps of its leather jesses, trailing beneath the hawk, marred its majesty. Koa silently urged the bird to vanish into the wild, but instead the 'io circled, awaiting its master's command.

The big man stooped to the wicker box and extracted a speckled dove. After spotting the hawk, he raised the dove over his head and released it. With a hurried beat of its wings, the little creature flew from his grasp. The man gave a sharp, loud command.

The hawk wheeled out of its circle and swooped, quickening the sweep of its wings, accelerating earthward toward the escaping dove. As the raptor closed the distance with astonishing speed, Koa felt his own body tense.

The dove, oblivious to the threat, flew toward safety. Too late it sensed the hawk and panicked, veering to the right. The hawk, its legs forward and its curved talons extended, plucked the dove from the air. In an instant, the raptor spread its wings, like air brakes, and descended swiftly to the ground, gripping its prize in vise-like talons. A single screech chronicled the savage killing.

The falconer walked slowly to the hawk, which was pecking disinterestedly at its prey, and extended his gloved fist. Koa felt a stab of regret as the 'io remounted the black fist and took morsels of food from its master. The hawk accepted the tasseled hood without protest, and the man reattached the leash to its jesses.

The show over, Jimmy restarted the car. Cresting a small hill in the center of the plateau, they arrived in front of a virtual castle. A huge open *lānai* with intricately carved *koa* balustrades fronted the two-story structure. Multiple windows soared from the roof of the *lānai* to gabled peaks.

Jimmy parked the Bronco at the foot of the steps leading up to the carved entrance doors. By the time Jimmy extracted his wheelchair, two Hawaiian retainers arrived to carry him up the steps to the *lānai*.

The falconer greeted Jimmy with obvious respect. He was casually, but expensively, dressed in Italian loafers and finely tailored slacks. Up close Koa could see that his short-sleeve silk dress shirt was embroidered with matching cream-colored thread.

Prince Kamehameha introduced his companion, Aikue ʻŌpua, before turning to Jimmy. "Mr. Hikorea, your reputation as one of the most knowledgeable and insightful Hawaiian archaeologists since Professor Kenneth Emory precedes you. It is an honor to welcome you to my home." The prince spoke in a refined voice with a touch of a British accent.

Aikue ʻŌpua, Koa thought, surprised to see him. First, he pops up looting antiquities from Kahoʻolawe with Reggie Hao, and now he's hanging out with Prince Kamehameha. What's more, ʻŌpua must have been in the house while the prince was out with the falcon. That reflected a degree of familiarity between the two men. Strange. He wondered if ʻŌpua had talked Reggie into risking his life.

"*O ke aliʻi wale nō kaʻu makemake* . . . my desire is only for the chief," Jimmy said. Although Koa knew the identity of his host, Jimmy's use of the word "chief" still surprised him, as did Jimmy's bow of his head. Such deference belonged to a bygone era. "Let me introduce my friend, Koa Kāne, chief of the Investigation Division of the Hawaiʻi County police. Koa, this is Prince Kamehameha."

Koa extended his hand to the descendant of the most powerful king in the history of the Hawaiian Islands, the ruler who, a thousand years after the first human habitation of the islands, had united them under one common dominion. The prince gripped Koa's hand with crushing force. Despite himself, Koa felt a touch of awe.

He quickly reasserted control over himself. The power of the prince's grip reminded him of Dr. Cater's hypothesis about the Pōhakuloa killer, tall and strong with nerves of steel. The prince fits the description, Koa thought wryly.

"Welcome to my home, Chief Detective Kāne."

"It is an honor, sir. That was quite a show with the hawk." Koa had seen ʻios around the island since his childhood but had never known anyone to take the endangered birds from their natural habitat. "I wasn't aware there were falconers on the island."

"I learned the sport in England during my Oxford days. From the time I first saw the sport, I wanted to hunt with an ʻio."

"They're endangered, aren't they?" Koa spoke softly.

"Yes, like my people and these islands."

Koa held his tongue. This man might be a prince, but he had nevertheless violated state and federal laws by taking endangered birds from the wild.

Koa turned to Aikue ʻŌpua, extending his hand. "I have heard much about your crusade to return the islands to native sovereignty." He scrutinized the heavyset activist, who wore a white Hawaiian dress shirt, jeans, and a belt with a Hawaiian flag buckle.

ʻŌpua wore specially made cowboy boots with underslung heels. The numerals "1893" were embossed on each side of the boot shafts, referring to the US annexation of Hawaiʻi in 1893. He sported a drooping cowboy mustache on his broad Hawaiian face. Koa found the *haole* facial hair strangely at odds with ʻŌpua's sovereignty clothing.

"Ahh, Detective Kāne, I fear my crusade, as you call it, will not succeed in my lifetime."

Koa wondered if those fancy cowboy boots had left the boot marks out at Pōhakuloa.

"Gentlemen," the prince said, interrupting Koa's train of thought, "let me show you to my sitting room, where we can talk." The servants lifted Jimmy in his wheelchair as though he were a child, and the prince led them across an entry hall and up a set of polished hardwood stairs. Koa listened to the clunk of 'Ōpua's metal heels hitting the floor as he walked up the stairs.

As they reached the second floor, Koa took in a cathedral-like room. Sunlight streaking through the windows sparkled off the polished floor and paneled walls. A log fire blazed in a shoulder-high stone fireplace on the interior wall. The arched wooden ceiling soared from fourteen feet at the exterior walls to twenty-four feet at its apex, where a row of skylights pierced a graceful vaulted arch.

Yet the breathtaking room was a mere vessel for its priceless treasures. Koa struggled to absorb the room's opulent objects. Life-size wax figures of Hawaiian warriors dressed in feathered regalia threatened to spring into battle from opposing corners. Next to one of the warriors, a majestic *kāhili,* a royal battle standard with an intricately carved pole, rose high to a lush crown of *'io* feathers.

A war canoe, complete with *pandanus* sails and *senit* bindings, occupied a place of honor. It had a rich, shiny black finish, and was balanced imperiously on carved wooden blocks as though sailing across the end of the room. Koa had a momentary flash of his ancestors building canoes for a long-dead king setting sail on an everlasting journey. He smiled to himself, thinking of his own racing exploits. He wasn't sure how fast he'd go in that monster.

The prince escorted them to a grouping of chairs in front of the fireplace. As Koa sat down, he took note of a desk with a computer, stacks of books, and a small stone dish. The dish held the remnants of several unfiltered cigarettes. Although he couldn't read them from across the room, the butts bore a tiny logo that caught his attention. They were likely Gauloises, the brand found in the Pōhakuloa lava tube. He'd have to find a discrete way to examine them more closely.

"As Mr. Hikorea knows, I entertain visitors rarely. You are guests because you hinted at some startling discovery. I trust you will not disappoint me."

"We are honored by your hospitality," Koa replied. "A murder case has taken a surprising turn. An anonymous call led us to a mutilated body, possibly a ritual killing." Koa locked eyes with the prince as he spoke but detected no discernible reaction. "We found the body in a lava tube in the Pōhakuloa Training Area. Jimmy's efforts unearthed a burial cave, what appears to be a royal burial cave."

The prince's eyes sparkled with interest. "A royal tomb? And what makes you think it's royal?"

"A burial canoe and a sorceress talisman."

"A canoe? What style is the canoe?" Koa looked to Jimmy to answer.

"It has the bow of a war canoe. The wood is no doubt *koa*, painted not the traditional black but red, the color of a king's canoe."

"A red burial canoe in the saddle lands. And the sorceress?" Excitement mounted in the prince's eyes.

"Typical female figure with crooked knees, except crowned with the head of a bird, all carved of black rock."

"The head of a bird?"

"Yes. An elongated head and beak. It's stylized but could be the head of a dark-rumped petrel."

"An *'ua'u* bird?" Aikue 'Ōpua interrupted. "And all this was discovered in the military training area . . . where the bombs of foreign devils disrupt the final sleep of an ancient Hawaiian king?"

"I fear that is so." Jimmy bowed his head slightly.

"The white man came to these islands and infected my people with Western diseases—our women with syphilis, our children with smallpox." Aikue 'Ōpua grew red-faced as his anger mounted. "They killed a quarter million of our people. The devils desecrated the archaeological treasures of Kahoʻolawe." 'Ōpua choked off his tirade, letting his hands fall downward in a gesture of hopeless frustration.

He's a fanatic, Koa thought. Of course, the *haoles* had disrupted the traditional Hawaiian ways, and done much damage in the process, but Westerners weren't the cause of all Hawaiʻi's problems. Reverting to a pre-1893 monarchy wasn't the answer. All that sort of talk made him roll his eyes. Did anyone really expect to give up their modern conveniences?

"What kind of king might have been buried in the saddle lands?" Koa asked.

The question seemed to surprise the prince, plunging him into thought. Koa tried to judge whether the prince was searching his memory or merely deciding how much to reveal.

The prince spoke almost offhandedly. "Story talk. No more than story talk."

"Stories are often rooted in real-life events," Koa coaxed.

"Just so," the prince smiled. "I heard a story passed among my elders when I was yet a child. Old men talked story of a community. A powerful and wealthy community of stonecutters."

"Who worked at *Keanaokekoʻi*, the adze makers' quarry on Mauna Kea?" Jimmy suggested.

"Mr. Hikorea, I have wondered about that name. *Keanaokekoʻi*. An interesting word." The prince became animated, talking with his face and hands as well as his voice. "One should translate *Keanaokekoʻi* as the cave of the adze makers. But where was this place? I have found no reliable historical record of its location." The prince spoke with authority. "When foreigners discovered adze makers' rock shelters on Mauna Kea they assumed . . . *assumed* that they had found *Keanaokekoʻi.*"

"Are you suggesting that the real *Keanaokekoʻi* may not have been the quarry site on Mauna Kea?" Koa asked.

"Yes, according to fragments from my childhood."

"As a child, you heard stories about another *Keanaokekoʻi?*"

"In a way."

"Can you recall these stories for us?"

The prince stared out to the east, as though his recollections came from there. "My elders talked of a powerful priest-king who ruled over a tribe of adze makers. A man of superhuman strength and great wisdom. A man who could judge stone with the eye of the kingfisher. A man who could wield the hammerstone with the cunning of the *manō* and the strength of the *koholā*—the instincts of the shark and the power of the whale.

"In the summer this priest-king and his stonecutters lived and worked under the stars around rock shelters upon the summit of the mountain where day first emerges from night." The prince paused. "And during the cold winter months, when men couldn't easily survive upon Mauna Kea, it was said that the priest-king and his adze makers lived where only *Pele* knows the way."

Koa and Jimmy looked at each other. *Pele* was the goddess of volcanic fury. "What does that mean?" Koa tried to keep the excitement out of his voice. "The words suggest a cave. Where might such a cave have been?"

"The story talk does not say."

"No hint at all?"

"Only that the priest-king made war under the banner of a strange *kāhili.*"

"Strange?"

"Yes, made with the tiny feathers of the baby *'ua'u* bird."

Koa, remembering the stick figure with an *'ua'u* bird in its hand, exchanged glances with Jimmy.

"Why might that suggest the location of the cave?"

"It doesn't necessarily, but it was said that the priest-king could fly higher than the *'io* and farther than the *'ua'u*, and yet, like the *'ua'u*, always returned to his nest."

"Higher than a hawk and farther than a petrel, yet, like the petrel, always returned to its nest." Koa repeated the prince's words.

"Higher than a hawk could easily mean the top of Mauna Kea. As a seabird, the petrel ranges far out over the ocean for months at a time, but the Hawaiian petrel always returned to the Big Island to nest in burrows under the crags of the Humu'ula Saddle," the prince elaborated.

"A cave in the Humu'ula Saddle?" Koa suggested.

The prince didn't venture a guess. "That's the best I can do for you, Detective Kāne."

"What happened to the priest-king and his craftsmen?" Koa asked.

"*Nalowale i ka 'ehu o ke kai* . . . lost in the sea sprays." The prince extended an arm toward the ocean.

"Disappeared?"

"It is said that they disappeared without a footprint. One day, the priest and his adze makers walked where only *Pele* knows the way and never returned to Mauna Kea or to *Keanaokeko'i*."

Koa studied the prince. Had this man revealed the extent of his knowledge? Koa doubted it. Hawaiians, especially the older generation, always held something back.

"Suppose we were to tell you we've discovered an underground workshop in the Humu'ula Saddle where ancient adze makers shaped tools . . . ?"

The prince straightened in his chair, leaning forward. "Is that true?"

"Yes. And there's more. In addition to the royal tomb and the workshop, a lava tube leads from the cavern some two and a half miles beneath the Saddle Road to the southern slope of Mauna Kea, where it emerges through twisted crevices into the bottom of an old cinder cone."

The prince stared off toward the east again, appearing to digest what he'd just heard. "They walked where only *Pele* knows the way. The tomb may well be that of the priest-king or one of his ancestors."

"Yes," Jimmy said, unable to contain himself. "And there is a rock carving on the cave wall—not a petroglyph, but an unusual carving, a carving in high relief, depicting a man holding an adze and an *'ua'u* bird."

"Higher than a hawk and farther than a petrel, yet, like the petrel, always returned to its nest," the prince mused.

"You knew nothing of this before we came here?" Koa asked.

The prince's wistful smile faded away. "Did you think otherwise?"

"Someone entered the lava tube and the underground workshop in modern times."

"How do you know this? Have they desecrated the site?"

"It has been looted. We're not sure when, but we assume the looting was recent. Where could the looted artifacts be sold?" Koa asked.

The prince didn't need to think to answer that question. "There are three main options—museums, private collectors, and shady art dealers. Museums used to grab every valuable historical item, but they've become much more circumspect, especially since the Native American Graves Protection and Repatriation Act protects the rights of native claimants." 'Ōpua nodded vigorously at this victory for his people.

"Private collectors are another story. Unfortunately, some collectors are grave robbers and others satisfy their passions from the most questionable sources."

Although he'd never before worked an antiquities case, Koa knew of people who collected artifacts. That did not, however, stop him from asking questions. Playing dumb was often the best way to get information. "Are there such collectors here on the Big Island?" Koa asked.

"Of course," the prince said, smiling bitterly. "There are ranchers who treasure objects taken from graves on their property, and there are the wealthy *haoles* who patronize us with their egotistic displays of our cultural wealth."

Now we're getting somewhere, Koa thought. "Have you heard of any recent acquisitions by such collectors?"

"No." The prince shook his head.

"And no one has approached you with artifacts of questionable provenance?"

"Absolutely not." Hardness crept into the prince's cultured voice.

"I meant no offense." Koa realized he'd breached etiquette with his suggestion that the prince might have bought looted objects.

"None taken, Detective."

"And what about shady dealers in Oceanic art?" Koa prompted, hoping to coax more from the prince. "I suppose there's a black market for that, too."

"International traffic is endemic to the art world. Just for starters, the British Museum acquired—many would say stole—the Elgin Marbles from the Parthenon. Sadly, here in the Pacific, the island governments have been criminally negligent in protecting their heritage. Ordinary objects sell for thousands of dollars and unique objects can bring millions. We have descended into a secular capitalist orgy where our cultural patrimony goes to the highest bidder on the international black market. And Westerners called us primitives."

The prince abruptly stood, signaling that the talk was over. Koa glanced at the desk, hoping for an excuse to examine the cigarette butts in the stone dish, but the prince shepherded them toward the door. The same two servants appeared to help carry Jimmy down the stairs.

"Prince Kamehameha," Jimmy said with the voice of a supplicant as the group descended the staircase, "would you honor us with a tour of the garden? I would especially like to see the aviary."

Koa smiled inwardly. Tradition required the prince to extend the utmost hospitality. Jimmy's was a request the descendent of a Hawaiian king couldn't refuse. As the prince walked with Jimmy's wheelchair toward the aviary, Koa fell in with Aikue 'Ōpua. He had another issue he wanted to discuss. "I understand you share the prince's interest in antiquities."

"In some ways. He's a collector. I'm compelled to preserve what the *haoles* took from my ancestors."

"Is that what you were doing on Kaho'olawe?"

Shock registered on 'Ōpua's face. "How do you know about Kaho'olawe?"

"Hook Hao is a friend. His son nearly died out there."

'Ōpua became guarded. "Kaho'olawe's out of your jurisdiction, Detective, and besides, I told my story to the Maui police."

"I'm not interested in prosecuting. I just want to help Reggie."

"Tell that to your police buddies on Maui." Bitterness dripped from 'Ōpua's voice as he turned away from Koa to join the others.

His little chat with 'Ōpua told Koa he'd only scratched the surface of the events on Kaho'olawe. Even allowing for the sovereignty activist's hostility toward authority, 'Ōpua had overreacted. Something ugly had happened out there.

The three of them—the prince, Koa, and 'Ōpua—stopped beside Jimmy under the spreading branches of the royal poinciana trees near the aviary. Koa had prepared for this moment. He pulled a pack of Gauloises from his pocket, rapped the pack against his knuckles so that two cigarettes slid partway out, and offered one to the prince.

The prince accepted. "You've traveled in Europe, Detective?"

Koa smiled inwardly. The prince had instantly recognized the unusual cigarette. Koa was prepared to bet a month's pay the butt in the ashtray upstairs was a Gauloises. He struck a match for the prince and lit up. "I'm afraid not. My addiction has a rather more mundane origin. I started smoking in the military, one of my only fond memories from those days."

"We have much in common." The prince drew deeply on his cigarette. "We, like my people, have inherited evil habits from the *haoles*."

There it was again, conveniently casting blame on others. Koa knew full well that smoking was a nasty habit. That's why he didn't smoke. He'd only purchased the cigarettes to tempt a suspect, and it had worked. The *haoles* hadn't forced the prince to smoke. He'd made that choice on his own.

As the group broke up, Koa noticed a cigarette butt in a corner near the base of the aviary. As he bent to pick up the trash, he saw that it too was a Gauloises. The prince not only smoked them but casually discarded the leftovers.

As Koa and Jimmy drove back down the twisting trail through the forest, Koa reflected on the interview. Koa's own criminal history made him suspicious of everyone, and his encounter with the prince gave him plenty to chew on. The prince's disregard for the protection of endangered hawks violated Hawaiian traditions and troubled Koa. Moreover, he smoked Gauloises and discarded the butts, like the one found in the adze makers' underground workshop. In addition, neither the prince nor 'Ōpua had asked about the murder victim. Experience told him that nearly everyone asked about murders.

'Ōpua's presence at the house was a surprising *pilina*, a connection. Two antiquities cases springing up together with the same actor appearing in both. His thoughts kept returning to 'Ōpua's fancy boots, and the boot prints they'd found out at Pōhakuloa.

For reasons quite apart from Reggie Hao, Koa decided that he would have a follow-up interview with 'Ōpua, alone. After all, a man known to hunt for native artifacts in one place could well have found other places to look.

CHAPTER TEN

FROM THE PRINCE'S castle Koa went to the doctor's office. After he had waited in reception long enough for fear to grow into a palpable thing, his turn with the doctor came. He stared at the surgeon's big hands and long, bony fingers. He'd heard Dr. Brower's words about preparation, anesthesia, recovery, and wearing a plastic collar afterward, but he could think of nothing but those fingers—fingers that would cut his neck and mess with his spine. What if they slipped?

"Listen, Doc, just tell me your success rate. How often does this surgery work?"

"It's all about the diagnosis. If we've got a good diagnosis, we have a 98 percent success rate." The doctor paused, taking a long, hard look at Koa. "But it doesn't do a goddamn bit of good to take out the wrong disk."

Christ, Koa thought, he didn't even smile as he said that. "And my diagnosis?"

"We know exactly what we're going after. You've got cervical osteophytes. In plain English it's a bone spur on your C7 vertebrae, and it's abrading the nerve that runs down your right arm. I showed you on your MRI. You're going to be okay, and a couple of months from now you'll be almost as good as new."

"So, I'll be able to compete in the Moloka'i Hoe?" Koa asked, referring to the grueling annual thirty-eight-mile outrigger canoe race across the Ka'iwi Channel from Ka'iwi Bay on Moloka'i to Waikīkī Beach on O'ahu.

"I said almost, Detective. If you're going to put seven-plus hours of unrelenting stress on your neck, we can schedule a second surgery for three years from now."

Ouch. But what choice did he have? "Okay, Doc, when do I go under the knife?"

The surgeon checked his calendar. "Two weeks from today. First thing in the morning."

Like a man awaiting execution, Koa had hoped for more time. "Okay, Doc."

Upon returning to police headquarters, he found Detective Piki practically jumping up and down in his office. "Boss, we got a lead on the Pōhakuloa victim. About time we nailed it."

Although Piki's instant conclusions didn't always justify his enthusiasm, the possibility of a break in the case lifted the dark mood Koa had brought with him from the doctor's office. "What have we got?"

"A Miss Julie Benson from the Alice Observatories filed a missing-persons report on Keneke Nakano, a twenty-nine-year-old Hawaiian astronomer. And," Piki added with a flourish, "he's been out of touch for the past ten days." He handed Koa a copy of the report phoned into the Honoka'a police substation.

Koa scanned the document. The ethnicity and the timing fit. Pōhakuloa wasn't that far—only about twenty miles—from the observatories on Mauna Kea. Piki was right: they might have nailed it. Within minutes, he had secured the license number of a nine-month-old black Isuzu Trooper registered to Keneke Nakano and directed Piki to put out an APB for the vehicle.

Koa's thoughts turned to Nālani. If the deceased were from the Alice Observatories, she'd likely know him and might have valuable insights. He tried her cell, but got no answer. She was probably in the dust-free "clean" room working on parts of the telescope's mirror. If so, she might be unreachable for hours.

The missing-persons report listed next of kin, and Koa immediately called Kimo Nakano, an uncle of the missing astronomer. Kimo agreed to accompany the police to his nephew's house in Honoka'a, a forlorn old sugar town north of Hilo. Koa collected Sergeant Basa, retrieved the key found at the Pōhakuloa crime scene, and headed for his Explorer.

"My guys have been practicing hard. You're gonna be paddling in our wake," Basa said.

Still caught in denial, Koa wasn't ready to tell his friend that he wouldn't be paddling. "You better practice so maybe you don't finish behind us like the last Moloka'i Hoe."

"Shit, you know we got caught in a squall and pushed off course," Basa protested. "Otherwise, we would've beaten your team by twenty minutes."

"Would've, could've. Excuses don't win races," Koa retorted with good humor. "You guys should have a good caller, like yours truly." Koa normally sat in the caller's seat, the number-two seat in a six-man canoe, determining how many strokes his paddlers would take on one side of the canoe before switching to the other side. The caller's skill kept the canoe racing forward without rolling over in heavy surf.

"We'll clean your clock next time, Koa. You just wait," Basa warned.

Being younger, the sergeant was more passionate about winning. Plus, they both knew that Basa and his crew were stronger. That's why Koa derived so much enjoyment from beating them.

But now his racing days, at least for bruising open-ocean contests, were likely over.

It took Koa and Basa only a few minutes to reach Kimo Nakano's house south of Hilo. A short, elderly gentleman with white hair and a leathery face answered the knock. His left sleeve hung empty where an arm had once been.

"Mr. Kimo Nakano?"

"Yes, that's me."

"I'm Chief Detective Koa Kāne. We spoke on the telephone."

"Oh, yes. You called to say my nephew is missing and you want me to go up to his place in Honokaʻa with you." The old man spoke in a concerned but scratchy voice. "I'm ready." He pulled the door shut behind him and started down the walk toward the police vehicle. He made his way slowly, hobbling in obvious pain.

"Automobile accident?" Koa asked as the old man levered himself into the rear of the Explorer.

"Heartbreak Ridge in eastern Korea, a little south of what's now the DMZ."

Koa nodded. As a former Army officer and student of military history, Koa knew the horrors of the battle that left thirty-seven hundred casualties on the American side. Koa admired the men who fought there. "I'm sorry."

"It was a long time ago."

Sergeant Basa easily steered through the sparse late-afternoon traffic on the Belt Road along the northeast coast. "Tell us about Keneke," Koa said, pulling out his notebook.

"He comes from good roots. His grandfather, my father, carved wood the old way, like his father and his father's father. Had a workshop, just a shed, really, near Hāwi. The gods guided his fingers.

"Keneke's parents were good people, but his father, my brother, he didn't have the gift. Miko couldn't carve, not like Keneke's grandfather. I don't have the gift either. Few men have. Miko managed a store in Hāwi, and Keneke's mother helped. They got along, not fancy, but okay."

"Where can we reach them?"

"They are with Keneke's grandfather. Miko passed away four years ago. Keneke's mother joined him within six months."

"I'm sorry."

"It happens that way when two people are very close. Keneke, their only child, gave them great joy. The gods blessed that boy. Blessed his mind. He had a gift for numbers, calculus, physics. Don't know where he got that gift, not from his father, maybe his grandfather." The old man began coughing, and it was several moments before he resumed talking.

"Keneke worshipped his grandfather. He used to sit in the old man's workshop for hours, listening to the old man talk story. His grandfather sure could talk story. The gods blessed him that way, too," Kimo noted with pride.

"The old man doted on Keneke. I guess it was natural. The boy was his only grandchild. There was quite a scene when the old man took sick . . . suffered a stroke. The old man was really agitated. At first, I thought he was afraid of dying. But that wasn't it. He wanted to see that boy.

"Keneke was at UH in Honolulu. Flew back to be at his grandfather's side. The old man was in a pretty bad way, but he had to pass his *hā*."

"His *hā*?" Basa inquired.

"Hawaiian for breath or breath of life, but it means much more than that. The old man literally breathed into Keneke's mouth, passing his *mana*, his life's power, to the boy. Kind of a last will and testament."

Koa had a long familiarity with the Hawaiian concept of *mana*. As a native healer, his mother treated the *mana* in sick neighbors with herbs, exercises, and a focus on what she called the good spirits within people.

Kimo fell silent, and when Koa turned around to look, he found him staring out the window. Seconds ticked by, becoming minutes, before he resumed speaking.

"Keneke led in his classes at UH, studying the stars. I remember him talking about black holes. I couldn't understand, but he did real well. Got himself into the University of California on a scholarship. Held his fellow students in awe . . . said he had to work three times harder than the smart ones from big-name colleges."

"When did he return to the Big Island?"

"He dreamed about working at Alice, but he always said he didn't have much of a chance."

"But he did end up working at Alice."

"That's right. He called me the day he got the job offer. It must have been about nine months ago. *He mau maka loaʻa ʻole*, eyes not easily obtained. That's what he said. Kind of a play on words, I guess. Just the sort of thing his grandfather would say, always toying with words," he noted with a chuckle.

"He came back here in July or August last year. I asked him to come live with me, but he wanted his own place."

"How often did you see him after he moved back here?"

"I only saw him three or four times. Felt bad about it, too. My brother would have wanted me to look after him, but Keneke worked hard—spent a lot of nights on that mountain." The old man tilted his head toward the rugged skirt of Mauna Kea rising to their left. "I tried to get him to spend Christmas with me, but he had a girlfriend in California, an Asian girl, another astronomer. Met her at the university. He went back to Berkeley to spend Christmas with her. Seemed pretty serious about her."

By the time Sergeant Basa had driven past the last of the abandoned cane fields that stretched along the highway, evening shadows covered Honoka'a. The town had bad memories for Koa. His father and grandfather had sweated out their lives in backbreaking labor at nearby sugar mills. One of those mills had crushed his father's life in a horrible accident. He'd slipped—or so Koa had been told—while loading sugar cane into the hopper and had been crushed, like the cane, between the giant steel rollers that squeezed the sweetness from the stalks. It had supposedly happened so fast that no one had been able to stop the machinery.

His father's coworkers had told a different story. They told Koa, sixteen at the time, that Anthony Hazzard, the mill manager, had arranged the fatal accident after a heated argument with Koa's father about labor issues. That had led to another turning point in Koa life—the killing of his father's murderer.

Basa turned the police Explorer into an unpaved driveway beside a modest duplex. An empty bird feeder stood on a pole not far from the steps. The blue bubble light atop the police vehicle immediately caught the attention of four neighborhood children, who gathered around as Koa, Basa, and Kimo climbed out and walked toward the house.

"You here to see Keneke?" one of the children called. Koa turned to a small bronze boy of about six, wearing only dusty white shorts. Koa sat down on the wooden steps, deliberately reducing himself to the same height as the child. He smiled.

"Yes, we're here to see Keneke, have you seen him?"

"He do a bad thing?" Fearless but inquisitive eyes searched Koa's face from beneath an inverted bowl of straight black hair.

"No, we just want to talk to him and make sure that he's okay," Koa reassured him. "Have—"

"I helped him feed the birds." The child pointed toward the bird feeder. "He taught me their names: silverbill, mannikin, and *'amakihi*." The child's face lit up with wonder. "One day we saw an *'amakihi*. We really did. Really. But the seed's gone and the birds don't come anymore. They went away."

Koa finally got a word in. "When did you last see him?"

"It . . . it was a long time ago," the child responded hesitantly, spreading his arms to show a big space. "He promised he would come to my *lā hānau* an' bring me a special present, but he never came. He broke his promise." The child looked down in disappointment.

"*Hau'oli lā hānau.*" Koa wished the child happy birthday. "Maybe it wasn't his fault," he added, sensing that he was nailing down the Pōhakuloa victim.

Basa ruffled the kid's hair. "You get a gold star for helping us." The boy screamed in delight and ran off to share his good fortune.

Turning away from the children, Koa approached the door to Keneke Nakano's little home and knocked loudly. No answer. After securing permission from his uncle to enter, Koa tried the Yale key from the Pōhakuloa murder site in the keyhole. The key turned effortlessly in the lock, and the door opened. Koa experienced a little jolt of adrenaline, while his brain asked how a twenty-nine-year-old astronomer could be dead for more than ten days without anyone, other than a six-year-old neighborhood kid, noticing.

"Where did you get the key? There is something that you haven't told me, Detective," Kimo protested. "Something terrible has happened to my nephew, hasn't it?"

Koa put a hand on the old man's shoulder and gently guided him into the house. He helped Kimo to one of the wooden chairs in the living room and waited patiently while he lowered his arthritic frame into the seat. From the moment Piki had shared the details of the missing-persons report, Koa suspected Keneke was the Pōhakuloa victim, but he'd delayed telling Kimo until he was sure.

Koa now looked the old man straight in the eye. "There is no easy way to say this, so I'll tell you straight out. We think your nephew was murdered. We found a body a couple of days ago in a cave out at Pōhakuloa. I'm terribly sorry for your loss."

Kimo's weary form sagged under the weight of the news, and he suddenly appeared more ancient, more frail. "The key . . ." Koa started to explain, but the old man wasn't listening. Koa watched him intently, fearful the shock might provoke a heart attack. Basa knelt beside the old man, checking his pulse, before nodding to Koa that Kimo was okay.

Koa turned his attention to the room. He stood for several moments, soaking up the feel of his surroundings. Beauty and history seemed somehow intertwined in the polished surfaces. Koa ran his fingers across the richly grained surfaces of the reddish *koa* wood furniture and felt a connection to his own ancestors.

He focused on a wood-framed oil painting hanging next to the staircase. It pictured an old man, intently shaping a wooden bowl with a traditional Hawaiian *k'oi*.

"Is that your father?" he asked Kimo, pointing to the picture.

Still coming to grips with his grief, the old man nodded, almost imperceptibly.

"And he made the furniture in this room?"

The old man nodded again. "He had the gift. The gods guided his . . ."—the old man's voice cracked—"his hands."

"An exceptional gift," Koa noted, although the praise sounded false, given the awful context.

He climbed the stairs to the second floor. A four-poster carved *koa* bed occupied one end of the large, open room. Sitting on the other side of the room were an oversized roll-top desk, its tambour curtain closed, and a bookcase. Books, carefully arranged in categories on the shelves, offered further insight into Keneke Nakano.

Astronomy and astrophysics selections filled more than half the bookcase. Koa recognized titles by Albert Einstein and Stephen Hawking, but none by any of the other authors.

Keneke had a collection of Hawaiiana and had devoted nearly half a shelf to materials on Kahoʻolawe. Congressional hearings, newspaper stories, maps, pamphlets from Protect Kahoʻolawe ʻOhana. Keneke had obviously been interested in Kahoʻolawe. But why? Could there be a *pilina*, a connection, between Keneke, Kahoʻolawe, and Hook Haoʻs son, Reggie? Aikue ʻŌpua had shown up in both cases . . . and now these books.

Making his way to the roll-top desk, Koa lifted one of the wooden handles, surprised at the ease with which the massive serpentine tambour rose in its wooden channels. Four objects were arranged on the richly grained desktop—a wireless modem, a silver-framed picture of an attractive Asian woman, a telephone answering machine, and a rock paperweight. The rock grabbed his attention. Although smaller than the preform found at the crime scene, it resembled the partially completed adze found near Kenekeʻs mutilated body.

"Do you know where Keneke got this rock?" Koa asked. By now the old man had come upstairs and was sitting on the bed, his shoulders slumped forward, his chin cupped in his bony right hand.

"Huh?" Looking up, the old man spoke with tears in his eyes.

"Do you know where Keneke got this rock?"

"I've no idea . . . from childhood, I guess." The old man's voice was barely more than a halting whisper. "He collected antique things . . . his grandfather collected things, too."

Koa looked around for a computer but saw none. Did he use a laptop? He examined the answering machine, noting that it registered the correct time and date. With the eraser tip of a pencil, Koa pressed the button to play back its messages. The dates ran from January 20 to January 27, when the tape ended. Keneke had received numerous and increasingly desperate messages from a woman, Soo Lin, imploring him to return her calls.

Replaying the tape for a second time, Koa noted calls from Thurston Masters on January 21, asking for a return call, and Gunter Nelson on January 25, requesting Keneke to reschedule a meeting. There were also two calls from Basically Books, asking Keneke to pick up a book he had specially ordered. Koa extracted the tape and slipped it into an evidence envelope. "We'll return the tape to you."

"Whatever . . ."

"We're going to need his medical records. Did Keneke have a doctor here on the island?"

"A pediatrician, up in Hāwi, kind of a friend of the family. That's the only doctor Keneke saw. So far as I know."

One by one Koa opened the drawers but went unrewarded for his efforts. He found no letters, no diary, no address book, and no computer. Using his handkerchief, he picked up the photograph. "His girlfriend?"

"That's probably Soo Lin, but I can't say for sure because I've never met her. Somebody's . . . somebody's going to have to tell her about Keneke."

"Yes. It would probably come a little easier from you, but we're going to have to talk to her."

"I'll call her. Keneke would have wanted me to do that."

Koa and Basa went through the whole place from top to bottom, not once, but twice. Even with Koa's sharp eyes attuned to anything out of the ordinary, they found nothing. Koa came away convinced the little house hadn't been the site of Keneke's murder. Otherwise there would have been some blood or sign of a struggle . . . something out of the ordinary. Besides, Honoka'a was a long way—over sixty miles—from where they'd found the body. Only a brave or stupid killer would transport a dead body that far.

CHAPTER ELEVEN

KOA WAS EAGER to see if *pōmaikaʻi*—the lucky happenstance of Nālani's job at the Alice Observatories—might give him some insight into the victim's workplace. Yet despite several attempts at reaching her, Koa was unable to talk to Nālani until late in the day, when she'd been driving to the Kīlauea Lodge. The 1930s-era Boy Scout Lodge was one of their favorite restaurants. Koa arrived first and was seated next to the Lodge's huge stone fireplace. He ordered white wine for Nālani and a beer for himself.

A few minutes later, she bounded into the restaurant with an excited expression and practically ran to the table. "Oh, Koa, it's so thrilling," she began before he could mention the Pōhakuloa case. "Director Masters has made a monumental discovery. It's all hush-hush for now, but he's brought in a verification team, six of the world's foremost experts. And guess what?"

He loved her enthusiasm, the eagerness in her eyes and the glow on her face. "What?"

"Director Masters asked me to assist one of the verification team members, Herr Doktor Reinhardt Schlingler from Heidelberg. I met him today . . . funny man. He looks like a chipmunk with a mouthful of acorns." She tried to mimic a man with heavy jowls, but only succeeded in making Koa laugh. "I can't believe Director Masters asked me to help. It's really exciting."

He raised his beer to toast her success. "Congrats."

"I want you to meet Herr Doktor Reinhardt Schlingler." She emphasized the "Herr Doktor," again making Koa smile. "In addition to astronomy, he's an opera expert. He makes all kinds of allusions to operas."

Koa had seen only a few minutes of opera on television, but that was more than enough. Action movies were more his style. "What's the discovery?"

"I'm not supposed to tell anyone. There's a press embargo until Director Masters addresses the North American Astronomical Society conference here next week."

He'd never seen her hold anything back. "So you're not going to tell me?"

"You don't share the details of your cases."

He held up his hands in surrender. "Speaking of cases, I tried to call you several times. We—"

She cut him off. "I know. I saw the calls. We spent the whole day in the mirror room putting the shine back on worn mirror segments. You know, I can't even take my cell in there."

"I know," he conceded. "I wanted to tell you we finally identified the Pōhakuloa victim."

"That's great, Koa. Who died out there?"

"Keneke Nakano. You might—"

"Oh my God, not Keneke," she said more loudly than she'd perhaps intended. "That's absolutely horrible!" The color drained from Nālani's face and tears came to her eyes. Other diners turned to see what had provoked her distress.

Koa put his hand over hers. "I'm sorry, my *ipo*. I didn't mean to shock you."

She choked back a sob and, by slow degrees, regained control. "He was the nicest, brightest young astronomer. I can't imagine why . . . why anyone would . . . and mutilated in a lava tube like that. It's horrible."

Her display of emotion surprised him, since he didn't recall her mentioning Keneke. Despite feeling badly for upsetting her, Koa needed to know more about this revered astronomer. "Tell me about him."

"Jesus, Koa, a thousand images come to mind. Happy, friendly, full of life . . . a fabulous storyteller. He spoke beautiful Hawaiian. Let me see, what else? He loved astronomy, robotics, archaeology—"

The last word grabbed him. He was beginning to get something useful. "Tell me about his interest in archaeology."

"Keneke loved Hawai'i. Knew its history, but he wanted to know more. He sought to use scientific methods to discover history's mysteries."

"How would someone use scientific methods . . .?"

"Spectrography to identify the source of rock samples. That would be an example."

"Like the spectroscopy police labs use to identify illicit drugs?"

"Yeah, it's the same concept."

"Sounds like a bright fellow."

"Amazingly smart, but not arrogant about it."

"You seem to have known him pretty . . ." The words popped out of his mouth before he realized that he sounded jealous of a dead man.

She reached across the table, covering his hand with hers. "He was a really nice kid, Koa, not a romantic interest." His face grew hot, and he felt like a fool. After a moment, he refocused. "Tell me about his relationships with his colleagues."

"He got along well with almost everyone, but especially the younger staff. They loved him."

"And the senior staff?"

"He worked a lot with Director Masters. Seemed to be one of the director's special protégés."

Something wasn't adding up. Nice kids surrounded by friends didn't wind up mutilated in lava tubes. He wasn't asking the right questions. "Was Keneke involved in this big discovery?"

"Not the big discovery. Masters used Charlie Harper on that project."

Koa felt his jaw muscles tighten at the mention of Harper's name, but he continued to follow up on Masters. "So what kind of things did Masters assign to Keneke?"

"Masters had him working on a new advanced adaptive optics program for the telescopes. It's the system we use to compensate for the distortion in starlight caused by the earth's atmosphere. Sensors read the earth's moving air currents and adjust one of the telescope's mirrors to remove the effect of the moving air. It makes the images a hundred times clearer. Not quite as good as the images from the Hubble Space Telescope above the earth's atmosphere, but almost. It takes really complex mathematics . . . genius-level stuff."

"But not related to Masters' big discovery?" he asked to be sure he understood.

"Only tangentially. Masters made his discovery using adaptive optics, but not the new system Keneke was working on."

"But they got along well?"

"Famously. Like I said, Masters has his protégés. Keneke belonged to that elite group."

"What about Charlie Harper"—he didn't even like to mention the man's name—"and the other assistant director. What's his name?"

"Gunter Nelson . . . poor Gunter."

"Why poor Gunter?"

"He so much wanted to be director, but never had a chance. He joined the Alice team just before the old director retired. A lot of the staff think he only took the job in hopes of a promotion. There's even a rumor, break room talk really, that someone on the foundation board promised him the job. Sometimes I think it eats him alive that he'll never be top dog." She paused as if she had just thought of something.

"But it's funny you should ask. Keneke and Gunter were big buddies for a while, but then something happened. They had some kind of falling-out."

At last, Koa thought, a lead he could pursue. "Falling-out over what?"

"I don't know, but the relationship cooled. You might say froze."

"Harsh words?"

"No, not that I overheard, but Keneke avoided him."

"And how did Gunter react to that?"

She made a little twirling gesture with her hands; one he'd seen before when she was trying to formulate a thought. "I think Gunter knew he'd done something to offend Keneke."

"What makes you think that?"

"I can't put my finger on it. Call it intuition."

The word "froze" stuck in Koa's mind. He plainly needed to give Gunter a closer look. He returned to a distasteful subject. "And Charlie Harper?"

"Nobody likes that pervert." Nālani frowned as she emphasized the last word.

"Anything in particular between Keneke and Charlie Harper? Keneke heard he hit on Polly, one of the other techs, not this last time, but the time before that. He offered to talk to Director Masters on her behalf, but Polly's so . . . so timid. That's why she's so vulnerable. Anyway, she refused to let Keneke say anything to Director Masters."

So, Koa thought, Keneke tried to stop the serial stalker. If Nālani
was right that Masters would have fired Charlie Harper for his unwanted sexual advances, Keneke was a potential threat to Harper's
position. And what else might Keneke have known about Harper?
"You think Charlie knew of Keneke's discussion with Polly?"

"Keneke may have had words with Charlie about it, but I don't
actually know for sure." She paused to sip her wine. "Oh, Koa, it's
awful. He was such a fountain of energy. Life is so . . . so tenuous."

He nodded. "Did Keneke have any enemies?"

"No, none that I know of."

*   *   *

Later that night, Koa sat bolt upright in bed. Asleep one moment,
he was now wide awake, thunderstruck by the connection he'd
missed. He must have been replaying the scene at the prince's
castle in his dreams, and his mind had stuck on Aikue 'Ōpua's
tirade—not on the words, but 'Ōpua's voice. He had heard that
voice before, and he knew where—the tape of the 911 call. After
returning from Pōhakuloa, he'd replayed the tape of the call, not
once, but several times. Aikue 'Ōpua had been out at Pōhakuloa.
The native-rights activist had called 911. Koa knew it, now he just
had to prove it.

An hour after dawn, he called Cap Roberts, the head of the police department's technology section, and then Zeke Brown, the
county prosecutor.

Koa was soon sitting next to Cap Roberts in front of a large computer screen. "It's him. I'm 90 percent sure." Cap pointed to two
jagged lines, one red and one black, on a graph. "This black spectro-
graphic line represents 'Ōpua's voice at his news conference on Hawai'i public radio, and the red line comes from the 911 tape. Here's

the word 'Pōhakuloa.' See how the lines match?" The screen shifted. "And here's the word 'devil.' He uses that word a lot."

"You can tell despite the pidgin?" Koa asked.

"Yeah. He used pidgin in the 911 call to disguise his voice, but I've got eleven words that match almost perfectly. There's a nine out of ten likelihood it's him."

Koa thought of an old law enforcement adage, particularly applicable to crimes of arrogance and greed: "Nobody does it just once." 'Ōpua had been hunting antiquities on Kahoʻolawe. There was every reason to believe he had other hunting grounds. His boots could well have left the tracks out at Pōhakuloa, and now Koa had a reasonably definitive voice match. "Is there a way to be positive?"

"Sure, with more samples I can get to a 99.5 percent probability, but you'd likely need a court order to get the samples."

Koa smiled. "Be careful what you ask for."

After meeting with the county prosecutor, Koa asked Sergeant Basa to join him for the afternoon. "Where we going?" Basa asked as they headed toward the saddle.

"To see Aikue 'Ōpua."

"The big-shot native sovereignty asshole?"

As with all Hawaiʻi policemen, Sergeant Basa had been through community sensitivity training, but he was still a *haole*, and many Westerners had little patience for native activists, especially loud-mouthed sovereignty types like Aikue 'Ōpua.

"That's him," Koa acknowledged before adding, "Some of his views about recreating the monarchy are a bit extreme."

"A bit extreme . . . hell, he wants to wind us back to the dark ages."

They drove up the slope into the saddle between the mountains before Koa turned off onto a dirt road. Stopping to open a gate, he drove through a pasture filled with grazing cattle and headed toward a weathered farmhouse. Aikue ʻŌpua stood on the *lānai*, watching as they parked the car and walked toward the house.

"You're trespassing, Detective." ʻŌpua wore the same boots with "1893" embossed on the shafts.

"It's official business," Koa responded evenly.

"Kahoʻolawe's out of your jurisdiction, Detective, and, like I said, I've already told the Maui police everything I'm gonna say."

"It's not about Kahoʻolawe. It's about Pōhakuloa." Koa saw a flicker in ʻŌpua's eyes. Surprise, maybe fear. A tell, in any case. "How about you show us a modicum of Hawaiian hospitality?"

ʻŌpua stared at them mulishly, and Koa thought he would refuse, but he finally shrugged. "Sure, Detective, even for a *hoʻohaole*." He stepped back, turning to usher them into his house.

Koa bristled at the slur. ʻŌpua had denigrated the authenticity of his Hawaiian heritage, attributing to him the ways of a Westerner. Yet Koa had heard the barb before. The sovereignty types frequently demeaned Hawaiian policemen as lackeys of their white oppressors. He let it pass, focusing on his mission.

They entered a simple ranch house filled with Hawaiian artifacts—a feathered cape, stone *kukui* nut lamps, and *poi* pounders. One wall held a collection of old knives, including whalebone *pāhoas*, or daggers. But the room also sported saddles, ropes, spurs, and other implements of cowboy life. Koa thought it an odd mixture of native and *haole* objects for a native-rights proponent. Cattle weren't native, and Hawaiʻi's *paniolo* cowboys had come from Spain.

ʻŌpua took a seat in a *koa* wood rocking chair, while Koa and Basa took the opposite ends of a wooden bench. As ʻŌpua hooked one leg over the arm of his chair, Koa caught the glimmer of a horseshoe-shaped tap around the heel. Before Koa could begin, ʻŌpua challenged his ethnicity more openly. "You know, you're not a real Hawaiian, Detective. You've sold out to the *haoles*, and you're out here doing their bidding."

Koa wondered if the sovereignty activist's baiting was intended to distract him and chose to respond with a hardball question. "Tell us how you discovered the body out at Pōhakuloa."

"What makes you think I discovered the body?" 'Ōpua responded coolly.

"Because you left boot prints before you made the 911 call."

'Ōpua looked toward his upturned boots, then chuckled. "There're thousands of cowboy boots with underslung heels on the island, Detective. The heel keeps a cowboy's foot from sliding through the stirrup."

"True," Koa agreed amicably, "but I doubt we'd get the same voiceprint match."

"A voiceprint. You don't have a valid voiceprint, Detective." Despite his nonchalance, what 'Ōpua intended as a statement sounded more like a question.

"Because you disguised your voice with pidgin? Guess again, Mr. 'Ōpua. We matched the words with your public statements. You seem particularly fond of the word 'devil.' You used it twice at Prince Kamehameha's, many times in your speeches, and four times in the 911 call."

'Ōpua tensed for just an instant before relaxing again. "What do you want, Detective?"

"To know what happened out at Pōhakuloa."

"I'm not interested in helping you, Detective."

"Mr. 'Ōpua, if you force me to do this the hard way, I'll serve the search warrant I have in my pocket for your boots. Then I'll serve a court order for further voice samples. Finally, we'll haul you before a grand jury. You'll have to answer questions, unless you want to invoke your Fifth Amendment rights."

The man was tough. He barely flinched. "And if I talk?"

"Unless you murdered that poor bastard out at Pōhakuloa, I have no interest in making your life difficult."

"Okay . . . okay, mister tough guy. I made the 911 call."

'Ōpua had locked horns with the authorities many times over the years, and he obviously knew when he held a weak hand.

"I knew it," Basa exclaimed, unable to contain his hostility toward the native activist.

'Ōpua scowled at the sergeant.

"And before that?" Koa asked.

"I was out riding."

"In the restricted area?"

"I don't accept that the white man can restrict what belongs to my people."

The words had a hollow ring, and Koa didn't miss the fact that they weren't responsive. Basa hadn't missed the evasion either. "That attitude won't protect you if your horse triggers unexploded ordnance," he chided.

"Whatever. Something spooked my horse. He trembled and shied. Then I got a whiff of a noxious smell. I investigated and found the body in the lava tube. I called 911."

Koa knew the Pōhakuloa site intimately. No one would have just casually ridden a horse over that nasty ground. 'Ōpua's visit had to have been deliberate. He thought about pursuing it but chose to bide his time. "Why call anonymously? Why disguise your voice?"

"The *haole* police and the *haole* courts discriminate against native Hawaiians. You've seen the statistics, Detective. Forty percent of those in jail are Hawaiian, way out of proportion to their share of the general population."

He was right, Koa had to concede. He had reason to avoid identifying himself.

"You touch anything in that cave?"

"The cave smelled of evil and I left."

The man had again avoided a straight answer, and Koa pursued the question. "Did you touch anything in the cave?"

'Ōpua hesitated. "No."

Koa sensed a lie. "You sure?"

"Positive, Detective."

"Did you know Keneke Nakano?"

'Ōpua stiffened and his eyes bulged. "You just used the past tense. Did something happen to him?"

"He died out at Pōhakuloa."

"*Koʻele nā iwi o Hua I ka lā.*"

It was an odd historical reference, meaning trouble would befall those who destroyed the innocent. "So you knew him?"

"Kawelo Nakano's grandson. He was *ʻohana huna.*"

The secret family, the same words that Hook Hao had used to describe Reggie's group. "When did you last see him?"

"I don't remember."

"Was he part of your Kahoʻolawe activities?"

"That's a question for the Maui police, Detective."

And, Koa thought, I'll be asking them, but he let it slide for the moment. "Any idea who killed him?"

"No."

"But you told Prince Kamehameha about the body, didn't you?"

"You'll have to ask him, Detective."

CHAPTER TWELVE

THE NEXT MORNING, Koa looked up to see Police Chief S. H. Lannua standing in the doorway to his office. As always, he was in uniform with all the creases pressed, as if his garments had just come from the dry cleaners. Given the sticky humidity in Hilo, Koa sometimes wondered if Lannua kept an iron in his office. The chief's tall, strapping presence surprised Koa because his boss usually relied on his senior staff to update him and rarely roamed the halls. In fact, Koa couldn't remember ever seeing Lannua in his office before.

Apparently, the chief likewise had no recollection of being in Koa's office because he looked around the room, taking in its contents. As its head, Koa had the detective bureau's only private office. Although it was no bigger than the offices senior detectives typically shared, the absence of a second desk and its end-of-the-corridor location with windows overlooking Hilo Bay made the room almost spacious.

Koa had chosen sparse decorations, replacing the usual official-issue pictures of the governor, mayor, and the police chief with a banner above his desk proclaiming: *I ulu nō ka lālā ike kuma . . .* Without our ancestors we would not be. The chief mouthed the words and nodded. Two framed Escher prints hung opposite Koa's desk. In *Reptiles* tiny crocodiles emerged from a pad and climbed over a book, a cube, and a brass cup before reentering the pad. In *Relativity* three sets of stairs arranged in a triangle created pathways into sideways and upside-down places. To these prints he'd added an eight-by-ten photograph of Nālani.

His colleagues understood the banner, reflecting Koa's respect for the people and history of the islands. His colleagues didn't disparage native Hawaiians in Koa's presence. To those who questioned his taste for Escher prints, Koa explained that *Reptiles* reminded him of the chameleon-like aspects of human nature, while *Relativity* taught him to think outside of the box. No one who knew Nālani questioned her presence.

Koa's battered wooden desk held only a stainless-steel thermos, a coffee mug, a telephone, and two stacks of papers, one of messages and the other of files.

Koa stood up. "What do you need, Chief?"

"The mayor heard about this Pōhakuloa killing and wants it solved."

Typical, Koa thought. Politicians expected him to produce results with a snap of his fingers. "It's a tough one, Chief, but we've identified the victim as a young astronomer."

"That only makes it more urgent. As usual, I'm counting on you to get the job done, Detective."

Koa massaged his neck as the chief retreated down the hall. He was no stranger to political pressure. It came with the turf. Just wait till he told the chief he was scheduled to go under the knife for the pinched nerve in his neck. He grimaced and turned back to the piles on his desk.

He poured coffee from the thermos and started in on the smaller pile, a sheaf of messages and reports from various police offices. The APB for Keneke's black Isuzu Trooper had so far produced nothing. Traffic stops on the Saddle Road and inquiries at the Army barracks at the Pōhakuloa Training Area had led nowhere. Koa had just turned to the files when Sergeant Basa appeared in his doorway. "Hey, Boss, I got a question for you."

"What's up?"

"Out there at 'Ōpua's ranch, he really had it in for you. What was with that *ho'ohaole* stuff?"

Koa flipped his hands outward in an exasperated gesture. "You know these sovereignty types, they're like that. They feel dissed by Western culture. Makes 'em confrontational, even with their own people."

Basa still seemed dissatisfied. "I thought it might be more than that. Figured he was trying to provoke you, maybe even create an incident so he could lodge an official complaint."

Koa, whose criminal past normally made him suspicious of others, realized that he hadn't paid sufficient attention to 'Ōpua responses. He leaned forward and encouraged Basa to elaborate.

"That's possible, but to what end?"

"I think 'Ōpua knows more than he let on."

Koa caught Sergeant Basa wistfully eyeing the thermos on his desk.

"Go on, Basa, help yourself." With mock reluctance Koa pulled a mug and a box of sugar packets from his drawer and pushed them across his desk. The sergeant uncorked the thermos and poured coffee almost to the brim of the mug before emptying four sugars and stirring it with his finger.

"Damn good coffee." Basa grinned. "Thanks, Chief."

Koa held his tongue about all that sugar and pushed Basa to explain his assessment of the activist. "So, what was 'Ōpua hiding?"

"I'm not sure, but he was evasive. I think he touched something in the cave."

"What?"

"Don't know, but he didn't answer your question and then he hesitated. And what was with that Hawaiian saying? I mean, he didn't seem all that surprised someone he knew had been murdered."

"You're right," Koa said, mulling over that point, "and neither he nor the prince asked about the murder victim."

As Basa left, Koa turned his attention to the old case files, looking for crimes committed with a similar MO. Then he stopped, overcome. His shoulder and arm blazed with an angry ache. Bone rubbing on a nerve between the vertebrae in his neck caused referred pain—that's what the doctors called it. It was similar to the way a short circuit in one room could kill the lights in another room. Yet if it was only referred pain, why did it hurt so damn much? He reached for his painkillers—not the Tylenol that had stopped working months ago, but the prescription Percocet stuff.

Koa needed to lie down. He locked his office door, moved the stack of files to the floor, and stretched out on his back where he could still reach the papers. He'd be better in twenty minutes.

One by one Koa read through an encyclopedic array of the island's most heinous crimes from the past thirty years. Drug-related killings, a kidnap-murder, the gang rape/slaying of a young tourist. At the bottom of the pile, he found several old cardboard case jackets, stuffed with police, laboratory, and medical reports, as well as dozens of faded yellow newspaper clippings, so old they'd begun to crumble. He soon came upon one that riveted his interest. "Damn," Koa swore softly as he began to read with intense concentration.

On February 14, 1983, four hikers, exploring the western slopes of Hualālai Mountain, had noticed noxious odors wafting from a hole in the ground. Investigating, they had discovered a mutilated, partly decomposed human body and summoned the police, who had recovered the remains of a fourteen-year-old boy, stripped naked and tortured to death. The Valentine's Day murder, as the press had dubbed it, had become an overnight sensation. "Child Tortured in Lava Tube." "Bloody Valentine's Day Victim Discovered." "Teenage Male Molested, Hacked to Death in Mountain Cave." The initial headlines started a feeding frenzy, not only on the Big Island but throughout Hawai'i.

The police had called in medical experts. Their findings bore an uncanny likeness to the report that Koa would soon be receiving from Dr. Cater. The doctors had detailed a brutal killing in the style of ancient Hawaiian human sacrifices. Multiple lacerations across the chest. Deep and straight, made with an antique whalebone dagger. "Like railroad tracks," it read. Exactly the same words Sam Cater had used. The cause of death grabbed Koa's attention—a six-inch puncture wound into the left cerebral cortex, administered with an ice pick-type instrument through the left eye socket.

The police had arrested one George Ray, who eagerly admitted to torturing and killing the youngster, but claimed to have done so at the behest of ancient spirits. Koa read the transcript of his confession with horrified fascination. Ray seemed to be from a different era and society. He called himself Pā'ao, a priest from Tahiti, and claimed: "I, Pā'ao, danced with the spear of the *pueo* and tattooed his eye."

Koa felt clammy when he finally stood and set the files aside. Walking to the window, he stood for a long time, looking out over Hilo Bay, thinking about George Ray. The human mind could pursue such peculiar paths. The real world, he had learned, was even more twisted than Escher's *Relativity*. When he finally turned from the window, it took him three calls and forty-five minutes to learn that Ray had died in 1995 while confined in the state hospital for the criminally insane. It was only an outside shot, anyway.

He then dialed Shizuo's number. When he finally got through, Shizuo responded with hostility. "I hope this isn't about that Pōhakuloa stiff."

"Shizuo, I need some help, okay?" Koa sounded more irritable than he felt, but his words had the desired effect.

Resignation resonated in Shizuo's voice. "Tell me what you need."

"Did you check for a brain injury? A deep wound to the brain?"

"X-rays did not show anything like that."

"Would X-rays show a puncture wound to the brain?"

"What are you getting at?"

"I've been researching case files and found an old one where some weirdo killed a boy. The killer raved about a ritual practice—tattooing the eye with the spear of *pueo*, that's what he claimed. The cause of death was a deep puncture wound through the eye socket."

"We weren't specifically looking for that, and X-rays might not show a puncture wound without bone involvement."

Koa didn't miss the use of the past tense, as though Shizuo considered the case over. "I want you to look specifically for such a puncture wound through the left eye socket."

"I suppose I can do that. I'm seeing patients this morning, though—"

"I need an answer this morning, Shizuo."

"No can do."

Koa stifled a sigh. He knew how to turn up the heat. "I'm briefing the chief, who'll be talking to the mayor later this morning. Shall I tell him you 'no can do'?"

"One of these days you will ask too much of me and I'll . . ."

Koa wanted to say retire, but he held his tongue.

Once the phone call ended, he returned to his former musings. He ticked off the similarities in his mind. Both corpses in lava tubes. Both bludgeoned beyond recognition. Both with an eye gouged out. Both sexually mutilated. Both cut in straight lines, like "railroad tracks." Both likely tattooed with the spear of *pueo*. The perp in the first killing had died, so this had to be a copycat killing. With one difference. He'd found no whalebone dagger at Pōhakuloa.

Going back through the file, Koa found a picture of the dagger used in the Valentine's Day murder. He suddenly had a vivid image of the knives on the wall in ʻŌpua's ranch house—steel knives and whalebone daggers. Everything clicked.

ʻŌpua had touched something in the lava tube. He had taken the *pāhoa* . . . now displayed in his ranch house.

Had he used it on Keneke? That was the question.

CHAPTER THIRTEEN

LATER THAT SAME day, patrol officer Johnnie Maru reported finding Keneke Nakano's black Isuzu truck in the Hilo airport parking lot. Finding the victim's vehicle at the airport puzzled Koa. He wondered whether Keneke had left it there or whether someone else had parked it at the airport to mislead the police.

If Nakano had parked the vehicle, he must have been planning to leave the Big Island. That would mean an airline reservation. Plus, if Keneke had been abducted from the airport, there should be witnesses. Koa instructed Basa to check the airlines for a reservation and have his men canvass the airport for potential witnesses.

An hour later Koa was standing under arc lights in the Hilo police garage. The blackened floor, sticky with oil, pulled at his shoes. The damp air was ripe with the smell of grease and transmission fluid. He watched a tow truck haul the black Isuzu Trooper into the shop.

Mickie Durban, a crime scene specialist, walked around the vehicle checking for prints before opening the driver's door. Unlocked, he noticed. "That's odd," he said. His voice had the rasp of a heavy smoker. "Most folks lock their cars at the airport."

He pulled the door open and whistled. "Better have a look, Detective." Mickie pointed to the passenger seat where car keys lay in plain view.

Koa pondered the implications of this unexpected discovery. Had Keneke been in such a hurry he'd left his car keys? Had the victim been abducted as he was leaving the car and dropped his keys? Had the killer parked the truck and left the keys, hoping a thief would steal the vehicle, creating a false trail for the police? It would help to know whether Keneke had made an airline reservation.

"Okay, Mickie. Let's see what else we can find," Koa directed.

Mickie dusted the steering wheel, door handles, gearshift, and other obvious places before searching the glove box and map pockets. When he climbed into the back and looked under the front seats, he found a large, thick envelope addressed to Keneke. It contained a book—a dog-eared copy of Martha Beckwith's translation of the *Kumulipo*, the Hawaiian creation chant. Inside, they found a handwritten note on flowery feminine stationery:

Dearest Keneke:

Thank you so much for loaning me your book. I had such a fabulous, wonderful, marvelous time with you at the hotel. Until next time.

Linda Harper

Linda Harper. Was that Charlie Harper's wife? Had the serial harasser's wife enjoyed a fabulous, wonderful, marvelous time with Keneke at some hotel? Were Keneke and Charlie Harper's wife having an affair? He recalled Nālani's reference to Charlie's bad marriage. He'd relish arresting Charlie Harper. But he reminded himself, sexual harassment wasn't murder.

Koa and Mickie spent another fruitless hour on the interior of the Trooper before Mickie closed all the doors in preparation for hoisting the truck up on the grease rack. "You know what's missing, Detective?"

"The entrance ticket to the parking lot," Koa responded.

"Yeah, he musta stuck it in his pocket. It woulda had a time stamp, showin' us when he parked the truck."

"Damn strange to take the parking ticket and leave the keys," Koa mused.

After raising the truck on the lift, Mickie scraped samples of dirt and dried weeds from its undercarriage. A police photographer, waiting on the sidelines, snapped pictures, popping his flash and adding blue-white illumination to the surreal brightness of the arc lamps.

"Detective Kāne," Mickie's raspy voice called across the enclosed space, "you better have a squint."

Koa moved in close behind the technician, who pointed a screwdriver at a broad swath of bright metal where some hard object had gouged the bottom of the differential.

"The driver bottomed out this baby on somethin' hard, like a concrete curbstone."

"Recent, too, would you say?"

"Yeah, it's recent. Lucky the son of a bitch didn't rip the differential out."

Koa remembered the jagged lava outcroppings along the Pōhakuloa jeep trail near where Keneke Nakano's body had been recovered.

"Take some scrapings or whatever you need. Check with Sergeant Basa and see if you can match these scrapings to the jagged lava outcroppings on the jeep trail in the Pōhakuloa Training Area."

"You got it, Detective."

Koa had no sooner mentioned Basa than he called. "Koa, I checked the airport," Basa said. "Keneke Nakano had a reservation on United to LAX on January 21, but, here's the thing. He never made the flight. A Robin Archer booked the reservation. She's at the airport now if you want to talk to her."

Koa dialed the number that Basa provided, and Robin Archer answered.

Identifying himself, Koa asked, "Ms. Archer, can you remember when Mr. Nakano made the reservation?"

"It's right here." Koa heard the clicking of a keyboard. "January 21 at 07:42 hours."

"What did he look like?"

"Who?"

"Mr. Nakano."

"Oh, I don't know. He made the reservation by phone."

"How do you know that?"

"Because I made the reservation for him myself."

"You remember the phone call?"

"Vaguely."

"You must make a lot of reservations. Is there some reason you remembered Mr. Nakano's phone call?"

"Well, sort of. He made the reservation at 7:42 for an eleven o'clock flight, and when he didn't show up, the gate agent made an announcement for him to board. That's why the name came back to me when your Sergeant Basa called."

"Did he happen to say where he was calling from?"

"Not that I recall, Detective. I usually ask for a contact number, but according to the reservation record, he didn't give one."

Koa thought for a moment. "Well, how did he pay for the ticket?"

"Credit card. Issued in his name. Visa authorized the transaction, and I issued an e-ticket for him."

"Was there a return reservation?"

"No. It was one-way."

Koa's hand went almost automatically to his sore neck as he thought about this new information. It narrowed the time of death. Dr. Cater had given him a window—forty-eight hours beginning at 1:00 a.m. on January 20. Given the time of the reservation, the window had closed to seventeen and a quarter hours starting at 7:42 a.m. on January 21, but more important than the hours, the new time frame ruled out the early morning hours of January 20. And since Keneke had eaten lamb shortly before his death and the crime had most likely occurred at night—the killing had occurred on the night of January 21.

But why a one-way ticket? Had something in Keneke's past drawn him to Los Angeles? Did the key to this crime lie outside Hawai'i? If so, there had to be something more. Maybe Keneke had talked with someone in L.A. Koa called Piki and asked the detective to check Keneke's cell phone records. "And while you're at it, get the call records for Thurston Masters, Gunter Nelson, and Charlie Harper."

CHAPTER FOURTEEN

KOA HAD BARELY set a foot back at headquarters when he got word that the chief wanted a briefing. The chief wasn't a man to be kept waiting, so Koa grabbed his notes off his desk and headed upstairs. Koa entered the police chief's office and took a seat at the round table. He hated the damn fancy chairs that supposedly gave the office class. They offered no back support, so he sat forward with his back straight to protect his neck. Slouching in a bad chair produced pain that lasted for hours. Basa came in a couple of minutes later.

Koa studied his boss as he finished a telephone call. For as long as Koa had known him, no one aspect of the chief seemed to explain the grip the shrewd official had on those around him. At times the chief's sway seemed to emanate from a certain patrician manner. Something intangible in his posture and demeanor made those around him defer, waiting for the chief to speak.

Unfortunately, despite his bearing, he possessed only one of the two qualities Koa considered essential for management of the island's police department: he had political clout. Chief Lannua's family had lived on the island for generations, had large landholdings, and commanded the respect of nearly everyone with political influence. Politicians thought twice before double-crossing Chief

Lannua or the Hawai'i County police. Koa had seen numerous instances where the chief's power and prestige had benefited the whole force.

But his strength was also his weakness. He was a politician. All too frequently, he shared details of police investigations with the mayor and the mayor's cronies, and sometimes thwarted investigations that cast the mayor in an unfavorable light. In Koa's view, he yielded too easily to supposed political realities. Too close to the mayor and the county council, he failed to fight for the funds the police department so desperately needed to maintain adequate levels of manpower and competence. And he was too old-school to embrace the technological changes needed to modernize the force.

Koa and the chief had a turbulent relationship. The chief, Koa knew, depended upon him to tackle the department's toughest cases. Yet they'd repeatedly locked horns over Koa's unrelenting push for a bigger budget, more detectives, and especially resources for police technology routinely used by mainland cops. But the real fireworks started when the chief tried to steer an investigation away from the island's power brokers. It had happened only twice—once in a murder investigation and once in a fraud case, but it drove Koa nuts. In Koa's experience, the rich and powerful surrendered to criminal impulses just as often as common folk.

Putting down the phone, Chief Lannua headed confidently across the room to join the two policemen at the table. As usual, he came directly to the point. "I requested this meeting to catch up on the Pōhakuloa killing. You have my attention."

Koa glanced down at his notes. "You know the crime scene details. A 911 caller alerted us to the body on January 29. The military police then located the deceased in a lava tube in the restricted area. The killer mutilated the victim, taking particular care to make identification difficult.

"The lava tube site is of archaeological significance. We had an archaeologist, Jimmy Hikorea, from the National Park Service out there."

"I know him—ex-marine and a good man," the chief said.

"In the back of the cave, concealed behind a rock wall, we found the entrance to an ancient tomb, complete with a burial canoe and a bird woman talisman. Probably the crypt of an ancient Hawaiian king.

"Through another rock wall, we discovered a huge underground cavern used, according to Hikorea, by ancient adze makers. A lava tube leads from that cavern under the Saddle Road to a collapsed *pu'u* on the southern slopes of Mauna Kea. We have no proof the site played any role in the killing, but we do know that someone entered the cavern in modern times."

"How do you know that?" the chief asked.

"We found a cigarette butt and wrapper in the adze makers' workshop."

Koa had the chief's undivided attention. "Go on."

"With Hikorea's help I talked to Prince Kamehameha."

At the mention of the prince, the chief's eyebrows shot up, and Koa knew he'd entered politically sensitive territory. "He played coy, giving us tidbits of Hawaiian history, but he knows something about the site, if not the murder itself. I'd bet a month's pay on it. Smokes Gauloises, the same brand as we found in the workshop. Now, how many people on this island smoke Gauloises? Not many."

"You're not suggesting that the prince was involved in this murder?" The chief's voice took on a hard edge.

"I have no real evidence, but he knows more than he let on about the site, and he had Aikue 'Ōpua with him—"

"Christ, we don't need trouble from the sovereignty crowd," Chief Lannua interrupted.

"According to the Maui police, 'Ōpua's involved in stealing artifacts from Kaho'olawe, and he's the 911 caller."

"What the hell. How do you figure that?"

"Boot prints and voiceprints."

"That's pretty thin."

"I talked to him. He admitted it."

"I'm surprised he talked to you."

"I didn't give him much choice. I had a warrant and a court order in my pocket."

The chief's eyebrows again shot up, almost meeting across the bridge of his nose. "Go on."

"So Prince Kamehameha's in the middle of this mess. I think he's been in the workshop. His buddy 'Ōpua's into stolen artifacts, and 'Ōpua just happens to stumble on the body. Sounds like a fairy tale, doesn't it?"

"Jesus, Koa, you'd better proceed with kid gloves. Prince Kamehameha's one of the true power brokers on the island."

"Yeah, well, he'll be less powerful if the feds find out he keeps endangered hawks."

The chief's voice took on a menacing tone. "Slow down, Detective."

"I need his cooperation," Koa insisted.

"There will be fallout. I need to talk this over with the mayor."

"Okay, but I do need to talk to him again," Koa insisted. "And we're going to execute a search warrant on Aikue 'Ōpua this afternoon."

"Why?"

"I think he has the knife used to carve up the victim."

The chief appeared thunderstruck. "Christ, the sovereignty crowd will go ballistic."

"I can't help that. I'm sympathetic to some of their goals, but they're subject to investigation like all other citizens."

The chief seemed to sag in his chair. "Go on."

"We've identified the Pōhakuloa victim. He's Keneke Nakano. Age twenty-nine. An island native. Educated at UH–Honolulu and the University of California. Employed for the past nine months as a staff astronomer at the Alice Observatories. His grandfather, a master wood carver, made traditional furniture in a small workshop outside Hāwi."

"Kawelo Nakano, the old wood carver . . . a legendary craftsman and a marvelous story talker," the chief interrupted.

"You knew Keneke Nakano's grandfather?" Koa's voice betrayed his astonishment.

"Yes, and so did Prince Kamehameha. He and old Kawelo were both steeped in the old ways and very close. The prince should want to help avenge the death of Kawelo's grandson."

"Good . . ."

"Many old Hawaiians knew Kawelo, and thousands have enjoyed his handiwork," the chief said, speaking in a reverential voice. "His work is in the Bishop Museum, but more than his artistry, he had a passion for preserving Hawaiian antiquities. As one of the founders of Protect Kahoʻolawe ʻOhana, he fought to stop the Navy bombing of archaeological and religious sites."

The chief paused, searching his mind for even more information. "He and ʻŌpua participated in the trespass protests during the mid-1970s. Old man Nakano must have been over sixty when he and eight others violated Navy restrictions. The Navy arrested and prosecuted them. The papers called them the Kahoʻolawe Nine. The old man drew a suspended sentence. A lot of us admired him."

"That explains the collection of stuff in Keneke's house."

"What stuff?"

"A whole bookshelf of legislative reports, bills, pamphlets, and news stories on Kahoʻolawe."

"*I ulu nō ka lālā i ke kumu*—the branches grow because of the trunk. Without our ancestors we would not be." The chief quoted the phrase in Koa's office.

"It's always been so," Koa acknowledged.

The chief redirected the briefing. "What does the county physician have to say?"

"It looked like a ritual killing, so we brought in a forensic pathologist from the US Army Identification Center."

"Shizuo asked for help?" The chief's voice registered surprise.

"I didn't give him much choice." Koa made little effort to hide his sarcasm.

"Is he going to complain to the mayor again?"

"I don't think so." Koa wanted to blast the incompetent coroner for starting the autopsy without him, but he knew it wouldn't do any good and decided to keep his powder dry for another day.

"He better not. Go on."

"The Army pathologist thinks the killer subdued the victim with a choke hold, then mutilated the corpse sometime later, maybe a couple of hours later. There is some doubt about the actual cause of death. Shizuo says it was strangulation; the Army doctor thinks it was a brain injury. Could have been the spear of *pueo* ... we're checking that now."

"Spear of *pueo*?"

"A deep puncture wound through the eye."

"Jesus."

"Forensic evidence places the time of death between 1:00 a.m. on January 20 and 1:00 a.m. on January 22. The killing most likely occurred in the late evening because the victim's stomach contained undigested lamb, and the activity out at Pōhakuloa most likely occurred after dark when intruders wouldn't be observed. The victim used his credit card to make a one-way air reservation to return to the mainland on the morning of January 21. And Detective Piki has confirmed the reservation call came from Nakano's cell phone. That narrows the time-of-death window to the night of January 21. That's our working hypothesis."

"How did you pin down the time of death into such a narrow range given the decomposition of the body?"

"The Army doctor used a new technique based on potassium in the eyeball. So far, we've kept the ritual killing part out of the press. In fact, outside the police department only the victim's uncle, Kimo Nakano, the next of kin, knows the true nature of his nephew's death. There will be an obituary tomorrow. You or the mayor are likely to get inquiries."

"Thanks, I'll alert the mayor."

"We've got a lot of investigating to do at Alice. I need to talk to the secretary who reported the victim missing. I'll have to interview the observatory staff. There's some evidence Keneke had a relationship with the wife of one of the assistant directors."

"Who?"

"Charlie Harper."

"Don't know him. What's the evidence?"

"A note . . . something about a fabulous, wonderful, marvelous time at a hotel."

"Jealousy is a good motive for murder, especially grisly murders."

Koa had known the chief would jump for the easy motive, especially if it pointed to someone the chief regarded as unimportant. "If he knew. Husbands are frequently the last to know. Anyway, I thought you might call the director to grease the way."

"You're talking about Thurston Masters."

"That's him. He's on Keneke's answering machine."

"Anything significant?"

"Just a message asking for a return call."

"Masters has been the director of the Alice Observatories for a while. A stuffed shirt. Arrogant, but smart and ambitious, with a pathological need for control. Married money, the daughter of one of the Honolulu elite." The chief paused. "You do what's necessary, but use good people and don't upset the astronomers. They're notorious prima donnas. Anything else?"

"Yes." Koa hesitated. "There's an uncanny resemblance to the last ritual killing on the Big Island, the 1983 Valentine's Day killing—"

"More than a superficial resemblance?"

"Yes. Both victims were found in lava tubes. Both mutilated, including identical genital mutilation. Both missing the left eye. Both victims bore razor cuts in straight lines . . . like railroad tracks. Both likely killed with the spear of *pueo*."

The chief gasped and stiffened in his chair. "Goddamn. You better arrest someone before this gets into the papers. The reporters will have a field day."

CHAPTER FIFTEEN

THE HEADQUARTERS OF the Alice Telescope Project occupied a prominent place along Waimea's main drag. A tribute to its designers, the ultramodern headquarters of the world's largest optical telescope blended seamlessly with the ranch architecture of the Hawaiian cowboy town. Thirty-six glass panes arranged in an arrow-shaped array of overlapping hexagons decorated the dormer above the entry doors. The thirty-six glass panels represented the thirty-six interlocking hexagonal mirrors of the Alice telescopes on the mountain, eighteen miles away as the crow flies, but nearly fifty miles away by road. Symbolically, the arrow pointed upward toward the heavens.

Koa wasn't admiring the architecture as he entered the building's small atrium on his way to see Thurston Masters. A cold, almost hostile, receptionist directed him toward the right wing of the building. NASA posters and paintings inspired by Russian science fiction writer Isaac Asimov decorated the hallway.

At the end of the hall, Koa entered the vestibule outside the director's office. An austere older woman glanced up from her computer monitor. "Detective Kāne?" Though they had spoken only briefly by telephone, Koa recognized her Boston accent. Her plain white blouse was buttoned to her neck, and she wore no jewelry.

Her brown hair, combed into a tight bun, gave her a stern, but efficient, appearance.

"Yes, I'm Koa Kāne. You must be Julie Benson." He smiled. "I appreciate your taking the time to see me. May I sit down?"

"Of course. It's awful about Mr. Nakano. Just awful." Koa registered her drawn-out New England pronunciation of the word "awful." He sat in the chair next to her desk and pulled out a small notebook.

"Your chief called the director, and he instructed me to help you in any way that I can."

"I understand that you reported Keneke Nakano missing?"

"Definitely . . . after his girlfriend, Miss Hun, called the director."

"Tell me about that, please." Koa jotted down notes as she spoke.

"I met Mr. Nakano maybe a dozen times. He seemed to know everything about the Big Island, all about its history before the Westerners. Anyway, he called one morning about two weeks ago. I get into the office promptly at seven thirty, and he called right after I arrived. I definitely remember that."

"What did he say?"

"He had to go back to the mainland. Something about his girlfriend. I remember he said he hadn't talked to the director. I told him I couldn't speak for Dr. Masters, but I did promise him I'd let the director know about his call."

"And you did that?"

"Definitely."

"How did Mr. Nakano sound? Was he excited . . . nervous?"

She pursed her lips before answering. "He sounded, uh, normal. Nothing out of the ordinary."

"Then what happened yesterday?"

"Miss Hun called."

"And what did she say?"

"She called just before I arrived at seven thirty and spoke to the director."

"But you reported Mr. Nakano missing."

"Yes, I did. The director told me Miss Hun had called and asked me to check up on Mr. Nakano. I called his home, but I got no answer. So I looked in his personnel file. He listed an uncle here on the Big Island as his next of kin. I tried the number but couldn't get through. So I checked back with the director, who told me to call the police."

"I see. Would Mr. Masters typically answer the telephone at that hour?"

"It's Dr. Masters, Detective," she corrected him. "Yes, that happens. I cover breaks for the receptionist, so the main lines ring in here. If no one picked up, the director would answer. He can't stand a ringing telephone. He insists I answer every call before the second ring."

"What exactly did Dr. Masters tell you?"

"That Miss Hun, Mr. Nakano's girlfriend, called looking for him ... claimed she hadn't heard from him in two weeks. Director Masters said she got pretty upset when he informed her Mr. Nakano had returned to the mainland."

"Anything else?"

"She's some kind of postgraduate fellow in astronomy. She told the director she'd been in Chile ... said Mr. Nakano had known about her trip there. I gather she got pretty upset."

"Can you fix the date of Mr. Nakano's call, the one when he said he had to return to the mainland and said something about his girlfriend?"

"I'm not really sure. It must have been after January 17. That's the day my mother—she lives with me—came back from Maui. I definitely remember telling her about it. Something about young men just running off on short notice. And I think he called a day or two before the verification team started on January 22, but I'm afraid that's the best I can do."

"That puts the call on or after January 18 and no later than January 21?"

Julie nodded.

Koa produced a calendar. "January 18 was a Sunday. You don't work weekends, do you?"

Julie shook her head no.

"Then it must have been Monday, January 19; Tuesday, January 20; or Wednesday, January 21. Does that seem right?"

"Yes, definitely. It must have been one of those days."

"Is there any way you could pin the date down—maybe telephone records or something?" She paused. "I don't think so."

Too bad, he thought, she couldn't pin down the date, especially since those days overlapped the date-of-death window he'd gotten from Dr. Cater. "Who supervised Mr. Nakano?"

"The staff astronomers work independently. The director has overall charge of the observatories and the whole staff. Deputy Director Nelson and Assistant Director Harper help Director Masters, but the professional staff really doesn't have supervisors."

"I'd like to talk with . . ." Koa paused. "Nelson and Harper after I see Mr. Masters."

"Dr. Masters," Julie corrected him again. "Deputy Director Nelson and Assistant Director Harper are usually here or on the mountain, but right now they're down at the hotel, helping set up for the NAAS meeting."

"The NAAS meeting?" Koa asked.

"The North American Astronomical Society. Dr. Masters is the keynote speaker announcing his big discovery." She bubbled with pride. Koa remembered his conversation with Nālani. Masters was making some big announcement.

"Oh. When is the big announcement?"

"Monday. Definitely the highlight of his career." She lowered her voice. "There's talk about a Nobel Prize. And there's a party Monday night after the speech. The whole observatory staff will be there."

That, Koa thought, would give him an opportunity to meet the staff, but Julie Benson wasn't the person to ask for an invitation. "Could you give me addresses and telephone numbers for Mr. Nelson and Mr. Harper?"

She picked up a memo pad and wrote the information in a precise, calligraphic hand.

"Thanks." Koa slipped the paper into his pocket. "Isn't it odd that nobody here at Alice checked on Mr. Nakano for over two weeks?"

She had an easy answer for that. "Things have been crazy here, what with Director Masters' big discovery. We've had media people calling from all over the world. The phone rang constantly for ten days. I guess nobody thought much about Mr. Nakano."

"Did Mr. Nakano have an office?"

"He has . . . had . . . a cubicle in one of our two workrooms here."

"What about a computer? Did Mr. Nakano have a laptop computer?"

"Definitely. The Alice Foundation provides laptop computers for all the staff astronomers."

"Do you know where we can find Mr. Nakano's computer?"

"I imagine he had it with him. Most astronomers carry them around like security blankets."

That explained the lack of a computer in his home. "I'd like to see his cubicle."

"Definitely." She stood and led him out into the corridor where they paused in front of three large photographs. "Dr. Masters is in the center; that's Gunter Nelson on the right and Charlie Harper on the left."

"Thanks," Koa said, studying each face to find a detail he would remember—Masters' square jaw, Nelson's shaggy facial hair, and Harper's almost cherubic round face. He rejoined Ms. Benson, and they entered a large workroom with eight small, partially enclosed carrels.

Julie pointed to the third one on the left side. "Mr. Nakano occupied that one." Only slightly larger than a library research desk, the space had an electrical outlet, but no personal computer. An autographed snapshot of Soo Lin Hun and a calendar hung from the corkboard above the desk. Five dates—January 4–5, 13, 20, and 22—had been highlighted with a yellow marker.

"You know the significance of the highlighted dates?"

"Those are observing dates, dates when Mr. Nakano had telescope time scheduled. It's more precious than gold."

"Isn't it odd for him to leave when he had observing time scheduled?"

"Definitely very odd. But it was also odd for him to leave without clearing his absence with the director."

As they walked back through the atrium, a silver Land Rover pulled into the parking spot reserved for the director. "That's Dr. Masters," Julie said, pointing. A tall, black-haired man with a strikingly square jaw emerged from the driver's door, followed by a boy, perhaps fifteen years old, who bounced out of the passenger side. Masters said something Koa couldn't hear and the boy broke out laughing. Masters smiled as the two shared the lighthearted moment.

"Who's the boy?" Koa asked.

"That's Danny, Dr. Masters' son. He spends a lot of time here when he's not in school on Oʻahu. If you'll have a seat here in the atrium, I'll come get you as soon as Dr. Masters is ready."

Minutes later, Julie Benson returned to inform Koa that Director Masters was on an important NAAS conference call. "I'm afraid

he'll be at least an hour. I'm so sorry. Let me show you to our kitch-
enette, where at least you can get some coffee."

Koa bristled. He didn't like to be put off, especially not for an
hour. The chief had pegged this Masters guy—arrogant enough to
put his own business ahead of an appointment with the police. Still,
he needed to talk to Masters, so he had no choice other than wait.
He followed Julie into the kitchen and got a cup of coffee. His
shoulder hurt and he wanted to lie flat on the floor, but he settled
for standing with his back pressed against the wall.

Hoping to see Nālani, he called her cell, only to learn that she
was once again in the mirror room at the observatories on the
summit of Mauna Kea. Like many Alice technicians, she split her
time between the headquarters in Waimea and the actual telescopes on the summit of Mauna Kea. She'd astounded Koa by explaining that the giant telescopes could be operated remotely and
that most astronomers never had to deal with the hostile conditions on the summit. Alice technicians, on the other hand, performed dozens of maintenance tasks that could only be done on
the mountain.

A voice at the door abruptly caught his attention. "Greetings,
earthling. I bring you tidings from the furthest reaches of the universe." The deep, computerized speech emanated from a contraption
nearly three feet tall, including a cubical head supported by a round
pipe on a box-like upper body. A large glass eye protruded from the
gadget's forehead. Stubby mechanical arms on each side ended in
pincer-like crab claws. The robot's lower torso, a round corrugated
canister, stood on four complex, multi-jointed metal legs.

Koa watched as the robot stutter-stepped toward him with tiny
movements of its metallic feet. "Who are you?" the machine asked
in a gravelly voice.

"Koa Kāne. And you are . . .?"

"Cepheid. My name is Cepheid, after the star Delta Cepheid in the constellation Cepheus, discovered by John Goodricke in 1784."

"And who is controlling you, Mr. Cep—Cepheid?"

"That is beyond understanding," replied the droid-like creature.

Koa shook his head. "Really?"

"Yes, earthling. You can neither see nor understand as Cepheid sees. Why are you here, earthling?"

Koa guessed the robot was Danny Masters' toy. "To talk to Director Masters," he responded.

"Are you a real cop?" the robot asked.

"How did you know that I was a policeman?"

The robot switched to a godlike voice. "Cepheid is all-knowing, earthling."

"Do you carry a gun?" With lightning speed, the robot extended one arm, pointing a crab claw toward Koa. "Zap . . . zap . . . zap," the robot intoned. "I beat you to the draw, earthling." It made a clucking sound as though trying to laugh.

Koa broke into a laugh of his own. "You are indeed quick on the draw. How do you manage such lifelike actions?"

"My circuits have 64-bit microprocessors with SIMD extensions, AI software, digital mapping, transistorized servo circuits, 256-bit telemetry, CCD lenses, and 64-channel audio." The robot cocked his head, inviting a compliment.

"Very nice. We could use you in police work . . . when my officers might otherwise be in danger."

"Cepheid arrests Keneke's murderer. That would make a nice headline." A line of LED lights across the robot's forehead flashed green as though the machine were pleased with itself.

"That's enough, Danny," Thurston Masters interrupted from the doorway. "I need to talk with Detective Kāne."

The robot released a long, hissing sigh. "Cepheid was helping the earthling solve Keneke's murder."

"That's enough, Danny." Masters' tone brooked no argument.

"You always say that just when it's getting fun." A string of flashing red lights across the robot's forehead signaled its irritation. It rotated and retreated from the room.

Koa faced the director of the Alice Observatories, once again noting his unusually chiseled jaw, black hair tinged with gray, and bright blue eyes. "That's quite a toy," Koa said, gesturing after the robot.

"It's not a toy," Masters responded coldly. "It's actually a test platform. We use a lot of robotics to control the telescopes and change the detectors that record what the telescopes see. What you call a toy was built with the aid of one of the experts who built NASA's moon rovers, *Spirit* and *Curiosity*." He paused. "Let's go back to my office where we can talk in private." Masters pointed Koa toward the hallway.

Still thinking about the robot, Koa asked, "What kind of test platform?"

"We use it to develop and test software we're going to install in the machines on the summit. It's also used to test artificial intelligence concepts. We generate so much astronomical data we're literally years behind in analyzing what we've already collected. We're using Cepheid to test ways of computerizing that process."

They entered a spacious office, and the scientist lowered his tall, lanky frame into a black leather chair behind his massive desk while waving Koa to a nearby chair. Koa scanned the office. The walls were covered with certificates—Harvard, MIT, and Stanford—as well as plaques, including an air force commendation for outstanding performance and a presidential citation, signed by Ronald Reagan. Koa immediately recognized Masters' "type"—a man defined by the plaudits of his admiring fans.

"We both want to find Keneke Nakano's killer. So sit down and let's get started," Masters said abruptly.

After having made Koa wait almost an hour, Masters was now all business. He hadn't even referred to Nālani, although he had to be aware of her relationship with Koa. Strange.

Koa squinted, noting one immediate disadvantage. The wall behind Masters was all glass, and looked out toward the sunlit mounds of the Kohala Mountains. Against the bright background, Koa couldn't read the man's eyes.

"'Grisly murder scene,' that's how Chief Lannua described it. I gather that the body was pretty badly decomposed?"

"Yes." Koa spoke slowly, organizing his questions in his mind. "There was substantial decomposition."

"You were able to determine the time and cause of death?"

Masters' interest in the details intrigued Koa. The players in this case were either uninterested in the murder, like the prince, or overly interested, like this man. But at least Masters had a legitimate interest. His employee had been murdered. "We're working on it."

"The murder of a staff astronomer is an outrage. It couldn't have come at a worse time with the NAAS people here. I want this crime solved. Fast." Suddenly, Koa understood Masters' interest in the details. He didn't want the murder to spoil his big party. Koa recalled Chief Lannua's words: pathological need for control. Keneke's murder was an annoyance this obsessive man couldn't control.

Masters paused, glaring at Koa. "Quite frankly, Detective, I question whether the Hawai'i County police are capable of solving such a crime. Shouldn't you bring in outside help?"

Koa met the director's gaze and chose his words carefully. "We have expert forensic help and have engaged certain resources of the FBI."

"Who's your forensic guy? Some GP from Hilo?"

Koa wondered briefly whether Masters knew about Shizuo or was simply disparaging the local medical community. "No, we brought in a forensic expert from the US Army Central Identification Facility on Oʻahu."

"Oh." Masters leaned slightly forward. "And has he been able to tell you anything?"

"He's running tests." Irritated by his sun-shot vantage point, Koa rose and moved to another chair. Masters raised his eyebrows as though seeking an explanation, but Koa didn't answer the implied question. From his new position, he had a good view of the director's face. The man's striking blue eyes were piercing and conveyed a directness that inspired trust despite his aggressive assertiveness.

Koa mentally reviewed his objectives: learn more about Keneke, get the lay of the land in this unfamiliar world of stargazers, and finally, to evaluate Masters as a potential suspect, although that was a long shot. The key with most witnesses, even the top 1 percent, was to get them a little off balance and then engage them in a conversation, minimizing their time to formulate answers.

"Dr. Masters, have you ever been in the Pōhakuloa Training Area?"

Masters hesitated, and Koa wasn't sure he was going to respond. "Not other than as Colonel Trippet's guest at a live-fire demonstration."

"Are you aware of any archaeological sites in the PTA?"

"Archaeological sites, no. What do archaeological sites have to do with this murder?" Masters' annoyance couldn't have been more obvious if the word had been stenciled on his forehead.

Koa ignored the question. "Did Mr. Nakano discuss archaeology with you?"

"No, not that I recall. What are you getting at?" Masters' annoyance clearly registered in his voice.

"Tell me about Keneke Nakano." For a moment Koa thought Masters might continue the tug-of-war for control of the interview, but then the director seemed to relax, sitting back in his chair.

"Nice young astronomer. Full of spark and energy. Not terribly strong scientifically, but extraordinarily cheerful. I liked him. Nearly everyone did."

"Explain what you mean by not terribly strong scientifically."

"Mr. Nakano earned his undergraduate degree at UH. He lacked the benefit of a scientific grounding of an MIT or Stanford. The University of California, of course, rounded out his scientific education, but, quite frankly, I didn't expect Mr. Nakano to develop any significant reputation as an astronomer."

Koa recognized the academic arrogance so openly displayed. If you weren't from Harvard, you were stupid. Funny, he didn't yet know much about Keneke, but the young astronomer hadn't won an assignment to the Alice Telescope Project by being stupid. "You could make that judgment so quickly?"

"Oh, yes. Résumés and interviews are worthless, but after working with a scientist for six months, I have a pretty fair idea of his or her talents."

Chief Lannua, Koa thought, should have added judgmental and conceited to his description of this man. "And you worked closely with Mr. Nakano?"

"Reasonably so. I assigned him a number of projects and reviewed his conclusions. He wrote a speech for me, but quite frankly, I don't assign speechwriting duties to the ablest astronomers."

"What kinds of observations did Mr. Nakano make?"

"Mr. Nakano was a staff astronomer." Masters leaned forward, focusing his bright eyes on Koa. "The staff concentrates on maintaining and upgrading the facility. Mr. Nakano was assigned to our adaptive optics team—"

"Adaptive optics?" Koa interrupted.

"Sophisticated computer-controlled mirror systems designed to correct the distortions caused by the earth's atmosphere," Masters responded, as though he were explaining things to a child.

"So Mr. Nakano worked on those systems?"

"Yes, but 'struggled' would be a better word. The mathematics involved is exceedingly complex. Unfortunately, Mr. Nakano hadn't mastered the intricacies of the requisite calculations."

Odd, Koa mused. Nālani described Keneke as one of Masters' special protégés, while Masters himself paints a less flattering view of the relationship. Yet that might just be a difference in perception. "Why did you select Keneke Nakano to join the Alice staff given your view of his education and mathematical weaknesses?"

"The world is not yet a meritocracy, Detective Kāne. We must still accommodate local prejudices."

Koa added "insensitive" to his description of the director, but he didn't let the slur slide. "Are you saying that Alice hired Keneke Nakano because of his Hawaiian ancestry?"

"We are in a conflict, a fight for survival with certain primitive Hawaiian forces, the so-called sovereignty groups. They would return the islands to the seventeenth century." Masters' face became rigid and his voice hardened. "Because of Mauna Kea's supposed religious significance to the early Hawaiians, these modern zealots would curtail or even shut down the observatories. In the face of this onslaught, Mr. Nakano's ethnicity worked to his—and our—advantage."

"Did he interact with the sovereignty groups?"

"We have public relations professionals for that. Mr. Nakano, like our many women astronomers, simply improved our demographics."

Koa wanted to laugh. Masters' insensitivity was nothing short of stunning. He had to know that Koa and Nālani were an item, yet he didn't hesitate to suggest she'd been hired to improve the observatory's demographics. At least, Koa thought, he's transparent about it. Koa took that as a mark of honesty. "I see." He kept his voice even. "Was Mr. Nakano under any particular stress?"

"Like most young astronomers, he was struggling to make a professional name for himself, but nothing out of the ordinary."

"But he wasn't succeeding?"

"That's not what I said, Detective Kāne. Contemporary astronomy is a complex field. In the short time Mr. Nakano had been with us, he couldn't have made a name for himself. I said in the long run I didn't expect him to develop a significant professional reputation as an astronomer."

"He spent a lot of time on the summit?"

"Yes, as our new adaptive optics program moved into its implementation phase, Mr. Nakano analyzed and adjusted the performance of the instruments on the telescopes. And that cannot be done remotely."

"He was allocated observing time for this work?"

"Telescope time, yes. Observing time, no." Once again Masters climbed on his high horse, as though lecturing Koa. "The implementation of any complex system requires a lot of trial and error, but in that process the telescopes are usually pointed at well-documented celestial objects. There's not much scientific originality in that kind of observing."

"And he had telescope time scheduled in the last couple weeks of January?"

"Yes."

"Wasn't it unusual for him to leave when he had telescope time scheduled?"

"Highly unusual, but astronomers do have emergencies."

"Any idea of the nature of Mr. Nakano's emergency?"

Masters spread his hands wide. "None. I had no idea he would be absent until Miss Benson informed me he'd returned to the mainland, and I still have no idea why he left in such a hurry."

"It appears that he never made it to the mainland."

"That would appear to be the case," Masters agreed.

"Director Masters, can you explain why the Alice Telescope Project, as Keneke's employer, failed to report his disappearance for two weeks?" Even as he asked, Koa saw from Masters' eyes that he'd anticipated the question. The man had to restrain himself so Koa could complete his sentence.

"Unfortunate, but understandable under the circumstances. Mr. Nakano and I had an appointment on January 21. I spoke to a science class at the Hawai'i Preparatory Academy early that morning. I had asked Mr. Nakano, who wrote my speech, to accompany me. I even called his house that morning to remind him."

Koa recalled Masters' message on Keneke's answering machine.

"When I got to the office, Miss Benson informed me that Mr. Nakano had called to say he needed to return to the mainland. Quite frankly, I expressed considerable displeasure. Our whole team was frantically preparing for our big announcement. In retrospect, I should have made further inquiries when he failed to return after a week. I just never thought of it in the whirlwind of activity."

That seemed to remind the director of something, and he reached into his pocket, withdrawing a slip of paper. Masters handed it to Koa:

1/21
7:32 a.m.

Mr. Nakano telephoned. Has some emergency. Must return to mainland. Absence not cleared. Told him I could not speak for D., but would convey message.

JB

Koa now had not one but two communications from Keneke on the morning of January 21—the phone call reflected in the note and the call for the airline reservation—reinforcing his belief that the astronomer must have been murdered later that day. "I'd like to keep it, if I may?"

"By all means, Detective."

"How did Mr. Nakano get along with others on the Alice staff? Any disputes or disagreements with his colleagues?"

"No. Nothing like that. As I said earlier, everyone liked him."

"Would you mind telling me where you spent the night of January 21?"

Masters smiled. "Wednesday afternoon, I flew to California for meetings at Caltech and the Alice Foundation. I stayed at the Checkers Hotel in L.A. Miss Benson can give you a copy of my bill."

If verified, that would be a conclusive alibi. Koa had thought it a long shot, in any case. "When did you last see Mr. Nakano?"

"I'm not positive. I think it was sometime around January 12. That's about when I assigned him to work on my HPA speech."

"Do you have any knowledge of any illegal activities of any kind by Mr. Nakano?"

Masters frowned as if it were a dumb question. "No, no, Detective. None at all."

"Any indication that Mr. Nakano was into selling Hawaiian archaeological objects?"

"Oh, heavens no." Masters' sharp jaw took on an even harder line. "The Alice project would never tolerate anything that might provoke the sovereignty fanatics."

They had already covered that. Koa switched direction once again. "Do you know where we can find Mr. Nakano's computer?"

Masters looked confused. "Not if it isn't at his house . . ."

Feeling that he had exhausted his questions, Koa rose. "I meant to start this meeting by congratulating you, Dr. Masters. I understand that you're about to announce an important discovery."

"Do you follow scientific developments, Detective?"

"In criminology, yes. Otherwise, only when they make the front page of the newspapers, I'm afraid."

"We all have our own orbits, I suppose. Would you like to attend the discovery announcement? You might learn a little about astronomy."

Koa was going to ask for an invitation, but Masters beat him to the punch. "I'd appreciate an invitation. And I'd also like to attend the party Monday night. I understand that most of the Alice staff will be there."

Masters smiled. "Sure, but I'd prefer you not come as a policeman. I don't want to cause unwanted speculation among our guests. You can join Nālani. Since she doesn't know all the scientists, I'll have Deputy Director Nelson escort you."

Koa liked the suggestion and responded, "That would be great." After what Nālani had told him about Gunter Nelson's falling-out with Keneke, he welcomed the opportunity to get a close-up reading on the man. Besides, the party would give him perhaps his only opportunity to size up the verification team—people who'd been around when Keneke disappeared.

CHAPTER SIXTEEN

Koa returned to Aikue ʻŌpua's farm with Sergeant Basa and Mickie Durban, one of the crime scene techs. Once again ʻŌpua, apparently alerted by some signal from the gate, greeted them on the *lānai*. "Ahh, Detective Kāne, what brings the *mākaʻikui* to my door?"

Why, Koa wondered, did this case involve slurs from both sides? The word meant detective, but literally translated as spying police. "Only the lawless fear the *mākaʻikui*."

"I do not fear you," ʻŌpua responded coldly.

"That's good." Koa turned to the business at hand. "We have a search warrant for your collection of knives." With some satisfaction, he detected a fleeting look of apprehension in the activist's eyes.

"So big *mākaʻikui* man, the *haole* cops have nothing better to do than harass us few true Hawaiians," ʻŌpua said bitterly, while making no effort to block their access to the house.

Koa ignored the challenge and walked directly to the far wall to examine the knives displayed in carved wooden holders. "That's quite a collection you've amassed," he said.

"I like old knives. There's nothing wrong with that," ʻŌpua shot back. "The *haoles* haven't yet outlawed knives, have they?"

Koa ignored the hostility and turned to the crime scene tech. "Mickie, start with the four whalebone knives, but check all of them."

Wearing plastic gloves, Mickie removed a long bone knife from the wall, placed it on a cloth, and illuminated a powerful ultraviolet light. No dark spots appeared, nor did they show up on the reverse side of the blade. He repeated the exercise with a second knife and got the same results. Only when he placed a whalebone *pāhoa*, or dagger, under the light did they see a black spot and streaks of black where the blade met the handle. The test had revealed probable bloodstains.

"Want to tell us where you got the *pāhoa*?" Koa asked.

"From my *makua kāne,* my father."

"Is that so?" Koa had seen many people dig themselves into a hole when they began to make up stories. If, as he suspected, the traces of blood on the dagger came from Keneke Nakano, 'Ōpua had just admitted to owning the knife before the murder. He wondered how deep a grave the man would dig for himself.

"How long has that *pāhoa* been in this display?" Koa asked.

"Many years."

"Ever butchered anything with it?"

"No. It's a family heirloom."

'Ōpua was digging himself in deeper. He's not half as clever, Koa thought, as he pretends. If the knife hadn't been used for butchering, how had it come to have blood on it?

Basa was now eyeing the activist with open disbelief, bordering on hostility. Koa wasn't surprised—Basa had good reason—but Koa wished his colleague weren't so obvious. The disapproval of a *haole* would only get 'Ōpua's back up.

The more he thought about it, the more confidently Koa believed the blood on the dagger was Keneke's. The young astronomer's murder appeared to be a perfect copycat inspired by the old Valentine's

Day murder. There was just one glaring exception—the absence of a whalebone dagger. A killer attentive enough to copy the earlier killing wouldn't have forgotten the dagger. Maybe ʻŌpua had done the killing and kept the dagger, but Koa doubted that ʻŌpua would kill a member of his own ʻohana huna—his own secret family. The sovereignty activists typically couldn't agree among themselves on the time of day, but it would be extraordinary for one of them to kill a member of their own club. That left the possibility that ʻŌpua—a collector of old Hawaiiana with an obvious fascination with knives—had filched the dagger from the murder scene before dialing 911.

"It's been in this display case for years. Is that what you're telling me?" Koa asked, deliberately letting the skepticism show in his voice.

ʻŌpua glared defiantly at Koa as he taunted, "So the mākaʻikui has become so corrupted by the haoles that he doesn't accept the word of his Hawaiian brother."

Koa had had enough of the slurs. He stepped forward, invading ʻŌpua's personal space, getting almost eye to eye with the activist. "The lab will tell us whether that's Keneke Nakano's blood on your dagger. You'd be well served to tell us now if the dagger came from the lava tube out at Pōhakuloa."

They stood inches apart, eyes locked in a staring contest for a long moment. Koa wondered if ʻŌpua understood that Koa was trying to help him, to give him a way out of the box he'd created for himself. Then ʻŌpua broke eye contact and turned away.

Still he hesitated. "No, mākaʻikui. It's been in my family since before the haoles stole these islands."

Some people were their own worst enemies. ʻŌpua could cast all the slurs he liked, because they amounted, like his sovereignty rants, to so much hot air. Koa lived in a world where hard facts had hard consequences. Even in the Hawaiʻi of old, a man was punished for murder.

CHAPTER SEVENTEEN

HEEDING THE CLARION call of Thurston Masters, the elite scientific community swarmed the Big Island like fans to a rock concert. The gathering of minds read like a virtual United Nations of learned men and women: optical engineers from Russia, university professors from South Africa, and science fiction writers from Europe. They represented every scientific discipline: Asian astronomers, South American astrophysicists, and American cosmologists. By late Sunday evening, 889 assorted scientists and camp followers had checked into the Waikoloa Hotel for the meeting of the North American Astronomical Society. Amid the throbbing of Hawaiian drums and the wafting scent of plumeria, the place buzzed with anticipation.

Koa arrived at the Waikoloa Hotel shortly after eleven o'clock on Monday morning. NAAS convention signs guided him to the hotel's huge Monarchy Ballroom, arranged like an auditorium. Masters had invited him to learn astronomy, but he had come to observe the Alice personnel and outside scientists who had been around when Keneke disappeared. Rarely did he miss an opportunity to observe potential suspects in their own private worlds. And he wanted to get some context before meeting up with Gunter Nelson, his escort for the NAAS party, where Nālani would join him. He staked out an inconspicuous spot against the left rear wall with a view of the entire room.

Rows of narrow tables set with light green linen, along with metal folding chairs, covered a seascape carpet. Each of the five hundred places was marked by an obligatory hotel notepad, a pencil, and a water glass.

Onstage, three armchairs flanked each side of the speaker's podium. Two giant, flat monitors hung from the ceiling on either side. Along the front, metal tripods held television cameras from which cables, taped to the carpet, snaked up the aisles.

Scientists and other assorted guests streamed in, chatting excitedly about the impending announcement. By 11:45, attendees filled every seat. By 11:55, the latecomers perched on the shallow steps and stood two to three rows deep across the back of the room.

The room dimmed and the television lights came on. As a woman ascended the stage, a disembodied voice announced, "Dr. Beverly Gottlieb, the Chilling Professor of Cosmology from Cambridge University." A buzz of voices erupted when Professor Jeremy Cocroft of the Institute for Advanced Studies at Princeton University followed Dr. Gottlieb onto the stage. "They're archenemies," Koa heard a man whisper. "I never thought I'd see the two of them on the same stage." Four more scientists took their seats as several people close to Koa expressed surprise at the awesome brain trust on the stage.

Following a brief introduction by the president of the North American Astronomical Society, Masters made his appearance. The man of the hour carried his six-foot frame with the confidence of a conquering hero. In a voice devoid of sentiment, Masters began speaking:

"Esteemed colleagues. Hubble defined a universe in which virtually every galaxy is receding from every other galaxy, an expanding universe. But at what rate? That question has haunted astronomers and cosmologists since Hubble's time. To determine the answer, we need to measure the distance to remote galaxies. Yet, as we know, great distances are extraordinarily difficult to judge from our position in the universe.

"Using the Alice telescopes, I have identified four vastly distant galaxies and determined the distance between them. But how, you ask." Masters activated the large LED screens at the corners of the stage.

The audience registered a collective "Wow."

"Look at the detail," someone said. Electronic flashes popped.

Koa didn't have the background to follow Masters' scientific discussion, but he knew enough to understand that Masters had panache. He played his audience like a concert pianist.

Equations filled the screens, followed by graphs and more equations. "With the newfound possibility of exact distance measurement to a pair of compact galaxies more than halfway to the edge of the universe, we programmed Alice's supercomputers to simulate the growth of the universe over billions of years." Pointing to the screen to his left, Masters continued, "This graph will show the results."

The vertical axis showed the size of the universe, while the horizontal axis displayed time in billion-year increments. A red line on the graph moved gradually, tantalizingly, upward, showing the expansion of the universe over time as Masters advanced in billion-year increments. Then the rate of expansion slowed, and the red line bent toward the horizontal until finally it peaked and began creeping down as the universe began to contract. A murmur rose from the audience, and then as people grasped the full significance of Masters' work, the noise swelled to a crescendo.

"It's closed! It's closed! The universe will end!" The shout came from somewhere out in the audience. People jumped to their feet.

More yelling and pandemonium ensued. The TV cameras panned to record the excitement. A full five minutes passed before the storm subsided. All the while Masters stood at the podium, basking in his glory.

"I declare the universe CLOSED . . . CLOSED," Masters' voice boomed. He began to speak more rapidly. "The universe will reach its point of maximum expansion in a mere 4.3 billion years, well before the death of our sun. Then it will begin to contract, accelerating into a headlong rush. We will head toward the Big Crunch. And perhaps another Big Bang. The Second Coming of the universe."

Over five hundred guests in the packed auditorium rose from their seats, and a thunderous applause swept through the room. It went on and on before Masters was finally able to resume.

Composing himself, Masters resumed speaking in a more restrained pace. "I want to offer special thanks to members of the verification team." He spread his arms, indicating the scientists sitting in the armchairs. "Each member has spent many nights with the Alice telescopes, checking and rechecking these observations. Together they have consumed thousands of hours of computer time checking my calculations, and they have verified my work beyond a shadow of a doubt."

*   *   *

On the terrace of the hotel bar, Koa popped two more pain pills and massaged his neck as he sipped an O'Doul's. As he waited for Gunter Nelson, he added up everything he knew about Keneke Nakano's disappearance. Just after 7:30 a.m. on January 21, a young astronomer calls his employer saying he has to return to the mainland—it's an emergency. Something to do with his girlfriend. But Nakano knows that his girlfriend isn't in the United States. She's at Cerro

Tololo in Chile. He misses an important event with his boss. At 7:42 a.m., he makes a reservation to fly to Los Angeles.

His SUV turns up at the Hilo airport. He's in such a hurry he leaves his keys in his unlocked car, but he fails to show up for his scheduled flight. His mutilated body is then found thirty miles away in an isolated lava tube. What drew him toward California? And what happened after he made that phone call to the Alice administrative offices and reserved his flight?

"Ah, Detective Kāne?" Koa turned to face a beefy man who offered a fleshy hand. "Gunter Nelson." He spoke softly, stretching his Germanic first name, robbing it of its guttural quality.

They shook hands. Looking maybe sixty-five, Gunter projected roundness with thick stubby legs, a beer drinker's sagging belly, a barrel chest, sloping shoulders, and a tree-trunk neck supporting a big head with an unruly mop of gray-white hair. A shaggy beard with an untrimmed mustache camouflaged the shape of his face. Folds of skin surrounded limp eyes, like those of a puppy.

"Will you join me for a fake beer?" Koa asked. "Or perhaps you want the real thing?"

"The real thing, from Holland," Gunter responded, motioning to the waiter as he lowered his bulk into the chair opposite Koa.

"Quite a show you astronomers are putting on."

"Colossal waste of time and money, all for the aggrandizement of our prestigious director." The hostility in Gunter's voice surprised Koa.

"You're not taken with Masters' discovery?"

"Oh, the discovery is genuine enough, but chance does not a Galileo make."

What had Nālani said about this man? It eats him alive that he'll never be top dog. She had that right. And resentment, in his experience, led people to do strange things. "You believe it was luck?"

"Masters is a glass mechanic, not an astronomer. He's an optics guy. This spectacle he's putting on? It's all optics."

"There you are." Nālani glided up to the table, looking radiant in a flowing Hawaiian dress adorned with a *pikake lei*. The jasmine flowers spread their rich perfume in a halo around her black hair and golden face.

"You look stunning." Koa stood to welcome her.

"*Aloha*." Nālani gave Gunter a smile. "I'm looking forward to this evening. This sometimes-excuse for a boyfriend"—she inclined her head toward Koa—"never takes me to a real party." The melody of her voice robbed the remark of criticism.

"Masters warned me not to say you're a policeman. How do you want me to introduce you?" Gunter asked.

"That's easy," Koa responded, "you can introduce me as a county employee."

"Fine, and you want most to meet the folks who worked with Keneke," Gunter responded.

"Yes, especially those who were around during the week of January 19."

"That would include members of the verification team."

"Yes. This may be my best opportunity to size them up."

"Through the looking glass and into the spectacle," Gunter quipped as the two men escorted Nālani toward the party.

Venus, the first bright planet of the evening, emerged from the twilight, and guests crowded the patio outside the ballroom. Flickering torches made shadows dance in the gathering dusk, and *pahu*—sacred coconut drums—beat out the ancient rhythms of Hawai'i. Waiters clad in Hawaiian prints glided through the crowd with champagne glasses and trays piled high with shrimp, sushi, and tidbits of *kālua* pig.

It resembled a gathering of Hawaiian royalty, Koa noted wryly. The governor and the two state senators passed as modern *ali'i*.

Around them gathered the *kahuna* of astronomy, attended by the *makaʻāinana*, the commoners, and served by the *ʻōhua*, the waiters. Only the *mōʻī*, the king, was absent. Dr. Masters was nowhere to be seen. That was just as well, Koa mused. He couldn't imagine an arrogant white guy as a Hawaiian king.

Gunter led them to a group that included a member of the verification team. "Let me introduce Koa Kāne and Nālani Kahumana, Dr. Yuri Andropovitchi."

Nālani extended her hand.

"Dr. Andropovitchi is a leading Russian astronomer, a man with many discoveries to his credit," Gunter said.

"Ah, Gunter, you do have an eye for beauty." Yuri's eyes dallied too long on Nālani as he took her hand in his long, bony fingers and bowed slightly to bestow a kiss upon it.

The man's fawning over Nālani annoyed Koa. First Charlie Harper and now this Russian ladies' man.

"Thank you, Dr. Andropovitchi." Nālani withdrew her hand.

As Koa shook hands with Yuri, Dr. Reinhardt Schlingler approached and greeted Nālani. "*Mein leitender stern* . . . my guiding star."

Nālani blushed at the compliment. "You are too kind, Herr Doktor."

"Dr. Schlingler and I share a common interest in opera," Gunter interjected.

"*Ja, ja.* When one understands opera, everything else, even cosmology, is child's play." Koa caught a twinkle in Dr. Schlingler's eye and sensed why Nālani had taken such an immediate liking to the German.

Koa turned his attention back to Andropovitchi. "So you and your colleagues have verified Dr. Masters' discovery beyond all doubt?"

The Russian seemed taken aback by the abrupt inquiry. "Nothing in science is beyond doubt, Mr. Kāne." He seemed to be trying to place the name. "But to answer your question, the evidence I have seen satisfies me that Dr. Masters has made a discovery of extraordinary, truly revolutionizing, significance. But the credit, I think, is not for Dr. Masters alone."

"Oh, why do you say that, Dr. Andropovitchi?"

"I am referring only to the telescopes. This discovery would have been impossible with any other instruments on the face of the earth."

"*Ja. Ja*," Herr Doktor Schlingler interrupted, "it is a magic instrument. Like the magic mirror in Handel's *Semele* that enhances the beauty of the beholder." The German startled them with the richness of his voice as he sung Juno's part from Handel's measured recitative in Act III, Scene 3 of *Semele*. "'Behold in this mirror. Behold in this mirror. Whence comes my surprise.'"

They all laughed. "*Ja*, Herr Doktor, it is so," Yuri responded.

"'Whence comes my surprise.' That's wonderful." Nālani's face bloomed with delight.

A man, actually more of an overgrown boy of perhaps forty-five, towing a reticent, somewhat younger woman, joined the group. A pained expression flickered across Gunter's face, and Koa recognized Charlie Harper's round face from the photograph at the observatory headquarters. "So Gunter, you're hitting on the observatory's Hawaiian babe." Charlie moved toward Nālani, extending his arm to encircle her waist, before Koa stepped between them, blocking the man's move with a subtle shove.

"Nālani doesn't appreciate your advances, Mr. Harper," Koa said evenly.

"Who are you?" Charlie asked.

"Not someone you want to mess with, Mr. Harper." Koa spoke softly, but with a touch of menace in his voice.

"Figures," Charlie snapped.

"And why is that?"

"Hawaiian birds of a feather flock together."

Koa restrained himself and ignored the slur. He'd accomplished what he wanted—warning off the workplace abuser. Instead, he turned his attention to Linda Harper, curious about the author of the apparently intimate note found in Keneke's truck. She gave every impression of hiding within the sunglasses that covered the upper third of her face. Koa wondered if she was concealing an injury. "Mrs. Harper," Koa began, "I understand you knew Keneke Nakano."

She tilted back in fright and shook her head.

"Leave my wife alone." Charlie Harper's moist breath, ripe with the smells of champagne and sushi, washed across Koa's face.

He knew, and he's jealous, Koa thought. Maybe the chief had it right, and Keneke had succumbed to a jealous husband.

Nālani intervened to relieve the awkward moment. "It's so exciting, the discovery and this party." She gestured to indicate the surrounding crowd.

"Perhaps, if you're Thurston Masters." Charlie lowered his voice to a conspiratorial whisper and again advanced into Nālani's personal space.

She adroitly stepped back before Koa acted on his impulse to block Charlie's path again. "Actually, I ran the gravitational lens survey that first located this odd collection of celestial objects. What Masters now calls the four aces."

"So it's your discovery?" Nālani raised her eyebrows.

Charlie, aware that Gunter was listening to this exchange, retreated from his boast. "Well, I couldn't exactly say that."

"And he helped Johann Sebastian Bach compose the 'Art of Fugue,'" Gunter said sarcastically.

Nālani fought to suppress a giggle.

"Damn, Gunter, that's not fair. I'm just explaining."

"Just the way Chancellor Bismarck explained his Kulturkampf to the Society of Jesus."

"Fuck you and your German history," Charlie muttered, turning on his heel and hauling his mousy wife away.

"Lovely fellow, and the two of you get on like France and Germany," Koa observed.

"Ah. Dostoyevsky had it right. Sarcasm is the last refuge." Gunter smiled.

His grin turned to a frown as a short, round blob of a man approached. Koa looked down on the top of the newcomer's head, where thinning hair lay in ironed streaks across a bald pate.

"You know it's a fraud, a shameful fraud." The little man seemed happy to convey this shocking news.

"What's a fraud?" Koa asked before Gunter could insert himself.

"This whole discovery. It's just like the moon."

"The moon? I'm afraid I don't understand."

"You don't really believe that men walked on the moon." It wasn't a question. "All a conspiracy, a government trick to raise taxes."

Koa smiled in amazement. What was a guy like this doing at an astronomical convention? Then again, maybe this sort of gathering attracted nut jobs.

"But what about all those pictures of Neil Armstrong walking on the moon?" Nālani interrupted.

"Hollywood trick. The government set up a studio up in the Haleakalā Crater, right over there on Maui." The man pointed to the northwest. "Took those pictures right here in Hawai'i." The little man stuck out his hand. "I'm Joseph Jeebers, president of the Cosmic Society for Scientific Veracity."

"Well, Joseph, what's wrong with Dr. Masters' discovery?" Koa asked.

"He's a government agent, you know. He worked for the Air Force and helped them fake the Star Wars interceptor test results. It was part of President Reagan's plan to steal billions from the taxpayers for the Star Wars defense contractors."

Koa shook his head in amazement at how some people could find a conspiracy behind every tree.

"My friends undoubtedly appreciate your insights, Mr. Jeebers," Gunter said, deftly steering the group away.

He seemed to be guiding them toward a woman with chalk-white skin, when Koa caught sight of a familiar head of snowy white hair. He excused himself and led Nālani by the hand.

"Good evening, Prince," Koa said respectfully. "May I introduce Nālani Kahumana?"

"Miss Kahumana, a distinct pleasure. You are most beautiful." The prince turned to Koa. "You have an interest in astronomy, Detective?"

"No special interest, but the Pōhakuloa victim was an astronomer at the Alice—"

"Terrible news about Keneke Nakano. He had such a great future ahead of him." The prince spoke in a flat tone, devoid of emotion.

He doesn't seem upset, Koa thought. "So you knew Keneke."

The prince ignored the question. "You were a bit rough on my friend Aikue 'Ōpua, weren't you?"

"The two of you could have told me about the discovery of the body."

"He had his reasons. The *haole* authorities don't treat our sovereignty brothers with the respect they deserve."

The prince hadn't denied having heard of the body from 'Ōpua. Koa began, "Did he tell you about the whalebone dagger—?"

Opera music blaring from the loudspeakers drowned out the end of Koa's question. The music sounded like something heavy and Germanic, maybe Wagner. Dr. Thurston Masters and his wife,

Christina, appeared high atop a long staircase. An elegant woman in her forties, she wore a sleek dark blue designer dress with subtle gold jewelry. Although she was a good ten years Masters' junior, they made a stunning couple. Someone began to clap as they descended. Others joined in, and the whole patio erupted in applause and cheering. The *mōʻī*, the king, had arrived with his queen, staging a sensational entrance.

Gunter rejoined Koa and Nālani, but he wasn't clapping.

Christina Masters stood apart as her husband moved easily from one adoring group to another. Thurston chatted casually with scientists and legislators, graciously accepting congratulations and posing for photographs with favored guests. The politicians especially, Koa pointed out to Nālani, wanted to be photographed with the great astronomer.

Koa shifted his attention back to Mrs. Masters. She stood alone on the fringe rather than in the center of the celebration. As he studied her athletic body, nicely outlined in a sleek midnight-blue dress with obviously genuine gold jewelry, Koa puzzled over the contrast between the couple's grand entry and Christina Masters' current isolation. He sensed she was estranged from her husband or maybe too shy to participate in this public gathering. Whatever the cause, she was plainly ill at ease. Slowly, a group of women coalesced around the director's wife. Suddenly, Christina Masters froze, her face twisting into a strange mask. Koa tried to decipher the fleeting expression. Anger? No. Contempt. Yes, scornful contempt.

Koa followed Christina Masters' gaze across the crowded patio to a stunningly beautiful young Hawaiian woman, wearing a simple white silk dress, expensively tailored to emphasize her voluptuous figure. The woman looked to be in her early twenties, with long black hair flowing over the soft golden skin of her bare shoulders.

Koa pointed her out to Gunter. "Who's that lovely young woman?"

Gunter rolled his eyes. "Miss Leilani Lupe. *Die Geliebte unseres prestigevollen Direktors.*"

Koa didn't understand. "What?"

"Just my German roots showing."

"What's it mean, Gunter?" Koa insisted.

"She's Masters' extracurricular entertainment, if you get my drift."

Koa looked back toward Christina Masters, but she had disappeared. Koa scanned the nearby groups. Movement on the stairs caught his eye, and he saw Mrs. Masters hurrying away toward the hotel lobby.

The following morning, Thurston Masters' discovery made headlines around the world.

CHAPTER EIGHTEEN

THE NEXT MORNING, roughly twelve days after Keneke's death, Koa arrived early at the old mission church near Hāwi to attend Keneke's funeral. Mourners came from the telescopes atop Mauna Kea, the University of Hawai'i, and a dozen other places. They filled the hundred-year-old church, overflowing onto the walk, the lawn, and the graveyard. People crowded close around the little church, straining to hear through its open windows. Koa stood in the crowd, watching the mourners.

As Keneke's uncle Kimo helped a young Asian woman from a black rental car, Koa recognized Soo Lin from the picture in Keneke's apartment. Even though dressed in black and barely able to hold back tears, her graceful—but proud—posture, subtle Asian features, and perfect skin made her beautiful in ways a photograph could never capture.

After escorting Soo Lin into the church, Kimo joined Thurston Masters and four others whom Koa didn't recognize in bearing a wooden casket up the narrow stone steps and into the tiny sanctuary. Koa paid particular attention to Masters. Although he had shown little emotion when discussing Keneke's death in his office, Masters' long face now bore a solemn, almost depressed expression bearing witness to his grief at the loss of his young protégé.

Just before the service began, an antique black Rolls-Royce stopped in front of the church. The Hawaiian driver sprang out to open the door for a tall, white-haired man in a black suit, who walked slowly up the stone steps toward the church. Without hesitation, the crowd parted, allowing Prince Kamehameha passage into the house of worship. Aikue 'Ōpua followed him up the aisle to the pew immediately behind Kimo and Soo Lin.

As a young Hawaiian minister mounted the pulpit and spread his arms, the chatter from the mourners receded. "The Lord giveth and the Lord taketh away. Praise be to the Lord." The preacher lowered his arms. "We are gathered together today to comfort and commemorate. We comfort Kimo Nakano, who has lost his only nephew. We comfort Soo Lin, to whom the Lord hath given, and from whom the Lord hath taken, the miraculous starlight of love. We comfort each other for the loss of a uniquely Hawaiian spirit that touched and intertwined too fleetingly with our own lives."

The minister's voice waxed and waned, but Koa paid little attention as he scanned the funeral-goers. He didn't expect to see signs of guilt, and he didn't. When the service reached its conclusion, Kimo, Soo Lin, and Prince Kamehameha gathered in a knot at the door. Other mourners, waiting to pay their respects, left a respectful space as the tall, white-haired father figure, the stooped war veteran, and the grieving young Asian woman exchanged condolences.

As the crowd flowed from the church, Koa walked to the prince's Rolls-Royce and, catching the driver by surprise, quickly slipped into the backseat. When the driver protested, Koa flashed his badge and said, "Inform the prince that Chief Detective Kāne is waiting for him." The driver got out and walked toward the church, and after a while the prince joined Koa in the back of the Rolls.

"Detective Kāne, does your chief condone his officers accosting people at funerals?" The prince's Oxford English didn't conceal his caustic tone.

"I thought you might favor discretion over a meeting in full view of all the worshipers."

"I would favor more respect for my privacy."

"Prince—" Koa began.

"This meeting is over, Detective. Kalā," the prince said, speaking to his driver, "could you help Detective Kāne out?" The driver sprang out and opened the door for Koa.

"I guess Chief Lannua made a mistake when he told me you'd help find Keneke's killer." Koa spoke the words softly, almost reluctantly.

The prince stiffened at the implicit warning. With an imperious gesture, he stopped the driver. He stared at Koa. When the prince lowered his gaze, Koa figured he'd realized that the matter would be pursued one way or another.

"Leave us alone, Kalā." The prince waited until the driver closed the door and walked away. "What is it that you want, Detective?"

"We both now know a vital fact I didn't know when we met at your estate." Koa wondered if the prince had picked up on the possible meaning of his use of the singular.

"And that is the identity of the Pōhakuloa victim?" the prince responded.

"Yes, and you must want to find Keneke's killer."

"Why should I be more interested than the next man?"

"You had a bond with Keneke's grandfather, old Kawelo, the woodcarver." Koa thought of *kūpaʻa*, the loyalty that governed the old *aliʻi*. "And Kawelo would expect you to help avenge the death of his grandson."

"One *kahuna nui*."

The response puzzled Koa. "*Kahuna nui*, a counselor to the high chief, not *kahuna kālai*, an expert woodcarver?"

"Both. The gods guided Kawelo's mind as well as his hands," the prince responded. "Old Kawelo was my friend."

The prince produced a pack of Gauloises and a Cartier lighter with tricolor gold banding. His hand shook as he sparked the lighter and touched the flame to the European cigarette. "Old Kawelo had a premonition that his line, a line that stretched back through many generations of Hawaiian heroes, would end in *mea kaumaha loa . . .* tragedy."

"A premonition?"

"Yes, Detective. Kawelo's nightmare begot reality, an unthinkable tragedy for the Nine."

Koa's mind raced. The Nine were the native Hawaiians who had defied the Navy by trespassing on Kahoʻolawe in 1976 to protest the desecration of the sacred island. Why had Keneke's death been a tragedy for the Nine?

"For the Kahoʻolawe Nine?"

"Kawelo and the others welcomed his grandson into the *ʻohana* and taught him the ways of the god *Kanaloa*—the secrets of the stars, the legends of the *huihui hōkū,* the constellations, and the skills of celestial navigation."

"So Keneke knew the Kahoʻolawe Nine?"

"He was *ʻohana,* family, to them."

"Including Aikue ʻŌpua?"

"Yes, of course. He is one of the Nine."

"Did Keneke know that ʻŌpua took Hawaiian artifacts from Kahoʻolawe?"

Surprise showed in the prince's eyes for a fraction of a second. "You've been in touch with the Maui police?"

The prince hadn't answered the question, so Koa repeated it.

"They have misjudged my friend Aikue."

Again, the prince had evaded answering. "How so?"

"The *haoles* cannot make preservation of our heritage a crime."

Koa tried a different tack. "What was 'Ōpua doing out at Pōhaku-loa? He didn't just stumble on Keneke's body by accident."

"What makes you say that, Detective?"

"It has something to do with *Keanaokeko'i*, the cave of the adze makers. You knew about the workshop before Jimmy and I came to your estate."

"I think you already established that, Detective." It was Koa's turn to be surprised. The prince's lips curled into a small smile. "That little trick in my garden with the pack of Gauloises. Not many Hawaiians smoke Gauloises, certainly not policemen. You were passing clever, Detective."

Koa could barely conceal his astonishment. He had to admire the man's savvy despite the rebuke. He thought of himself as more than "passing clever."

"When were you last in the workshop?"

"It shouldn't have been necessary."

"Why is that?"

"Don't be stupid, Detective. To visit a secret grave risks disclosure. There are eyes everywhere. There are many evil ones who would disrespect the ancient *ali'i kāne*, the ancient kings."

"But it was necessary. Why?"

"Because, as the *haoles* say, there was a security breach."

"How did you learn of this security breach?"

"In the same way that I learned that you do not smoke Gauloises. *Ka 'io nui maka lana au moku.* The great *'io* with eyes that see everywhere on the land. Little escapes my notice." A shadow of a smile flickered across the prince's face.

Koa understood. Someone in the prince's network—a retainer, a loyalist, a friend—had alerted the prince to something that aroused his suspicions.

"And you went to see for yourself?"

"Yes."

"When?"

"In December. I walked where only *Pele* knows the way and entered *Keanaokeko'i*. Four hundred moons, more than thirty years, had passed since I had last entered *Keanaokeko'i*. The evil one had preceded me."

"The evil one?" Koa inquired.

"An expression, Detective. *Ka po'e kahiko*, the people of old, attributed all man-made evil to the poisonous priest Pā'ao, who brought human sacrifice to the islands."

"The evil one was a trespasser?" Koa asked.

"Worse, a grave robber."

"A recent grave robber?"

"Yes."

"Couldn't the open grave chamber off the workshop have been robbed years, even decades, ago?"

"No. Evil just recently walked where only *Pele* knows the way."

"How do you know that?"

"*Ka 'io nui maka lana au moku*. Believe me, Detective, I know."

"What stranger walked where only *Pele* knows the way?"

"I wish I knew. Someone was up on Mauna Kea with explosives. When word first reached my ears, I thought they must be hunters, but they were not hunters. Someone was setting off explosive charges."

Koa recalled the fragment of explosive cord and the heavy yellow paper that Piki had found near the cinder cone. "Explosive charges, plural?"

"Yes, at least ten of them scattered along the southern side of the mountain."

"Why would anyone plant explosive charges up there?"

"I have no idea, Detective."

"How did you make the connection between the explosive charges and unauthorized entry into the lava tube?"

"*Mehue*, footprints. There were footprints leading to and from the entrance."

"Did you track them?"

"Yes."

"And?"

"*Nalowale*, lost. The trail disappeared in the lava rocks."

Koa pictured the scene around the cinder cone. An intruder would disturb the loose cinders, at least until the wind smoothed them, but would leave no trail once he reached the surrounding bedrock. "Did he come back?"

"Not after my visit in December."

"So you sent Aikue 'Ōpua out to Pōhakuloa to see whether anyone had been poking around out there." Koa saw from the prince's eyes that the guess had hit the mark.

"Not a bad deduction, Detective."

"You knew before Hikorea and I came to your home that we had found the workshop?"

"Of course."

"You planted the electronic detector." The prince's reaction showed in just the slightest flicker of his eyes. Koa would bet a month's pay that he had surprised the man.

"You left it in place, didn't you?" the prince asked, conceding the point.

"That's how you know that the grave robber hasn't been back. You had the detector installed after your visit."

"Yes. You left it in place, didn't you?"

Koa ignored the repeated question. "So your apparent surprise when we disclosed the existence of the underground workshop was an act?"

"In part. I was aware of the workshop, and I knew that there were burial crypts nearby, but I'd never been inside the crypt with the red canoe. I had no idea about the bird woman. You see, if the grave robber had come back, I would have stopped him."

Koa had followed the Zimmerman-Trayvon Martin killing in Florida and other so-called self-defense killings. He disliked vigilantes. Intensely. "Stopped him? How?"

"That's a hypothetical question, isn't it, Detective?"

"Is it?"

"What are you suggesting?"

Prince or no prince, Koa had a golden opportunity he wasn't about to pass up. "I've been told that *ka po'e kahiko*, the people of old, would kill a stranger who trespassed on the grave of a Hawaiian *ali'i kāne* and mutilate his body as a warning to others who might trespass."

"I did not carry the spear of *pueo*."

The admission hit Koa like a jolt of electricity. If Aikue 'Ōpua's *pāhoa* had sliced Keneke's body and the prince knew of the spear of *pueo*, had one of them killed Keneke? Why? Because Keneke knew something about the Pōhakuloa workshop or the looting of Kaho'olawe? Was 'Ōpua part of the tragedy of Keneke's death? Was the prince covering for his friend 'Ōpua?

"How did you know about the spear of *pueo*?" Koa watched the prince intently as he posed the question.

"That is not a secret."

"It was known only to the police conducting the investigation and to the killer. So I ask you again: How did you know the precise way that Keneke died?"

The two men stared at each other for a long time before the prince broke the silence. "The mayor told me."

"Damn!" Koa swore before he could stop himself.

Had the mayor really been so indiscreet? Or, Koa considered, had the prince made up a clever cover story, knowing that Koa would never cross-examine the mayor?

Koa wrestled with a host of new revelations as he left the prince and walked back to his Explorer. The prince and Aikue 'Ōpua were up to something on Kaho'olawe. They had worked together to protect the Pōhakuloa adze makers' cave. 'Ōpua had discovered the body. He had the dagger. And the prince knew about the spear of *pueo*. The myriad of connections sparked Koa's deepest suspicions. Collectively, it was almost enough to make an arrest.

CHAPTER NINETEEN

THE DAY AFTER the burial service, Uncle Kimo accompanied Soo Lin, Keneke's girlfriend, to police headquarters. As they set up in a conference room, Koa took two more pain tablets and brought in a straight-back chair. He wanted to conduct this interview without the nagging distraction of pain running across his back and down his arm.

Although Soo Lin knew of the murder, Kimo hadn't been able to bring himself to burden her with the hideous details of her lover's death. Koa could see why. Her red eyes and dark circles told him she'd been crying and probably hadn't slept. His heart went out to her, and he wondered if she would be able to get through the interview.

Against this background, neither Kimo nor Koa expected her insistence on knowing the details. "I want to know everything. I want to know exactly how he died." Koa looked at Kimo, the official next of kin, whose permission he needed before revealing confidential police information to anyone outside the legal family.

"Soo Lin is the closest Keneke had to family. She's entitled to know, but"—Kimo turned to the young woman—"Soo Lin, Keneke died a horrible death. Maybe it would be better for you, if you didn't pursue it."

Soo Lin bit her lip and fought to control her emotions.

"Do you know the story of 'Ōhi'a and Lehua?"

"Of course," Koa responded. All Hawaiians knew of the love story of the handsome 'Ōhi'a and the beautiful Lehua. So much did 'Ōhi'a love Lehua that he rejected *Pele's* advances, angering the old fire witch, who burned the couple to death in a fit of jealousy. Later, feeling guilty, *Pele* turned 'Ōhi'a into a tree and Lehua into its magnificent red blossoms, forever joining them in the *'ōhi'a lehua* trees that grace the island forests.

"Keneke and I were like 'Ōhi'a and Lehua. That's how we met. He called me Lehua and told the story of the *'ōhi'a lehua* tree. Later he admitted it was the craziest thing he'd ever done, approaching me like that, but by then we were in love. I loved him very much and I have to know how he died."

Koa told her about their discovery of Keneke's body, neither emphasizing the grisly details nor omitting any significant facts. She listened in grim-faced silence, occasionally pressing her palms against the sides of her head. She recoiled when Koa told her of the missing left eye and the spear of *pueo*. Koa withheld information about the burial cave, the adze makers' workshop, and the passage to the collapsed *pu'u* on the side of Mauna Kea. When he'd finished, the three of them sat in silence for what seemed like an eternity.

Virtually all police officers dreaded notification of next of kin, and Koa found the first interview with a grieving lover just as difficult. He had to ask hard questions and still tread gently to avoid aggravating a wound that hadn't even started to heal. He watched Soo Lin's face as she forced back her tears. Her large black eyes took on a determined look. Finally, he said, "If you are up to it, I must ask some questions."

"I want to help bring the animal who did this to justice. Does Hawai'i have the death penalty?"

"No. I'm afraid not."

"It should for crimes like this."

"You're right about that," Kimo added.

Koa's feelings about the death penalty were complex, but he agreed that life in prison was too good for anyone who sliced up a man and left him in a lava cave. "When did you last speak to Keneke?"

"Monday, January 19. We talked on the phone that evening before I left for my observing run in Cerro Tololo, Chile."

"What did the two of you talk about?"

"I was excited and a little anxious about Cerro Tololo. Keneke encouraged my enthusiasm and tried to calm my anxieties."

"And that's the last time you spoke to him?"

"Yes. I tried to call many times from Cerro Tololo, but never reached him. I guess he was already dead, wasn't he?" She looked down and again held her head in her hands, slowly shaking it. Just above a whisper, she said, "I was angry at him for not answering."

"We know that he called the Alice Observatories and made plane reservations between 7:30 and 7:45 a.m. on Wednesday, January 21. We don't know what he did for the rest of the day, but we're pretty sure that he died that night."

"I tried to call him that afternoon," Soo Lin said, wringing her hands as she talked.

"I know. We have the answering machine tape." Soo Lin turned to what had puzzled Koa. "I just don't understand why he would go to Los Angeles." Anger crept into her voice. "He knew I had left for Cerro Tololo, and that I lived outside San Francisco, not Los Angeles. He had no family or relatives in L.A."

"That's right," Kimo added. "We've never had a single relative in the Los Angeles area."

"Tell me about his relationship with the observatory people—Masters, Nelson, Harper, and the others," Koa asked.

"He viewed Masters as a compulsive, driven genius, but Masters taught him a lot about adaptive optics. He respected Masters."

"Did he ever talk about any tension or disputes with Masters?"

"No. Masters pushed him to perform, but no disputes."

That aligned with what Masters had told him, albeit filtered through the director's massive conceit. "How about Gunter?"

"That's more complex. At first Keneke and Gunter got along well and spent a lot of time together. Keneke shared his archaeology theories with Gunter—"

Koa leaned forward at the mention of a link between these two worlds. "What archaeology theories?"

"Keneke believed that *Pele* had buried archaeological treasures beneath the overlapping lava flows in the Humuʻula Saddle. He wanted to X-ray the whole saddle." She was suddenly engaged and stopped wringing her hands.

"What?"

"An astounding idea, isn't it? Isn't it strange, he said, that we have powerful telescopes to search out the mysteries of the distant universe, but no machine to show us what's right here under our feet?"

"He shared these theories with Gunter?"

"Yes. They spent a lot of time together out in the saddle. Then Gunter disappointed Keneke and their relationship cooled. Keneke's attitude toward him changed."

"What happened?" Koa asked.

"I don't really know, but Keneke said he couldn't trust Gunter. He said something about Gunter's bitterness getting the better of him."

"Bitterness?"

"Yes. Gunter's failure to become director ate at him like battery acid. I think those were Keneke's words."

Keneke's assessment of Gunter's state of mind lined up with Koa's own impressions, but did nothing more to answer the more important questions: Had Gunter's resentment driven him to act, and if so, how?

"What about Harper?"

Soo Lin's lip curled and her eyebrows dipped. She obviously shared Nālani's distaste for Harper. "Keneke thought Alice should fire Charlie Harper." The hand wringing started up again.

"That's pretty strong. What did Keneke say?"

"That Harper was lazy. He did sloppy work. He treated his wife like a pet bird, and he couldn't keep his hands off the female astronomers and techs. Keneke really disliked the man."

Koa recalled Linda Harper's note to Keneke. He pondered how he could ask the question delicately. "Did Keneke ever meet Linda Harper?"

"Sure. Keneke belonged to a historical society. Linda Harper showed up at one or two of their meetings. Keneke described her as the most timid human being he'd ever encountered."

"So there was no . . ."—Koa struggled for the right word—"inappropriate relationship?"

Soo Lin stopped wringing her hands and looked him in the eye. "No . . . not a chance. Keneke felt sorry for her, but he didn't much care for weak women." There was a tiny twinkle in her eye for just an instant.

Koa nodded as he thought of his own interaction with Linda Harper at the astronomy party. For her, a wonderful, marvelous time might be nothing more than an intellectual conversation with a normal man. But Charlie Harper must have feared more had happened, given his reaction at the party. A paranoid's jealousy could still motivate murder.

"Did Keneke have words with Charlie Harper?"

"I'm not sure about words, but Keneke wasn't subtle in his dislike for Harper."

"Any problems with the younger staff, or with anyone, for that matter?"

"No. Keneke had no enemies. I never heard him down on anybody, except Harper . . . and Gunter after their falling-out."

Koa paused momentarily to check his notepad of questions. "Tell me about Keneke's interest in Kaho'olawe."

Soo Lin smiled for the first time that morning. "You might say that Keneke inherited his interest. You know his grandfather violated Navy regulations by trespassing on Kaho'olawe to dramatize his religious and environmental beliefs."

"Yes, we know that Keneke's grandfather was part of the Kaho'olawe Nine."

"Did you know that Keneke also planned an expedition to Kaho'olawe?"

"No!" Koa couldn't keep the surprise out of his voice. "What attraction did Kaho'olawe hold for him?"

"Keneke had this theory that ancient Tahitian toolmakers, searching for new sources of stone, brought adze-making technology to Hawai'i, initially to Kaho'olawe. He hoped to find links between stone quarries on Tahiti, Kaho'olawe, and Mauna Kea. Tying it all together—the South Pacific, Kaho'olawe, and Mauna Kea—that was his holy grail. That's why he wanted to dig at Pu'u Moiwi."

The connection hit Koa like a tire iron. Keneke and Kaho'olawe. Hook Hao's son, Reggie, and Kaho'olawe. Aikue 'Ōpua and Kaho'olawe. It couldn't be a coincidence. He needed to talk to the Maui police and interview Reggie, especially since 'Ōpua wouldn't talk to him about Kaho'olawe.

"Did he actually go exploring on Kaho'olawe?"

"I urged him not to go. I was afraid of the bombs, but I don't know whether he actually went."

"When are you returning to California?" Koa asked as he prepared to end the interview.

"Not for a while."

"What are you going to do?"

"Kimo has graciously allowed me to stay in Keneke's house in Honokaʻa, and I talked to my professors at UC. That's where I did my graduate work in astronomy. They've arranged for me to work at Alice for a while."

"I don't like it," Koa burst out, unable to contain his concern. "We don't know who killed Keneke or why. You shouldn't be walking in his footsteps until we've caught his killer."

"There's something I haven't told you, Detective. When I got to Cerro Tololo and checked my e-mail, I had a message from Keneke. He said he was sending me something important that I should safeguard. Nothing more, just that I should safeguard what he was sending. Then when I got back from Cerro Tololo, I found a package from Keneke, mailed on January 19. It contained data, digital pictures made with the Alice telescopes, but no note or other explanation. I think the data has something to do with Keneke's death, and I'm going to find out how. I owe him that."

This woman was one revelation after another. "Tell me about the data."

"It's detailed analyses of images of star clusters. By itself, the data is unremarkable, except that there is a duplicate of each image—well, almost a duplicate. There are slight differences in each pair of images that I don't yet understand. I need to get up to the Alice Observatories to replicate Keneke's observations."

Koa saw her jaw harden and a look of determination fill her bright eyes. He could tell that he wouldn't be able to dissuade her, and he had no legal basis to stop her. He settled for what he could do.

"You should keep in touch with me. Let me know if anything, anything at all, makes you feel threatened. And come by my office in the morning. We'll give you an emergency beacon. The police communications center will monitor the frequency twenty-four hours a day. Once you activate it, we'll be able to locate you and hear whatever happens around you. Okay?"

"Thanks, Koa." She rose from her seat. "I'm tougher than you think."

After she left, Koa stretched out on the conference room floor to rest his neck, replaying parts of the interview and shuffling the deck of suspects. Charlie Harper, the pervert, and Gunter Nelson, the resentful loser, remained strong suspects, although he still needed to find out what had happened between Gunter and Keneke. He made a mental note to see what Detective Piki had learned from the telephone records of the observatory people.

But it was the Kahoʻolawe connection that most intrigued him. Reggie Hao, Aikue ʻŌpua, some felon who had taken the Fifth, the prince, and now Keneke were all connected to an illegal hunt for artifacts on an abandoned Navy bombing range. One of them was now in a coma and another dead. Contacting the Maui police moved to the top of his agenda.

CHAPTER TWENTY

Koa had often visited Nālani at the Alice administrative center, but their plans for a trip to the summit kept getting postponed. Koa's work had never taken him to the remote 14,000-foot mountaintop some fifty miles from the nearest town. Thus, despite all his years on the Big Island, Koa had never been to the summit of Mauna Kea.

The afternoon of the Soo Lin interview, he finally drove up the mountain. Rounding a bend two-thirds of the way up the mountain, he came upon the gray stone buildings of the Onizuka visitors' center and dormitory complex. Koa turned into the parking lot for the dormitory complex. He'd called ahead and upon entering the main building, he found Gunter Nelson standing in the doorway waiting for him.

"Welcome to the mountain, Detective. I see you survived the medieval circus down at the hotel," Gunter said. He wore a checkered flannel shirt that made Koa wish he himself had dressed more warmly for the cold air at 9,000 feet.

"Yes," Koa said, trying to ignore Gunter's bitterness. "Nālani and I had a rather good time."

"I understand you want to go up to the observatory."

"Yes," Koa responded, "but first, I'd like to find out what was served for dinner up here on Tuesday, Wednesday, and Thursday the week of January 19."

"Sure. Let's go talk to Lucrezia."

"Lucrezia? The food's that bad?" Koa asked.

"Worse." They walked down a few steps into and across the cafeteria, past the daily menu scrawled on a blackboard, and through a swinging door to get to the small but well-equipped kitchen. A grotesquely overweight man of Polynesian ancestry, standing before a counter chopping carrots, told them that Graham Gravel, the regular cook, was vacationing on the mainland. To Koa's disappointment, they learned Gravel kept the menu schedule in his head, and had left no contact number. They'd have to await his return to find out what he'd served for dinner on those key nights.

Unsatisfied, Koa turned to Gunter. "Will you see if you can find a phone number? Maybe his employment records show family he's visiting."

"Sure, what's next?"

"I'd like to see where Keneke kept his possessions before we go to the top."

They had to break the padlock on Keneke's locker yet went unrewarded for the effort. They found no computer and nothing else of interest to the investigation.

The two men climbed into Koa's Explorer for the trip to the summit. From the dormitory complex, an uneven, rutted gravel road cut back and forth in a series of long switchbacks up the side of the mountain. They passed through a band of clouds, and nearly all vegetation disappeared. Large and small cinder cones abounded. The big Ford engine protested both the grade and the increasingly thin air.

"Tell me about Keneke Nakano," Koa asked casually.

"A wonderful young man. Keneke had depth. Lots of astronomers never learn the mythology of the heavens, but Keneke knew the Greek and Roman legends. Like Johannes Vermeer's *Geographer*."

"Vermeer's *Geographer*?"

"A seventeenth-century Dutch painter from Delft. Painted a picture of an early geographer, kind of a symbol of a renaissance man . . . that was Keneke."

Gunter obviously loved the sound of his own voice, and Koa was happy to encourage him. Verbose suspects made his job easier. "Sounds like you knew him pretty well."

"We were professional colleagues. I spent some off-hours with him. There's not much to do here except talk. Keneke did much of the talking, a real *minnesinger*."

"*Minnesinger*?"

"A bard, a minstrel, a troubadour, a storyteller in the oral tradition. A Polynesian Tannhäuser, a lyric poet of the Pacific."

"Really."

"Yeah, sometimes after dinner we'd sit in the cafeteria. Keneke would start rubbing his *pōhaku 'aumakua* and after a couple of minutes, it was like he'd entered a different world."

"Did you say *pōhaku 'aumakua* . . . his stone god?"

"Yeah, he wore a tiny carved stone on a string around his neck. Said it had belonged to his grandfather. Called it his *pōhaku 'aumakua*. I never saw him without it."

"And he told stories?"

"In six or seven months, I must've heard Keneke tell fifty stories. Stories about stonecutters, the mythical Hawaiian *Menehune*, Kamehameha's battles to consolidate the islands, the exploits of the god Maui. I don't know where they came from or how he memorized them all, but he had an unlimited capacity for story talk."

"Did tools—hammerstones or adzes—often have a role in his stories?" Koa asked.

Gunter pulled at the long gray-white strands of his beard, and then patted the thicket back into place as he mulled over the question. "Yes, come to think of it. In many of Keneke's tales real or imaginary tools empowered the actors. He used to say the same thing about Alice. That the telescope created its creators, imbuing them with Herculean qualities."

"Like Director Masters?"

The brightness in Gunter's eyes dimmed. "Yeah. I suppose that's an example."

Koa didn't want to stop the easy flow. "When did you last see Keneke?"

"Gee, that's tough. Let me think. It must have been about two weeks ago. We had dinner. I'm pretty sure that's the last time I saw him."

"What date or day of the week?"

Gunter produced a pocket calendar and thumbed through the pages to the week of January 19. "Must have been Tuesday, January 20. That's the only night that week that I ate up here. Thursday evenings I teach an advanced astronomy course at UH in Honolulu. I wasn't on the mountain again until Friday, January 23."

"Where did you spend the rest of that Tuesday evening?"

"In my room here."

As they drove up the winding gravel road toward the summit, the Explorer hit a rough patch and bounced. Koa gritted his teeth and braced his neck against the headrest, but Gunter didn't seem to notice.

"Where did Keneke go after the two of you finished dinner Tuesday night?" Koa asked.

"He had machine time on Alice to work out some software wrinkles. Astronomers never miss their time slots," he pointed out. "It's just not done. Telescope time is precious."

"Software wrinkles. I don't understand."

"Masters had Keneke testing software for an experimental adaptive optics technique. Not real astronomy, just one of Masters' pet projects. Mathematically, analytically, it was whiz-kid stuff. Our existing adaptive optics cancels out a lot of the distortion caused by the earth's atmosphere, but Masters wanted to do better. That was Keneke's big project—to give the Alice telescopes new eyeglasses, enabling them to see just as well as the Hubble Space Telescope."

"That's funny. Masters said he doubted Keneke's intellectual prowess."

"Masters believes he's the smartest guy in the universe. No one else comes close," Gunter responded disparagingly.

"Did you see Keneke go up to the summit?"

"No, but his picture, along with the entry time, will be on the security tape. Everybody goes in and out past a security camera. It's motion activated so the tapes last for weeks."

That would be useful, but Koa still had more questions before their ride up the mountain ended. "What about fights, enemies, and disputes? Keneke involved in anything like that?"

"Nothing. Keneke charmed everybody. He had a gift for winning people over."

"How about your relationship with him?"

"We got along great. Like I told you, Keneke was a Polynesian renaissance man—witty, educated, entertaining. He had a wide range of interests—astronomy, history, literature, geology . . . a genuinely diversified intellect."

"Any rough spots in your relationship with Keneke?"

"None. Like I said, we got along great."

He's lying, Koa thought as his suspicions came to a boil, comparing Gunter's glib assurances with what he'd heard from Nālani and Soo Lin. What was the man hiding? "Did you and Keneke work together on any archaeological projects?"

That made Gunter sit upright, jerking the carriage of Koa's own seat. "Uh, no. What makes you ask?"

"I thought you and Keneke went exploring out at Pōhakuloa."

"That would be pretty dangerous. It's a live-fire area."

He wasn't answering the question. "Did the two of you go exploring anywhere in the saddle despite the danger?"

"Nope, never."

Another lie. Soo Lin had said that Keneke and Gunter had spent a lot of time in the saddle. Gunter wouldn't own up to an interest in archaeology or any falling-out with Keneke. Koa needed to understand why.

As the Explorer passed over a small rise, they saw several telescopes. "And there's what you drove up here to see," Gunter announced.

Pretty awesome, Koa thought, as he got his first view of the Alice telescopes. The two sparkling white domes stood so close together that they seemed to embrace. From their common base, each of the 125-foot-wide domes rose nearly a hundred feet high. Although their width-to- height ratio gave them a slightly fattened, squat aspect, it enhanced rather than marred their peculiar beauty.

As they approached over the barren volcanic soil, the distance between the domes seemed to increase. The huge shutters and exterior catwalks became more prominent. The catwalks rose and angled, rose and angled, following the contour of the dome to tiny platforms mounted on either side of the great shutter. "Anybody ever climb to the top of the dome?"

"Sure. I've even climbed up there once. The height isn't too bad unless you suffer from acrophobia. The real problem is the oxygen level. We're at 14,000 feet, and above 12,000 feet the air is dangerously thin. There's a serious risk of high-altitude pulmonary edema. Children and pregnant women aren't even allowed up here."

"Am I going to be okay?" Koa asked.

"Most people are fine if they move slowly, but don't go running around. Let me know if you get nauseous. That's the first sign."

They parked the vehicle, stepped out into the freezing air, and approached the giant white domes, looming like bloated igloos above them. Gunter led them through a door with a glass window into the service building. As they passed into a small anteroom, Koa noted the opposing video cameras watching everyone who entered or departed. Alerted by Gunter's reference to motion detectors, he spotted a pair of infrared sensors. "These sensors activate the cameras?"

"Right. The opposing sensors are designed to detect any motion in the anteroom, but as a failsafe, a light beam shines between the sensors. If the motion detectors don't trigger the cameras, a person breaking the light beam starts the videotape."

Koa was impressed. He should have such aids in all his cases. "Pretty neat. The video recorder has a date and time function?"

"Right—the date, time, and camera are electronically recorded, along with the image. We use security tapes with a prerecorded background track. Makes tampering impossible. We got the specs on the system. I can get you a copy."

"Great. I'd appreciate that."

From the anteroom, they entered Alice I's office-workshop wing, passing a machine shop, an office, and a computer room. As they strolled down the corridor, Cepheid turned the corner and stutter-stepped toward them. "Good afternoon, earthlings," the robot intoned.

"Good afternoon, Cepheid," Koa responded.

"I see you've met Thurston Masters' second son." Gunter's voice took on a disparaging tone.

"His second son?"

"Like I told you, Masters is a technician, a software engineer, an optics guy, not a real astronomer. He loves robotics and that thing . . ."—he pointed to Cepheid—"is a robotic test platform. In some ways this whole telescope is one big computerized robot. Computers and robotics control the shape of the mirrors; computers and robotics adjust the mirrors thousands of times a minute to eliminate most of the earth's atmospheric distortions. Computers and robotics allow astronomers to operate the telescopes from anywhere in the world."

"Yeah, Nālani explained that astronomers don't actually have to come to the summit."

"And many of them don't."

"I had quite a conversation with Cepheid yesterday while I was waiting to chat with Masters." Koa noticed a short, curly wire, like a car phone antenna, protruding from the top of the robot. It had to be radio controlled. He wondered how close the transmitter had to be.

"Don't sell that contraption short. Its computer brain ranks as one of the most advanced artificial intelligence platforms in the world. Masters even had Keneke working to program Cepheid to tell right from wrong . . . to give it a conscience."

"Really? How could that possibly work?"

"Well, Detective, have you ever read Isaac Asimov's *I, Robot*?"

"No."

"Asimov's robot followed three simple laws: First, a robot must never injure a human. Second, a robot must obey humans, except if doing so would violate the first law. Third, the robot must protect itself unless doing so violates either of the first two laws. Those simple principles form the basis of an ethical system that could be reduced to computer code."

Koa was still shaking his head over Gunter's description of Cepheid as they entered the telescope control room, located just outside the space reserved for the telescope. A long glass window overlooked the interior of the dome, giving Koa his first glimpse of the world's largest optical telescope.

He'd seen a model at the Alice headquarters, but nothing about the tiny replica prepared him for the enormous size of the telescope. The wing-like platforms that had extended no more than two inches from either side of the model were two stories above the observatory building floor and stretched farther than the wings of a Boeing 727. While the crisscrossed cage of metal girders in the model couldn't have held a mouse, the cage of this telescope extended over forty feet across and soared more than ninety feet upward toward the crest of the dome.

"God, it's gigantic."

Gunter smiled. "Not an uncommon reaction. Let me introduce..." Koa reluctantly tore his eyes away from the twelve-story telescope to focus on a pug-nosed blonde woman in her late twenties. "Polly Safer, one of our technicians. Polly, this is Chief Detective Koa Kāne of the Hawai'i County police."

"Nice to meet you."

Gunter turned to the woman standing next to Polly. "And, of course, you know Soo Lin Hun, visiting from our mother ship at the University of California." Soo Lin looked different in jeans and a long-sleeve woolen shirt beneath a down-filled vest.

"Polly, give Detective Kāne the VIP briefing, the short, nontechnical version."

Polly smiled and launched into a smooth tour-guide spiel, explaining the computer keyboards, monitors, and printers through which astronomers received the data collected by the telescope.

When Polly finished, Gunter led Koa into the icy-cold dome. They rode a small elevator cage up through two levels of steel decking to emerge on a platform level with the huge gimbals the telescope pivoted on.

"The dome weighs about seven hundred tons and rotates along with the telescope," Gunter explained. "The telescope pivots up and down on these gimbals." He pointed to the massive bearings that supported the telescope in its yoke. "By rotating and pivoting, the telescope can be pointed toward any part of the sky."

As Gunter pointed out the components, Koa gradually made sense of the forest of pipes and bars. He recognized the huge open-framed hexagonal cylinder of the telescope with its unique segmented mirror. "Thirty-six segments of Schott Zerodur glass make up the primary mirror, which has an aggregate diameter of 10.95 meters."

"Why is it so cold in here? Doesn't the heat work?" Koa asked, shivering.

Gunter laughed. "There is no heat. In fact, our air-exchange system replaces the entire volume of air in the dome with outside air every five minutes. We do that to keep the temperature of the telescope equal to the outside temperature. Otherwise, when we opened the shutter at night to observe, the temperature difference would distort our observations. Besides, all the astronomers work in the heated control room."

"A side of beef would freeze in here," Koa persisted.

"That's true. Most nights the temperature dips well below freezing." Gunter pointed upward toward the secondary mirror hanging high in the center of the open frame. "We call that secondary mirror a 'rubber' mirror. Actuators driven by our adaptive optics computers deform that mirror to compensate for the effects of atmospheric turbulence. It focuses the light gathered by the primary mirror back through the aperture in the center of the primary mirror to various detectors."

"You mean, nobody actually looks through the telescope?" Koa asked.

"That's right. We use detectors, frequently charge-coupled devices. They're sophisticated and expensive variations of the chips in video cameras. And they're thousands of times more sensitive to light than the human eye, particularly at this altitude where asphyxia, or oxygen deprivation, diminishes the eye's ability to discern light."

"How much did this thing cost?" Koa asked.

"If you have to ask, you can't afford one," Gunter chuckled, before adding, "about a hundred million, more if you count the adaptive optics enhancements and the detectors."

Koa was starting to shiver involuntarily.

"Seen enough?" Gunter asked.

"I don't know about that, but I'm plenty cold enough."

"I assume that you want to see the security video."

"Yes, for the night of January 20. That would be helpful."

Gunter took Koa and Soo Lin through the workshop-office area into a small office with a television monitor, where everyone except Koa settled into several chairs. The chairs didn't have much back support, so he stood against the wall.

"If you'll come with me, Detective, you can watch me extract the videotape."

Koa followed Gunter into a medium-sized computer room containing rows of computer cabinets. Gunter opened a large gray box mounted on the wall, revealing a control panel and a video recorder. Gunter pushed a button and an aluminized tape cassette ejected from a slot.

"Doesn't that disable the system?"

"No, there's another tape in Alice II that continues to run. In addition, a non-erasable ejection character is embedded on the tape so that you can always tell if a tape has been ejected." Gunter took a blank tape from a cabinet and inserted it into the slot before closing the door.

They returned to the office with the tape cassette, which Gunter inserted into a video player. After rewinding and viewing several sections, he located the security camera recordings from the evening of January 20. Each segment of tape contained four pictures, one in each quadrant, split down the center by a quarter-inch white band containing red numbers in sequence.

"The tape records four cameras?" Koa asked.

"Yes, the two security cameras at the entry door for Alice I feed the right-hand pictures; similar cameras in the entry area of Alice II feed the left side of the screen. The white band makes the tapes virtually tamper-proof."

The first picture on the right-hand side, in surprisingly clear color, showed Polly Safer entering the observatory at 17:34:56, shaking out her blonde hair and disappearing through the second door. "Polly must have been the duty technician on January 20. Our rules require a duty technician on site whenever anyone operates the telescope. The duty technician is responsible to make sure nothing gets damaged and to shut the observatory down in case of weather problems or electrical difficulties."

"How often does the weather shut you down?" Koa asked.

"Not too often. More in the winter, less often in the summer."

"Usually snow?"

"No, it's usually wind. Sometimes the jet stream drops down and we get gale-force winds across the mountaintop. We shut down when the winds exceed forty-five knots. That happens a fair amount in the winter. Also, two or three times a year we get enough snow to make the roads impassable, and in the mid-eighties, a blizzard closed off the whole mountain for fourteen days."

"Jesus, I'd hate to be up here in a blizzard."

The next figure at 18:44:19 was a young man with a crest of thick black hair and an easy smile on his roundish face. Gunter punched the stop button and the figure froze in mid-step. "That's Keneke."

Soo Lin gasped, and Koa turned toward her. She appeared shaken. "I'm okay. His sudden appearance just surprised me, that's all."

"Play the whole segment," Koa directed. Gunter pushed a button, and they watched Keneke enter the building, pull off his brown mittens, stuff them in the pocket of his parka, and head through the interior door. Near the end of the segment, one of the cameras caught a decent close-up of Keneke's face. Gunter once again pressed stop, capturing the portrait. Deep, wide forehead; large, clear black eyes that seemed to twinkle even in the inadvertent picture. Flared nose, rounded brown cheeks, thick smiling lips fading into dimples, neat porcelain-white teeth, and a heavy, wrinkled chin. A Hawaiian face—jovial, but not overly handsome.

"Looks like a fellow without a care in the world."

"Keneke was like that. Nearly always happy, like he was retelling one of his stories in his own mind," Gunter responded. As he spoke, Koa watched Gunter's face, looking for some kind of tell, but read nothing, except maybe a sense of loss in the man's sad eyes.

Koa turned to Soo Lin. "See anything unusual?"

She shook her head. When she spoke, it was in a choked, halting whisper. "There's . . . there's nothing unusual. He was always so . . . so happy." She lowered her face into her cupped hands and rested on the table. After a few moments she lifted her head, revealing a sheen of tears in her eyes. "I didn't think this would . . . would be so hard."

"Want to stop and come back to it later?"

"No."

"Replay the segment three or four times," Koa instructed. As Gunter worked the remote control, they watched Keneke enter the facility. Once. Twice. Three times. Each time Koa concentrated on the fleeting glimpse of Keneke's animated face he'd previously known only as the bloodied, one-eyed pulp in the Pōhakuloa lava tube. The picture reinforced his determination to find Keneke's sadistic killer. The left side of the television screen came alive. Over white digits displaying 18:51:50, three male figures, one in a sweater and two in jackets, filed through the entry door and anteroom of Alice II. Koa recognized Director Masters. "Who are the two men with Masters?"

"That's Rick Cooper and Gil Gaylord. Gaylord's a tech—a really sweet guy. He works a lot with schoolkids, trying to get them interested in astronomy. He must have been the duty technician for Alice II that night. Rick Cooper is one of our longtime staff astronomers. Been here at least four years. Works a lot with Masters, kind of his protégé."

"I'd like to have Sergeant Basa talk to Gaylord and Cooper."

"Okay. He can meet them at the dormitory complex or we'll send them down to Hilo."

When the next picture appeared on the television monitor, the white digits read thirty-four minutes after midnight, and Cooper exited Alice II. "That's probably just a break. Most astronomers get a little stir-crazy and take a stretch outside during the night." And sure enough, twelve minutes later Cooper reentered Alice II.

At 01:12:10, Keneke walked across the right side of the monitor, leaving Alice I. "That's probably Keneke's break. It was a regular thing with him. He went out to eyeball the *huihui hōkū* for a few minutes."

"*Huihui hōkū?*" Soo Lin asked.

"A flock of stars. What we call constellations. Keneke knew dozens of Hawaiian star stories."

But Gunter was wrong. Keneke didn't return to the observatory. The next pictures showed Polly Safer exiting the building at 02:17:47 and reentering at 02:20:14.

"Polly is not supposed to leave the facility," Gunter said, annoyed. "That's against policy."

Then the security tape showed Polly leaving Alice I at 06:45:17, followed a few minutes later by footage of Gaylord, Cooper, and Director Masters leaving Alice II at 06:55:39. They rewound the tape and checked again, but they'd made no mistake. Keneke had left the observatory at 1:12 a.m. on January 21 and hadn't returned.

"Why would he leave at that hour? Would his observing time have been over?" Koa asked.

Gunter shook his head. "It's unlike him or any other astronomer to walk out like that. I can't explain it."

"Play the 1:12 a.m. segment again." As Gunter rewound the tape and replayed the segment, Koa watched closely, trying to glean some clue from Keneke's movements or the expression on his face. "Do you see anything out of the ordinary?"

"Nothing, except he wasn't wearing his mittens."

"Probably still had them in his pocket."

"Soo Lin, you see anything odd?"

"Nothing. He seems to be stepping out for a break. Keneke loved the night sky. He once said he'd never spent a whole night inside an observatory without getting outside to see the stars, and he hoped he never would."

"But he didn't go back. That's the last time he appears on the security tape," Koa said.

"I just don't understand." Soo Lin let out a deep sigh. "Can I see both segments again?"

"Sure. Gunter, can you run them again, please?"

As they watched the first segment, Soo Lin burst out, "Stop!" Gunter stopped the tape. "Can you back up a couple of frames?" Soo Lin stood up and headed toward the television monitor. The picture flickered as Gunter slowly reversed the tape. "There." The picture froze, not on Keneke's happy face, but on a full-body shot when Keneke was about two steps inside the first entry door. Soo

Lin pointed at the bottom of Keneke's parka, where a black triangle extended below the hem of his jacket. "That's his computer bag."

"You're right. It looks like his computer bag," Gunter agreed.

"Now play the exit tape," Soo Lin requested. Gunter replayed the exit scene, stopping it several times for them to study the pictures. "I don't think he took his computer out with him," she concluded.

"But he wouldn't have taken the computer on a break," Gunter responded.

"Exactly," Soo Lin agreed. "But he would have taken his computer if he was leaving the mountain. It's like he took a break and never came back. Something isn't right."

"Well, if he had the computer when he came in and not when he left, it should be here," Koa reasoned. "And if he was just taking a break, Polly must have been surprised when he didn't come back." Koa turned to Gunter. "Can you ask Polly to come down?"

"Sure." Gunter picked up a telephone and spoke into it. "She'll be right down. You want to take the tape?"

"Yes, I do," Koa replied, taking the cassette from Gunter.

Koa thought about what he'd just seen. On the surface, it looked like Keneke had simply walked away from his job. Yet Soo Lin had identified a critical discrepancy. Why hadn't he taken his computer? And what had happened to it?

"How would Keneke have gotten up here from the dormitory complex that night?" Koa asked.

"He always drove. He loved his 4x4, called it his big black canoe," Gunter responded.

"And you never saw him again?"

"Nope. Not after Keneke got up from the dinner table Tuesday night."

When Polly arrived, Koa excused Gunter. "Polly, you were the duty technician on Tuesday, January 20, right?"

"Yes." She drew the word out, reflecting a hesitancy that put Koa on alert.

"And Keneke had observing time on the telescope that night?"

Beneath blonde bangs, she had large blue eyes, a small nose, and narrow lips. "Well, not exactly." She paused. "Keneke was working on adaptive optics software. He was testing some new programs."

"Okay, but he was up here with you?"

"Yeah."

"Did he have his computer?"

The question seemed to take her by surprise. "Gee, I assume so. I mean he always had his computer with him. He must have had it that night."

"Do you remember seeing his computer?"

"He must—"

"Don't speculate. Tell me only what you actually remember."

She paused, and then spread her hands in a gesture of uncertainty. "Gee, I can't say for sure that I saw his computer that night."

"Do you know where we can find his computer?"

"I have no idea. It's not up here." Again, she hesitated. "Someone would have found it by now."

"Could it have been stolen?"

She looked quizzical. "From up here? I don't think we've ever had a theft up here."

"Are you aware that Keneke took a break that night?"

Her eyes went wide, taking on a deer-in-the-head-lights quality. "Yes." She paused. "He always took a break, but . . . but . . ." she stumbled, "he didn't come back."

"What did you do?"

Polly looked apprehensive. "Can this be between us, Detective?"

Koa suddenly understood her predicament. She was afraid she'd be punished for violating the observatory rules. "I'll treat it as confidential, if I can."

"Thank you." She became a bit more sure of herself. "The duty technician is never supposed to leave the building. It's a cardinal rule. But I was concerned about Keneke. He left sometime after midnight, and he didn't come back. It was awhile before I realized that he hadn't. I went out to check on him. I looked for his black canoe—I'm sorry, his SUV. It was gone, so I knew that he'd driven off the mountain. It was odd. Not at all like Keneke."

For Koa, this information only deepened the mystery. Keneke had unexpectedly left the observatory a little after 1:10 a.m. About six hours later he had called the Alice headquarters to say he planned to return to the mainland and then made plane reservations. He apparently drove to the airport but never checked in for the flight. Was he running from something—something that caught up with him at the airport? What had caused him to flee the observatory?

"Polly, did anything else unusual happen that night?"

She thought for a moment. "No. Nothing struck me as odd."

"Did Keneke get any phone calls or have words with anyone?"

"No. Not that I saw."

After allowing Polly to return to her work, Koa sat mulling over the strange sequence of events from that night.

As Koa left the room, he ran into Director Masters and Nālani. "Detective," Masters began, "can I have a word with you and Nālani?" They stepped back into the same room where Koa had been with Polly, and Masters closed the door. "I want to apologize to you and especially Nālani on behalf of the Alice Observatories and the Foundation."

"Apologize? Why?" Koa asked.

"Polly Safer tried to tender her resignation this morning."

Nālani's hand flew to her mouth.

"At first," the director continued, "she wouldn't tell me why, but then it came out that Charlie Harper has been harassing her with sexually suggestive comments and worse. This afternoon I talked to some of our other women employees." Masters looked at Nālani. "I understand he tried something inappropriate with you and you slapped him. I'm sorry you didn't knock his teeth out. Anyway, I have spoken to Mr. Harper in terms he won't soon forget. He's on probation, and quite frankly he'll be gone as soon as we find a qualified replacement. It won't happen again, and you have my sincerest apology."

Nālani expressed her first concern. "Is Polly going to stay?"

"Yes, I talked her into withdrawing her resignation."

"Thank you," Nālani said, and Koa echoed the sentiment.

Later, the two of them walked out of the observatory into perhaps the most stunning sunset in Koa's memory. Far off to the west, trails of vaporous mist played eerily over the deeply shadowed valley where night had already fallen between the Hawaiian mountains. Across the channel, Haleakalā on Maui seemed to rise from the mists of some unseen netherworld. Hues of red, orange, yellow, and pink glorified the darkening sky. No edges separated the colors. A continuum of subtle shades simply slid softly together in the ever-shifting light of the dying day.

Behind them the huge shutters of the Alice telescopes rolled open. One of the domes turned slowly. A laser beam for the adaptive optics snapped on, sending a bright line of orange light toward the heavens. The giant eyes peered deep into space and backward in time to a younger and more violent universe.

For Koa, his current universe was plenty violent enough. Some malevolent current had swept Keneke away from Mauna Kea in the middle of the night, prompted him to make plans to return to the mainland, and then unexpectedly carried him to a ritual death and mutilation in a Pōhakuloa lava tube. There had to be some connection to the observatory. Otherwise, why would Keneke leave in the middle of the night?

Koa's mind suddenly focused on a contradiction he had previously missed. According to both Nālani and Soo Lin, Keneke and Gunter had a falling-out, Soo Lin saying that Keneke didn't trust Gunter, and Nālani sure that Keneke avoided Gunter. But according to Gunter, they had dined together shortly before Keneke's disappearance. Had they reconciled, or had something happened at that dinner to launch Keneke on his flight from the observatory?

CHAPTER TWENTY-ONE

THE NEXT MORNING, Hook Hao called Koa to say that Reggie had regained consciousness, and that Lieutenant Baxter of the Maui police wanted to interview Reggie. Koa groaned at the mention of Baxter's name. He knew the Maui lieutenant from his military days as a condescending asshole with a nasty attitude toward minorities. They had sometimes worked together as police officers, but Koa had no fond memories of those times together.

He called Baxter to ask him to hold off until he and Hook could get to Maui. After ringing off, Koa booked and boarded a Hawaiian Airlines flight. Hook was waiting for him when he entered the terminal at Maui's Kahului Airport.

"Hey, Brah, some good news, no?"

"The best." Koa gave Hook two thumbs-up. "You get any more on his medical condition?"

"A little. He's conscious and his vital signs are normal. He's out of immediate danger."

"That's great. I want to talk to Lieutenant Baxter and then we'll go to the hospital. Okay?"

"Sure."

Koa's cell phone chirped and he answered, "Detective Kāne."

"This is Detective Wanabi. Baxter asked me to pick you up. I'm in a brown Ford Explorer in the pickup lane outside the Hawaiian terminal."

"Great. See you in two minutes," Koa responded. They met Wanabi and made their way to downtown Kahului. Massive traffic jams choked the streets and created gridlock at the intersections. "The town, hell, the whole island, has become a parking lot," Wanabi complained.

"Yeah," Koa agreed. "You could change a flat tire and not lose your place in this line of cars."

Wanabi chuckled as he fired up the siren and illuminated the blue bubble light. Koa ignored the misuse of police emergency powers as Wanabi blared and weaved toward Maui police headquarters.

When they finally made it to the modern concrete-and-glass building, Koa asked Hook to wait in the lobby while he walked upstairs to see Lieutenant Baxter.

"Hey, man, long time no see. You been hidin' 'cause of the dinner you owe me?" Tony Baxter grinned, revealing bad teeth. The man was seriously overweight and wore a wrinkled uniform with grease spots on one sleeve. With officers like Baxter, it was little wonder that a lot of the population had little regard for the police.

Koa went along with the teasing. Playing buddies with Baxter was a small price to pay for the favors he wanted. "That's not my fault. I bet you a dinner in Hilo, and my sources tell me you've been too busy chasing Hawaiian babes to collect."

"Your sources ain't worth shit. You think just because you've found your Hawaiian pussy, it's off-limits for the rest of us."

The crass description of Nālani bothered Koa, but he let it ride. "Just hurts my feelings that you think it trumps dinner in Hilo."

Baxter gave him a wry look, like Koa should be glad he hadn't collected. "And now you're here lookin' for more favors. This time, it's dinner in Wailuku. I'm not givin' you another fuckin' out."

"Deal. Tonight after we talk and I see the kid up at Maui Memorial?"

"Deal. I been thinkin' the Waterfront over on Māʻalaea Bay." Baxter grinned.

He's an asshole, Koa thought. The Smith family, who owned and managed the eatery, had their own fishing vessels and served the day's catch at top prices, making it the most expensive place in town. "You looking for seared ʻahi or ono en papillote?"

Baxter looked disgusted. "I don't eat that shit. Martinis and steak, that's man food."

Koa chose not to challenge the man's claims to culinary expertise. Instead he got directly to the point. "Tell me about this thing with Hook's kid."

Baxter shifted in his seat, accepting the change to serious talk. "Damn funny business. The Navy shore patrol spotted a guy waving a makeshift flag from the pali above Kanapou Bay on Kahoʻolawe. The flag waver turned out to be Aikue ʻŌpua, the native-rights oracle. He led the shore patrol to Reggie Hao, who got tangled up with a fuckin' unexploded bomb up near the Puʻu Moiwi. A Navy rescue helo airlifted Reggie back to Maui Memorial."

"You brought ʻŌpua in for a statement?"

"You bet. According to him, he's Saint ʻŌpua, out to save Hawaiʻi for the restoration of the old ways, the resurrection of the aliʻi, the rebuilding of the heiau, and the reestablishment of the taboos . . . all that shit. He's a fruitcake, but it'll be hard to convict him of trespass, let alone looting antiquities. The fuckin' sovereignty loonies are already beating their tom-toms. Some big muckety-muck from the Big Island called the mayor, trying to get ʻŌpua a pass."

Koa let his puzzlement show. "Who called from the Big Island?"

"Prince Kamakamakama or something like that. Supposed to be the descendant of some dead Hawaiian king."

"Prince Kamehameha?"

"Yeah, that's the big-ass dude."

The news surprised Koa. The prince seemed to have his fingers all over the antiquities cases on both Maui and the Big Island.

"How many times did 'Ōpua and the others go out to Kaho'olawe?"

"'Ōpua says this was his virgin outing. More bullshit, but what would you expect? I mean, why tumble to multiple trespass charges when we got evidence of only one?"

"They find anything?"

"'Ōpua says they found squat. Still more bullshit, but that, too, is what you'd expect. I mean, trespass is a misdemeanor, but looting antiquities—that could get you real time in the big house."

"You don't believe him?"

Baxter's smart-ass grin showed exactly what he thought of the sovereignty people. "Hell, if he said the sun was shining, I'd check the window. Besides, the Seabees went back after the rescue. Found a blue backpack, mostly fishhooks and stones, volcanic glass, and some 'aumakua objects . . . you know, little family idols. We may not be able to prove they came from Aikue's dig, but it would be a real strange coincidence if they didn't."

"You don't seem to like Mr. 'Ōpua."

"I'd love to put that little cocksucker and his toadies away. These islands are part of the United States, one of the fifty states, for God's sake, and this little snake wants to crank us back to the fuckin' Middle Ages. Who cares if the captain of some whaling ship raped his great-great-grandmother?"

The vehemence of Baxter's outburst surprised Koa. The man's animosity toward minorities had plainly gotten worse, but Koa held his tongue. Baxter was badly maladjusted. "There was a third guy?"

"Yeah. One Garvie Jenkins. We didn't even find out about him until we took 'Ōpua's statement."

"Didn't the shore patrol pick him up with 'Ōpua and Reggie?"

"No. He didn't hang around for the rescue and left 'Ōpua and the injured kid. Hoofed it over to the Kaho'olawe preservation office and hitched a ride out on a supply boat."

"He abandoned Reggie after the dud exploded?" Koa was incredulous.

"So it seems. But I guess it ain't too shocking, since the dude's done time in the big house."

That didn't sound good for Reggie. "Really? Where?"

Baxter grinned. "He did a stretch at Kūlani."

"He's from the Big Island?"

"Yeah. Ran some kind of financial scam in Kona. Bought himself an all-expenses-paid trip to Kūlani. Gave us a Kona address when we picked him up."

Koa was already thinking ahead—he had to tell Hook about his son's unsavory friends. "So what does this model citizen have to say for himself?"

"That's the weird part. He refused to talk."

"Because he's facing a misdemeanor trespass charge that we can prove through other people. That doesn't make sense."

"It's not an ordinary trespass charge." Baxter grinned. "Under code section 13-260 Kaho'olawe's a restricted place. The penalty's a year in the can, plus a thousand dollars a day."

Koa was unimpressed. "It's still a misdemeanor. His stonewalling tells me he found loot or something worse. He's worried about a felony charge."

"Probably, but it gets still more peculiar."

"How?" Koa cocked his head.

"He's represented by T. Gordon Wheeler, *the fuckin' Esquire*."

"The celebrity criminal lawyer?"

"The very same."

This new entry astonished Koa. "Wheeler charges twenty-five grand to answer the phone. Garvie wouldn't hire him for a trespass violation. Hell, I doubt that Wheeler would take a pissant trespass case. Garvie's got to be worried about something involving serious time."

"Maybe, but unless we can tie 'Ōpua or Garvie to the backpack, I've got three misdemeanor raps. Makes me think I missed a turn someplace. It just doesn't compute."

"You've talked to Wheeler?"

"I didn't exactly *talk* to Mr. fuckin' Esquire. He called me to say that he represents Garvie and will handle all questions. When I suggested the county prosecutor might bring Garvie before a grand jury, Mr. Esquire asked me if I had ever heard of the Fifth Amendment. That's a fuckin' dead end."

"What about Reggie?"

"He's been in a coma since the Seabees hauled him out. Hasn't uttered a word. They did find an 'aumakua in his pocket, a small stone turtle, but that don't prove zip. Half the Hawaiian population carries an 'aumakua. It's like a key ring back on mother mainland. What's your deal with this kid, anyway?"

Baxter obviously didn't understand that 'aumakua represented personal or family gods, but that wasn't surprising. He was a cultural illiterate. So far Koa had presented himself only as a family friend because he feared Baxter would become territorial, but now that he understood better what had happened on Kaho'olawe, he needed to go further. "Like I explained on the phone, I've known the kid and his father for more than a decade. The father has helped us a bunch of times. But I'm also working a murder case, a ritual murder. It's got an archaeology angle, and now that you've explained what happened out there, I've got a feeling that there could be a *pilina*—a connection."

"How?"

"I haven't put it together yet, but we found an archaeological site on the Army training ground at Pōhakuloa looted. We haven't established a connection to the murder, but it can't be a coincidence. Now you've got another possible looting, one that attracts T. Gordon Wheeler, Esquire. I've been on the force a dozen years. In all those years, I haven't seen a single looting of antiquities case. Now there are two of them and they're not connected? I'm not buying."

"So you're goin' up to the hospital to see *my* witness?"

"Yeah, Hook and I are going to see Reggie."

"He's *my* witness." Baxter looked Koa straight in the eye. "*My* witness, Detective."

Koa nodded reluctantly. The case belonged to the Maui Division because Kahoʻolawe was their territory. Baxter might be a professional friend, but he, like all police officers, had a turf-conscious commander. Baxter's possessiveness nevertheless surprised him. It was bad police work. Enlisting the aid of the father and a family friend was far more likely to get the young man to talk. Koa decided to bide his time. "I understand. I'll follow your lead."

"Deal."

They collected Hook and drove up Mahalani Street to Maui Memorial Hospital. A Hawaiian matron in a flowing *muʻumuʻu* directed them to the general medical ward on the fourth floor, and a nurse in the ward pointed them toward Reggie's room.

The hospital room usually held two patients, but the hulking young man was alone. Hooked up to an IV and various monitors, he had a tired, bloodless appearance. A thick band of padded gauze wrapped his forehead, and a cast covered his left arm from above the elbow to his wrist. "*E kuʻu makua kāne . . .* Father," he said in a hoarse croak.

"*E ku'u keiki kāne*... my son." Hook leaned over the bed and the two embraced awkwardly. "Good to see you *ua ala*... conscious."

"Good to be awake. At least it would be if my head didn't hurt."

"You need medicine?" Hook asked anxiously. "No. They gave me something a while ago."

Baxter stepped forward. "I'm Lieutenant Baxter of the Criminal Investigations Unit of the Maui Police. I need to ask you some questions."

"Okay," Reggie croaked with a grimace.

"I must tell you that we are investigating crimes, and anything you say can and will be used against you in a court of law. You have the right to an attorney and the right to remain silent. Do you understand your constitutional rights?"

"I guess so." Reggie's voice was almost inaudible, and he had a pained expression.

"You were on Kaho'olawe?" Baxter's careless, overbearing technique surprised Koa. If one of his detectives had accepted an I-guess-so response to a Miranda warning, Koa would have hauled him out of the room for a lecture. Even Piki, who was often too exuberant, knew better. Besides, Reggie had obviously suffered serious trauma and was drugged up on painkillers. Nothing he said to Baxter would be admissible in court.

"Yes, I kinda remember landing on the sacred island."

"With 'Ōpua and Garvie?"

"I think so. It's not too clear, but it seems like I was with Aikue 'Ōpua and maybe someone else. It's all kind of confused in my head."

"Why? Why were you on Kaho'olawe?"

"Trying to protect our sacred... Hawaiian heritage."

"You mean, lookin' for artifacts?"

"Arti... arti... artifacts?" Reggie closed his eyes.

"What happened out there?" Baxter's voice hardened.

"I kinda remember landing on the sacred island at dawn . . . soft gray light from the east . . . I remember walking . . . then dark . . . the darkness of *pō*." Reggie closed his eyes and seemed to go to sleep.

Hook stared at the police officer with barely contained hostility. "I think you better let him rest."

"Shit," Lieutenant Baxter swore, "I'm not gettin' shit."

"Might give it some time," Koa suggested. "We could let you know if his memory comes back." He took a first step to leave, meaning to draw Baxter away. The two walked out of Reggie's hospital room into the hall.

"Okay," Baxter said, plainly dissatisfied, "I'm going back to my office. Let me know if he remembers anything—an' don't hold out on me—got that?"

"Yeah, I got it." Koa suppressed his annoyance.

"Good, Koa, do you or Mr. Hao need a ride?"

"*Mahalo*, but no. We're going to hang out with Reggie. Then figure out our next move. The steak place down by the bay at six thirty?"

"Deal. *Aloha*." Baxter got into the patient elevator and the huge double door closed.

"That's a friend of yours?" Hook asked skeptically.

"We need to talk." Koa pulled Hook into one of the *'ohana* rooms for visiting family. "Baxter acted like an asshole. It wasn't even decent police work, but this thing is serious. It's more than just trespassing, and I'm not sure, but I think it's more than preserving Hawaiian history. Garvie was into something . . . probably the looting of antiquities. That's a felony."

"Oh, God." A worried expression furrowed Hook's massive brow.

"But the fact that Garvie isn't talking might be a blessing. He's got a record. His criminal record and the fact that he turned tail without helping Reggie should make him the real target." Koa talked more rapidly as he continued. "I was watching Reggie's eyes. I think he remembers more than he told Baxter. You need to get Reggie to tell us what he knows."

Hook stared at Koa for a long time before responding softly, "There is a risk he'll incriminate himself, isn't there?"

"Yes, and I won't mislead you. The risk is real. Baxter wants a case. He doesn't like 'Ōpua, but knows he'll have trouble getting a conviction. There's a lot of sympathy for the sovereignty movement even if there's no real political support." He gave Hook time to digest that information, and then continued. "He's gonna ask the prosecutor to file charges. I'll bet a month's pay on that. Just trespassing or more serious—that's the question and it depends on witnesses. Of the three potential witnesses—'Ōpua, Reggie, and Jenkins—the one who talks first and helps the police is going to get the best deal and maybe, just maybe, walk away."

Hook sat with his head in his hands. "I don't know, Koa. I'm scared for him. He's all I have. Let me go talk to him alone." The old fisherman rose heavily from his seat and walked slowly out of the room. He was gone for a long time.

While Hook talked to Reggie, Koa called Sergeant Basa. "You staying out of trouble, my friend?"

"Yeah, I'm working on it," Basa responded cautiously.

"For you, that's a full-time job, isn't it, Sergeant?" Koa chuckled.

"Cute, boss . . . real cute. And now I'll bet you want a favor."

"Yeah, run a records check on one Garvie Jenkins, G-A-R-V-I-E. He did time at Kūlani."

Ten minutes later, the phone rang. "It's Basa. I put Jenkins in the computer. One Garvie Jenkins pled a 708-852, class C felony. Drew an indeterminate ten years. Did his time at Kūlani. Paroled about four years ago."

Koa thought for a minute. "Forgery?"

"That's the code section."

"What'd he pass? Bad checks?"

"I don't think so. The computer file says 'forged documents.' That's not records speak for a phony check rap. You want me to pull the file?"

"Yes, and call me back as soon as you get something." He rang off. He considered going back to Reggie's hospital room, but thought better of it. An hour crept by.

Finally, Hook returned to the ʻohana room and sat down. He took his time in collecting his thoughts.

"Koa, my telling you something, well, it's not like Reggie telling you. I mean, I can't incriminate him, can I?"

The old fisherman had been around. He was smart, and nothing mattered more to him than protecting his son. "No. I could use what you tell me as a police officer, but I don't think a prosecutor could use your statement against Reggie. It'd be hearsay."

"And you're going to help Reggie?"

Although Koa and Hook had reached this sensitive point a number of times over the years, Koa felt obligated to restate the ground rules. "Any way I can, consistent with my obligations as a police officer. As we've talked before, there's a line I can't cross."

Again, Hook paused. Koa watched him struggle to come to a decision. "Okay, you were right. Reggie remembers more than he told the detective. Baxter spooked him. It's complicated. Reggie and his friends were into the sovereignty thing. That's how he met Aikue ʻŌpua."

Koa nodded, knowing how that worked.

"Anyway, ʻŌpua got Reggie all worked up about Kahoʻolawe. You know about December 8, 1941?"

"The day after Pearl Harbor? No."

"That's the day the United States seized Kahoʻolawe, forced the residents off, built a mock airstrip, and started bombing. It wasn't hard to get Reggie stirred up. It's not hard to get anyone who respects the land . . ."

Koa saw anger flare up in Hook's eyes and inflame his cheeks. Koa understood. Hawaiian society before Western contact had revolved around respect for the land and the ocean. That respect indelibly marked the Hawaiian people, and Hook was Hawaiian to the core.

"Anyway," Hook continued, "Aikue got Reggie excited about saving his native heritage. Introduced him to other traditionalists— some in the sovereignty movement an' others just interested in preserving the old ways. They had meetings. It's mostly talk an' more talk.

"Somehow Jenkins shows up in this group. Reggie remembers seeing him with 'Ōpua and some of the others, but he's not sure how Garvie got hooked up with 'Ōpua. He had some *pilina*— some connection to archaeology—but wasn't part of the sovereignty crowd.

Jenkins was carrying books, articles, and texts about things used by the people of old. Some of it was the usual fishhooks, poi pounders, and stone bowls, but Jenkins mostly talked about things used by the *ali'i*. He wanted to find the treasures of Hawaiian history." Hook's face twisted with dislike.

"Reggie didn't know Jenkins was a bad dude. He swore to me he didn't know. He says Jenkins talked like a professor, not a convict. Jenkins talked about preserving things. Anyway, they went out to Kaho'olawe maybe a dozen times. Didn't find much at first, but on the third or fourth trip they found a rock shelter. On the next trip they found a small burial cave."

"They looted a burial cave?" Koa didn't bother concealing his surprise.

Hook looked down, not meeting Koa's eyes. "Jenkins wanted to preserve everything. 'Ōpua agreed and Reggie went along. They stashed things in a cave on the Big Island for safekeeping."

This was adding up to a felony. There was no excuse for grave robbing. "They always brought things back?"

"I don't know about every trip. On one trip they found a tiny figure carved from a sea urchin spine. Jenkins got excited. He knew something about it. Said that Kahoʻolawe was the only place in the Pacific where the natives had carved sea urchin spines."

"And they brought it back to the Big Island?"

"Yes. And obsidian. They found some obsidian beads. According to Jenkins, obsidian beads were rare in Hawaiʻi."

Koa had misjudged ʻŌpua. The high and mighty sovereignty activist was a thief—or worse. "And they kept going back?"

"Yes. The rock shelter wasn't far from the coast and away from the bombing range, but Jenkins wanted to explore Puʻu Moiwi. He told Reggie about quarries near Puʻu Moiwi."

"Quarries?" Koa felt a tickle of excitement.

"Yes, adze quarries. Reggie wasn't keen on going that far upslope into the bombing range, but Jenkins insisted. Said that's where they might find really interesting stuff."

"How did Jenkins know about the quarries?" Koa asked.

"According to Reggie, Jenkins had done research and knew a lot about Kahoʻolawe."

"Did Reggie say more about Jenkins's background?"

"He was in some kind of business. It had some kind of connection to research. Reggie didn't know the details."

Research support for grave robbing came to mind. "Okay, so they went up toward Puʻu Moiwi?"

"Yeah. They worked their way *ma uka*, up toward the ridgeline. They were careful. It took time. They found the Puʻu Moiwi adze quarry. It's just an open pit covered with partly made tools and stone chips, nothing special. Reggie was disappointed. He had taken a risk going that far inland and they found nothing. That's when Jenkins told them about a cave where the ancients dug volcanic glass."

"Jenkins told them to look for a cave?"

"Yes, a cave with a—what do you call it—a band, a section—?"

"A vein?"

"Yeah, a cave with a vein of volcanic glass."

"Did they find it?"

"Not on that trip. But on the next trip, Jenkins used a machine. According to Reggie, it was the size of a package." Hook used his hands to illustrate a rectangular shape about briefcase size. "It had a short folding antenna. Garvie also had many peg-like things with antennas. They drove holes into the ground and placed the pegs in a straight line about three hundred yards long.

Garvie fiddled with some controls on the box and then set off a small explosive charge in the middle of the line of pegs." Koa instantly recalled the windswept slope of Mauna Kea where Piki had found a piece of fuse cord and wax wrapping from an explosive charge. There was a connection to the Pōhakuloa cave, Koa thought excitedly.

"Go on . . ."

"They moved the line of pegs and repeated the whole thing five or six times. Jenkins told them that analysis of the data would help them find the cave."

"Did it?"

"On the next trip Jenkins had a detailed map of Pu'u Moiwi, more detailed than any map of Kaho'olawe Reggie had ever seen. It showed positions for the pegs and explosive charges and two possible caves. This time Jenkins had a different machine, like a small electric lawn mower with a computer attached to the handle. Jenkins rolled it around over the possible cave sites. Then they started digging. That's how they found the cave, a cave untouched for centuries."

Koa's cell rang, and he snatched it up. It was Basa. "Koa, I've got the R&I file on Garvie Jenkins. It wasn't bad checks. He operated—"

"Slow down, Basa. Let me make some notes." Koa hadn't been taking notes as Hook spoke because he hadn't wanted to spook the old fisherman, but now he extracted a small notebook and began scribbling. "Okay, go ahead."

"Jenkins operated a bookstore in Kona, a place called The History Buff. An upscale place, selling expensive items, old prints, maps, lithographs, rare books, and an occasional artifact." Koa could tell that the sergeant was proud of his digging.

"Seems like Jenkins couldn't get enough inventory. He started printing his own old maps. Printed them on an ancient newspaper press—sold expensive forgeries to wealthy tourists. One of his marks turned out to be a well-connected New Yorker. This buyer takes Garvie's maps to a dealer in New York who tagged them as forgeries. The mark had friends in the FBI and raised a shit storm.

"The feds called the county prosecutor, who raided Garvie's shop. His records showed the sale of more than forty-five phony maps. He netted almost a hundred fifty grand. We initially charged him under 708-854, possession of the implements of forgery, as well as 708-853 for forgery. He pleaded out the forgery rap. Does that help?"

"It fits a *lei* on a *hula* dancer." Koa smiled for the first time since he'd walked into the hospital. "Anything else?"

"Nope."

"Okay. I want a complete workup on Jenkins—employer, bank accounts, known associates, travels, the works—and Basa, you remember that blasting stuff we found on Mauna Kea?"

"Yeah."

"See if our federal friends can figure out the manufacturer, the dealer, and the buyer. Tell them it might have come from a seismic testing company, maybe in the oil or mineral exploration business, and check to see whether anybody uses that stuff here in the islands."

"Your wish is my command."

"Save the sarcasm for your drinking buddies. And Basa, send someone back up Mauna Kea where Piki found the blasting materials. Have them do a grid search for more materials of the same type. Got it?"

"I got it."

"Good. Now let me go. I'm in the middle of something." Koa hung up and turned his attention back to Hook. "So what happened when they opened up the cave?"

"There was lots of dust, maybe two inches thick over everything, like it had flaked off the walls, maybe from the bombing. One of the walls had a glassy black color an' showed marks where it had been chipped away. Garvie said it was obsidian, a kind of volcanic glass."

"So they found an ancient volcanic glass mine?"

"Yeah. They had battery-powered lights and began digging through the dust. That's when they found the glossy black figures, figures of the Hawaiian god *Kanaloa*. Some of the figures were three inches high, but another stood nearly a foot tall. It gleamed. Reggie said it was beautiful. Jenkins became really excited, yelling and whooping."

"I'll bet. Obsidian *Kanaloa* figures must be worth a fortune on the black market."

"Jenkins was into the black market?" Hook asked incredulously.

"I think so, based on his criminal record, but I still don't know what happened out there—how Reggie got hurt."

"Jenkins said something about selling the *Kanaloa* statues to a collector he knew. Reggie objected. They argued, and then they were screaming at each other. Reggie called him a traitor. They fought. When Jenkins pulled a knife, Reggie ran. Jenkins chased him, screaming that he wasn't going to let a fuckin' Hawaiian ruin his chance for a fortune. That's when Reggie triggered an explosion. He remembers a blinding flash and then nothing."

"He's lucky it didn't kill him." Koa put his hand on Hook's shoulder. The two men sat in silence as Koa sorted through this gigantic mess.

"What do you think?" Hook finally asked.

"I think Reggie's going to come out of this okay, but we got some work to do. I'm out of my jurisdiction, and I don't trust Baxter. You need to get Reggie a lawyer, Hook. Try Bernie Ponabi. He's got a lot of credibility with the authorities."

Hook frowned at the suggestion. "What can Ponabi do?"

"He can negotiate immunity for Reggie in exchange for his testimony against Jenkins."

"You mean, Reggie's gonna be a snitch?"

Koa gave his friend a hard stare. "It's better than going to Kūlani on a felony charge."

The gravity of the situation was sinking in for the old fisherman. "Okay, Koa, I'll talk to Bernie Ponabi. I'll see what he thinks."

"Good. Now, where is the equipment that Jenkins used? Is it on the island or in Reggie's boat?"

Hook hadn't thought of that. "I don't know. Reggie didn't say."

"Go back and ask him. Another thing. Ask him about a blue backpack, full of fishhooks and stones, volcanic glass, and some 'aumakua objects. The Navy found it out there."

"Okay." Hook disappeared into Reggie's room, but returned a few minutes later. "Reggie last saw the box and the pegs when they unloaded back in Hilo after the last trip. The lawn mower device was at Pu'u Moiwi when the dud exploded."

"That's odd. The Navy didn't report finding anything like that."

"Can't help you. Reggie says they pushed it off to the side when they started digging."

"And the backpack?"

"Each of them had a backpack. Reggie had a red one. 'Ōpua had a blue backpack. Jenkins had two packs, both black. They carried them on each of their trips."

So where was all the potential evidence? "Something's fishy. Something doesn't add up." Koa thought for a moment. "Go back to Reggie. Get the location of the cave."

Hook didn't emerge from Reggie's hospital room for nearly ten minutes. "He says it's east of Pu'u Moiwi. He's not sure about the exact location, but it's south of most of the pegs."

* * *

Koa wasn't looking forward to dinner with Lieutenant Baxter, but he knew he had to honor his commitment. He prided himself on dealing fairly with his colleagues, but wanted them to meet him halfway. Baxter's racist attitude was completely out of control, infecting both their collegial relationship and Baxter's professional performance. That crossed Koa's red line. He'd help Reggie, and not think twice about screwing Baxter and his headlong rush toward an unfair prosecution.

He caught a taxi for the ten-mile trip across the narrow neck of the island to Māʻalaea Bay. He looked for Baxter inside the Waterfront restaurant before spotting him on the patio overlooking the bay. He was flirting with a Hawaiian waitress who had just delivered the overweight lieutenant his second, or maybe his third, martini.

"Am I interrupting something?" Koa asked as he slid into the chair across the table from Baxter.

"No. Alana here was just gittin' me anotha martini on your tab," Baxter said, slurring his words. "What's ya drinkin', Koa, my man?"

Koa ordered a beer. The waitress had barely left the table before Baxter asked, "That snot-nosed kid tell you anything?"

Koa shook his head. Baxter's conceit wouldn't allow him to believe that a native detective could get information that had eluded him. So be it.

"Didn't think so. He was lyin' through his fuckin' teeth this afternoon. I'm gonna teach that little cocksucker. I'm gonna git his butt locked up. Maybe one of the hard timers at Kūlani will do his ass for him . . . serve the little cocksucker right."

Koa could ill afford the $170 tab when it came, but the dinner did have one saving grace. It wiped out any guilt that Koa might otherwise have felt for going behind Baxter's back. That night he called Hilo to brief his chief on what he had found and what he intended to do. The chief wasn't keen on his plans, but neither did he veto them. Koa was going to Kahoʻolawe, and, if Reggie was telling the truth, he'd turn Baxter's case on its head and get Reggie out of a nasty jam.

CHAPTER TWENTY-TWO

AFTER A LITTLE wrangling with Rear Admiral James B. ("Happy") Cunningham, commander of the Coast Guard's Fourteenth District, Koa arranged for a ride to Kahoʻolawe. At six the following morning, he was back at Kahului Airport, watching a red-and-white Coast Guard Aerospatiale HH-65 Dolphin helicopter settle onto the pad outside the FAA control center. When the side door slid open, he crouched low to avoid the spinning rotors, grabbed his neck to avoid pain, and eased himself aboard, glad that Nālani was unaware of his latest adventure. She didn't like helicopters, considering them unsafe as well as a serious threat to the native bird population.

Jimmy Hikorea, who had readily agreed to join the proposed outing, grinned from ear to ear. He introduced Navy Specialist John Carter above a deafening roar as the chopper leapt into the air. The machine turned south, skimmed across the saddle between the Maui mountains, flew almost directly over the Waterfront restaurant, and left the coastline, heading toward Kahoʻolawe.

As they approached the center of the low-lying island, huge arrow patterns of white stones pointed toward the central target area formerly used by US warplanes. Acres of barren, eroded red earth marked the impact area where thousands of warheads had exploded and countless duds waited like time bombs. Within this wasteland lay the Puʻu Moiwi quarry, damaged by explosives and the ravages of time. As they neared the quarry, Koa saw a makeshift landing zone laid out on the hillside, where four seamen were waiting for them. Admiral Cunningham had pulled out all the stops. Koa hoped that the effort wasn't going to be wasted.

After landing downslope from the quarry and unloading Jimmy's wheelchair, Koa, Jimmy, Specialist Carter, and the four seamen gathered for a conference. "I appreciate your help," Koa began. "We're here to find a cave, one recently opened by three trespassers. The intruders used seismic technology to locate the cave. We should find multiple lines of holes from data recorders and the remains of several small explosive charges. If we can find that stuff, we can probably locate the cave. I don't need to tell you to be careful. There is unexploded ordnance all around us."

"We have metal detectors," Specialist Carter responded. "They'll slow the search work, but no one is to move an inch outside the area we sweep. What kind of search pattern do you want us to use?"

Koa had no idea how far east of the quarry the cave might lie. He did, however, know that Jenkins had laid out parallel lines of sensors about three hundred yards long. He planned to send out teams on radial lines along the eastern slope below the quarry, looking for evidence of disturbed ground. He explained his thinking and asked for suggestions.

"You might be able to see something from the air," the chopper pilot, who'd been standing off to the side, volunteered. "The HH-65 is auto-stabilized for search operations. I could run a pattern east of the quarry. An observer with binoculars might be able to spot what you're looking for."

Jimmy volunteered for the job. "I'm useless on the ground, but I can sit in the chopper and my eyes are sharp."

"Great, go for it," Koa encouraged him.

The pilot helped Jimmy into the copilot's seat, Specialist Carter handed out radios, and the seamen started searching. Soon the chopper was hovering in the air, zigzagging back and forth east of the quarry. Over the next hour, the hello spiraled slowly outward with remarkable precision while the ground searches moved farther east.

"Koa!" Jimmy's shrill radio call sounded excited. The second call came simultaneously. "Detective Kāne, this is search team two." Both the chopper and search team two were off to the south along the ridgeline that formed the backbone of Kahoʻolawe. The search team had found the remnant of one of the explosive charges, and Jimmy had spotted several points, in a line perpendicular to the ridgeline, where the earth had recently been disturbed.

Koa called in the other search teams, and they moved their base of operations to the ridgeline. He pointed to a large round boulder in the midst of an area chewed up by the Navy's target practice. "That rock will be the center of the search area. Let's see if we can find the other peg lines and the cave."

Over the course of the next two hours, the search teams carefully swept the ground for unexploded ordnance. They found four more lines of peg holes parallel to the first line, but no cave. The burning sun rose high in the sky, and the search teams grew tired and frustrated before Koa called them together for a break.

"According to Reggie," Koa advised them, "they had a map showing the peg lines and two possible cave locations. They rolled some kind of device over the possible locations, identified something of interest, started digging, and found the cave. We've been over every inch of ground inside the peg lines, and we've found no indication of digging and no cave. What are we missing?"

"Maybe the cave is outside the peg lines," one of the seamen suggested.

"Maybe," Koa responded, "but if the pegs were seismic recorders, and I think they were, they record energy reflected from layers in the ground. I don't think they would record much outside the pattern of pegs."

"Maybe," a voice squeaked, "we're standing on top of the cave."

The men turned in unison toward Jimmy. The archaeologist, who was sitting in his wheelchair, had fixed his gaze off to his left. The men turned to follow his gaze, but saw only the hillside that they'd been combing for the last two hours.

Koa struggled to keep the irritation out of his voice. "Come on, Jimmy. This is no time for riddles."

The archaeologist seemed unperturbed. Slowly, he raised his arm, extended a finger, and pointed toward the boulder that marked their starting point. Once again, the men looked out on the ground they'd already covered.

Then Koa saw it. "The boulder. They covered the entrance with the boulder!"

"Dead-on, Detective," Jimmy squeaked with a smile.

In that instant Koa knew his instinct to bring Jimmy had been correct. The former marine had an uncanny sixth sense for archaeological sites.

The heaviest of the seamen put a shoulder to the boulder, but pushed without success. "Give me a hand," he urged. The other three seamen jumped to his aid, and the four of them rolled the boulder far enough to reveal a man-sized hole.

"Son of a bitch," Specialist Carter swore, "we walked right past it twenty times."

"Dead-on, Specialist. It's always hardest to find a thing in plain sight." Jimmy grinned.

Using a rope from the helicopter, the seamen lowered Koa down into the hole. He'd repelled out of helicopters and climbed ropes in the military, but this time he had the sailors lower him carefully to minimize the pain in his neck and shoulder. His powerful electric light revealed striated layers of rock as he descended. Five feet down, the shaft widened into an underground cavern. The cave floor was still ten feet below. There, he spotted something sitting in what seemed like a pile. Pieces of wood, something curved . . . a collapsed rope ladder. Down they lowered him, until he was standing next to it.

At Koa's direction, the seamen lowered Jimmy and his cushion down the shaft into the mine. Together they surveyed their surroundings using Koa's beam of light. A metallic sheen caught Koa's eye, and he steadied the light on a contraption resembling a lawn mower. There was no doubt now. They had found the trespassers' cave. Beyond the contraption huge patches of the cave wall glistened, as though they were wet.

"Obsidian, pitchstone, volcanic glass," Jimmy said, identifying the thick, shiny black vein. The cave had been dug following the vein, which ran along the wall thirty feet from where they stood. Ancient miners had hacked into the obsidian, leaving pits chipped in the wall. Jagged chunks of black glass lay in piles on the floor, half-buried in dust.

"What's this thing that they used to find this place?" Koa asked, stepping over to the lawn-mower-shaped machine. Jimmy hopped after him. "Don't touch it until we can get it dusted for prints," Koa warned.

Jimmy peered at the contraption, which bore the logo "Pathfinder GPR." "GPR . . . GPR," Jimmy repeated the letters. "Ground Penetration Radar. It's used in mineral exploration, and I've seen articles about archaeological uses, but I didn't know they made portable units. Pretty nifty, and since they found this place, it must work."

"So they used seismic testing to get the general lay of the land and then ground penetration radar to find the exact location," Koa said.

"Dead-on, Detective."

"Wow!" Koa exclaimed. "This is a sophisticated operation. There's got to be real money behind it."

"This little techno-jobby must have cost several grand, and more for the software. I mean, the software would have to be state of the art to locate a cavern in the middle of a barren ridgeline."

That meant the machine was relatively rare. "I wonder if we could trace it."

"It's got to have a serial number." Jimmy started to reach for the machine.

"Don't." Koa stopped him. "I want to bag it and take it back to the lab."

Specialist Carter lowered plastic sheeting, and Koa laid it over the machine before tilting it back on its handle. When he moved to fit the plastic around the bottom of the device, he saw a large black canvas backpack concealed underneath. It had to be one of Jenkins's backpacks, Koa thought, eager to see what was inside.

"Hold the light," he instructed Jimmy as he slipped on a pair of evidence gloves and opened the zipper. He pulled out an object wrapped in heavy cloth and slowly peeled away the protective covering. His efforts revealed a thin, gleaming black object pointed at one end. Koa didn't need an archaeologist to identify an obsidian knife blade.

"Wow," Jimmy squeaked, "look at the workmanship. I've never seen anything like that in the islands."

Jimmy's exclamations continued as Koa carefully removed and unwrapped three small polished black figurines of a seated god with a wide mouth and a tall headdress. "They're beautiful, absolutely beautiful," Koa said in rapt appreciation.

"And worth a fortune on the black market."

That reminded Koa of another part of the tale, and he began methodically scanning the space with the electric torch.

"Missing something?" Jimmy asked.

"Yes, according to Reggie Hao, they found a big god statue, roughly a foot tall and polished until it glistened."

"I'd love to see that," Jimmy responded.

"So would I, so would I," Koa murmured, not finding the relic. "That and the second backpack that Jenkins was carrying. He must have taken it with him. We'll have to get a search warrant for his place on the Big Island."

CHAPTER TWENTY-THREE

KOA AND BAXTER sat on opposite sides of Maui County prosecutor Iwikua Oliwa's conference table. Zeke Brown, the Hawai'i County prosecutor, was participating by phone. A burly man with an easy smile, Iwikua presided from the head of the table. His family, originally from Poland, had come to Hawai'i to work on irrigation systems for the sugar plantations in the 1800s. He had a reputation as a tough, but fair, prosecutor.

"Okay, gentlemen," Iwikua began, "Lieutenant Baxter has proposed that this office prosecute three men—Aikue 'Ōpua, Reggie Hao, and Garvie Jenkins—for trespassing on Kaho'olawe. The charge is a misdemeanor, which carries a maximum one-year jail sentence."

"It's a straightforward case based on solid evidence," Baxter added helpfully.

"However," Iwikua said, ignoring the interruption, "we have a rather unusual proffer from Bernie Ponabi, Reggie Hao's attorney. In exchange for immunity, he would testify that although he and the others trespassed on Kaho'olawe and used some sophisticated equipment to locate valuable Hawaiian artifacts, he committed this violation to secure archaeological treasures for posterity. He would also testify—and this is the interesting part—that when he learned that Garvie Jenkins planned to sell artifacts for profit, he tried to stop Jenkins. Jenkins pulled a knife. Hao ran for his life, but Jenkins chased him into a target area, where a dud exploded, injuring Hao. Other evidence would further suggest that 'Ōpua assisted in the rescue of Hao, but that Jenkins fled." All of them realized how this version of events changed the stakes.

"If this proffer of testimony were corroborated, Jenkins could be prosecuted for attempted looting and assault in addition to trespass. Those are serious crimes, felonies, for which we would need Hao's testimony."

"Yeah, but the proffered testimony is bullshit. Hao's lawyer," Baxter's inflection showed his disdain for lawyers, "says that Hao remembers what happened out there. He didn't remember shit when I interviewed him. His lawyer says they used sophisticated equipment. We didn't find no sophisticated equipment. Did it disappear in thin air? His lawyer says they found a cave. We ain't seen no cave. He says they found priceless treasures. We found a bunch of fishhooks and junk in a backpack. It's all just fuckin' bullshit."

"You think Hao fabricated this story?" Iwikua asked, allowing him his say.

"Damn straight, he fabricated it. Must think we're a bunch of idiots. Let's just nail the three of them for trespassing."

Iwikua held up his hand. "Whoa. It may not be so easy to convict 'Ōpua. Do you know his history?"

"You mean, like he's a big fuckin' native Hawaiian activist?"

"'Ōpua was one of the Kaho'olawe Nine, one of the nine Hawaiian men who occupied Kaho'olawe in 1976 while the Navy was still bombing. A historic event—Hawai'i's version of the sit-ins during the civil rights marches. Many Hawaiians regard 'Ōpua as a hero. And besides, he apparently saved Hao's life."

"He broke the fucking law by going out there without a permit. An' Hao got hurt 'cause he was trespassing. You can't let 'Ōpua off because he did the same thing thirty-plus years ago. He's a goddamn recidivist!"

Once again Iwikua held up a hand. "Detective Kāne, you haven't said a word. What is your take on this?"

Koa spoke slowly in a controlled voice, deliberately distinguishing his tone from Baxter's over-the-top bravado. "First, there are two investigations, not just one. We're investigating a murder and an archaeological looting on the Big Island. Evidence found there suggests that looters located the Pōhakuloa cave using seismic testing. When I first heard that a similar technique might have been used on Kahoʻolawe, I thought there might be a connection. I secured Admiral Cunningham's help to search the Puʻu Moiwi site." Baxter's head shot up, but Koa pretended not to notice. "What we found plainly proves that my hunch was right. There is a clear connection between the looting on Kahoʻolawe and at Pōhakuloa, and that looting may well be related to the murder. Let me explain.

"There is an obsidian mine near Puʻu Moiwi. The trespassers used seismic and ground penetration radar to locate it. We found their equipment, a portable ground penetration radar machine, in the mine. Although we have to do some more checking, I believe the equipment came from the Big Island and was used near our Pōhakuloa murder site. We also found valuable obsidian artifacts in a black backpack that matched Hao's description of Garvie's backpack. So there is plenty of corroboration for Hao's story."

"You sorry son of a bitch." Baxter mouthed the words so that only Koa heard them.

"Well, gentlemen," Iwikua began, "that does change the picture."

"Yes, and there's more." Zeke Brown's rich baritone voice boomed from the speakerphone. "As you know, Jenkins has a criminal record. We convicted him of selling forged maps to wealthy tourists. Based on his criminal record, evidence of seismic testing on Mauna

Kea and Kaho'olawe, the looting at Pōhakuloa, and the Kaho'olawe trespassing, we got a search warrant for his home, telephone records, and bank accounts."

"What did you find?" Brown had captured Iwikua's undivided attention.

"Some interesting stuff." The voice from the speakerphone blasted so loudly that Iwikua turned the volume down. "We found a black backpack with wrapping materials similar to those found in the cave on Kaho'olawe. And most significantly, we found unexplained cash deposits to Jenkins's bank account. We're talking more than a quarter million dollars. We're in the process of tracking the deposits, but I'm guessing that many, maybe even most of them, came from sales of the looted items. Jenkins could even be our murderer."

Iwikua whistled softly. "We just entered major crimes territory. Jenkins might give us a window into the archaeological black market."

"That's exactly what I think," the telephone voice shouted. "There is another possible link as well. We didn't find any expenditure for the ground penetration radar device. The machine that Detective Kāne found in the obsidian cave runs at least twenty grand. If Garvie didn't buy it, then he had an accomplice."

"With all this evidence, we don't need Hao's testimony." Baxter glared at Koa as he spoke. "We can take Hao down on the trespassing rap and still go after Jenkins on the more serious charges."

Iwikua held up his hand. "I don't think so. True, we have a lot of evidence against Jenkins, but Jenkins has hired a top-flight lawyer. Wheeler may be an arrogant bastard, but he's the best trial lawyer in the islands. We need a live witness to lay things out for the jury. And with his attempt to stop Jenkins and his injury, a jury will sympathize with Hao."

"You need him more than you think." They turned to listen to Koa. "According to Hao's proffer, they used the machine to find the cave, but set it aside when they began digging. When the dispute erupted, Jenkins chased Hao until the dud exploded. The machine should have been on open ground beside the shaft they dug." Koa tied the ends together with a logical conclusion.

"When we got out there, we found the machine and a backpack containing the artifacts hidden inside the carefully concealed cave. Garvie hid the machine and sealed the cave while Hao was unconscious."

"Hmmm," Iwikua thought for a moment. "Are you suggesting that the assault, the chase, the injury, the hiding, and Garvie's flight might add up to an attempted murder charge?"

"Yes, and you need Hao's testimony to make that case. You might also offer 'Ōpua immunity for his testimony. He can tell you what happened while Hao was unconscious."

"Shit," Baxter interrupted in an angry tone, "you just want to spring your friend Reggie Hao out of a trespass rap. You haven't owned up that Hook Hao's your buddy."

"Enough," roared the speakerphone, "I will *not* have you impugning Detective Kāne's integrity!"

Iwikua's hand shot up. "Gentlemen, gentlemen. Please." When he'd given tempers a few moments to cool, he went on. "On the one hand, we've got trespassing, which is a minor offense and one that is hard to prosecute against native activists. On the other hand, we've got serious criminal offenses—looting of antiquities, assault with intent to do bodily harm, and perhaps even attempted murder by a known felon. Moreover, by focusing on Jenkins, we'll be helping the Hawai'i County police, who've helped us in the past. Following up on Jenkins may even lead to the murderer." By now everyone knew which way he was going to decide.

"This office needs to focus on serious crimes and known criminals. This office will work out an immunity deal with Hao's attorney.

After we interview him, we will revisit the question of ʻŌpua. We'll get our stones lined up, and then we'll see whether Wheeler wants to fight or play nice. That's my decision, gentlemen."

Koa resisted the temptation to smile as Baxter stormed out. Instead he focused on the next step, and it involved Jenkins. Given the similarities, Jenkins had to be in on the Pōhakuloa looting, and that meant he might be the killer, or at least might provide a break in the Pōhakuloa murder case.

CHAPTER TWENTY-FOUR

THE NEXT DAY Nālani took Koa to a special cocktail party at the Alice headquarters, where Director Masters planned to recognize all those staff members who had assisted in his big discovery. Gunter Nelson attended, as did a noticeably subdued Charlie Harper. Dr. Masters greeted Nālani at the door and thanked her for her aid to Dr. Schlingler in verifying his discovery. He personally welcomed and expressed his appreciation to each of the other guests as they arrived.

When all the astronomers and technicians had assembled with champagne glasses, opera music filled the room, a spotlight snapped on, and Cepheid minced into the center of the room. The robot tapped its champagne glass with its other claw, and the chatter of the guests died down.

"I have come," the robot said, using its godlike voice, "at the behest of the Alice Foundation, that faraway body that funds much of our research, to express the trustees' thanks for your loyalty and devotion to our mission. Without your support, Dr. Masters' momentous discovery, which has brought great honor to the foundation, wouldn't have been possible. The trustees salute and honor you." The robot raised a claw to its forehead and snapped off a sharp salute. Laughter rippled through the group.

Conversation erupted as Cepheid marched out. Masters' guests radiated good humor. "He's clever," Koa said softly to Nālani. "Just think of the goodwill he's won tonight."

"Well, I'm happy," Nālani smiled.

Koa wandered across the room to where Gunter Nelson stood alone watching the other guests. "Good evening, Gunter," Koa began, "you hear about our discovery?"

"No." Gunter looked puzzled.

"We found an adze makers' workshop and graves near Keneke's body out at Pōhakuloa."

For an instant Gunter looked like a rat caught in the beam of a flashlight. Then he recovered. "Really?"

"Yeah, unfortunately, grave robbers got there ahead of us."

Again, Koa thought he had caught Gunter off guard. "You're kidding."

"Keneke ever say anything to you about archaeological sites out at Pōhakuloa?"

"Like I said, Detective, I don't remember talking to Keneke about Pōhakuloa."

Well, Koa thought as he walked away, I gave him a second chance.

Before Koa left with Nālani, Director Masters drew him aside. "Any progress on the investigation, Detective?"

"Some, but we don't have a suspect."

"My people giving you their full cooperation?"

"Yes, at least from my perspective."

As they left, Julie Benson gave each of the honored guests a small tote bag emblazoned with the Alice logo. Inside her bag, Nālani found a plaque inscribed with a letter of appreciation from the CEO of the Alice Foundation. Nālani was one of those people for whom respect and appreciation mattered almost as much as money, and she was thrilled.

When they arrived home that evening, Koa had an answering machine message from Zeke Brown, the Hawai'i County prosecutor. When Koa returned the call, Zeke answered on the first ring. "Zeke Brown," the prosecutor's voice boomed through the handset, which Koa quickly pulled away from his ear.

"Hey, Zeke, it's Koa. You looking for me?"

"Yeah, sorry to bother you at home, but the duty sergeant said you'd split. Got a minute?"

"Sure, what's up?"

"I wanted to bring you up the curve on this Kaho'olawe obsidian thing. You know we found cash deposits to Jenkins's bank account, a whole bunch of them, ranging from $7,000 to $9,000 and totaling a whopping two hundred and sixty-two grand."

Koa couldn't believe that number. It pointed to some kind of organized crime ring. "You figure out where Jenkins got that kind of cash?"

"Not yet, but we may be closing in on it. First, we've got the time frame."

"What's that?"

"Last two and a half months, and there are multiple deposits on some days, like he was trying to avoid the Treasury cash-reporting rules."

"But no indication where he got the money?"

"Not from his financial records or from the bank."

Brown was jerking his chain a little. "Don't make me pry it out of you."

"We got his phone records. He didn't make many calls, except there are a couple dozen calls, all to the same number, starting about twelve weeks ago."

"Now that's interesting. Whose number?"

"It's a bar in Hilo, a place called the Monarch."

"The Monarch?" An image of the bar popped into Koa's mind. "That joint hasn't seen a coat of paint in the past half century. Maybe Jenkins is into the drug trade. It's that kind of establishment."

"I've got no idea, but I thought you might want to check it out. Oh, and one other thing."

"What's that?"

"We traced the serial number on that GPR machine. Manufactured in Texas. Cost forty grand. They're checking their records to see who bought it."

"Great, let me know when they ID the buyer."

"I will. Call me if you learn anything at the Monarch."

"You got it."

The Monarch had a good crowd when Koa walked in a little after ten. The odor of stale beer and cigarette smoke hung heavy in the air. A classic Wurlitzer jukebox pulsed neon colors as it filled the room with Peter, Paul and Mary's "Blowin' in the Wind." Koa hadn't heard that one in a long time.

Judging from the frayed clothing and work boots on the thirty or so patrons, Koa figured them to be stevedores, forklift operators, and cargo handlers from the nearby port. Most were beer drinkers, but a few guarded shot glasses. They were mostly spread out in ones and twos at separate tables, but five rough-looking men with weather-beaten faces and sunburned arms, and a rougher-looking woman with heavy wrinkles and what appeared to Koa to be skin cancer, had a poker game going at one of the large round tables. They announced their bets loudly and swore like sailors when the cards disappointed them.

Koa scanned the room as he moved slowly toward the bar. He recognized Drake, the bartender, but the patrons were strangers. He saw no pay phone and no phone visible on the bar or the wall behind the bar.

A large, ratty black cat slept on the bar, oblivious to the noise. It looked to be infested with fleas. Koa eased up to the other end of the bar, watching while Drake filled a half-dozen beer mugs that looked none too clean and carried them to the poker players. A cockroach scampered across the bar, not far from the sleeping cat. Koa wondered how many years had passed since the last health inspection.

"What'll ya have, my man?" Drake turned toward the detective. He was in his late sixties. Yellowish white hair hung almost shoulder length in tangles. His gray eyes had a dull, glazed quality that made Koa think of untreated cataracts. His black T-shirt displayed beer stains that even the color couldn't hide.

"A draft and some information." Koa laid his police identification on the bar.

"Ah, shit."

"You don't like the police?"

"Cops ain't good foah business, my man."

"You give me what I need and I'll be gone."

Drake moved to the tap, picked up an unwashed mug, drew a beer until the head overflowed, and slid it down the bar to Koa. "You gonna run a tab?"

Koa ignored the stupid question. "You got a phone under the bar?"

"Huh?"

"You got a phone, a telephone, under the bar?"

"Huh, you need a phone. County forgit to pay its fuckin' phone bill?" Drake laughed nervously. "Yeah. I got a phone." He reached under the bar and lifted an old black telephone, the kind with a rotary dial, onto the bar. Koa examined the circle in the middle of the dial, but couldn't read the telephone number through the encrusted grime.

"This telephone have a number, Drake?"

The barkeep seemed surprised that Koa had used his name. "You bin in here 'fore?"

"What's the telephone number?"

"327-6867." The number matched the one that Jenkins had called over a dozen times.

"Who uses this phone?"

"Me, I use it foah supplies and stuff."

"Anyone else?"

The crow's-feet at the corners of Drake's eyes crinkled ever so slightly. "Customers might use it sometimes."

"You get calls from Garvie Jenkins?"

"Nevah heard of no Garvie Jenkins."

That's what Koa expected him to say. He pulled out a faxed photograph of Garvie Jenkins. "Recognize this man?"

"Nah."

Koa always found it useful to have something to hold over a witness, and the Monarch was a gold mine of leverage. "Let me see if maybe I can jog your memory, Drake. Suppose I get the health department in here. What do you think they'd say about the cockroaches and that ratty black beast on the bar? And what do you suppose the licensing bureau would do about the gambling over at that poker table?" Koa nodded at the poker players. "And you know what? Maybe you'd like to lock up and come down to the station to help you concentrate on my questions."

"Aww, shit. I knew ya was gonna hassle me."

"Maybe if you'd answer my questions, I might overlook the roaches and the unwashed dishes you got behind the bar." Koa tipped his head toward the stacks of unwashed mugs and shot glasses.

Drake picked up the picture of Garvie Jenkins. "I swear on my mother's grave, I ain't seen this here dude, least I ain't got no memory of it."

"But one of your customers got a bunch of calls on this phone, starting back in October." Koa saw a dim light dawn in Drake's dull eyes. The man knew something.

"Might've been a customer." The same evasive drawl.

"This customer have a name?"

"Sure he must got hisself a name, 'cept I ain't got no memory of it."

Koa started to drum the top of the bar, one slow, loud tap at a time. "What's he look like, this mister no name?"

"Little guy, greasy hair. Wears dem tourist shirts from Hattie's."

Koa broke off the tapping. "Look, Drake, we can do this two ways. Either you give me what I need, or you deal with the boys downtown tonight and the health department and the licensing bureau guys tomorrow. It's your choice."

The bartender was looking a lot older and a lot paler. "Okay, okay. There's a dude. I swear on my mother's grave I ain't got no memory of 'is name, but he's in here a few times. Okay, more than a few times. He's in here. He gets calls."

"And you answer the phone when it rings?"

"Yeah, most times I do. I answer it."

"And so how do you know the call is for this dude . . . this dude in the Hilo Hattie shirts?"

Again, Koa detected the slightest brightening in Drake's glassy eyes.

"Oh. The caller, he asks for the fuckin' private eye. He always asks for the fuckin' private eye."

"Then what happens?"

Drake was getting upset, realizing that he'd been used by one of his customers. "Shit, man. He's bin sitting at the bar, so I jus' shove the fuckin' phone in his ugly face."

"What's he say?"

"How am I supposed to know that?"

"Well, you're standing right there, you shove the phone in his face. You got ears. What does he say?"

"Hey man, I got a bar to keep. I ain't got time to listen to some toadie in an *aloha* shirt talkin' story on the fuckin' phone."

Koa wasn't buying that line for a second. "How many health and safety violations you think the inspectors could find in here, Drake? A hundred, maybe? Two hundred? At five hundred bucks a pop, that's somewhere between fifty and a hundred grand. You got that kind of bread, Drake?"

"Shit, I don't know." The bartender wrestled with his conscience, but Koa had made his way crystal clear.

"'Gar'—nah, that's not right. 'Garv' . . . 'Hi, Garv.' Something sorta like that, best as I kin recall."

"That's good, Drake. Maybe I won't need to call the health department." Koa held out a carrot. "Tell me about the conversation?"

"What fuckin' conversation?"

"The conversation that's going to keep your bar open."

"Shit, I ain't got no memory . . . the box . . . PI kept saying he got the box. Yeah, the box . . . like he owed Garv something, some kinda thing in a box. I don't know, man, somethin' like that."

"What else did they talk about, Drake? Think on it, man . . . think hard."

"I ain't . . . the pod. I heard private eye ask 'bout the pod. 'Does she . . . does the fuckin' pod tell you anything,' like the pod was talking."

Suddenly, a patron at the poker table yelled, "Drake, you sorry son of a bitch, git me another motherfuckin' beer."

"I got customers. I got a bar to keep . . ."

"Go on, Drake. I'll wait while you take care of the customers," Koa reassured him. "I just have a few more questions."

Koa waited while Drake served more beer in unwashed mugs. He hadn't touched the draft still waiting at his elbow. With any luck he might catch a new strain of hepatitis in this joint.

When Drake returned, Koa asked, "So Garv and the private eye talked about some kind of pod?"

"Yeah."

"Okay, when the PI came in here, was anyone else with him?" Again, Koa thought he saw a flicker in the old man's eyes. "Who? Who'd he talk to, Drake?"

The old man looked defeated. "Jus' that chopper fellow, Skeeter." He winced as he gave out the name. "He flies them rich tourists over the national park."

"What's this Skeeter's last name?"

"Ain't nevah asked 'is last name."

Koa could believe that. "What did they talk about, Skeeter and the PI?"

"Dunno. They sat by theirselves in the far corner. Nevah did hear them talking, but . . ."

"But what, Drake?"

The bartender instantly pulled back. "Nothing."

"Bullshit, Drake. You heard something or saw something. What was it?"

"Okay, okay. I saw the chopper dude giving something, some kinda box, a black box 'bout the size of one of dem movie tapes. Givin' it to the fuckin' private-eye dude."

"Okay. Just a couple more questions. What did the PI fellow and Skeeter drink?"

Drake brightened, obviously happy to be on a familiar subject. "Scotch, Cutty Sark. The two of them can kill a whole bottle of Cutty Sark."

"Who buys?"

"Skeeter runs a tab, but sometimes . . . sometimes the fuckin' private eye buys, though he bitches 'bout it. Hell, Cutty Sark ain't cheap."

"And how does private eye pay for it?"

"Mostly cash."

"Mostly, meaning sometimes he used a credit card?"

"Maybe, maybe a time or two."

"You got the credit card slips?"

The old man sighed. "Shit, man, I got a whole pile of that crap in the back."

"Okay, Drake. I'm done for now, but in the morning, you're going to meet Sergeant Basa and help him find those credit card slips. You understand?"

"And you ain't gonna call the health department?"

"Not if you and Sergeant Basa find those credit card slips."

* * *

When Basa finally returned to the police station the next morning, he found Koa just getting up from the floor of his office. "You suffer from insomnia last night, boss?"

Embarrassed, Koa decided to fess up. "No, my friend, I've got a pinched nerve in my neck. Lying on the floor helps control the pain."

Basa's face showed genuine concern. "Ah, so that's the problem. I thought something might be wrong from the way you've been moving. You seeing a doctor?"

"Yeah. Looks like I'm going to have to go under the knife. But keep that to yourself for now."

"Jesus, I'm sorry, Koa. Let me know if there's anything I can do."

"Thanks." Koa forced a smile. "The doc says I'll be stronger, faster, and better looking after the surgery."

"He better be some kind of doctor."

Koa turned to business. "Tell me about your new friend at the Monarch."

"My God, that place is filthy. It's infested with roaches. We ought to get the health department in there before he starts an epidemic."

"I promised we wouldn't bring the law down on him if he cooperated."

"Cooperated!" Basa snorted. "That son of a bitch is too dumb to cooperate. He's lost his driveshaft, and his carburetor is sucking air."

"But you got the private-eye dude's name?"

Basa made a mournful face. "Yeah, after two hours going through a crate full of credit card slips and mouse droppings. You owe me big time for this one, Koa."

Koa grinned. "Okay, Basa, I owe you. I owe you big time. Who's the dude?"

"You remember Ricky Kling?" Basa asked.

An image of Kling wearing a cheap tourist shirt flashed into Koa's mind. Years ago, Koa had caught Kling extorting a married man who'd visited a prostitute. The sleazy private eye had escaped jail only by giving up his private investigator's license. "Jesus, that creep? We pulled his ticket years ago. Was he the private-eye dude on the phone with Jenkins?"

"He fits Drake's description, if you can call 'a little guy with greasy hair and tourist shirts' a description, and he used his credit card in the Monarch on two of the days when Jenkins called."

"And he's just the sort of lowlife who'd hang with a convicted felon like Jenkins," Koa added, happy with the way this was falling together. "How about Skeeter? Does the FAA have a line on a helicopter pilot by that name?"

"Skeeter Slade owns Fantastic Air Tours. One of those Kohala tourist sightseeing outfits."

"I wonder what Garvie Jenkins and Skeeter Slade have in common," Koa mused.

"You think it's something more than an acquaintance with Ricky Kling?" Basa asked.

"I'll bet you a *malasada* there's more. Have we got an address for Kling?"

"Yeah, a rental apartment on Hoku, around the corner from the Monarch. You want me to bring him in?" Koa thought about their odds. "We don't have enough for a warrant and Kling isn't the co-operative type. No, I'd like to talk to Mr. Skeeter Slade. You have an address for him?"

"I've got something better than an address." Basa grinned, obviously proud of his sleuthing. "I got his flight plan. He's flying tourists over the volcano and lands out at the airport about noon."

CHAPTER TWENTY-FIVE

A FEW HOURS later Koa and Sergeant Basa stood on the observation deck of the Hilo airport as Skeeter's Fantastic Air Tours chopper circled away from the active runway and settled onto a landing pad. Skeeter Slade climbed out of the cockpit and opened the side door for his passengers. A couple with four children emerged and followed Skeeter across the tarmac to the Fantastic Air Tours office.

Koa and Sergeant Basa were about to walk down to confront Skeeter when they saw him come back out of the office and head back toward his helicopter. Reaching the machine, Skeeter looked around before dropping to the ground to slide between the skids under the belly of the whirlybird.

"What's he doing?" Basa asked.

"I can't see. Maybe he's checking something or performing maintenance," Koa responded. Yet he was hoping that the pilot was doing nothing of the sort.

Skeeter pulled himself from beneath the chopper, emerging with a black box the size of a videotape cassette. Once again, Skeeter looked around before strolling back across the airport apron. Instead of returning to the office, he skirted the side of the building and headed toward a security gate leading to the employee parking lot.

"He's going for a drive," Basa said. "I'll go grab him."

"Tail him instead, and let me know where he goes. I'm going to have a look at that helicopter."

While Sergeant Basa followed Skeeter, Koa secured access to the tarmac and walked out to the whirlybird. He gently lowered himself to the ground and, holding his neck, squirmed his way beneath the machine just as Skeeter had. He spotted an electronics pod installed on the chopper's belly. So here, he thought, is the pod Drake overheard Kling talking about. The front part of the pod appeared to have hinged access doors, like small versions of the doors covering the landing gear on an airplane, but Koa couldn't see any way of opening those panels. Toward the rear of the pod, four small latches held another access panel in place.

Cautiously, Koa released the four latches and swung the panel open, revealing what appeared to be a data recorder with an empty slot. It must have contained the cassette Skeeter had carried away. Koa replaced the panel and crawled out from under the machine.

His cell phone buzzed as he walked back to the terminal building. Basa spoke in an excited voice. "He's headed toward the Monarch."

"Watch from outside. Keep track of who goes in and out. I'll be there in fifteen minutes." Koa rang off quickly and called the Monarch's bar phone.

"Monarch bar," Drake answered.

"It's Detective Kāne. Skeeter's coming into the bar. If you don't want to do that health department tango, you won't let on that we talked. Understand, Drake?"

"Yeah, man, I got the picture."

Koa caught a taxi and minutes later joined Basa across the street from the Monarch. "Guess who's in there with Skeeter?" Basa grinned.

"Ricky Kling, the private eye in the Hilo Hattie shirt?"

"Bull's-eye. Your buddy Ricky Kling arrived about five minutes after Skeeter."

"He's gonna be my buddy sooner than he'd like."

They waited twenty minutes before Kling emerged from the Monarch carrying a black box. He walked up the street and turned the corner toward his apartment.

"Let's go meet Mr. Slade." Koa reviewed what he'd learned from Basa about the helicopter pilot as he led the way into the Monarch. Skeeter Slade had been a medevac pilot in Iraq, and like many former military chopper pilots had started his own tourist business after mustering out. Basa had also discovered that Skeeter had filed a police complaint after vandals had damaged one of his choppers, but the responding officer hadn't done much.

They crossed the room toward a table in the rear corner, where Skeeter sat with his back to the wall, eyeing a half-full bottle of Cutty Sark and a half-empty shot glass. Koa had been at the scene of a number of helicopter crashes and didn't like seeing this pilot hit the bottle.

"Mr. Skeeter Slade?" Koa asked.

"Who the fuck wants to know?"

It was the wrong way to start. Koa had been prepared to go easy on the former military pilot, but Skeeter's hostility was quickly going to make him change his approach. "Detective Kāne and Sergeant Basa, Hawai'i County Police."

"Is this about the fuckin' vandals?"

"We want to ask you some questions," Koa responded nicely, still hoping to do this the easy way.

"I ain't got time foah questions. I gotta git back to the airport. I got customers."

That was the last straw. There was no way Koa was going to let this drinker get back in the cockpit after multiple shots of scotch. "Mr. Slade, we're taking you into custody and down to the police station."

"What the fuck—"

Koa read the man his Miranda rights.

"You rotten, no-good fuckers. I want my attorney."

"You can call your attorney as soon as Sergeant Basa completes a Breathalyzer test." Koa smiled as the light dawned in Skeeter's eyes.

"Oh, shit," was all that he could manage.

Koa and Basa took him to the police station and stashed him in an interrogation room. An hour later, after getting test results showing blood alcohol way over the limit, Koa walked back in to confront him. A long wait in an isolated room typically annoyed suspects, and Skeeter was no exception.

"I thought you said I could call my lawyer," Skeeter challenged.

Koa eyed the pilot. His bloodshot eyes and red face confirmed the Breathalyzer test. The man was a serious drinker. Yellowing in the whites of his eyes likely meant liver damage. Koa still felt an urge to help the former military pilot, but not if it put innocent tourists at risk. "You can call a lawyer, but maybe you might want to hear me out before you run off half-cocked," Koa responded. People in an interrogation room, especially after waiting alone for a while, wanted out, and if you could give them a path, they were often surprisingly cooperative.

Some of the hostility disappeared from Skeeter's face, leaving him with an almost pathetic look. "Go on."

"I talked to the FAA. There are two ways to handle this. We can book you for flying under the influence, in which case the FAA will start license revocation proceedings and you'll be out of business."

"Or?" Slade asked suspiciously.

"You can give us the information we want, and if you weren't involved in criminal activity, we can let you voluntarily check yourself into the FAA's alcohol rehabilitation program. If you're dry for thirty days, they'll lift the suspension and you can go back to flying with periodic sobriety checks."

Skeeter was looking a lot more attentive. "What'd you want to know?"

"We want to know about your dealings with Kling and Jenkins."

"This ain't about the vandals?" A puzzled look came over Skeeter's face.

"It's about Kling and Jenkins."

"I nevah heard of Jenkins."

"Then it's about Kling."

"And if I tell you about Kling, you won't charge me?"

"We won't charge you with operating an aircraft while under the influence so long as you check into the FAA program. If you've done something else, we'll have to evaluate that separately."

"I ain't done nothing illegal with Kling."

"We'll be the judge of that."

Skeeter still looked confused, but finally he gave in. "Okay. It's really pretty simple. Kling approached me last year. Wanted me to mount some equipment on my chopper and take readings on flights across the island. Paid me $300 for each trip."

"You did it for the money?"

Skeeter suddenly looked like a schoolkid caught with dirty pictures. "It wasn't just the money."

"What then?"

"Kling knew I'd cheated on my wife . . . he had pictures."

Koa felt more sympathy for Skeeter and a flash of anger at Kling. Kling was a recidivist, continuing to use the same MO that had cost him his license. Koa would deal with Mr. Kling shortly. Maybe this time he'd be able to put the little snake behind bars.

"Tell me about the equipment?"

"It's an electronics pod that Kling provided. I wasn't supposed to open the sealed unit, but I had a little look-see—wide-angle camera, magnetometer, and ground penetration radar. Takes readings every few seconds and records the readings on a data cassette. I delivered the cassettes. Kling paid me. Simple."

"What did Kling do with the data?"

"He never said, but I figured they was looking for something out at Pōhakuloa."

Koa's heart rate jumped. "On the Army's Pōhakuloa Training Area?"

"Yeah, Kling had me flying parallel runs across the saddle land, recording while I was over the PTA. Parallel lines like a fuckin' search pattern."

"How did you know what lines to fly?"

"Kling gave me a fuckin' map with GPS coordinates, precise coordinates. Fucking Kling told me that I had to fly the exact path or they wouldn't pay for the next run."

"You said you figured 'they' were looking for something and 'they' wouldn't pay you. Who are they?"

Skeeter put up his hands in a display of innocence. "Kling nevah said, but I figured he was nothin' but a front man. I mean, he didn't know shit about the 'quipment. He had to be selling the data to someone with brains. Shit, Kling ain't smart 'nough to figure out something that complicated."

Koa agreed with that assessment. "Who mounted the pod on your chopper?"

"I did. It's a standard pod, just bolts on."

"We're gonna confiscate it and the search map. You want to help the police technician take it off?"

"Damn straight. I don't want no amateur messing with my bird."

"Okay, Detective Piki will take you and the tech out to the airport. I'll talk to the FAA. You'll be free to go after we get the pod and the map, but your license is suspended. Don't get in the cockpit until the FAA clears you."

"Shit, I can't afford being grounded for a month."

"You can't afford to be caught flying. You won't get another chance."

CHAPTER TWENTY-SIX

KOA SPENT AN hour with the county prosecutor, drafting the affidavit necessary to support a search warrant for Ricky Kling's premises. When they were finally armed with the warrant, Sergeant Basa asked, "You want me to pick him up?"

"No," Koa said, "let's go see him on his home ground. We may learn something. I'll get Detective Piki to help with the search." Koa wanted the black box that Kling had carried out of the Monarch and hoped to find records connecting Kling and Jenkins.

The three policemen parked a block away and walked to the address on Hoku Street, a decrepit three-story rooming house. A crooked hand-lettered sign advertised furnished rooms for rent by the week or month. There appeared to be two rooms per floor. They climbed two flights of creaky stairs and found a door bearing the words "Consulting Security Services" above a logo of an eye. Piki, ever the eager beaver, drew his weapon, but Koa waved him off. "Put that away," he whispered. "Kling's an asshole, but he's not violent." Piki holstered his gun.

Koa knocked and a voice responded, "It's open."

Koa, Basa, and Piki entered a closet-sized office barely large enough to hold a desk, two chairs, and a filing cabinet. Ricky Kling, clad in an *aloha* shirt, sat behind the desk.

"Well, well, well," Kling said, sporting a phony smile, "if it ain't my old buddy, Detective Kāne, with his cronies. To what do I owe this prestigious honor?" Kling was a little man—not more than 5 foot 2—and thin, with long, greasy blonde hair pulled back into a ponytail. He wore his trademark cheap Hawaiian shirt along with a ridiculously insincere smile.

"The state revoked your PI license, Kling." Koa examined the room as he spoke. There were no pictures on the walls, no visible files, no sign of any business conducted in the space. Just a book on the desk, but a book that Koa had seen before: Kirch's *Feathered Gods and Fishhooks*.

"Don't need no license for a security consulting business. Guess they didn't teach you that, huh, Detective?"

Koa picked up the book.

"When did you get into archaeology, Kling?"

Kling's eyes narrowed. "Man ought to understand the history of the islands, don't you think?"

"Especially if he's dealing in looted artifacts," Koa shot back.

"You accusing me, Detective?"

Koa switched directions. "You've been hanging out at the Monarch, Kling?"

"What's this about?"

"Have you been hanging out at the Monarch?"

"Maybe, it ain't unlawful."

"Use the phone there?" Again Kling's eyes narrowed.

"Couldn't say. I might have, but I don't rightly remember."

"You rightly remember meeting Skeeter Slade?" Koa shifted gears again, trying to keep Kling off balance.

"Skeeter Slade, Skeeter Slade . . ." Kling bought time by repeating the name. Koa could almost see Kling's wheels turning. "Yeah, I met

Mr. Slade. He's worried about weirdos vandalizing his helicopters. He was lookin' for my security services."

"What about Garvie Jenkins?" A surprised expression flashed only fleetingly across Kling's face, but Koa caught it and knew that he'd struck home.

"What's . . . what's this all about, Detective?"

"Did you know he was a convicted felon?"

"No." Again Kling's face showed surprise. "Er, I mean I'm not so sure I know any Jenkins. What's his first name again?"

"Garv. You called him Garv when you took his calls on the Monarch bar phone?"

"You bin tapping my phone, Detective?"

"I asked you about the calls from Garvie Jenkins, those you took on the Monarch bar phone."

"I need to know what this is all about 'fore I answer any more questions. I got constitutional rights, you know," Kling responded.

"And you're going to have a chance to use them unless you help us."

"Are you threatening me, Detective?"

"No, Mr. Kling, I'm seeking your help to track down criminal activity. I'm sure you want to help the police in any way you can."

"Absolutely, but I think I've provided all the help I can today."

"Not quite, Mr. Kling." Koa pulled the warrant from his pocket and handed it over. "This is a search warrant for your premises."

"You can't do that," Kling protested.

"You can complain to the judge," Koa pointed out helpfully. "His name's on the bottom of the warrant."

"But these are confidential files," Kling protested.

"What makes 'em confidential, Mr. Kling?"

"The law . . ." Kling's voice died away as he realized the import of what he was about to say.

"The law doesn't protect the files of security service providers, does it, Mr. Kling?"

"I wouldn't want them to become public," was the best Kling could manage.

"We'll protect them from public disclosure, Mr. Kling, unless, of course, they become part of a court record." Koa smiled.

The little investigator was beginning to panic. "What do you want to know? I'll tell you."

Koa stared hard at Kling.

"You want to tell us how Garvie Jenkins got you and Skeeter Slade to run aerial surveys over the Pōhakuloa Training Area looking for ancient burial caves?"

Kling slumped in his chair.

"No, I didn't think so." Koa answered his own question as he opened the filing cabinet next to Kling's desk and pulled out a black box, probably the one that Kling had carried out of the Monarch.

* * *

Much later, when Koa returned to his office, he found Detective Piki poring over maps and papers spread across Koa's desk. The young detective didn't see Koa enter the office and jumped when Koa spoke.

"You been promoted to chief detective, or you just borrowing my office?" Koa's smile robbed the question of any hostility. If people took pride in their work, Koa respected them, irrespective of their position. Everyone at police headquarters knew that.

"Sorry, Koa, I needed a place to spread these maps. Besides, you're going to love what I found."

"What have you got?"

"The maps from Slade's helicopter. Look at these lines." Piki pointed at a large-scale map of the Pōhakuloa Training Area. Red lines about three-fourths of an inch apart started on the western side of the training area and ran in parallel across the entire PTA. Each line began and ended with a set of numbers representing geographic coordinates. About half of the coordinates on each end of the lines had been crossed out with a slash.

"Looks just like Slade described," Koa said.

"That's right. I figure Slade crossed off the coordinates when he started and completed each run so he wouldn't get confused and run the same path twice."

"Good guess."

"So look at this spot." Piki pointed at a spot near the eastern side of the PTA. "This here line passes directly over the lava tube where we found Nakano's body. And the slash marks show that Slade completed his run down that line. I'd guess Slade gave Kling GPS, magnetic, and radar data covering that lava tube where we found Nakano, and Kling passed it on to his buyer."

"I agree, that sounds right. Check with Slade. See if you're right about the slashes."

CHAPTER TWENTY-SEVEN

LATER THAT AFTERNOON the weather turned nasty. Koa turned off the highway toward the harbor where Hook's fishing vessel, the *Ka'upu*, rocked uneasily on her moorings. Rain squalls whipped in from the ocean, and swirling whitecaps topped giant gray swells. Even at full speed Koa's wipers struggled to clear the Explorer's windshield.

Hook had called an hour earlier to offer Koa "a real nice *a'u* for Nālani." The suggestion of fresh fish contained a coded message. Hook had important information, something big enough to justify the use of the special *a'u* code word and to require a personal meeting. To request a meeting in this weather, the message had to be vital.

Koa parked as close as possible to the pier. The rain gods seemed even angrier close to the bay, and the wind nearly wrenched the car door out of his hand. Luckily, he wore thick rubber boots and a rain slicker. Conscious of the treacherous footing and the near-gale-force winds, he trod cautiously along the battered planking of the ancient pier, lined on both sides with oceangoing trawlers. The last thing he needed was a fall that would wrench his already damaged neck. With relief, he stepped across the gangway to the *Ka'upu* and onto the well-worn deck. Slipping around to the side of the wheelhouse, he pulled the heavy door open and entered the warm, dry space inside. Hook, who had been working at the chart table, turned to greet him.

"*Aloha*," he exclaimed warmly. "Climb out of that slicker and make yourself at home." Hook motioned to one of the two chairs bolted to the deck and poured two cups of hot coffee from a thermos. "Something to ward off the *nukumaneʻo*, you know, the malignant spirits?" Hook held up a flask, and when Koa nodded, he added a dollop of amber liquid to each cup.

Koa took one of the cups and held it aloft. "To the *puhi*." He grinned, recalling their first meeting.

"The *puhi*." Hook smiled. They touched cups and drank.

"How's Reggie, Hook?"

"He's doing well. Looks like he might be released from the hospital in the next couple of days. The head doctors say he'll be back to normal in a couple of months."

"That's great."

"I'm still worried about the legal thing. I don't trust Baxter."

"Baxter's an asshole," Koa acknowledged, "but Iwikua, the prosecutor, controls what happens to Reggie."

"I know. Reggie's lawyer says the same thing, but I won't stop worrying until Reggie's in the clear. That's why I called in this foul weather."

"This has something to do with Reggie?"

"There's a *pilina*, an' Reggie gets credit for this *aʻu*, okay?"

"You're telling me the information comes from Reggie?"

"Reggie remembered something an' I did some askin' around. Dock talk . . . you understand. The information is solid. Reggie gets credit; you'll make sure of that?"

"If it's solid, Reggie gets credit."

"Reggie remembered seeing Garvie with another dude, a little Japanese guy, Tony something, with a fishhook scar on his face. A

Japanese Tony don't mean nothing to me, but the fishhook scar, that triggered a memory. I've seen that dude. He's been around the docks. He did time up at Kūlani for smuggling dope." The two exchanged a glance. A criminal engaged in one enterprise didn't have much problem turning to another.

"So I get to thinking—what's Scarface doing with Jenkins? Maybe they met in the big house . . . maybe they're in business together. "Fishermen have ears. If you know who to ask, you learn things. Scarface runs an import-export business." Hook paused. "Now if you wanted to move drugs or looted treasures, you need a shipping business, maybe, a freight business run by an ex-con, an ex-con who did time with you. I checked. The two of them were cell mates at Kūlani."

"What's the name of this import-export business? Where's it located?" Koa asked.

"Hold on, Koa. I ain't done serving *aʻu* yet."

"There's more?"

"Early December Scarface shipped a package, a container for Jenkins, on a barge out of Kawaihae Harbor through a freight forwarder on Oʻahu to a Hong Kong address."

"How did you discover all this?"

"You really don't want to know." Hook grinned. "What you should know is that another shipment is scheduled tomorrow, another container out of Kawaihae."

"How can I identify it?"

"It will be on a flatbed pulled by a transporter from Starfish Shipping, consigned through TransPacific Freight Forwarders to Orient Reprocessing in Hong Kong. The container arrives at Kawaihae Port for loading tomorrow morning. The barge is supposed to be under tow by 11:00 a.m."

Koa felt the pace of the investigation accelerate. Jenkins had taken a large god-like obsidian figurine from the Kahoʻolawe mine, and with the police making inquiries, he would want to fence his loot as quickly as possible. It could easily be in that container. "Where's the container now?"

"Don't know. I just know where it's going."

"This is reliable?"

"Would I ask you to come down here in this stinkin' weather if it weren't reliable?" Hook grinned. "More coffee?"

This could be a long-awaited break in the case. "No. I'd better get going. I've got some arrangements to make before 11:00 a.m. tomorrow."

"*Mahalo.*"

"*Mahalo*, my friend."

Koa was already concentrating on logistics as he donned his slicker and stepped out of the wheelhouse. How could he search the container? He doubted that he had enough for a warrant, certainly not without laying out Hook's long-term reliability as an informer, and the judge might well ask how Hook had gotten the information. He needed to find a way without a warrant. Suddenly, the answer came to him.

By seven o'clock the following morning, Koa and his men were in position. Koa himself was in the operator's cab of an unused crane, high above the harbor. Spread out below him like a map, Kawaihae lay tucked along the northern coastline of an elbow-shaped bay off the 'Alenuihāhā Channel between Maui and the Big Island. The manmade harbor enclosed an oblong rectangle of water, bordered by a single wharf with only two commercial vessels. Almost directly below Koa an oceangoing barge, stacked high with containers destined for Honolulu and beyond, strained at its hawsers. At the ocean end of the dock, a powerful sea tug, the *Ali'i Mano*, or Shark-Chief, lay snugged up against the timbers, awaiting its daylong tow to O'ahu.

Koa picked up his binoculars and surveyed the scene, looking first up Kawaihae Road, the most likely route for an approaching flatbed truck. Nothing. He refocused his binoculars on a small shed, not more than twenty yards from the loading area, which concealed Detective Piki and a uniformed patrolman.

Refocusing yet again, he peered toward the guard shack by the entry gate, where Sergeant Basa stood. He was in civilian dress, armed with a clipboard, ready to assist the port security officer verifying the entry authority of incoming vehicles. Basa would be the first to identify the suspect container and alert the others.

Trucks turned into the port area and discharged their containers, but none bore the Starfish logo. Time passed. Periodically, Koa scanned the road, but no more trucks appeared. At 10:15 four sailors arrived in a blue Ford van and boarded the tug. Several minutes later, Koa heard her engines cough and burble to life. Koa looked at his watch; it was 10:25 a.m. Time was running out. Maybe Hook had gotten it wrong.

He swung his field glasses back to the highway, and there, barreling down the blacktop, came a flatbed truck bearing a single twenty-foot container. "Truck approaching," Koa radioed his team. The truck came on at high speed, racing through the outskirts of the village, braking hard just before the turnoff into the dock area. Koa heard the hiss of air brakes as the vehicle slowed and swung around the corner to an abrupt halt in front of the guard post.

Koa focused the field glasses on the truck. His heart raced at the sight of a starfish overprinted with the words Starfish Shipping. Movement caught his eye. He adjusted the binoculars. There were two men in the cab of the truck. Koa didn't recognize the driver, but the second man wasn't a total stranger. Koa knew Garvie Jenkins from a police mug shot.

The driver jumped from the cab with a handful of papers and sprinted into the security building. He emerged moments later with the dock guard and Sergeant Basa. Koa held his breath as he watched a magnified view of Basa checking and rechecking the paperwork, the truck, and its container. The police sergeant seemed to be taking forever. Something must be wrong.

Suddenly, Basa's hand, the one holding the clipboard, shot up into the air. It was the prearranged signal—the expected container had arrived. "The box is in the bag," Koa radioed to the team waiting at the dockside. "On your toes, everyone. The second man, riding shotgun, is Garvie Jenkins."

As soon as the truck cleared the guard shack, Basa's voice crackled over the radio. "Koa, you're not going to believe this. The shipper is the Alice Telescope Project. The bill of lading describes the cargo as used machine tools, computer parts, servos, and other miscellaneous industrial parts."

Koa whistled softly. Could the Alice Telescope Project be linked to Garvie Jenkins and possible archaeological looting? The contents of that container should be most interesting. He began climbing down from his perch as the flatbed rolled alongside the barge.

Koa approached as an excited Piki and a uniformed officer emerged from the shed, split up, and surrounded the truck. Piki gesticulated as he exchanged words with the driver, who looked back and forth from Piki to the uniformed officer, before reluctantly climbing down from the cab.

"What's the matter? This here container's got to be on that barge before she sails."

"Not until we inspect it," Piki responded with a flourish.

"You can't open it. It's locked."

"Then, we'll have to break the lock," Piki shot back. He brought his fist down on his hand, like he was already smashing the lock.

"You got a warrant?" Jenkins asked, descending from the tractor.

"We don't need one, Mr. Jenkins," Koa intervened, enjoying Jenkins's look of surprise at the mention of his name.

"Who the fuck are you?" Jenkins shot back.

"Detective Koa Kāne, Hawai'i County Police."

"I know my rights. You can't search this container without a warrant." Jenkins had the cocksure arrogance of a jailhouse lawyer.

"Didn't you read the sign as you came through the gate? All containers entering this port facility are subject to inspection. You consented to a search when you entered." A look of consternation flickered across Jenkins's face, but he recovered astonishingly quickly. "So, go ahead an' search the fuckin' thing. You won't find no contraband." His casual assurance surprised Koa.

Piki and the uniformed officer turned their attention to the container, breaking the seals and smashing the lock. Piki summoned two dockworkers to manhandle a crate out of the shipping container and down to the wharf. With crowbars and hammers they ripped it open, exposing more packing material—chunks of Styrofoam and cardboard boxes. Koa watched as Piki opened the first of the boxes, scattering plastic peanuts to the wind, and stared intently at the object inside.

"Koa, you better have a look."

Koa, who had been watching Jenkins as the search operation proceeded, joined Piki. The young police officer looked crestfallen as he held up used machine parts.

Koa looked back at Jenkins, who sported a cocky grin. "You found my used machinery, just like it says on the manifest. Satisfied, Detective?"

"Excuse me, excuse me, if you blokes don't git this here container on that barge, we gonna be sailin' without it. We gotta git under way, so's we kin keep the schedule." Koa turned to see a sailor, presumably the tugboat captain, standing in front of him. The man had a massive wad of chewing tobacco in his mouth and a distinctly unhappy expression.

"I'm Chief Detective Koa Kāne of the Hawai'i police. We're going to finish inspecting this container. It's not going anywhere until we're satisfied."

"You're not thinkin' of detaining us, are you, Detective?"

"You know what's in this container?"

"Nah, we jis haul the buggers. We don't take no responsibility for packin' 'em."

"Then I'm not thinking of detaining you."

"We can't wait much longer, Detective. The tide's going out an' it's twenty-two hours across to Honolulu. We got a goddamn schedule to keep."

"That's a lawful shipment," Jenkins said. "You've seen for yourself. It's a shipment of used industrial equipment. You have no right to stop it. I'll sue the county. I'll sue you and the fuckin' county." Jenkins's voice rose with his threat.

Koa knew that he was on shaky ground. He didn't have a warrant. If he held up the container and found nothing, Jenkins could sue the county. Koa's defense would require him to give up Hook as an informer.

Still, Hook's information had always been right on the mark. The container had appeared exactly as predicted, and Garvie Jenkins had been riding shotgun. The ex-con hadn't come all the way across the island just to protect a shipment of used machinery. And he had initially objected to the search, only to back off with a smug expression. Something was fishy, and Koa intended to find out what.

Koa turned to Piki and his team. "Get the rest of the boxes out of the truck and open them up."

"I'm gonna sue you for every penny you've got," Jenkins threatened.

"We've got to get under way," the tugboat captain insisted.

"Your choice, Captain. Shove off now without this container or wait till we're done."

The man backed away before turning to walk back to the tug. "We'll be casting off and taking up the tow."

"Every fuckin' penny," Jenkins threatened again.

The tug cast off, whistled farewell, and sailed out into the channel. An hour passed before the police officers and dockhands had unloaded and unpacked eight huge boxes, all of which were heavy and well crated. Detective Piki shook his head as they finished the last crate. "It's all machine tools, computer parts, electro-mechanical devices, and other industrial parts, just like it says on the manifest." All of Piki's previous energy and enthusiasm had left him.

"Fuckin' satisfied now, Detective?" Jenkins snarled.

If Jenkins's hostility was meant to deter Koa, it had the opposite effect. He was more determined than ever to outsmart the asshole.

Something wasn't right. Koa couldn't believe that Hook had failed him. He climbed into the empty container. No false bottom. No false top. He rapped the side panels. No hidden compartments. He paced its length—four, five, six strides, plus a couple of feet—a standard twenty-foot container. He examined the rivets—nothing out of the ordinary.

He climbed down out of the container and walked around the truck. A standard twenty-foot container on a standard truck bed, just like the one parked across the way. He compared the two rigs. They appeared identical—tractor, flatbed, container flush with the back of the flatbed. Then he saw the discrepancy. The container on the Starfish truck wasn't flush with the back of the flatbed. It hung over the back, too long for the truck. A short extension had been welded to the front of the container. Koa understood immediately: it wasn't a standard twenty-foot container. The container had a separate compartment, not accessible from the main compartment.

Koa walked back to Detective Piki. "Get a crane operator out here and lift that container off the flatbed. We're going to have a look at the other end."

"Why?" Piki looked puzzled.

"Because Jenkins is a clever bastard."

Soon a crane operator had lifted the container off the Starfish truck. When they finally had access to the front of the container, both Koa and Piki could just barely see the welds where an extra compartment had been attached. But there appeared to be no access, no door, no way of getting inside.

"Want me to try the top?" Piki asked, once again bubbling with enthusiasm.

"Sure." Two dockhands boosted Detective Piki up onto the top of the container.

"Nothing, no access from the top," Piki reported. "Guess we'll have to cut the son of a bitch open with a blowtorch." Piki made a back-and-forth gesture like he was ready to wield the welding torch himself.

"Let's try the bottom before we call for a welder," Koa suggested. The crane operator once again lifted the container, letting it swing gently eight feet off the ground. When the two detectives walked underneath, they immediately spotted the bolts holding the bottom of the attached compartment in place. They both spoke in unison. "We need to lay it on its side."

The crane operator complained loudly that the police had lost it, but with the help of two dockhands and cables attached to one side of the container, they managed to turn the steel box on its side. Fifteen minutes and eighteen hex-headed steel bolts later, they had the attached compartment opened. They saw more crates, specially designed to fit snugly inside the hidden compartment.

Piki admired Jenkins's handiwork. "Pretty neat setup. No customs agent would ever find that compartment."

"You're right about that. I'll bet he's moved a lot of contraband in that box. The state police and the FBI will want to trace its previous movements. But right now," Koa directed, "we need to see what's in those crates."

Piki and the uniformed officers went back to work pulling crates before attacking them with crowbars. More cardboard, more Styrofoam peanuts, then bubble wrap. Soon the young detective had unpacked a dozen objects from the first of the crates. Koa felt his heart skip a beat. Spread before the detective on the wharf, each on its own sheet of plastic bubble wrap, were a dozen stone implements, hammerstones, adzes, a stone bowl, a *kukui* nut oil lamp, and a stone mask, unlike anything Koa had previously seen.

Piki, still kneeling, looked up at Koa. "Think these are from that cave you and that park service archaeologist discovered out at Pōhakuloa?"

"It's a good bet. I mean, look at the different artifacts—bowls, hammerstones, and other things. That stuff didn't come from the obsidian mine on Kahoʻolawe. And we know Jenkins got data from Skeeter and Kling related to Pōhakuloa. Where else could this stuff have come from?"

Koa paused and thought for a minute. "Get on the horn to Jimmy Hikorea, and get him up here as soon as you can. He can help you inventory the stuff. We'll want a seizure order, so we'll have to submit an affidavit with a listing to a judge."

"Okay, Koa. What are you going to do?"

"I want to look at the paperwork for this container and have a word with the driver. Then we're going to book Mr. Garvie Jenkins."

Koa retrieved a sheaf of documents, including the bill of lading, from the cab of the tractor and flipped through them. Just as Sergeant Basa had said, the international bill of lading identified the shipper as "The Alice Telescope Project" and described the contents as "used machine tools, computer parts, servos, and other miscellaneous industrial parts." The shipment had been consigned to a freight forwarder in Honolulu for transshipment to a Hong Kong address for Oriental Reprocessing. Scrawled, almost illegibly, in the bottom right-hand corner of the bill of lading was the shipper's authorized signatory.

Koa noticed Jenkins watching him as he walked over to speak to the forlorn trucker. The trucker, too, noticed Jenkins and turned his back on his employer. Koa regarded that as a good sign.

"Am I under arrest?"

"I haven't decided yet. Where did you pick up the load?"

"That Alice place. You know, the HQ up in Waimea."

"Anybody supervise the loading?"

"Not really."

"What does that mean?"

"The container, she was all packed and buttoned up. This guy, Charlie, one of the Alice guys, he signs the paperwork. He's got a big red face, like he drinks. Ya know the type."

Koa nodded crisply. Even though Charlie Harper, the pervert, was on probation, Koa couldn't suppress a tingle of satisfaction.

"The container was locked and sealed when you picked it up?"

"Yup."

Koa couldn't decide whether the driver was borderline dumb or complicit. "Anybody tell you what was inside?"

"Just astronomy stuff, like it says on the lading."

"Who told you that?"

"Mr. Jenkins."

"You work for him?"

"Yup, sometimes. Like whenever he needs a driver, he calls me. Might be a couple times a month."

The man answered without hesitation, and Koa began to think he might be no more than a hired driver. "When was the last time you worked for him before today?"

"About ten days back when I hauled the empty container up to that Alice place so them astronomy guys could pack it."

"You left the container on the truck bed?"

"Yup. They ain't got no derrick up there at that Alice place."

If the container hadn't been moved off the flatbed at Alice, the secret compartment must have been packed before the vehicle had reached Alice. "Where did you pick up the truck?"

"Jenkins's place, a shop near the docks in Hilo."

"You know about that hidden compartment?"

"No, honest. I didn't know nothing about it."

Again, no hesitation, just a straightforward response. "But you knew that the container didn't fit right on the truck. You knew that, didn't you?"

The driver shrugged, and his expression remained unchanged. "Yup. I asked Mr. Jenkins about that. He said it was just an old container made before they standardized 'em."

"And you believed him?"

"I didn't think much about it. Honest, I didn't."

That had a ring of truth. "Give your name and address to the detective over there. Give him a complete statement. Everything just like you told me. Understand?"

The wrinkles in the man's brow smoothed, but Koa saw no indication that he thought he had pulled a fast one. "Yup, I understand."

"Then you can go."

"I ain't gonna git paid?"

"That's not my problem."

Koa turned to Garvie Jenkins. "You are under arrest. You have a constitutional right to remain silent—"

"I heard that shit before," Jenkins interrupted.

"Yes, I know, but I'm not going to be happy until you've heard it again," Koa responded, before continuing with the standard

Miranda warning. He handcuffed Jenkins, placed him in the back-seat of a police vehicle, and instructed Basa to take Jenkins to Hilo for booking on illegal antiquities charges.

Eager to pursue the next link in the chain, Koa headed up the hill toward Waimea and the Alice administrative offices. On the drive, he called Police Chief Lannua, who expressed great interest in the container with the secret compartment. Koa had no doubt that the state police and the FBI would soon be tracing all its previous movements. Although chomping at the bit to confront Charlie Harper, Koa knew he had to exercise caution. If the secret compartment had been packed before the container arrived at Alice, Harper could be innocent, but then again, why would a premier outfit like Alice use a slime ball shipper like Starfish?

CHAPTER TWENTY-EIGHT

A CALL TO Julie Benson, Director Masters' assistant, told Koa that Charlie Harper was "on the mountain" adjusting a detector on Alice I, so Koa headed for the summit of Mauna Kea. On the way, his car phone rang, and he answered to the booming voice of Zeke Brown, the county prosecutor.

"I hear you busted Garvie Jenkins. Nailed him while in possession. Nice work."

"Word travels fast."

"Your chief called, said Alice was the shipper. Is that right?"

"Yes, for the legitimate cargo, but I'm not sure about the artifacts in the separate compartment." Koa explained what they had found. "The way I see it, that hidden compartment must have been loaded in Hilo. Jenkins may have been using Alice to cover up his movement of artifacts. I'm on my way to talk to Harper now. He signed the bill of lading."

"Hmm, that's good,"—Koa held the phone away from his ear to avoid being deafened by Zeke's voice—"but I've got news for you. Remember the GPR machine? We traced the serial number."

"And?" Koa asked. As he listened, his eyebrows shot up at the content of Zeke's report. The portable GPR machine had originally been purchased by the Alice Telescope Project.

* * *

After gaining entry to Alice I, Koa stopped in the control room to see if he could catch Nālani. She was surprised and delighted when he popped in the door. Since she was alone, they embraced, sharing a kiss. Releasing her, he asked her where he could find Charlie Harper.

"You're not going after him for harassing me, are you?" she asked, concern flashing in her eyes.

"No. It's about a shipment of stolen antiquities we just stopped."

Her hand went to her mouth. "Charlie? I know he's got roving hands, but antiquities theft?" She looked dubious. "He's into *hula* dancers and martinis, not Hawaiian history or artifacts. Gee, Koa, he's the last person I'd suspect of looting graves." She added that Harper was inside the dome, working on the telescope.

Koa walked across the floor of the dome, looking up at the huge telescope, before entering a small elevator cage. The lift carried him up two floors to the platform surrounding the telescope. Charlie, wearing headphones, sat with his back to Koa, hunched over a laptop connected to a large box. Koa steeled himself. One part of him wanted to hammer Charlie Harper for his unwanted advances toward Nālani, but he forced himself to put his personal feelings aside.

"Mr. Harper?" No answer. "Mr. Harper?" Koa yelled.

"Oh." Charlie Harper turned and removed his headphones. "You're Nālani's date. What are you doing here?"

"Mr. Harper, I'm actually Chief Detective Koa Kāne of the Hawai'i County police. I need to ask you a few questions."

"Did that bi—" He caught himself.

Koa was ready to pound him for that. "Did you say something, Mr. Harper?"

"Nothing important. Have I done something wrong? Do I need a lawyer?"

"I don't know, Mr. Harper." Koa forced himself back down to his regular calm. "Is there someplace we can talk?"

"We can talk here. Besides, I got this detector opened up. I can't leave without closing her back up."

"Okay. You shipped some used parts to a Hong Kong reprocesser?"

"Right. Anything wrong with that?"

"You make such shipments often?"

"Not often, maybe once or twice a year. What's this all about, anyway?"

"Who packed the container?"

"Most of the stuff came from up here. Some of it was packed up here. Techs packed the rest at the admin offices. Something wrong with the packing?"

The man seemed oblivious to the import of Koa's questions. Or maybe it was an act to throw him off. "Who put the boxes in the container?"

"I don't know. Techs and some day laborers at the admin offices. Did the container break open? Was there an accident?"

"They packed the container while it was on the truck?"

"I suppose they must have. We don't have a crane at the admin offices."

"Who arranged for the shipment?"

"I did. That's part of my job."

"What company did you use?"

"Jesus, I don't rightly remember. StarFreight, StarLight, Star something. What difference does it make?"

Koa didn't like the evasion and probed harder.

"Has the Alice Telescope Project ever used that company before?"

"How would I know?"

"Didn't you arrange the previous shipment?"

"Sure."

"Did you use the same company?"

"No, I don't think we did."

Harper wasn't acting as Koa had expected. He seemed genuinely confused. "Why did you choose Starfish Shipping?"

"That's it. Starfish. I knew it was Star something."

"Why did you choose Starfish?"

"What difference does it make?"

Koa had had enough of the man's questions. "Mr. Harper, I'm asking the questions. Why did you choose that particular company?"

"I didn't."

"Who did?"

"Deputy Director Nelson handled it while I was over in Oʻahu at a symposium."

That answer would need to be checked. In the meantime, Koa wanted to move on to another subject. "What do you know about ground penetration radar?"

"GPR? Not too much. We have a machine. I know that."

"Why would Alice have a GPR machine?"

"Because of the old graves."

Koa's ears pricked up at the mention. "Graves?"

"Ancient Hawaiians viewed this mountain as sacred. It's historical mumbo jumbo, but Director Masters doesn't want to roil the damned native sovereignty crowd, so whenever we construct something, we can't touch old grave sites. But nobody knows where the bodies are buried, so to speak. We check the construction areas with the GPR machine."

Didn't any of these astronomers ever get sensitivity training? Koa wondered. "When was the GPR machine last used?"

"I don't rightly remember. Maybe eighteen, maybe twenty months ago, somewhere around then."

The lead that Zeke Brown had given him didn't look so damning now. "Where's the machine?"

"One of the storage rooms."

"I'd like to see it." Koa's request was a clear command.

"What? You want to see the GPR machine?"

"Yes and now." Koa's voice brooked no opposition.

"I've got to button this detector up. It'll take me a few minutes."

"Go ahead. I'll wait."

Harper unplugged several electrical cables from the detector, replaced covers, and latched the device closed. Then Koa followed Charlie down to the main floor into the storage wing of Alice II.

"Should be in here," Charlie said as he unlocked a storage room. Yet when they looked, they didn't find a GPR machine. They searched three other storage rooms, but the machine was nowhere to be found.

"Jesus Christ," Harper exclaimed, "the machine's gone, and I'm responsible for the physical plant. Masters is gonna hang me by my balls when he finds out." A light seemed to dawn in his eyes. "Hey, you knew it was missing. You knew, that's why you asked. You found it, didn't you? You found it and traced the serial number."

Koa ignored Harper's questions. "Who has access to these storage rooms?"

"Gee, the director and the assistant directors have keys to everything. So does the duty tech. Anybody could borrow the duty tech's keys. They're kept in a drawer in the control room."

"When were these storage rooms last inventoried?"

"Uh, I don't rightly remember."

Koa frowned. The man was responsible for the physical plant and didn't remember the last inventory. That didn't make sense. "You were responsible for the inventory, weren't you?"

Harper hesitated. "Yes."

"Then you must remember when the last inventory was taken."

"Yes, but . . ."

"But what?" Koa's voice took on a hard edge.

"Well, sometimes the inventory isn't done that carefully."

"Are you telling me you faked the last inventory?"

Charlie didn't answer, but his sheepish look and downcast eyes were all the confirmation Koa needed. Damn, he thought, Harper's either incompetent or he's covering something up.

"So you have no idea when the GPR machine went missing? Or who took it?"

Charlie shook his head.

The reading he was getting on Harper was inconclusive, but he did seem like a natural-born loser. Koa decided to use the opportunity to check whether the man had an alibi. "Where were you on Wednesday night, January 21?"

"That's my poker night. Five of us get together every Wednesday night."

"Where?"

"Pete Chalmers's house in Hilo. He's a buddy I met on the golf course."

"You there all night?"

"Naw, I got bad cards and went home about midnight."

That fit the time frame. "And you were home the rest of the night?"

"Uh-huh."

That didn't sound convincing. "What do you know about the relationship between Nakano and your wife?" Koa asked the question with a steely edge in his voice.

Harper opened his mouth and seemed to shrink away. "I didn't…"

"You didn't what, Mr. Harper?"

"I didn't like her hanging out with that fuckin' history group."

"So, what did you do about it, Mr. Harper?"

"Nothing." The anger in his eyes telegraphed the lie.

Koa remembered Linda Harper's huge sunglasses at the astronomy party. He'd wondered then if the sunglasses covered an injury. Maybe Linda Harper was a battered wife. Koa framed the question unfairly and took a certain pleasure in it. "Did you take it out on Keneke Nakano or your wife, Mr. Harper?"

Harper's face turned red and his chin quivered. After a moment's hesitation, he fessed up. "Okay. I hit her. I didn't like the bitch hanging around with that history club crowd. It was just wrong, them meeting at a hotel and all. Hell, I don't even like her going out on her own. Made me nervous. But I didn't kill Keneke. I swear, I didn't."

CHAPTER TWENTY-NINE

THE FOLLOWING MORNING, Koa counted no fewer than fifteen law enforcement officers outside the ramshackle garage of Starfish Shipping in Hilo's warehouse district. Two unmarked cars and six agents from the FBI, two cruisers and four uniformed officers from the state police, and two DEA vehicles. Zeke Brown, the county prosecutor, had an investigator with him.

"Christ, they need twenty officers to serve a search warrant on an empty building?" Koa asked rhetorically.

"They all want credit for your Jenkins bust. They think he's a drug kingpin," Basa responded.

"They're in for a disappointment."

"Why? You don't think Jenkins was moving drugs?"

"Oh, he was moving drugs and other contraband. FBI chemists found traces of marijuana and cocaine in that phony container. I just don't think they're going to find anything."

"Why?"

"Jenkins is an ingenious bastard. His forged map scheme, the secret compartment in that container, the way he hid the Kahoʻolawe obsidian mine . . . he's cunning. He almost fooled us on Kahoʻolawe."

"So you think he's got another hideout?"

"I don't know, but I'd bet a half-dozen canoe lengths in the next race that he's covered his tracks."

"We'll know soon enough."

Zeke Brown banged on the front door. "Police open up."

There was no response. On Zeke's signal, his investigator hit the door with a sledgehammer. The door shattered with near-explosive force and swung inward, banging violently against a counter. Two FBI agents, guns drawn, entered the building. "Clear . . . clear . . . clear" sounded three times. One of them hit the light switches while the other found the controls for the bay doors, which groaned upward on rusty tracks.

Koa entered the garage and stood alone in a corner watching the officers comb through the place. The building consisted of four rooms—a small office area with a customer service counter, a large double bay equipped with a single hydraulic lift, a cramped equipment room for the air compressor, and a tiny bathroom littered with filthy rags and other refuse.

Battleship-gray paint splotched with petroleum stains covered the uneven concrete floor. Steel beams embedded in the walls supported a mobile hoist on rails near the ceiling. It was a well-equipped shop, where mechanics could easily have modified the sham container.

Zeke's investigators, the FBI men, and the DEA agents ransacked the place. They emptied a small file cabinet at the back of the office and rummaged through the cupboards under the counter. Two DEA agents methodically sorted through the tool chests. One of them pulled the cover from the electric arc welder, as though he expected to find a cache of contraband inside. One of the Bureau boys drew the nasty job of searching the filthy bathroom, only to be rewarded with a couple of dog-eared girlie magazines.

The team examined every nook and cranny of the service shop and the adjacent spaces. The oft-repeated words "shit" and "I can't

believe this bastard's clean" reflected a rising level of frustration. After three hours they'd found nothing incriminating. As the crowd
was getting ready to pull out, Koa walked over to commiserate. "A
bust, huh, Zeke?"

"I was sure we'd find something. This dude can't be clean after
what you found on Kahoʻolawe and in that phony container."

"He's not clean," Koa responded. "We just haven't found his stash."

"Well, it's sure not here. I'm clearing out and going back to my
office."

"Leave the warrant papers with me, will you, Zeke?"

The prosecutor looked quizzically at Koa. "You think we missed
something?"

"I don't know. His forgeries and that bogus container tell us
something about Jenkins. He's wily and knows how to keep secrets."

"Here," Zeke said, handing Koa the papers. "Bust your ass."

Koa waited until they were all gone, except Basa. Then he began
walking around the shop. "There's something here, there has to be."

"Where?"

"I don't know. Jenkins modified that container. He's somehow
modified this space."

"I don't see how. It's a simple rectangular building. This shop oc-
cupies most of the floor space. The compressor room and the john
take up all the space on one side, and the office uses all the space on
the other side. There's no place for a hidden room."

"I know. I already paced off the distances. Still, that cocky son
of a bitch has something hidden here. I wish we had a set of floor
plans."

A light sparked in Sergeant Basa's eyes. "You know, Koa, there
might be a set of drawings up in the planning office."

The idea gained traction in Koa's thinking. "It's possible. Can
you check?"

While Basa drove back to the Hilo government complex, Koa roamed the building, once again pacing off the dimensions of each room. He checked the walls. He walked and measured the outside perimeter of the building. He checked the floor for any hidden access doors. His hopes of finding anything dimmed.

Nearly an hour later, Basa walked back into the garage with two thick files. "You found floor plans?" Koa asked.

"Yeah, I got 'em, but it cost me a pretty penny."

"Why?"

"You gotta fill out a form and it takes a week or two. The files are in storage boxes in the basement."

"So what did you do for the clerk?"

"Parking tickets. The clerk's mother has three unpaid tickets. I told him I'd see what I could do."

"The chief's not going to be happy if he finds out."

Basa looked pretty unhappy himself. "You want the files or not?"

Koa took the files. The first one contained the plans and permits for the existing building. "Looks like they renovated this place four years ago."

"Isn't that about when Jenkins got paroled?"

"You're right. Jenkins must have renovated this place right after Kūlani cut him loose. I wonder where he got the money."

Basa make a face and gestured around them. "Not much of a renovation. It still looks like shit."

"Except for the garage," Koa interjected. "That's a first-class service area."

Koa spread the plans on the counter in the office. He traced the outlines of the building and checked the dimensions. Still, he didn't find any discrepancies large enough to permit a hiding place. He shook his head. He had the same feeling he'd experienced on the dock that morning. "We're missing something. I wish I knew what." He refolded the plans and returned them to the file.

The second file contained the original plans for the building, which appeared to be almost identical to the renovated structure. Again Koa traced the outlines of the building and the dimensions. Again, he was unable to find any clue to a concealed space. He started to refold the plans—and stopped. Slowly, he spread the plans back out on the counter and stood staring at the old, pre-renovation plans.

"What is it, Koa? What do you see?"

Without uttering a word Koa walked back into the shop. Picking up a steel rod, he moved to the head of the truck bay without the hydraulic lift. He raised the rod and let the end fall to the floor with a thud. He moved a foot down the bay, lifted the rod, and let it fall to the floor again. He moved again and repeated the exercise with another thud. On the fourth repetition, the rod struck with a different sound.

"It sounds hollow." Basa's voice registered surprise. Koa repeated the exercise three more times, confirming the hollow sound.

"You think there's a space under the concrete floor?" Basa asked.

"The old plans, the ones before the renovation, show two hydraulic lifts. Why would an operator remove a hydraulic lift from a truck service bay?"

"They wouldn't," Basa responded thoughtfully.

"And why would a garage paint the bay floors battleship gray?"

"Maybe to hide a concrete patch," Basa suggested.

"That's what I think."

"But how would anyone get under the concrete?" Basa asked.

Koa again studied the service bay. His eyes moved from the arc welder to the tool chests, then to the belts and other parts hanging on the walls, and finally to the hydraulic tire changer. Nothing. He saw no possible entrance to an underground chamber. Then his eyes lit upon the hydraulic lift in the adjacent bay. He pointed to it. "How do you operate that lift?"

They found the switches for the compressor and the controls for
the lift. When Koa pressed the lever, the lift rose, exposing a deep
pit, nearly ten feet wide and eighteen feet long. As the lift jerked to
a stop at its maximum elevation, Koa picked up a flashlight from
one of the workbenches and examined the walls of the pit. At one
end, a set of iron rungs formed a ladder. Koa turned and started
down the ladder.

"Be careful, Koa. I don't trust this lift. Mechanics have been
crushed under these things."

Koa stopped. "It should be okay. There's no weight on it."

"Sure you don't want to get some experts out here? Maybe from
fire and rescue?"

"Let's see what we find first."

"Be careful . . . be damned careful."

"Okay." Koa held his damaged neck as he climbed slowly down
into the pit. He swung the flashlight around, examining the floor
and the walls. The front wall, back wall, and side wall closest to the
office appeared to be solid concrete, but he spotted something on
the pit wall closest to the second bay. It was hard to make out in the
dim illumination. Koa edged toward it.

"There's a metal plate here. It's covered with grime." Koa ran his
light around the edges of the large steel plate. "Looks to be about
five feet tall and maybe thirty inches wide."

"Sounds like a door. See any way to get it open?" Basa responded
from above.

"This light's terrible. Is there an electric torch up there?"

Moments later Basa dangled a hooded electric work light over the
edge of the pit. "Yeah, here you go."

Koa caught the cord and held the light close to the steel plate.
Moving slowly, he examined its entire outline. "I don't see anything
on the plate. No bolts, no rivets. Wonder what holds it in place?"

"What about the frame? Any kind of catch or locking mechanism?" Basa asked.

Koa moved the light around the edge of the steel panel. "Wait a minute, there's a recess here with a hole. Could be some kind of keyhole. You didn't see a key anywhere, did you?"

"Nope."

"Hand me a crowbar. I'm going to see if I can pry this plate loose."

Basa handed Koa a long, heavy crowbar and glanced overhead. "Be careful, Koa." Koa hooked the blade under the edge of the steel plate and put his weight against the bar. The plate creaked, but didn't move. He threw his weight against the bar. Suddenly the plate gave way and began to swing outward.

"Look out!" Basa screamed.

From the corner of his eye, Koa saw the hydraulic lift coming down. He dove for the opening where the plate had been moments before.

The underside of the hydraulic lift hit the edge of the steel plate. The shriek of twisting metal rent the air, followed by a thunderous crack as tortured metal bent beyond the breaking point. The concrete floor shuddered. A shower of blue-white sparks flared from the severed electrical cord. The torch died, plunging the pit into darkness. The smell of burned rubber and ozone filled the pitch-black pit.

"Koa...Koa...can you hear me?" Basa screamed. "Koa, can you hear me?" Basa's voice rose to a near panic. Grabbing his cell, Basa dialed the emergency center. "Betty, it's Basa. I've got an officer down. It's Koa Kāne. I need fire and rescue with heavy equipment." He gave the address.

"Koa...Koa...can you hear me?" Basa screamed again.

Koa found himself in utter blackness. At first, he thought he might be dead or unconscious. He tried to move his fingers, and to his surprise, they responded. He rolled over and carefully sat up. His neck and shoulder were shrieking with pain. He remembered banging his face against something and reached up to feel for blood. Ouch! No blood, but he was going to have the mother of all bruises and a shiner as well. Nālani was going to be livid with him for risking his life. He heard Basa's voice: "Koa, for God's sake, answer me!"

"I'm here." Koa's voice echoed off the walls as though he were in a tiny chamber.

He didn't have to see Basa to recognize his tremendous relief. "Are you okay?"

"I think so."

"Where are you?"

"I'm not sure. It's pitch black. I can't see my hand in front of my face."

"I'll get a torch."

"Watch out. I think the lift severed an electrical wire. Don't get electrocuted." Koa heard footsteps on the concrete above him and then a small noise in the pit.

"There's no electric power. I'm going to lower a flashlight."

Koa saw a dim glow coming from a gap along the floor. Basa was lowering the light into the pit, but something didn't make sense. With a start, Koa realized that he was no longer in the pit with the hydraulic lift. He remembered diving into the hole behind the steel plate. He was in another space altogether—the pit for the second hydraulic lift before it had been covered over during the renovation.

He crawled to the hole previously covered by the plate, now half-blocked by the shattered metal undercarriage of the lift. No more than six inches separated the bottom of the undercarriage from the floor. He realized with a shudder how close he'd come to being crushed. He'd been exceptionally lucky.

"I'm going to need help getting out of here. You'd better call the fire and rescue guys."

"They're already on the way."

Still on his hands and knees, Koa peered through the gap, but the flashlight dangled far out of reach. "Lower—drop it down a foot more and over this way."

At last he caught the flashlight and pulled it into the chamber where he knelt.

The batteries must have been old, but the weak yellow beam cast enough light for Koa to identify a dozen or so bales stacked against the wall. He didn't need a chemist to know that he'd found several thousand pounds of marijuana. Alongside the bales were numerous plastic bags, most likely containing cocaine. The room held a fortune in illicit drugs.

Koa aimed the dim yellow beam toward the other end of the room. He felt a chill. Adrenaline jolted his system. Shiny black eyes seemed to reach through time, eyes both beautiful and sinister. Below the eyes were heavy breasts, weighted down with age and drooping nipples, and open legs, crooked outward at the knees. Human, yet not human. The twin sister of the bird woman from the Pōhakuloa burial cave, standing on a small desk. He shook himself free of the bird woman's stare. Next to her lay a bound ledger, perhaps a book of accounts.

"You'd better get Zeke on the horn," Koa called upward. He recalled the ridiculous gang of officials who'd tried to search the building and smiled. "The feds are going be scraping egg off their faces for months."

"That wouldn't be a bad thing." Koa heard the mirth in Basa's voice, then the sirens of emergency vehicles in the distance. They wouldn't be able to extricate him for quite a while, so he might as well use the time.

Lowering himself into the chair in front of the desk, he rubbed his sore shoulder before slipping on a pair of plastic gloves and opening the ledger. He aimed the slowly dying light toward columns of numbers, weights, and amounts—large amounts. Drug deals, by the look of it.

He flipped through pages and pages of weights and amounts. No doubt about it—they had stumbled onto a major drug kingpin. He continued flipping the pages until he came upon blank pages and more blank pages. He almost closed the book, but some stray thought made him flip to the end. There. A different accounting system, and a list of objects—talisman, adze, carved bowl, feathered ornament, figurine, hammerstone, etc. At the end of the list, he found numbers, large numbers, many times his annual salary, and a name—a name he recognized.

CHAPTER THIRTY

KOA, BASA, AND an accompanying uniformed officer found Gunter Nelson sitting at his desk inside the Alice headquarters in Waimea. He looked up when the men entered unannounced.

"Gentlemen, to what do I owe this honor?"

"Thought you might be expecting us."

"Can't say I was."

"Your buddy Garvie Jenkins sends his regards."

Gunter gave away no tell at all. "Garvie Jenkins?"

Koa was sick of all these smart guys thinking they could get away with anything. "Save the stage acting for the courtroom, Mr. Nelson. You want to tell us a little bit about your trafficking in archaeological artifacts?"

"Perhaps I should consult a lawyer."

"We have a warrant for your arrest for violations of the Hawai'i antiquities laws." Koa read him his rights. "Please come with us. You can call your lawyer from the police headquarters in Hilo."

After handcuffing Gunter Nelson and sending him off to Hilo, the officers executed a search warrant on the neat white clapboard house Gunter called home. Located halfway up a large *pu'u* in Waimea's version of Nob Hill, it overlooked the little cowboy town and the dry grasslands beyond.

The mess of books and clothes strewn about inside contrasted not only with the simple building but also with Koa's image of German correctness. For Koa, the disorder reflected the conflict between Gunter's public persona as perhaps the second most senior astronomer on the island and Gunter's corrosive unhappiness at failing to win the Alice directorship. Frustrated ambition was written large in the way the man kept his home.

The disarray inside slowed the search, but didn't stop them from turning the place inside out. While Koa reviewed Gunter's financial records, looking for evidence of proceeds from the sale of artifacts, Basa searched the house and the garage.

"Koa," Basa called, excitement palpable in place of his usual calm, "we've found something even bigger than we thought. Come look." Koa walked down the back steps to an unusually large detached workshop-garage. A heavy lock lay smashed on the ground, and the door to a brightly illuminated work area stood open. Inside, a long table occupied the center of the room while workbenches lined three of the four walls. A number of stone artifacts lay scattered on the table and the workbenches.

Koa stood in the room surveying its contents. Three heavy-duty computers, a printer, and a giant monitor occupied one of the workbenches, and immediately to one side stood a commercial graphics plotter, capable of handling poster-sized sheets. A rack on another wall held an array of electronic equipment and a set of aluminum tubes, each about two feet long and three inches in diameter, pointed on the bottom, with whip-like antennas mounted on top. Koa guessed they'd found the seismic testing gear Gunter had used on Mauna Kea, and that Jenkins had employed to find the obsidian mine on Kahoʻolawe.

Huge sheets of corkboard affixed to the walls above the benches held giant, highly detailed geologic maps. Pinned here and there atop the maps were extraordinarily high-resolution satellite photographs and long strips of graph paper covered with multiple wavy black lines, like seismograph readings after an earthquake.

Upon examination, the maps displayed tiny sections of the Big Island, portions of the southern slopes of Mauna Kea, the saddle lands, and Mauna Loa. Various points on the maps bore large and small circles, penned in yellow ink, while four or five other locations were marked with bright red X's. Koa noted a red X on the collapsed *pu'u* on the south side of Mauna Kea where the tunnel emerged from the adze makers' workshop.

Another map seemed to be a duplicate of the one Piki had found in Skeeter Slade's helicopter. It bore the same straight red parallel lines across the Pōhakuloa Training Area with the same coordinates at the ends. Unlike Slade's map, this one featured a large red X over the lava tube where they had found Keneke Nakano's body. As Koa had guessed from the ledger in the hidden space beneath Jenkins's truck shop, Jenkins had been feeding the data that Skeeter collected to Gunter, who had the skill to analyze it for the location of hidden caves. And this map proved Gunter's knowledge of the cavern where they'd found Keneke's body.

As he thought back on his encounters with Gunter—Koa had developed a rapport with the man—he reflected on Escher's *Reptiles* etching on his office wall. Gunter was a chameleon—an upstanding, even esteemed, member of the community by day and a grave-robbing thief by night. It was so often that way. Everyone harbored secrets. Most were just human foibles . . . but once in a while you came face to face with real depravity. Koa had yet to figure out the litmus test to tell one from the other. Maybe Gunter could shed light on that quandary. Koa was looking forward to interviewing the German.

The evidence pointed to Gunter as Keneke's killer. Gunter knew of the remote cave where they'd found the body. He'd had a falling-out with Keneke, mostly likely because Keneke had discovered Gunter's thefts of antiquities. Fearing disclosure, Gunter would have had a powerful motive to kill the young Hawaiian. Gunter had no alibi. Still, Koa doubted that Gunter had the physical strength or the steely courage to have committed the grotesque murder. Then he remembered Dr. Cater's caveat that if the killer were less than six feet tall, he might have applied a choke hold as he pulled Keneke over backward. Still, Koa wasn't sure . . . he just couldn't see the puppy-eyed Gunter killing and mutilating the Polynesian Tannhäuser, as Gunter had dubbed Keneke.

"What is all this stuff?" Basa wondered aloud.

"Our friend Gunter Nelson is an archaeological treasure hunter. He used all this electronic gadgetry to locate burial caves."

"You mean like the oil guys use to find gas and oil deposits?"

"Exactly. Except we have a high-tech grave robber."

"Don't the oil guys use explosive charges or something?"

"Yeah, and I'll bet that we'll find some around here someplace."

It was a good bet. In a small shed behind the garage, they found two crates of small explosive charges from a Houston oil industry supply company.

Gunter had a lot of questions to answer.

CHAPTER THIRTY-ONE

WITH NĀLANI, KOA always minimized the dangers he faced as a police officer. Yet there was no hiding the huge black-and-blue bruise on his face from his dive beneath the power lift in Jenkins's shop.

"Oh my god," Nālani said, "what did you do to yourself?" That comment reflected her concern, while "Why the hell didn't you let the fire and rescue boys check it out?" signified her blazing anger at the risk he'd taken. He could laugh it off with his colleagues but not with Nālani. She made him go to the hospital and swear on his Hawaiian heritage he'd never again do something so stupid. It made for a rough start to the day, but he loved her for caring.

* * *

The two sides sat across the table in the police interrogation room. Gunter Nelson, out on bail and looking older than his sixty-three years, sat on the far side with Aka Kaka, his criminal defense lawyer. Koa and Zeke Brown sat facing the accused. A police technician stood behind a camera, ready to videotape the interview.

"As we've explained to your attorney," Zeke began, "we're looking at both the unlawful removal of ancient artifacts from state lands and the murder of Keneke Nakano. You are a principal target of the antiquities case and a suspect in the murder investigation." He used his booming voice to special effect during criminal interviews, and Gunter drew back, seemingly pained by the volume directed at him.

"Your attorney has advised us that given the overwhelming evidence against you in the artifacts case, you wish to dispose of that matter. Your plea bargain on an artifacts charge will not affect your status in the Nakano murder investigation. You will remain a subject of that investigation. Do you understand that?"

"Yes."

"We are prepared to charge you with over fifty felony counts of unlawful removal and sale of archaeological artifacts, having an unknown value in excess of one million dollars. We have agreed to allow you to plead guilty to a single felony count, carrying a term of no more than ten years' imprisonment, in exchange for your full cooperation, including the recovery of any artifacts and restitution. Do you understand?"

"Yes."

"Koa, you want to take over?"

In this tag team, Koa was the hard guy, even though his voice was much less penetrating. "Yes. Tell us in your own words, Mr. Nelson, how you got into looting artifacts."

The astronomer grimaced at the word "looting," but seemed ready for a full confession. "It's a long story, an unhappy one. I've long been interested in archaeology. When I was working at the Kitt Peak National Observatory in Arizona, I met a petroleum geologist with similar interests. Together, we tested seismology techniques widely used in oil exploration to see how they worked on archaeological sites. My interest intensified after I settled in Hawai'i."

Gunter let out a long sigh, pulled at his beard, and patted it back into place. "We are our own worst enemies, I'm afraid. When I came here, I wanted to be the director. It became my personal holy grail, and it slipped from my grasp. I knew Masters would force me out and then where would I be? Sixty-three, sixty-five years old, unemployed and unemployable. I became bitter, corrosively bitter."

Koa was grimly amused by all the penetrating self-knowledge on display—which would never have emerged if Gunter hadn't been caught.

"I got serious about archaeology. I spent all my free time hunting for caves, using what I'd learned in Arizona. I found an anomaly, a place on Mauna Kea where the data showed a discontinuity, a small cave with a burial vault. I couldn't believe I'd developed a way to see through the earth, to find things that had been hidden for hundreds of years. I found a carved wooden idol, an ancient female dwarf with pendulous breasts. She became my protostar, the seed of my future."

"You did this searching alone?"

"I went out with Keneke a bunch of times, but then one day we went back to a little cave where we'd found a few insignificant stone tools. Keneke thought some of the tools we'd seen on our first visit were missing. He got suspicious that I was taking things. After that I always went alone."

Koa thought about what Soo Lin had quoted Keneke as saying: "We have powerful telescopes to search out the mysteries of the distant universe, but no machine to let us see what's right here under our very own feet. Yet Gunter had devised such a machine and put it to what use?—grave robbing. He was indeed his own worst enemy."

"I took the female dwarf to a man in Honolulu, a collector. He paid me $60,000."

"How did he make the payment?" Zeke interrupted.

"Cash, hundred-dollar bills, six hundred of them."

"Go on," Koa directed. "While Keneke and I were still talking, he shared a lot of his archaeological ideas. He thought the archaeologists were all wrong about Mauna Kea. He just couldn't accept that the stonecutters disbursed back to their villages in the winter. He was convinced the stoneworkers were a cohesive community and worked together all year round. He had a theory about the saddle lands, that it had been a crossroads, that there had to be caves out there.

"I got really excited about that idea. I mean, if they were a community, there'd have to be artifacts, likely valuable ones. But I had this problem. Individual seismic shots cover only tiny areas. I needed more data, and I wanted data from inside the Pōhakuloa Training Area. I needed an aerial survey, like they use in the oil business. I noticed one of those tourist helicopters—a perfect platform for survey equipment. I didn't want to risk approaching pilots, so I hired this security consultant."

"Ricky Kling?" Koa asked, using one of his favorite tactics to extract the truth. If you could make a suspect believe that you already knew the facts, the person revealed more for fear of being caught in a lie.

"Yeah, but how—"

"Never mind how we know. Just continue."

"Kling found a pilot, and I paid Kling each time he brought me a data cassette. The data was pure gold, really detailed. Keneke was right. I found indications of a cave system in the saddle, but I couldn't figure how to get to it. I mean, it was in the middle of the Army training area." Gunter paused and pulled at his beard.

"All the while I continued my seismic testing. That's how I discovered the tunnel. I wandered around that collapsed *pu'u* on Mauna Kea for an hour before I discovered the entrance to the tunnel. Then I discovered the workshop. My retirement was in the bag. I was free of that son of a bitch Masters. And that was before I discovered the king's burial vault."

"Did you sell anything from the stonecutters' workshop?" Zeke Brown put in.

"*Ja*, but not the same way. I asked my contact in Honolulu what kind of volume he could handle, and he turned queasy. He refused to handle any volume, only individual pieces, but he put me in touch with Garvie Jenkins—told me Jenkins was a fence."

"Go on."

"Then I discovered the burial vault off the workshop, the grave of some really high chief. Unbelievable feather cape and the black stone bird woman. You've seen the bird woman?"

"The one you sold to Jenkins?"

"*Ja*, frightened the living crap out of me the first time I saw it— like it's almost alive."

"Yeah, we've seen it," Koa acknowledged. "So you and Jenkins went into business together?"

Gunter dropped his head into his hands. He sat in silence, lost in some personal misery. "*Ja*, a treacherous, conniving man, but he was willing to handle volume and paid good money."

"Treacherous?" Koa asked.

"He wanted to know my methods and sources. I think he wanted to cut me out and take the whole shebang for himself."

Koa decided to blindside the old astronomer. "Whose idea was Kaho'olawe?"

"You know about Kaho'olawe?" Gunter was genuinely surprised and paused. "His idea initially. He'd read about an obsidian mine, and wanted to apply seismic techniques to locate it. He promised me 25 percent if I helped with the seismic work. So, I taught him how to shoot seismic. I let him use my equipment. I still did the analysis."

Koa set a trap for Gunter. "What equipment?"

"A seismic box and charges"—Gunter hesitated—"and a GPR, ground penetration radar, machine from the observatory."

"How did Keneke discover that you were smuggling artifacts?" Koa asked the question naturally, as though it followed perfectly from Gunter's recitation.

Gunter stopped fiddling with his beard and looked directly at Koa.

"I didn't kill Keneke. Let me say it again. I did *not* kill him. I don't know how much he discovered about my activities. He never confronted me. He just stopped talking to me, and mostly stayed away."

"You lied to me about discussing archaeology with Keneke."

Gunter remained unflinching. "*Ja.*"

"And you lied about exploring the saddle with him. You were out there in that cave where we found his body, weren't you?"

Gunter hesitated, but then confessed, "*Ja*, but . . . but nothing happened. That was weeks before his death."

"Bullshit, Mr. Nelson, you had a falling-out with Keneke."

Gunter became more assertive in the face of this challenge. "That's not accurate. I think he suspected me of taking artifacts, but he never confronted me. He just stopped talking to me about archaeology and generally avoided me."

"And you lied to me about that too."

"But I didn't kill him."

"You're telling us that Keneke suspected you of stealing Hawaiian treasures, and he did nothing to stop you. Is that what you're asking us to believe?"

"That's what happened . . . that's the truth."

"You've lied and lied and lied. Why should we believe you now?"

"Because now I'm telling the truth."

CHAPTER THIRTY-TWO

TWO HOURS LATER, Chief Lannua, Koa, Sergeant Basa, and Detective Piki met in the chief's office to discuss the Nakano murder. Koa gave up any effort to disguise his pinched nerve and stood against the wall while everyone else gathered around the table. The chief took no note, and Koa wondered if Basa had said something to him.

Before they could get started, the chief's assistant entered, saying that the National Weather Service had issued a severe weather warning. Heavy rains and high winds were expected, with wintery conditions at higher altitudes. The chief thanked her and turned to the detectives.

Koa laid out a rich stew of suspects and crimes, starting with the grave-robbing ring: Gunter Nelson, trafficker in antique treasures stolen from state lands. Ricky Kling, unlicensed private eye and a go-between for Gunter. Skeeter Slade, drunken helicopter pilot and collector of geologic data while flying tourists over the Pōhakuloa restricted area. Garvie Jenkins, ex-con, map forger, dope smuggler, and black-market antiquities dealer.

Koa then enumerated the other suspects: Charlie Harper, bizarrely jealous husband, serial sexual harasser, and possible accomplice on the Starfish shipment and the GPR machine. Prince Kamehameha, guardian of the Pōhakuloa adze makers' cave, sworn to kill any trespasser. Aikue ʻŌpua, Hawaiian activist, owner of the whalebone *pāhoa* used in the killing, and the man who had called 911 after finding Nakano's body.

But who'd actually killed Keneke Nakano? That was the question.

The chief looked at Koa. "I take it from your list that Masters is in the clear?"

"Yeah, he's got an ironclad alibi for the night of Wednesday, January 21, when Keneke was killed."

"Okay, that's good." The chief never wanted to see any of the island's important people in the police spotlight. He turned to Piki.

"Detective Piki, who's your suspect?" Koa had seen the chief play this game before, asking each of his officers to state and defend an opinion. And the chief liked to put young Detective Piki on the spot.

"Aikue ʻŌpua," Piki responded forcefully, confident he'd nailed it. "The lab ran tests on his dagger. His *pāhoa*'s got Keneke's blood on it, and he admits ownership. Unless someone snuck into his house, stole the dagger, and returned it after the killing, he's our killer. It's an open-and-shut case."

"So why haven't we arrested him?" the chief asked.

"Because," Koa responded, "I have doubts. The Kahoʻolawe Nine, including ʻŌpua, accepted Keneke into their *ʻohana*, their family. I just don't see ʻŌpua killing Kawelo Nakano's grandson. Besides, ʻŌpua saved Reggie's life on Kahoʻolawe. That's not the act of a killer—"

"But what about the *pāhoa*?" Piki interrupted loudly.

"I agree that the *pāhoa* is powerful evidence," Koa acknowledged, "but I think ʻŌpua lied. He collects old knives and couldn't resist taking that blade when he discovered Nakano's body."

"You're making excuses because he's a native-rights activist," Piki challenged.

Koa wasn't about to stand for that nonsense. He glared at the young detective. "His political activities have nothing to do with my opinion. Maybe you need to learn to look beyond the obvious."

"Ouch," Piki responded. "I'm sorry. I didn't mean to offend you."

"Who's your second choice?" the chief asked, again pointing at Detective Piki.

"Garvie Jenkins," Piki said, a little more hesitantly. "He'd know people who'd gladly cut your throat for pocket change. Strong motive . . . he was making a fortune smuggling. Nakano must have stumbled onto the grave-robbing scheme, and Jenkins killed him or maybe had him killed."

"Sergeant Basa?" the chief asked.

The sergeant scratched his head. "The whiz kid makes a good case, but I don't buy it. It's true that Garvie has nasty associates, but he has no personal record of violence."

"That's not quite right," Koa interrupted. "According to Reggie Hao, Garvie chased him with a knife out on Kahoʻolawe."

"Fair point," Basa conceded, "but still, we have no evidence that he and Nakano ever met or even knew of one another. No, I put my money on Charlie Harper."

"Harper?" The chief's tone sparkled with surprise. "What's his motive?" The chief seemed to have forgotten that Harper was once his favorite suspect.

"Jealousy, one of the strongest motives around. Harper kept his wife locked up like a glass figurine in a museum case. That marks Harper as a covetous man, a jealous man. He knew that Nakano met his wife at a hotel. Figures they shacked up and got nasty. It eats at his manhood. He beat up his wife over Keneke and he must have been out to get even. He's big and he's tall, capable of getting behind Nakano, locking 'im up in a choke hold and crushing his windpipe. And his alibi is a lie."

Koa turned in surprise. "How do you know that?"

"I checked with his friend Pete Chalmers. It's true that he got cashed out of the Wednesday night poker game, but a parking ticket on his car issued at 5:00 a.m. on January 22 outside a sleazy bar in Hilo says he wasn't far from where we found Nakano's truck, and he lied about going home."

Koa nodded. The sergeant had made a good case. Koa once again hoped Basa would work toward becoming a detective.

"Koa?" The chief almost always called on him last, both out of concern that the others would follow his lead and because Koa had an uncanny ability to get it right.

"Well, Chief, I'm not betting on Jenkins or Harper."

"Explain."

"Nakano was last seen at the observatory. We don't have a shred of evidence that Garvie had anything to do with the observatory or Nakano's sudden departure. There are too many missing links for me to pin it on Jenkins."

"What about Harper?"

"Sergeant Basa is right that Harper kept his wife like a caged bird. The SOB has the morals of a mongoose, and jealousy is a potent motive. But even if Harper threatened Nakano, and we have no evidence of that, it's hard to believe that Nakano would leave the observatory in the middle of the night and make reservations to return to the mainland. That would be a pretty extreme reaction."

"What about Gunter? We know," the chief began, "that his relationship with Keneke soured, because Keneke suspected that Gunter was looting Hawaiian grave sites. He has no alibi. As an Alice insider, he'd know Keneke's habits. He's been in the cave where we found Nakano's body. His cock-and-bull story would have us believe that although Keneke suspected him of stealing treasures, Keneke did nothing about it. And he's lied repeatedly."

"He's the obvious suspect, but I'm just not sure, Chief," Koa responded.

The chief didn't like to be contradicted, but he and Koa had disagreed so often the chief wasn't surprised. "Why?"

"There are pieces that don't fit right."

"Like what?"

"Keneke's computer. He appears to have left it when he walked out of the observatory. Why didn't we find it there? Gunter's only motive would have been to protect his illegal trade in ancient artifacts. Where does Keneke's computer fit into the motive?"

"Maybe Keneke had computer files about Gunter's activities," Basa suggested.

"Maybe, Sergeant Basa, but the logic of his doing that escapes me."

"What else doesn't fit?" the chief asked.

"The package Keneke mailed to Soo Lin on January 19. She says it contained astronomy files. Why would Keneke hide astronomy files from Gunter?"

Chief Lannua sighed heavily, nettled that his suspect wasn't holding up. "You got good instincts, Koa. You've spent time with Gunter Nelson. You interviewed him and toured the summit with him. What's your gut tell you?"

Koa hesitated. Rational analysis led inexorably to Gunter Nelson as the probable killer, but the chief had asked a different question, a question of gut instinct. "No, on a gut level I can't see Gunter Nelson killing Keneke Nakano and stuffing his body in that lava tube."

The phone rang, and Chief Lannua answered before handing the receiver to Basa. "It's one of your patrolmen. Says he's sorry to interrupt, but he's got something on the Nakano case."

Basa took the receiver. "This better be good, Maru. You interrupted me in the chief's office." As Basa listened, a surprised look spread across his face. "You're sure?" Another pause. "You show him the pictures?" More silence. "None of them? Is this Kessler guy sure?" Another pause. "Okay, ask him to come down to headquarters. What? He's got a rush job and can't come until this afternoon? I don't care. Get him in here now, and tell him to bring his work records, so we can pin the date down."

Basa put down the phone and turned back to the group. "Maru turned up a mechanic out at the airport. Guy named Kessler worked late one night about two weeks ago and nearly collided with Nakano's Trooper at five, maybe five thirty, as Kessler was leaving the airport. Maru's bringing him in for an interview."

"That's interesting," Koa responded. Why, he thought, would Nakano call for an airline reservation if he was already at the airport?

"What about Skeeter or Kling?" They all turned toward a grinning Detective Piki.

"It couldn't be Koa's buddy Kling." Sergeant Basa dismissed the idea with a wave.

"Why not?" Piki retorted.

"That little dick is too weak, too short, too creepy, and too much of a fuck-up to have killed Nakano and carried his body out to the PTA."

"What about this Slade fellow?" the chief asked. "I don't know him at all."

"He's an alcoholic helicopter pilot, and runs a tourist air sightseeing business," Koa said. "Someone, probably an anti-helicopter crazy, vandalized his equipment. He hired Kling to find the culprits. Kling paid him to fly Gunter's seismic pod over the Pōhakuloa Training Area."

"So he's a possible, Koa?"

"Possible, but unlikely," Koa responded. "We'd need a lot more than what we've got on him."

"What about the prince? He would have killed anyone who discovered the Pōhakuloa workshop," Piki suggested.

"That's true," Koa responded, "except Nakano's grandfather asked him to look after the kid." He'd already thought this thread through. "If it is the prince—and as a Hawaiian, I'd hate to believe one of our icons had fallen so far—I don't think the workshop provides the motive."

"Explain," the chief demanded with a quizzical expression on his face.

"The prince and 'Ōpua are like *kaikua'ana* and *kaikaina*, brothers, and the prince must be involved in 'Ōpua's Kaho'olawe activities. I mean, the prince tried to intervene with the Maui authorities to get 'Ōpua a pass. It's probably all sovereignty driven, but 'Ōpua hung with Garvie, and Garvie acted as a fence. It's got a bad smell."

He still hadn't decided whether this Garvie angle had all been 'Ōpua's doing and the prince knew nothing about it. He just couldn't see the prince condoning the sale of antiquities from his heritage. Then again, he found it surprising that 'Ōpua would do it either. "If 'Ōpua and the prince were really into something rotten on Kaho'olawe and Nakano discovered it, then we'd have a motive." Koa adjusted his back against the wall and stretched his neck, then added, "I wish I knew whether he lied to me about the spear of *pueo*."

"What lie?" the chief asked sharply.

"The prince let it slip that Nakano died by the spear of *pueo*, a fact we never released publicly. He claimed the mayor told him. I suppose it's possible, but if not, he moves to the top of my suspect list."

Koa had already brainstormed through all the suspects they had discussed without reaching a resolution. He had an uneasy feeling that he had missed something, but as hard as he tried, he couldn't pinpoint the source of his anxiety.

"I can find out for you," the chief responded. After making the offer, he looked hard at Koa. "Something's bothering you, Koa. What is it?"

"Chief, I'm worried about Soo Lin. Everything that night points to the observatory. She's been up there for four days. We gave her an emergency beeper and she calls twice every day, but I don't like it. I'll feel better when she's off that mountain."

"Why don't you bring her down?"

"We don't have any basis."

"She won't listen to you?"

"No. I've tried, but she's determined to find out why Nakano sent her the astronomy data. She thinks it's the key to his murder, and there's a good chance she's right. But that just makes me more anxious to get her off that damn mountain."

"So what's the next step?" the chief asked.

"I'm going to talk to the Kessler guy from the airport," Koa responded.

CHAPTER THIRTY-THREE

As Koa well knew, there came a moment in most cases when the pieces snapped together. That afternoon produced such a moment. The process began with a book. When Koa first removed it from the interoffice envelope, it mystified him. Why would anyone send him a book entitled *Scientific Fraud: Past and Present*? Then he saw the note and remembered Keneke's answering machine messages from Basically Books. One of Basa's patrolmen had collected the book from the store.

Although Koa enjoyed—was that the right word?—a familiarity with common fraud and thievery, he knew little about scientific hoaxes. Yet, on the book's dust jacket, scientific crimes paraded before him: The Loch Ness monster, the Piltdown Man, cold fusion, medical fraud. The list of scientific crimes and misdemeanors seemed endless.

Koa reflected on the book. What an odd choice of reading material. Why would Keneke Nakano have ordered a book on scientific frauds? For general information or curiosity, perhaps? Surely, Keneke wasn't planning a scientific fraud. Could he have discovered a scientific fraud? Could there be a connection between the book and the data he'd sent Soo Lin? Now, there was an intriguing idea.

Koa took the book into Chief Lannua's office. "Keneke ordered this book just before he died. Turns out to be a book on scientific fraud." He handed the book to the chief, who thumbed disinterestedly through the volume.

"What do you make of it, Koa?"

"It's probably nothing, but it got me thinking whether Keneke might have uncovered some kind of scientific fraud."

Chief Lannua appeared startled by the suggestion. "Isn't that quite a leap from the fact that he ordered this book?"

"You think I'm grasping at straws?"

"I think you'd better put your thinking cap back on." Koa dropped the book back on his desk and went down the hall to interview Herb Kessler, the witness from the airport. Dressed in grease-smeared coveralls, Kessler wore his hair in a crew cut, strangely at odds with his short goatee. He looked to be in his forties. "Thank you for coming in, Mr. Kessler. I understand you nearly collided with a black Isuzu Trooper a couple of weeks back?"

"I don't know why you blokes hauled me down here. I ain't done nothing wrong. I stopped in time. There weren't no accident."

"I understand. We aren't investigating an accident. Tell me what happened."

"Like I told the officer who came by the hangar, I worked late on a tourist helo. The control linkage was all fucked up. I wrapped up about five a.m. an' was drivin' out of the employee lot. Suddenly, this here black Trooper wheels around the corner. Drivin' fast, real fast. I slam on the brakes and skid some. But there weren't no collision."

"The Trooper was going into the airport?"

The mechanic's face took on a look he might have used with a stupid child. "Of course, he was comin' in. You think I'd near collide with a car leaving the airport?"

Koa ignored the sarcasm. "Can you describe the driver?"

"It happened real quick an' we didn't git out, so I was lookin' through the windshield. The dude had black hair. I'm sure about that. Age is tough, maybe fifty, but I could be ten years out."

Koa handed him a sheaf of photos. Kessler went through them one by one, rejecting all except one—a picture of Charlie Harper. "This one looks sorta like the driver. Might even be the guy, 'cept I kinda think the driver was older an' his face weren't so . . . so fat, and his jaw was kinda square." He handed Koa the photograph.

Koa shuffled through the photos, putting Nakano's picture in front of Kessler. "It wasn't this man?"

"No, the driver weren't no Hawaiian. No way."

The mysterious airport link was getting even murkier. "Can you fix the date of this near collision?"

"Yeah, I got my work records here. Haven't looked at 'em." Koa noticed the grime under Kessler's nails as he shuffled through a package of time sheets. "Yeah, here it is. January 20, I was working on the control linkage—"

The date surprised Koa. Keneke's calls to Alice and the airline reservation desk had occurred between seven thirty and seven forty-five on January 21. Those calls had been made from Keneke's cell phone, and his credit card had been used for the airline fare. On that basis, Koa had assumed that he was alive on the morning of January 21, and had died that night. But if someone else had parked his truck at the airport at around five o'clock in the morning on January 21, that changed the picture. "Did you say January 20— Tuesday, January 20?"

"Yeah, the time sheet's for that day, but the near collision happened early the following morning on January 21."

"You're sure?"

"Hell, yes. These work records are gospel. Even gave 'em to the FAA once. They've gotta be right."

Koa couldn't have explained the exact source of his inspiration.
He'd been ruminating on Keneke's astronomy data, and the book
had introduced the idea of scientific fraud. Then Kessler's certainty
about the timing of his near collision had cast doubt on the timing
of Keneke's death. In any event, it suddenly occurred to Koa that
Masters might be a viable suspect after all.

"Stay right here, Mr. Kessler. There's a picture I want to show
you. I'll have to get it from my office." Thurston Masters had been
in L.A. the night of January 21, so his picture wasn't included in
the original group.

"Yes, sir. I'll be sitting right here."

Koa hurried down the hall only to find Sergeant Basa in his office.

"Koa, I got something on Nakano. You better hear—"

Koa cut him off. "The near accident between Nakano's Trooper
and the airport mechanic occurred early on the morning of January
21, and someone with black hair, but not Hawaiian, was driving
Nakano's truck. Nakano might have been abducted or dead before
five on January 21."

"That fits . . . that fits like an outrigger on a canoe," Basa exclaimed.
"You remember, Koa, you told me to get on to Graham Gravel, the
cook up at the observatory cafeteria—the guy Gunter calls Lucrezia? Well, he got back from vacation this morning, and guess what?
The cafeteria served lamb—big chunks of lamb—for dinner on January 20. If that Army doctor is right about lamb in his stomach,
then Keneke died that night shortly after he left the Alice I Observatory around 1:00 a.m."

"Christ, that nails it," Koa said emphatically. "Nakano died in
the early hours of Wednesday morning—before the Wednesday
morning calls to the Alice headquarters and United Airlines.
Those calls were faked to make us think Keneke was still alive on
Wednesday morning."

Koa stopped and held up both hands, demanding silence. The case had changed fundamentally. He felt like the rug had just been pulled from beneath his feet. He had seen it happen in other tough cases, like his investigation of a murder by a councilman's son, and knew what was required. He had to step back, reexamine every piece, rethink every step.

Keneke had died between 1:12 a.m., when he left the observatory, and 5:00 a.m. on January 21, when the killer had driven Keneke's SUV into the Hilo airport parking lot—a span of three hours and forty-eight minutes. He mentally replayed the key sequence as outlined by Dr. Cater: choke hold . . . spear of *pueo* . . . movement of body . . . mutilation. He then focused on the timing: perhaps fifteen minutes to kill and load the body, an hour from Mauna Kea to the remote Pōhakuloa jeep trail; perhaps another hour to carry the body to the lava tube and perform the mutilation; perhaps fifteen minutes to dispose of the clothing; and another hour from Pōhakuloa to the airport parking lot—a total of three and a half hours. Close enough.

Koa was now certain that Keneke had died on the mountain. He hadn't run from the observatory. He'd stepped out on a break as he had in the wee hours of every night he'd spent there. He hadn't taken his computer because he expected to go back inside. But the killer had been waiting for him. The pieces fit like the workings of a well-oiled clock.

Koa explained his thinking to Basa, ending with his conclusion. "The killer is an Alice insider—someone intimately familiar with Keneke's routines."

By the time Koa finished, Basa was nodding in agreement. "And the call to Benson kept the Alice staff from asking questions about Nakano's disappearance," Basa added. "This killer's a devilishly clever bastard."

Basa's mention of the Benson call reminded Koa of the telephone call analysis that Piki had performed. That work, too, would have to be updated in light of the revised time of death. He sent Basa to get Detective Piki, along with the telephone records they'd assembled.

While he waited for Basa and Piki to return, Koa's mind raced. He was sure the killer had been waiting outside Alice for Keneke. In that case, the evidence pointed to either Gunter Nelson or Charlie Harper. Neither had been working at the observatory that night, and neither had a good alibi. He now added Masters to the list, too, although his review of the observatory tapes showed that Masters hadn't left the Alice II facility. And of the three, only Harper and Masters had black hair. But one discordant fact still nagged at Koa—Keneke had left his computer inside the observatory and it had disappeared. Did the killer have an accomplice?

Koa's eyes fell on the book that Keneke had specially ordered. The back of the dust jacket listed more than twenty scientific frauds, and near the bottom of the list, the words "Star Wars Program" jumped out. He picked up the book and found the relevant section. The first paragraph of the Star Wars chapter summarized the fraud:

A private defense contractor named Thurston Masters, sometimes called Mr. Star Wars, helped the defense department fool the Russians into believing the United States could track and destroy incoming missile warheads. He did so by developing computer software to fake the interceptor test results. Congress investigated and uncovered the fraud, but the Justice Department never pursued the case. It couldn't. Masters and his friends had destroyed all the test records. It's been an open secret in Washington for years, but it fooled the Russians.

Basa returned with Piki in tow. Basa had barely cleared the door before he announced, "It's got to be either Gunter Nelson or Charlie Harper. They weren't working that night and their alibis aren't worth shit."

Piki was more emphatic. "It's Charlie Harper. It's got to be. He made two cell phone calls between midnight and five a.m. He sure wasn't sleeping."

Koa surprised them with his question. "What about Masters?"

Piki looked confused. "I haven't even looked at his cell records. He has a rock-solid alibi. The security cameras show he spent Tuesday night, January 20, at Alice II, entering at dusk and leaving at dawn. It can't be Masters."

Basa caught on more quickly. "Koa, are you suggesting that Masters tampered with the security video?"

Koa held up Keneke's book. "Masters was 'Mr. Star Wars.' He helped fake the air force interceptor missile tests. He fooled the Russians. Maybe he also fooled us."

"What motive would he have?" The question came from Sergeant Basa.

"Just suppose"—Koa leaned forward, elbows on his desk—"just suppose that there's some fraud involved in his big discovery. Some fraud that Keneke uncovered or maybe was close to uncovering. That would explain Keneke's need to protect his astronomy data by sending it to Soo Lin. Maybe he didn't send an explanation to Soo Lin because he hadn't completed the work or maybe he didn't have time. It would also explain the removal of Keneke's computer—"

"But," Sergeant Basa objected, "those famous scientists all verified his discovery . . . six of the top guns in their fields . . . even a master at deception would have trouble fooling a bunch of pros."

Koa smiled grimly. "And who picked the verification team?"

While Koa outlined his theory, Piki had been frantically sorting through telephone records. "Masters only made one telephone call that night—at 5:05 a.m. from his cell phone."

Precisely, Koa thought, the time when the killer was at the Hilo airport. "Give me the number," Koa demanded as he picked up his cell phone and dialed as Piki read off the number.

The phone rang four times before a woman answered in a honeyed voice, "*Aloha*, this is Leilani Lupe."

Although he had heard it only once before, Koa instantly recognized the name and pictured the beautiful young Hawaiian woman who had spooked Christina Masters at the astronomy party. Gunter had made some crack about her in German and identified her as Masters' mistress. He hesitated, then disconnected.

Soo Lin was still on Mauna Kea. She could easily become Masters' next target. He tried calling her without success.

Koa weighed his options. Could he arrest Masters? On what charge? He didn't have nearly enough for murder. There might be fraud in Masters' great discovery, but Koa had no evidence. And with the findings of the verification team, it would take one hell of a lot of evidence.

But even fraud in the discovery wouldn't prove Masters guilty of murder, especially since the tapes showed that Masters hadn't left the observatory on the critical night. Even an identification by Kessler wouldn't be enough to overcome the security tape evidence. Damn, he had forgotten Kessler. Was he still sitting in the interrogation room? He grabbed Masters' picture and started toward the room, signaling Detective Piki and Sergeant Basa to join him.

He couldn't arrest Masters, but he could at least put him under observation. He turned to Detective Piki. "I've got three assignments for you. First, I need this Leilani Lupe woman's address. Second, get ahold of the telephone company and find out what cell tower carried that five o'clock call from Masters. And I want you to arrange a tail on Masters . . . loose and discreet, just enough so we know where to find him."

"Okay, I'll take care of it."

When he entered the interrogation room, Koa wasn't surprised to find it empty. He had Sergeant Basa send one of his patrolmen out to the airport with Masters' picture. As soon as he had Leilani Lupe's address, Koa headed for her garden apartment in the south part of Hilo. On the way, he repeatedly called Soo Lin without success.

Why did people make his job so hard?

Leilani answered his knock, Koa identified himself, and she led him into the living room of her apartment. Although he had seen Miss Lupe at the astronomers' party, she still surprised Koa. Her long, flowing black hair, unblemished light brown skin, even white teeth, and big sparkling black eyes made her an extraordinarily beautiful young woman. Even in this casual setting with an unexpected visitor, she wore a designer sundress that showed off the curves of her voluptuous form. Taking his eyes off her, Koa noted more elegant and expensive furnishings and artwork than typical for a Hilo apartment. Nor did he miss the decanter with two wine glasses set out in expectation of a visitor.

"What is this all about, Detective?" She spoke with a soft, almost girlish voice, adding an aura of innocence to her loveliness.

"We're investigating a homicide, and we believe that you may have some information that could help us."

She looked at him with soft black eyes. "Go on, Detective."

"Telephone records reflect that Dr. Thurston Masters called your number at 5:05 a.m. on the morning of Wednesday, January 21. Do you remember that call?"

He saw her jaw tighten at the mention of the astronomer's name. A young girl came out of the back of the apartment and cuddled next to Lupe, who put her arm around the child. "I have an autistic daughter, Detective. I don't want to have any trouble with the police."

Koa had to reassure this woman and get her to talk. He considered his words carefully. "Miss Lupe, we are aware that you have some sort of relationship with Masters. We are not investigating that relationship and have no interest in pursuing you on account of that relationship, whatever it may be. We just need your help to understand what happened during and after that telephone call."

Her face betrayed neither emotion nor any hint of her thinking. "All right," she said, nodding as she spoke, "ask your questions."

"You do have a relationship with Masters, am I correct?"

"Yes," she answered forthrightly. "We see each other regularly. He's very good to my daughter . . . pays her medical bills and school tuition. And he buys me nice things, like this." She fingered her circular gold necklace, embossed with diamonds. "Is that what you wanted to know?"

With that bit of background, Koa went for the jugular. "Did you talk to Masters about five o'clock in the morning on Wednesday, January 21?"

"I'm not positive about the date, but there was one night . . . it must have been that week . . . when he called and asked me to pick him up. His car had broken down and he needed a lift back to Mauna Kea."

"His car broke down?"

"Yes, out by the airport."

Now that link was tied up. "Hilo airport?"

"Yes. I picked him up at the commercial terminal."

"What time?"

"As soon as I could get dressed and drive over to the airport. Maybe fifteen minutes after his call."

"And you drove him back to Mauna Kea?"

"Yes, to that dormitory place. I didn't want to wake up my neighbor, Virginia Thorpe, who usually cares for my daughter, so I took Hannah with me." She hugged the girl next to her.

Koa wanted to be absolutely sure. "Can you pin the date down?"

"It must have been Tuesday night, or rather, Wednesday morning. Yes, it was early Wednesday morning. After I dropped him off on Mauna Kea, Hannah and I had breakfast and then went to the farmers' market, so it had to be Wednesday. That's the day of the Hilo market." Koa handed her a calendar. After looking at it for a few moments, she said, "Yes, Wednesday morning, January 21."

"Thank you, Miss Lupe," Koa said, as he left to race back to police headquarters. He was angry with himself for having been fooled by Masters, and was now desperately concerned for Soo Lin's safety. Masters had killed Keneke to preserve his Nobel prize-winning discovery.

Koa wasn't sure how Keneke had stumbled upon the fraud. The answer was undoubtedly in the data he'd sent to Soo Lin. And she was now on the mountain in harm's way. Masters wouldn't think twice about doing the same to Soo Lin.

Koa nearly collided with Sergeant Basa as he tore into his office. "We found Kessler. It's—"

"Masters," they both said in unison.

Seconds later Piki came running down the hall. "Koa . . . Koa!" Piki was so excited that he could hardly talk. "The five o'clock call from Masters originated in Hilo. He must have done a Star Wars number on the observatory security tape—because he didn't call from the observatory."

"We've got to find Masters and get Soo Lin off that mountain." Koa was emphatic. "If she's successful in following in Keneke's footsteps and uncovers proof of Masters' fraud, he'll kill her. She's our first priority . . . we've got to get her off that mountain."

CHAPTER THIRTY-FOUR

HEAVY RAIN DRENCHED Koa and Basa as they sprinted out to Koa's Explorer. Basa flipped on the emergency lights and activated the siren before they were out of the parking lot. They raced out of Hilo toward the Saddle Road. Using the SUV's mobile phone, Koa called for backup vehicles and additional police officers. He then asked to be patched through to Soo Lin at the Alice Observatories.

After repeated tries, the desk officer reported dead communication lines to the Alice Observatories and severe weather on Mauna Kea, deteriorating fast. All the observatories had ordered their personnel off the summit, but no one from Alice had acknowledged the directive or come back to the dormitory facility.

"Goddamnit!" Koa swore.

They turned onto the access road and roared up the mountain.

Seconds later the desk sergeant called back. "We've received an emergency beeper signal from Soo Lin."

Koa's worst nightmare was becoming real. "Patch the voice signal through to this telephone," Koa ordered. They listened with growing apprehension to scratchy sounds, relayed from Soo Lin's tiny transmitter through a series of microwave towers to police headquarters and then back over the airwaves to the speeding police vehicle. Koa could feel prickles dancing on the back of his neck as she spoke the name he now knew so well.

"Director Masters, I didn't know that you were in Alice I tonight. I was looking for Gaylord."

"Gaylord won't be bothering us anymore." They barely heard Masters' voice.

"Where is he?" Koa heard panic in Soo Lin's voice.

"Why did you come to Alice? What did Keneke Nakano tell you?" The voice was louder. Masters must be moving closer to the transmitter.

"N-nothing."

"Don't lie to me." Masters' voice cut like a whip. "Nakano figured out that the adaptive optics distorted observations at great distances. He was using an Alice computer to check the effect of the error on my discovery. He told you the discrepancy invalidated my calculations, undercutting my discovery." It was a statement, not a question.

"What are you talking about, Dr. Masters?" Koa guessed she was deliberately repeating his name for the transmitter. He realized she must have hidden the transmitter someplace on her person. Smart girl. Seconds passed. "Don't touch me. Don't touch me, you bastard."

Soo Lin's scream made Koa cringe. If only he'd figured it out earlier . . . or had persuaded her to get off the mountain.

Crack! It sounded like a vicious slap. Koa wanted to jump through the speaker to her rescue. It was his fault—if only he had been smarter.

The voices stopped, replaced by sounds of a struggle. Sobs? "Damn you . . ."

Silence. Sergeant Basa drove as fast as he dared up the steep Mauna Kea access road through heavy rain and thick, swirling white mist. As they neared the astronomers' dormitory the rain changed to snow and graupel, a form of alpine precipitation resembling soft hail. The police vehicle began to slide on the steep slopes.

Koa was desperate to reach the summit, but he doubted they could get all the way up in the icy weather. He racked his brain for alternatives. For the first time in his life he thought about chains and snow tires, but nobody used snow tires in Hawai'i. Maybe the Mauna Kea support facility, it occurred to him, used chains. He grabbed his cell, leaving the vehicle speakerphone hooked to Soo Lin's transmitter, and started to punch in the number for the support facility. Then a thought struck him.

He dialed Lieutenant Zeigler. Moments later he heard the Army officer's sleepy voice. "Christ, Koa, don't you ever sleep? It's close to midnight, for Christ's sake."

"How fast can you get an armored personnel carrier up the Mauna Kea access road?"

"What?" Zeigler's astonishment registered in a single word.

"We have a police emergency on the summit of Mauna Kea. Lives are in danger. We've got blizzard conditions, gale-force winds, and blowing ice. How fast can you get a tracked vehicle up here?"

There was a long pause at the other end of the line. "Well, if you tell me it's a life-or-death emergency, I'll do it."

"Do it. Soo Lin's life is hanging in the balance."

More noises from Soo Lin's transmitter: an overhead door grinding open, the howl of the wind, ice pellets bouncing off the dome. The sounds grew louder. They heard a rumble, like the building shaking with the intensity of the wind. A rending sound signaled something breaking loose—metal clanging against metal—and something clattering to the concrete floor.

"Damn," Koa swore, "the building is starting to disintegrate."

New sounds filtered through the speaker, maybe a motor, like a diesel engine. The sound grew louder. More engine noises, then whirring and clanking. A loud crack startled them.

"What was that?" Sergeant Basa asked.

"What are you doing?" They heard Soo Lin's voice again. "You'll damage the telescope."

"Exactly." Masters' voice slashed across the radio like a laser.

Something heavy thudded against the concrete floor.

"You bastard. You're going to destroy the observatory to cover up your fraud."

"Fraud, Miss Hun?"

"Your calculations were false. You just told me you failed to real-ize that the adaptive optics introduced errors that invalidated your research. Or did you introduce the error to get the results you wanted?"

"Very good, Miss Hun, but you confuse the proof with discovery."

"Oh, I see," she said. Her voice turned sarcastic. "Having con-ceived your great discovery, it was okay to falsify the proof."

God, Koa thought, she's gutsy. She's making him confess.

"The discovery is real. It ranks with the greatest achievements of astronomers throughout the ages—Copernicus, Galileo, Kepler, Einstein, Hubble, Hawking."

"But when other astronomers can't replicate your observations, they'll know you falsified the data."

"Not without these observatories. Without the power of the Al-ice twins linked together, astronomers won't have the capability to replicate my observations. The verification team has validated my discovery, and no man will challenge it for decades."

"The verification team will tear you apart when they learn you tricked them."

"Really? The best and the brightest, wined and dined, given a special preview . . . honored to verify the greatest discovery of their time. Thoroughly co-opted."

"You killed Keneke and . . ." The shrieking wind tore away her words.

"Yes, Miss Hun, and cleverly too. I hoped his body would rot in that desolate lava cave, but I couldn't take chances, so I replicated the Valentine's Day murder."

The pride in Masters' voice turned Koa's stomach. Masters' mention of the Valentine's Day murder reminded Koa of the extensive media coverage the crime had attracted, reflected in the file he'd studied.

"Valentine's Day murder?"

"It happened years ago while I was hospitalized on Maui with a broken jaw. It fascinated me and I read all the stories. Some wacko mutilated a kid. I copied his style. It gave me the excuse to destroy Keneke's face and fingerprints."

"The security tapes show that you spent the whole night at Alice II."

Koa heard Masters laugh. "Technology, Miss Hun. I rewired the motion and infrared sensors. Touch a remote control and nothing triggers the camera. Flip it back on and everything returns to normal."

"You killed him on his break."

"I was waiting when he came out of the observatory. The fool was just gazing up at the stars. I got him in a choke hold. Just like in air force survival training. And then I stabbed him in the eye. It was painless. He didn't suffer like you're going to. I trained at Pōhakuloa and knew about the lava tube. An ideal place to stuff a body, don't you think?"

"The telephone calls. You faked the telephone calls."

"Something important has come up." A different voice came over the transmitter, one Koa knew only from the words. "It's my girlfriend. I've got to go back to the mainland to California for a few days."

"Miss Hun, you've met Cepheid." Masters' voice resumed its cultured tone. "Cepheid, say hello to Miss Hun."

"Good evening, Miss Hun."

"You used that thing to call the airline to make a reservation in Keneke's name."

"A nice touch, don't you think? The security cameras gave me an alibi for the night of January 20, but I went to California on January 21."

"You fooled the security cameras."

"Child's play. Fooling the Russians about our capability to shoot down their missiles, that was hard. That took talent. Fiddling with the cameras was mere child's play."

"Tell me why. You had everything—a prestigious position, money. People respected you for your genius in adaptive optics. Why fraud? And murder?"

"I'll go down in history as the greatest astronomer of all time . . . a modern-day Hubble, Einstein, and Hawking all rolled into one towering giant of astronomy—the man who proved the universe will end! The name of Thurston Masters will be celebrated for centuries."

"You will never get off the island."

A burst of static obscured Masters' answer.

More static . . . the transmitter seemed to be failing.

"There's no record of my being here today, Miss Hun, and I'll be gone before this building explodes in flames. Cepheid will see you to the end."

Suddenly the static cleared. "You're mad."

"Mad, Miss Hun? No. Just clever."

More static . . . more static . . . and no more voices.

CHAPTER THIRTY-FIVE

AT THE DORMITORY complex, Koa and his men fought their way through blinding snow and flying ice to get to the entrance. "Who's in charge here?" he bellowed, throwing open the front door. Koa hadn't expected the polar bear of a man who stepped forward—Gunter Nelson, still out on bail. The two men glared at each other until Gunter broke the silence. "I'm afraid you're stuck with me, Detective Kāne. I'll help you any way I can."

Koa had no alternatives. He was running out of time and options. It might already be too late. "Let's go, we've got to get to the summit." Koa turned toward the Explorer.

"You'll never make it in this weather," Gunter responded. "At least put strap chains on your vehicle."

"Get them," Koa directed. While two policemen fastened spiked straps to the rear wheels of the Explorer, Koa again called Zeigler.

"I've got a Bradley Fighting Vehicle on the way at top speed," Zeigler said. "I had 'em load night-vision goggles and arctic gear. You'll need it on that fucking mountain. I hear they got whiteout conditions. The vehicle commander, Sergeant Pete Lomi, will report to you, but he retains command of the vehicle. It's on the access road, no more than ten minutes south of the dormitory complex."

"Thanks. Sergeant Basa, Gunter Nelson, and I are going on ahead. Tell your vehicle commander to pick up the rest of my men at the dormitory complex and make for the summit, but keep an eye out for my Explorer. I'll transfer to the Bradley when it catches up."

Koa struggled out to the Explorer. Even at the 9,000-foot altitude with some shelter from the surrounding cinder cones, the wind howled, driving pellets of soft ice through the air like big BBs. God only knew what it would be like at 14,000 feet. The Explorer lurched up the mountain road, frequently spinning its wheels. They ran the defroster and the wipers at full blast, but still strained to make out the edges of the road ten feet in front of the bumper.

"Who's left on the summit?" Koa asked.

"Gaylord and Soo Lin were the only Alice people on the summit. We tried to get them off the summit at the same time the astronomers and technicians from all the other observatories evacuated, but we couldn't get through and then the communication lines failed," Gunter responded. "I don't know, but I think they're still up on the summit."

"What about Masters?"

Gunter gave Koa a puzzled look. "He wasn't on the mountain today."

"You're wrong about that," Koa said grimly. "When was your last contact with Soo Lin?"

"About an hour ago, then we lost contact. The storm must've knocked out the communication system."

"Any way to evaluate conditions up there?"

"We still have a data link. Instruments report sustained winds of fifty miles per hour with frequent gusts in excess of seventy-five miles per hour. Temperature in the low twenties and falling, heavy precipitation—ice and graupel, intermingled with snow. Video surveillance shows near-zero visibility. The National Weather Service predicts deteriorating conditions for the next several hours. It's as bad as I've ever seen it, Detective."

"Goddamnit!"

"One other thing..."

"What else?"

"We got a sensor signal showing an open shutter on Alice I. That building is in trouble."

"What does that mean?"

"The dome was designed to withstand these conditions, but not with the shutter open. At speeds of eighty to a hundred miles per hour, the wind could rip the dome off and destroy the telescope."

"Shit!" Koa exploded. Things were getting worse by the moment.

As Basa nursed the Explorer up the slippery incline, the rear wheels hit an icy patch and spun freely. *Thwackkkk!* Thwack! Thwack! The strap chains tore free from the tires, slapping hard against the wheel housings. Basa fought to control the heavy vehicle, but it turned sideways, and a wheel dropped off the road before the SUV stopped. They were stuck with no option but to wait for the Bradley. Worse, the stalled Explorer blocked the access road.

Minutes later, they heard the sound of a tracked vehicle clambering up the steep road. An olive drab hulk emerged from the swirling snowstorm, and an M2 Bradley Infantry Fighting Vehicle lurched to a stop behind the disabled Explorer. It looked like a small tank, twenty-one feet long and ten feet wide, carrying a turret with a 25mm Hughes chain gun. Huge sprockets at the front corners of the track housings delivered power to the heavy metal tracks, which rode on a series of smaller spring-tensioned bogie wheels.

With the churn of the hydraulic pumps, the rear hatch cracked open and dropped slowly to the ground. Five men dressed in thick white pants and hooded white parkas emerged from the vehicle. Koa recognized three of his officers, noting that they now wore military combat boots in addition to arctic gear. Koa silently thanked Lieutenant Zeigler.

"I'm Sergeant Pete Lomi, the vehicle commander." The white-clad figure stood nearly six feet tall. "I suggest you climb in the back and get into some winter gear. You're gonna freeze your butts off out here dressed like that."

Koa and Basa were only too happy to comply. Even Gunter, who already had a parka, put on arctic pants.

Four police officers, straining with all their might on the slippery road, couldn't budge the Explorer. Finally, Koa asked, "Sergeant Lomi, can the Bradley push it out of the way?"

"Sure can, Detective, but the Bradley weighs thirty tons, and the controls ain't that precise. It'll likely rip the shit out of that piece of tin."

"We'll take that chance. We've got to get to the summit."

Under Sergeant Lomi's direction, the driver edged the front of the Bradley forward. Sergeant Lomi held up his hands so that the driver could judge the distance, but when he applied his foot to the gas, the 506-horsepower Crimmins four-stroke diesel engine roared and transferred power to the tracks. The armor-clad fighting vehicle hit the back of the Explorer with a crunch that crumpled the rear bumper, shattered glass, and ripped a gash across the back of the Explorer. The SUV came loose, flipped on its side, crashed off the edge of the road, and rolled down the embankment. "Jesus," Koa said as he stared down at the wreck.

Having cleared the obstruction, the driver backed off, picked up Koa and Sergeant Lomi, and headed up the access road. The engine screamed and the tracks clanked. The vehicle shook violently on the rough washboard of the unpaved mountain road. Inside, the noise was deafening, and the jerking and twisting triggered blinding pain in Koa's neck, shoulder, and arm. He gritted his teeth, just hoping they would make it to the summit in time.

Sergeant Loma kept the vehicle out of the ditches and away from the edges, where the ground often dropped a harrowing five hundred feet. Under his skilled direction, the Bradley maintained a remarkably fast pace up the steep slopes and around hairpin turns.

As the vehicle lumbered up the mountain, Koa had to scream to make himself heard. "Okay, here's the situation. Masters has Soo Lin and Gaylord captive in Alice I. He's going to destroy the building."

Gunter opened his mouth in astonishment, but he remained silent.

"We have to see what's happening inside without detection, if possible. Gunter, you know the buildings. How can we get a look inside?"

"The main entry door and an overhead service door lead into the dome, but either way, anyone inside would see you," Gunter responded.

"Any other way?"

"You could enter Alice II, go down into the interferometry tunnel, and get under the Alice I telescope. You'd have the best chance of being undetected if you went in through the tunnel."

"You'd come out in the Alice I dome?" Koa couldn't visualize it.

"No, you'd be under the Alice I dome with the ability to see what's happening inside. There's an ocular, an opening under the center of the telescope. We could use a mirror, like a periscope, to see what's happening inside the dome."

"Okay, we'll try it," Koa screamed over the roar of the bouncing vehicle.

They finally crested the last ridge and moved into position near the observatories. As they prepared to dismount, Sergeant Lomi handed each man a headset attached to a cigarette pack–sized transceiver. "If you put these on, we'll be able to maintain communications."

Koa took over from the Army sergeant. "Sergeant Lomi, you stay with the Bradley. Sergeant Basa, take two men and stand by just inside Alice I. Gunter and I will go through the tunnel and reconnoiter Alice I. Let's go."

When Sergeant Lomi lowered the hatch, the wind blasted them with astonishing fury. Bent double, the men could barely stagger toward the entrance to Alice II. The thin air and cold quickly sapped Koa's strength, so he had to force himself to plod forward. They were only halfway there when Koa heard Gunter exclaim, "*Verdamnt*." Looking to his side, he saw the German astronomer pointing upward. Following Gunter's upraised arm, he saw the Alice I shutter standing open. Hurricane-force winds had shredded material from inside the dome. Even as he watched, Koa could see the dome bulge with the gusting wind. Time was running out.

"Keep moving," Koa ordered.

When they reached the door, Gunter fumbled with the lock before they raced into the main corridor. Partway down the hall, Gunter flung open a door. The overpowering smell of diesel fuel and gasoline hit them. "*Verdamnt!* Something awful is happening." The smell grew stronger as the men ran down a flight of stairs into a long tunnel filled with workbenches, mirrors, and sensors. Gunter led the way past the work areas toward the opposite end of the tunnel. He stopped and raised a hand just before they reached the far end of the space. "We're under Alice I," he whispered through his communicator.

Looking up, Koa saw light from inside the Alice I dome coming through a hole in the ceiling. He watched as Gunter quickly clamped two mirrors to a long rod. After adjusting the mirrors, he mounted the assembly into a vise on the bench and slowly extended the rod upward until the top mirror, angled at forty-five degrees, passed through the hole into the dome above. As he did so, Gunter pointed to the mirror near the bottom of the rod.

In the bottom mirror, Koa saw the inside of the dome. For an instant, he had trouble making sense of the forest of pipes and brackets, but then his mind took in the picture. The mirrors enabled him to look outward from a spot near the floor in the center of the dome. He saw the base of the telescope, the railing separating the telescope from the open space around it, and then the inside wall of the dome. Nothing appeared out of the ordinary.

As Gunter slowly rotated the rod, Koa saw oil drums tipped on their sides, surrounded by a massive slick of diesel fuel and gasoline with propane tanks scattered around. Koa's breath caught in his throat as Gaylord's prostrate form came into view. The man appeared to be dead. His heart sank as he realized they were too late to save Soo Lin. The mirror turned. More overturned fuel drums. The place would explode in an inferno, hot enough to melt the steel frame of the telescope.

The picture changed. Koa almost missed the significance of the canister-like shape behind one of the overturned oil drums. "Cepheid," he muttered, "Masters' robot." The mirror turned farther, revealing the rest of Cepheid, and Koa gasped. "Holy Mother of God." The robot held an acetylene torch aloft in his left pincer. The tip of the torch glowed with a small flame, fed by a rubber hose attached to a tank. If the robot dropped the torch into the diesel and gasoline slick, the entire observatory building would go up in flames.

Cepheid was the trigger, like the detonator of a bomb. With a single command to the robot, the observatory was doomed. But Cepheid was a remote trigger, and Koa instantly recognized its significance. Masters had fled. He was going to destroy the observatory electronically from a remote distance.

"Faster. Turn the mirror faster. We're running out of time."

Gunter rotated the mirror until Koa commanded, "Stop."

Soo Lin came into view. She was alive, bound to a telescope support and surrounded by a pool of fuel, still struggling to free herself.

"Swing around again. Stop." Koa studied Cepheid standing still with his mechanical arm outstretched and his pincers holding a flaming torch. His mind flashed back to his first encounter with the robot outside Masters' office. The robot had moved with lightning speed when it had pretended to beat him to the draw.

How could they disable the robot? They couldn't risk shooting it. The chances of knocking it over or causing the torch to fall were too great. How was it commanded? He remembered the curly antenna atop its head. Danny had controlled it using some sort of remote radio. He recalled the huge glass eye, some sort of camera. He wondered if the robot had seen the mirror. God, he hoped not.

They had to disable the robot. But how? Koa again flashed back to his encounter with Danny. How had the boy responded? "Cepheid arrests Keneke's murderer. That would make a nice headline."

Danny Masters might hold the key. Koa wondered if he could get in touch with the boy.

He hurried back down the tunnel. "Sergeant Lomi, do you read me?"

"Yes, sir, loud and clear," his voice crackled over the radio.

"Get hold of Lieutenant Zeigler. Get him to patch a telephone hookup to this radio net. Can you do that?"

"Yes, sir."

Koa waited. The seconds seemed like an eternity before he heard Zeigler's voice.

"Lieutenant Zeigler here. What do you need, Koa?"

"Two things, Jerry. First, I need to jam the transmissions from a controller to a mechanical robot."

"What kind of transmissions?"

"It's radio controlled."

"What's the frequency?"

"No idea. Can you jam all frequencies?"

"We don't have a frequency jammer on the Bradley. I'd have to transmit a jamming signal to the Bradley and have it retransmit. I'd be lucky to get enough power to jam a narrow frequency band."

"Okay, let me try to get the frequency. There's a kid, Director Masters' son, Danny Masters. He should be at Punahou School on Oʻahu. Get him on the phone. Soo Lin's life may depend on it."

While he waited, Koa briefed the others on the team. He divided the team into two groups. He ordered one team to assemble quickly and quietly in the service bay outside the Alice I dome and the other team to stand by in the corridor near the other entrance to the dome. Gunter told them where to find firefighting equipment. "Be damned careful. The object is to rescue Soo Lin, if possible, but that place is going to go up like a lava fountain. I don't want any of you hurt."

"Hello," said the voice of a young man.

"Danny . . . Danny Masters?" Koa asked.

"Yes. Who is this? Why did you get me up in the middle of the night?"

Koa could hear the sleepiness in his young voice. The kid had been rousted out of bed.

"Danny, this is Detective Kāne. We met at the observatory headquarters. Do you remember?"

"Yes, I remember."

"I need your help. It's about Cepheid." Koa had the boy's undivided attention. "We need to stop Cepheid from doing something wrong. Is that possible?"

"Why?"

Koa hesitated before deciding to go with the truth. "Cepheid's being used to commit a crime. If we don't stop him, a young astronomer will die."

"Who's using Cepheid? It's my father—he's using Cepheid, isn't he?"

Koa hesitated. The boy was his best hope, and he was slipping away. "Yes," Koa answered slowly. "We believe that your father is controlling Cepheid, and we need your help to save a young astronomer. Please, Danny. Please help us." He should have expected the boy to be torn.

"Should I help you or my father?"

"That's the most difficult decision you'll ever have to make, Danny. All I can say is that your father is going to use Cepheid to kill a young woman, and I need your help to save her."

"Are you going to hurt my father?"

"No, Danny, not if I can help it. Listen, we need the frequency used to control Cepheid."

"I guess it's okay to help you," the boy said slowly.

"You're going to try to jam the frequency?"

"Yes. Will it work?"

"Maybe. Cepheid operates on channel 89 at the top of the 75-megahertz band. The frequency is 75.970 megahertz."

Koa had his answer. "Thank you, Danny. You may have saved a woman's life."

"There's one more thing, Detective Kāne. You remember that Keneke worked on Cepheid's software?"

"Yes."

"Keneke created an artificial intelligence program designed to prevent Cepheid from hurting either a human or the robot himself. If you can trigger that program, at least theoretically Cepheid won't harm anyone. Keneke and I tested the program, but never in a real-life situation." Koa listened for another thirty seconds as Danny explained how to activate the program he and Keneke had designed into the robot's electronic brain.

Lieutenant Zeigler, who'd been listening, spoke up. "We'll try jamming that frequency, but I'm not sure we'll have enough power to block any command signals, especially if the command transmitter is close by."

"It has to be close by. Masters can't have gone too far in this weather."

"I'll do the best I can, but I'm warning you, you better have a plan B."

Koa, Gunter, a patrolman, and Private First Class Caulder gathered at the main entrance to the Alice I observatory with heavy fire extinguishers. The extinguishers had wide black nozzles capable of laying down a blanket of foam. Sergeant Basa and two more police officers also equipped with fire extinguishers went to the service bay entrance to the dome.

Koa spoke softly over the radio net. "On my command, everybody goes. Sergeant Lomi, you start jamming. Firefighters, lay down foam on the gasoline slick. Concentrate on the area around Soo Lin. Sergeant Basa, you go for Soo Lin. Cut her loose and get her out of there. I'm going to try to neutralize the robot. Got it?"

"Ready to start jamming," came the reply from Sergeant Lomi.

"Soo Lin, your time has come."

The deep, cultured voice from inside the dome surprised Koa. He had been sure that Masters had fled. Where had he been hiding? He must have been on the platform above Koa's line of vision.

Now he would have to contend with both Masters and Cepheid. Plus, Masters would be armed. Jesus, the operation, already difficult, had become impossibly dangerous.

"Please wait," Soo Lin pleaded. "Please, I need to know why."

"Why? To achieve immortality . . . to be remembered for a thou-sand generations . . . to be a modern Hubble." Masters' deep voice boomed through the dome.

In that instant Koa realized his mistake. The voice was too unnat-urally loud. Masters wasn't inside the dome. He was speaking through Cepheid.

"Now! Launch now!" Koa commanded.

He sprang through the door, followed by the others. He scanned the interior. God, the dome was huge, much larger than he'd re-membered. He spotted Cepheid behind several overturned oil drums. The robot remained stationary. The jamming must be work-ing. Yet when he started toward Cepheid, the robot's arm jerked. Some commands must be getting through. The acetylene torch flared, sending a narrow tower of flame upward.

Christ, the jamming had failed, Koa groaned. He was too far away to stop Cepheid. The robot's arm jerked again, starting downward.

"EVIL. Danny says you're doing an EVIL thing." Koa used the commands he'd learned from Danny Masters. Although yelling, Koa forced himself to space the words. "You cannot take a human life. You cannot do EVIL. You must NOT take a human life."

The robot turned its head, focusing its huge glass eye on Koa. Cepheid's arm stopped moving. The flame roared upward at a 30-degree angle.

"EVIL." Koa began to repeat the litany, shouting at the top of his lungs. All the while, the firefighters sprayed foam everywhere. Koa was heartened to see Basa reach Soo Lin.

"There is no evil in obeying my commands . . . you must obey." Masters' deep voice boomed from Cepheid's speakers. "Cepheid, you must obey."

The words seemed to reestablish Masters' control over Cepheid. The robot's arm jerked. The flame shot straight out, almost licking the petroleum-covered floor.

"EVIL!" Koa shouted. "You must not take a HUMAN LIFE." The robot's arm stopped again.

The firefighters spread foam wider and wider, but there was diesel fuel and gasoline everywhere. Basa sliced at the ropes holding Soo Lin. Christ, Koa cursed, why couldn't he move faster? They had to get her out. They themselves had to get out before the place went up in flames.

"Obey."

"Evil!"

The conflicting words kept the robot frozen. Then Cepheid's arm moved, but not as either man intended. In one swift movement Cepheid turned the acetylene torch back on itself, and the flame cut through the side of the robot's head. Its huge glass eye transmitted the blue-white color of superheated acetylene before its circuit boards melted. Cepheid destroyed himself before Koa got to the valve on the acetylene tank to shut off the gas.

With the immediate threat of being burned alive removed, Gunter managed to restore power and slowly closed the shutter of the Alice I telescope.

Koa, Soo Lin, and three police officers gathered inside the office. Soo Lin, now bundled in a grossly oversized arctic parka, shivered almost uncontrollably.

"Masters wasn't scheduled to be up here today," she said, speaking in a hushed whisper, "but somehow he snuck into the building. At first, I thought the storm had cut off the power and the communication lines, but it was him. He cut the lines. Then he hit me and tied me up out there." She pointed through the window between the control room and the telescope. "The bastard killed my Keneke because he was close to revealing the flaw in Masters' big discovery. Masters admitted it . . . he admitted killing Keneke. And Gaylord too . . . he killed poor Gaylord. I saw him dragging the body. He was going to destroy the telescopes and leave me here to die . . . all for the sake of his phony discovery. He's a maniac, drunk on the desire for glory . . . for immortality."

"Do you know where he went?" Koa asked. "How he planned to get off the mountain?"

"He left the telescopes. I saw him go. He said something about a car in the hills above Waimea. He's going to pretend he was never here."

Koa, still wired into the radio network, spoke into his microphone. "Sergeant Lomi, this is Koa. Can you hook up a telephone patch to police headquarters?"

"Yes, sir," came the reply, followed by a series of clicks and pauses.

"Koa, this is Desk Sergeant Kanewa. What's happening? The chief has been calling me every five minutes for the past two hours. He's about to blow a gasket."

"Listen carefully, Sergeant Kanewa. Thurston Masters killed Keneke Nakano and an observatory technician named Gil Gaylord. He tried to destroy the Alice telescopes. He's on foot trying to escape down the western slope of Mauna Kea toward Waimea. He must've stashed a vehicle, probably off one of the jeep trails in the hills behind Waimea. Get some officers up there. Set up roadblocks. Consider him armed and dangerous. Don't let him get out of there."

Koa turned his attention to another force at his disposal. "Sergeant Lomi?"

"Yes, sir."

"Can the Bradley track Masters down the slope through this storm?"

"Sure. It'll be slow going—that's brutal terrain—but the Bradley can handle steep grades and rough terrain, and we've got thermal detectors. They'll pick up a man's heat, especially in this weather."

Koa was hot to catch Masters. After instructing PFC Caulder, together with one of his patrolmen, to keep watch over the facility, Koa left Gunter with Soo Lin in the telescope offices. He took Sergeant Basa and the other police officers through the still-intensifying storm to the Bradley. Sergeant Lomi fitted Koa with thermal goggles. The two men stood in the turret as Sergeant Lomi directed the big tracked machine down the slope. They advanced cautiously, avoiding large boulders and other obstacles. The wind tore at them, flinging pellets of ice that frequently obscured their visibility.

Koa and Lomi scanned the blizzard-torn night with their thermal glasses, searching for any gleam of heat. To check his glasses, Koa turned back toward the Alice telescopes. The heat radiating from the support facilities lit up the glasses like a movie screen.

Yard by yard, the Bradley tracked down the icy slope. Twice Sergeant Lomi stopped, directing the driver to back up and turn to avoid some obstruction or particularly difficult slope. Five minutes, then ten. Koa estimated that they had gone four hundred yards down the mountain when a point of light flashed in his goggles.

He grabbed Sergeant Lomi and pointed. Lomi directed the driver to swing left toward the source of heat. Both men stared through the night as the image grew from a blob of light and gradually took on shape—a thick, long body, then a head. Almost simultaneously, both men recognized the image—a cow.

Sergeant Lomi pointed the driver back to the right. They came to the edge of the ancient Mauna Kea adze quarry. Sergeant Lomi, intently aware of the risk of running the vehicle into one of the huge pits hacked into the side of the mountain, inched the Bradley forward, skirting a giant pit's edges.

As they neared the lower limit of the quarry, the storm abated somewhat. Visibility improved from a few feet to a few yards. Koa scanned the ground ahead. Still no sign of Masters. He wondered if they might have missed their prey. Maybe he hadn't headed toward Waimea at all. Perhaps he was still near the observatories. The thought sent a chill down Koa's spine.

Koa keyed his microphone. "PFC Caulder, what is your status?"

No response. "PFC Caulder, what is your status?" Koa repeated. No response.

"He's backtracked. He must be back at the observatory." Even before Koa finished speaking, Sergeant Lomi signaled the driver into a wide turn. As the Bradley came around, Sergeant Lomi ordered the vehicle to full power. The Bradley jerked violently forward like a spooked horse, the noise rising to a deafening clatter. The vehicle shook as it reached top speed and raced up the mountain.

The Bradley bucked as it crested the ridge, stopping so abruptly that Koa banged against the steel ring of the turret. Ignoring the searing pain in his shoulder, he levered himself out of the turret, swung down to the ground, and took off at a dead run through the snow. Suddenly he felt weak and remembered what Gunter had said about dying of oxygen deprivation. It didn't matter. He had to save Soo Lin. His lungs burned and he fought down nausea. He drew his Glock automatic and hobbled as fast as he could into the Alice II building and down the hallway. Turning right and then left, he entered the Alice I service bay.

"You!" Soo Lin screamed.

"Yes, Miss Hun." Masters' voice retained its arrogance. "You seem to have escaped your fate, but you won't be so fortunate the second time."

"What are you doing?"

"Exactly what I originally planned, except this time I will personally ignite the fire that will consume this observatory and you along with it."

The sound of Masters' voice led Koa toward the overhead door into the Alice I dome. His eyes instantly absorbed the scene. The blackened hulk of Cepheid. Soo Lin bound on the floor. The police officer he'd left behind unconscious next to PFC Caulder's limp body. Gunter struggling with a knife in his shoulder. Masters standing near the main door with the acetylene torch in his right hand.

"Stop, or I'll shoot." Koa's voice boomed through the dome.

In reply, a flame bloomed from the tip of the acetylene torch, sending a plume of fire four feet into the air. To Koa the action seemed to unfold in slow motion. Masters raised the torch, preparing to throw it into the lake of diesel fuel and gasoline covering the floor. At the same time, Masters' left hand, holding a gun, swung toward Koa.

Koa's pistol bucked. He brought it down and fired again. Masters jerked as the first bullet slammed into his shoulder. Masters' gun flashed, but Koa's bullet had disrupted his aim, and a glass segment in the primary mirror of the telescope shattered. Yet the lighted torch sailed upward in an arc, headed for the pooled diesel fuel and a conflagration that would consume them all. They were about to die.

"*Whoooosh!*" The sound of escaping gas filled the dome. The rubber hose from the acetylene tank whipped through the air like a wild snake. The flame died just before the torch hit the floor. Only then did Koa see that Gunter had crawled over and cut the acetylene hose.

His gun at the ready, Koa cautiously approached Masters' body crumpled on the floor. Squatting down, Koa checked for a pulse.

There was none. Koa's second shot had killed the would-be modern Hubble.

*   *   *

Koa, Nālani, and Soo Lin met three days later for dinner at the Queen's Court restaurant overlooking Hilo Bay. Chief Lannua joined them. Hook Hao, the master of all Hilo waterfront secrets, somehow learned of their dinner and showed up with two bottles of Russian River chardonnay. They made a place for him at the table, and he offered the first toast. "To Koa Kāne, who never forgets a friend in need." They raised a glass to Koa.

As they discussed Reggie's Kahoʻolawe escapade, Koa gave Hook credit for tipping off the police to Jenkins's secret shipment of artifacts. "You know," Koa mused, "if Reggie hadn't gotten hurt out there, we might never have solved the Pōhakuloa antiquities case. Reggie led us to Jenkins, who led us to Kling, Skeeter, and ultimately Gunter. The Maui prosecutor nailed Jenkins for attempted murder. When he gets out, we'll prosecute him for antiquities theft, and then the feds will have their turn on drug charges. And that little rat Kling will also be serving time."

"I was sure Gunter murdered Keneke," the chief interjected, "but once again, Koa, you proved me wrong. Here's to the best detective in Hawaiʻi!" Again they drank to Koa.

"How did you do it, Koa?" Soo Lin asked. "How did you stop Cepheid?"

"Keneke saved your life. He built Cepheid's artificial intelligence software and programmed the robot to distinguish right from wrong. He gave it a conscience. Danny, Masters' son, told me how to trigger the program. In the end, Cepheid refused to be an instrument of murder."

"What's going to happen to Gunter?" Nālani asked.

"He'll serve some time, but not as much as he would have without his good deeds on the mountain," Koa responded. "The courts simply can't overlook grave robbing and antiquities theft."

They sat in silence pondering Gunter's fate before Koa changed the subject. "Funny how ambition destroyed two careers. Masters committed murder in pursuit of immortality, while Gunter's thwarted ambition led him to rob graves. Somebody once said, 'Whether we fall by ambition, blood, or lust, like diamonds we are cut with our own dust.'"

Just before they were ready to pay the check and leave, Prince Kamehameha walked up to the table. They rose to greet him, but he waved them back to their seats. "I've come to pay tribute to Detective Kāne, a true Hawaiian who solved three cases in one fell swoop. Old Kawelo Nakano is singing his praises in the great beyond. I honor him for stopping the thief who desecrated the graves of my ancestors."

The prince cracked a small smile. "Even my friend Aikue, who didn't much like testifying for the Maui police, acknowledges that Detective Kāne prevented the looting of treasures rescued from Kahoʻolawe. Koa Kāne is *hanohano*, honorable. There is no higher tribute."

Koa thanked the prince, but felt a chill inside. Those around him might think him honorable, but he couldn't think of himself that way. He'd killed a man and escaped punishment. He hadn't acknowledged his crime or paid his debt to society as he demanded of others. His life was a charade. Yet, he knew he'd achieved a bit of redemption ... a small down payment ... in bringing Keneke's killer to justice. Still, he had much left to do before, if ever, he deserved to be *hanohano*.

EPILOGUE

KOA ARRIVED HOME early one August afternoon to find Nālani at the door with a smile on her face. They kissed. "Sit down right here on the steps, where you can look out over the forest. I've got something wonderful to show you," she beamed.

He sat and leaned back against the railing, wonderfully free of the pinched nerve that had dogged him for years. The surgeon had been true to his word, and Koa was as good as new—well, almost.

Nālani disappeared into the house briefly before returning with a letter in her hand. Addressed to Detective Koa Kāne and Nālani Kahumana, it bore a California return address. Koa slipped the letter from its envelope and unfolded a single sheet of paper, covered on both sides with tiny, but legible, handwriting.

August 30

Dear Koa and Nālani:

I write with exciting news. Keneke Kawelo Nakano came into this world at dawn a week ago. Eight pounds, four ounces. He looks just like his father, black eyes, black hair, face as brown and round as his father's. And already he has

*eyes for the stars. He's a precious miracle. I'm not exactly
sure how he happened. Maybe the Hawaiian gods worked
their ancient magic.*

*Dr. Maples, the new head of the Alice Telescope Project,
has extended an invitation to join the Alice staff. I have
accepted, and we're returning to the Big Island. I want
Keneke Kawelo to grow up in the land of his father and his
great-grandfather, to know the Humuʻula Saddle and the
trails of Mauna Kea. I want him to know he, like his
father, is a descendant of a great chief, the chief of the land
of the hafted adze and the ʻuaʻu bird.*

*Prince Kamehameha has convinced the state of Hawaiʻi
and the Defense Department to create the Keneke Nakano
National Historical Site at Pōhakuloa. Many treasures
that Gunter stole will be returned to their rightful place,
and the adze makers' cavern will be open to the public.
Keneke Kawelo will one day see his heritage, so long
hidden where only Pele knows the way.*

*Love,
Soo Lin*

Only when Koa finished reading did Nālani hand him the photograph of little Keneke Kawelo Nakano. Soo Lin was right—he did
look just like his father.

AUTHOR'S NOTE

There is an adze quarry, damaged by Navy bombs, near the Puʻu Moiwi cinder cone on the island of Kahoʻolawe, a place of great cultural significance to Hawaiians. Archaeologists theorize that ancient South Pacific explorers first brought adze making technology to Puʻu Moiwi, and from there it spread to the Big Island.

No matter how the requisite skills reached them, the adze makers of Mauna Kea had a formidable presence on the mountain where the summit soars roughly 14,000 feet above sea level and was glaciated during the ice ages. Volcanic eruptions under its icy slopes created a particularly hard form of lava called hawaiite. Ancient Hawaiians discovered veins of hawaiite along the upper surfaces of Mauna Kea and mined them to make stone tools—items highly prized in their time. The quarries are expansive, stretching more than seven miles, and are organized into different work areas, not unlike a modern manufacturing plant. There were many workers, who, collectively, would have been a potent societal force.

Harsh weather undoubtedly drove these intrepid craftsmen off the summit during the winter months. Although the adze makers' workshop that Koa Kāne discovers is a product of the author's imagination, archaeologists, in truth, have never satisfactorily solved the mystery of where Mauna Kea's adze makers spent the Hawaiian

winters. Nor have historians explained their disappearance long before Western contact.

The adze makers may have returned to their villages during the
winter months, but they may also have relocated to the 6,000-foot
saddle between Mauna Kea and Mauna Loa. Stone chips and partially formed stone tools have been found in small lava-tube caves
on the saddle plain; and additional caves, perhaps even whole work-
shops, could easily be buried under the many overlapping lava flows
from the two mountains.

While the summit of Mauna Kea was an important industrial
area for the ancients, it is today the premier astronomical observation site in the northern hemisphere. The two 10-meter,
segmented-mirror Keck telescopes are among the most advanced
and productive observational instruments in human history.

Adze makers and astronomers form the historical backbone of
Death of a Messenger, bookending the astounding changes in the
250 years since Captain Cook became the first European to reach
Hawai'i. Keneke Nakano, the victim in this murder mystery, bridges
these disparate points in time and mirrors the tragedies suffered by
the Hawaiian peoples.